Archie®

1000 PAGE COMICS-PALOOZA

Archie®
1000 PAGE COMICS-PALOOZA

Published by Archie Comic Publications, Inc.
325 Fayette Avenue, Mamaroneck, New York 10543-2318.

ISBN: 978-1-936975-86-0

Holly G! / Yoshida / Grossman

EGAD! WHAT IS THAT STENCH?!
WOOSH!
SNIFF!
SNIFF!
IT'S SO PUTRID, I CAN'T TELL WHICH LOCKER IT'S ORIGINATING FROM!
25

BUT, IT'S ONE OF THESE FIVE...
24
25

SOMETHING MUST BE DONE AT ONCE!
MR. WEATHERBEE
PRINCIPAL

WILL THE STUDENTS OF LOCKERS 22, 23, 24, 25 AND 26, REPORT IN FRONT OF THEIR LOCKERS AT ONCE!

I WONDER WHAT THE BEE IS BENT OUTTA SHAPE 'BOUT THIS TIME?
WE'LL FIND OUT SOON ENOUGH!

EITHER OF YOU KNOW WHAT THIS IS ABOUT?!
WHO CARES? IT GOT ME OUT OF TRIG!
I HAVE A STINKING SUSPICION WHAT IT COULD BE!
YEUCK! REG, DON'T YOU SMELL THAT?!
WHAT?!
WITH THE AMOUNT OF COLOGNE REG WEARS, IT'S A WONDER HE HAS A SENSE OF SMELL AT ALL!
TEE-HEE!
WHAT?!
I SEE YOU STUDENTS SMELL THE PROBLEM AT HAND!
BOY, DO WE!
WHAT?!
NOW I WANT THOSE LOCKERS OPENED AND CLEANED OUT! I HAVE A FEELING SOMEONE OVERLOOKED END OF THE YEAR SCHOOL LOCKER CLEANING!
WE'LL START WITH LOCKER NUMBER 22!
THAT'S ME!
3

CLICK
CLACK
CLICK

RIVERDALE

MAYBE *THAT'S* WHERE THE SMELL IS COMING FROM... ARCHIE'S PHOTOS! HAW-HAW!
WE KNOW WHO'S A BIG *STINKER* AROUND HERE!
OKAY, REGGIE! ENOUGH JOKING AROUND! I BELIEVE YOUR LOCKER IS 23!

THERE! CLEAN AS A WHISTLE!
ER... YES! YOU MAY CLOSE YOUR LOCKER NOW!

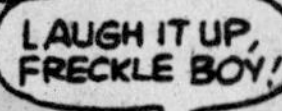
LAUGH IT UP, FRECKLE BOY!

GEE, REG, IT'S A WONDER YOU CAN GET YOUR TEXT BOOKS IN YOUR LOCKER WITH ALL THOSE PHOTOS OF YOUR *FAT HEAD!* HA HA!
SLAM!
STOP IT, BOYS! THIS SITUATION SMELLS BAD ENOUGH WITHOUT YOUR *ROTTEN* INSULTS! ARCHIE, YOU'RE NEXT!
SORRY, SIR!

... 2-3-4, ARCHIE ANDREWS! THERE ARE MORE PHOTOS OF BETTY THAN ME IN HERE!
ER...UH...
RIVER

ER... I KEEP MORE OF YOUR PHOTOS IN MY WALLET! SEE! I CAN CARRY YOU AROUND WHEREVER I GO!
MM-WELL, OKAY!
MISS LODGE!

THIS LOCKER IS NEAT AND CLEAN!
TA DA!

IT SHOULD BE, I HAVE A MAID COME IN AND CLEAN IT ONCE A WEEK!
FIGURES!!

YOU KNOW WHAT THIS MEANS, JUGHEAD!
ER...

OKAY, MR. S.! READY YOUR MOP!
READY FOR ANYTHING, MR. W.!
WAIT!
5

I DON'T THINK THIS IS SUCH A GREAT IDEA!
OPEN THAT LOCKER, MR. JONES, OR IT'S A MONTH'S DETENTION FOR YOU!!
OKAY! OKAY!
THAT'S RIGHT, BOY! I'VE CLEANED EVERYTHING!
CLICK CLICK CLANK
CHIPS
DUNKER
MR. SVENSON HAS FAINTED!
MR. WEATHERBEE -- ARE YOU ALL RIGHT ?!
THIS IS TOO GROSS!
GEE, MAYBE I FORGOT A SANDWICH OR TWO! HEE! HEE!
DON'T JUST STAND THERE! CALL THE FIRE DEPARTMENT TO HOSE US DOWN!!!
END

Betty and Veronica
The Secrets of Veronica's Diary
RIVERDALE
WHAT ARE YOU SCRIBBLING, BETTY?
JUST ENTERING SOME THINGS INTO MY DIARY.
WOULD YOU LIKE ME TO PROOFREAD IT FOR YOU?
NOT ON YOUR LIFE!
YOU KNOW DIARIES ARE SUPPOSED TO BE PRIVATE.
OH, ARE THEY?
SCRIPT & PENCILS: DAN PARENT
INKS: JIM AMASH
LETTERS: TERESA DAVIDSON
COLORS: BARRY GROSSMAN
EDITOR-IN-CHIEF: VICTOR GORELICK
PRESIDENT: MIKE PELLERITO

YOU SHOULD HAVE A DIARY, VERONICA!
I'M SURE YOU COULD FILL IT WITH ALL SORTS OF GOSSIP AND TANTALIZING THOUGHTS!

WE'LL SEE.
HA! LITTLE DOES BETTY KNOW...

I'VE BEEN KEEPING A DIARY FOR YEARS! I'VE JUST CHOSEN TO NOT LET ANYONE KNOW.

AFTER ALL, IF PEOPLE KNEW ABOUT IT, THEY'D WANT TO KNOW WHAT WAS IN IT!

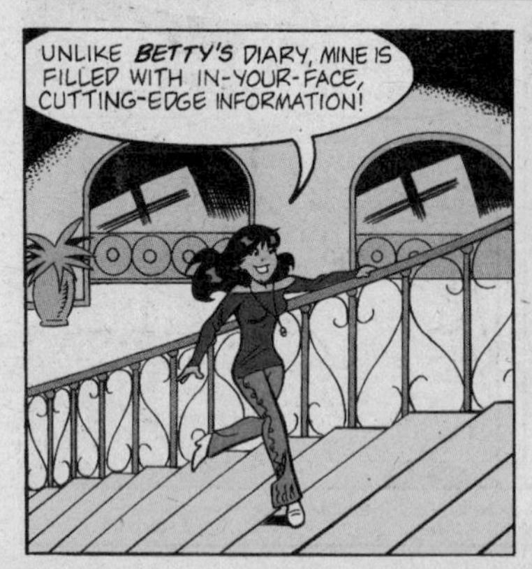
UNLIKE BETTY'S DIARY, MINE IS FILLED WITH IN-YOUR-FACE, CUTTING-EDGE INFORMATION!

PLUS, SOMEDAY, WHEN I'M FAMOUS AND I WRITE MY AUTOBIOGRAPHY, I'LL HAVE THIS WEALTH OF INFORMATION TO REFER TO!
V

TIME TO MAKE AN ENTRY IN THE DIARY!
I'LL JUST OPEN UP THE SAFE!

OPEN UP THE JEWELED ENCASED FIREBOX...

...AND, VOILÀ!
HELLO, DIARY!
Veronica's Diary
V

NOW, LET'S SEE... WHAT SHOULD I WRITE ABOUT TODAY?
OH, YES! DIARY, YOU WON'T BELIEVE THE HIDEOUS DRESS MIDGE HAD ON TODAY...

SO...
WOW! THIS DIARY IS ALL BEAT UP!
I THINK I'D BETTER GET IT REBOUND.
Veronica's Diary
V

I'LL BRING IT DOWN TO OFFICE-MANIA. THEY'LL DO IT WHILE I WAIT!
SNAP!

THAT WAY IT WON'T GET OUT OF MY SIGHT!
THIS IS TOP SECRET INFORMATION, AFTER ALL!

SO...
COPIES
WE'LL HAVE YOUR BOOK REBOUND SHORTLY, MISS LODGE.
THANK YOU!

HI, RON! WHAT BRINGS YOU TO SUCH A COMMON PLACE LIKE THIS?
Oh, um, NOTHING! JUST GETTING A BOOK BOUND FOR MY MOTHER!
COPIE

I'M GETTING A BOOK BOUND, TOO! I CALL IT, "REGGIE: BOOK ONE".
WHAT'S IT ABOUT?

IT'S JUST HEADSHOTS OF ME! I HAVE SO MANY, I CAN'T KEEP TRACK OF THEM!
IT'S PERFECT IF I JUST WANT TO KICK BACK AND LOOK AT MYSELF FOR AN EVENING!

SOUNDS CAPTIVATING.
YES, I AM!
Sale

HERE YOU GO, MISS LODGE.
THANKS! AND GOOD LUCK WITH YOUR BOOK OF... YOURSELF!
COPIE

LATER
I THINK I'LL CHECK OUT MY BEAUTIFULLY BOUND NEW DIARY...
Hmm... WHAT'S THIS?

PHOTOS OF REGGIE ?!
OH, BROTHER! THEY GAVE ME HIS BOOK INSTEAD OF MINE!

OH, WELL, THAT MUST MEAN HE HAS MY DIARY...

EEEEEEEEEEEEE!!
OH MY GOSH! THIS COULD BE WORLD WAR 3!!

PLEASE LET HIM NOT HAVE LOOKED IN THAT BOOK YET!

ZOOOM!
WHAT WAS THAT?
MRS. MANTLE! IS REGGIE HERE?
HE WENT OVER TO POP TATE'S!
THANKS! I'LL FIND HIM THERE!
ZOOM!
AND TO THINK I NEVER TRIED OUT FOR TRACK!
I'M HERE!
LET'S HOPE I CATCH HIM BEFORE HE READS IT!
POP'S
HI, REGGIE! DO YOU HAVE MY...
DIARY? WHY, YES! I GAVE IT A READ...

AS WELL AS THE REST OF US, VERONICA!
≡GULP!≡ I WONDER IF I CAN GET A ONE-WAY TICKET TO THE FAR EAST RIGHT NOW...
VERONICA, THANKS FOR CALLING ME PATHETIC AND MOUSY!
AND SAYING YOU DON'T KNOW WHY YOU HAVE SUCH A GOOBER LIKE ME FOR A BOYFRIEND!
AND YOU CALLED ME DUMB!
AND ME DUMBER FOR GOING OUT WITH HIM!
7

SHE SAID MY DESIGN SENSE WAS DISCOUNT STORE AT BEST!
SHE SAID SHE COULD OUT-SING ME ANY DAY!
POP'S

SHE CALLED ME A DATELESS BRAINIAC!
WHAT DID SHE SAY ABOUT YOU, JUGHEAD?
POP'S

THAT I WAS A BUFFOON AND A GLUTTON, BUT SHE SAYS THAT TO ME EVERYDAY ANYWAY.
HA! HA! C'MON, GUYS! THERE WERE GOOD THINGS IN THERE, TOO!

YEAH, ABOUT YOURSELF!
WELL, THAT'S A START!

C'MON, GANG! LET'S LEAVE!
AW, C'MON!
POP'S

JUGHEAD, YOU'RE THE ONLY THING RESEMBLING A FRIEND I HAVE LEFT!
HOW DO I FIX THIS?

I HAVE AN IDEA! LET ME GO TALK TO THEM.
THANK YOU!
THE NEXT DAY...
WE'VE COME UP WITH A SOLUTION!
YOU NEED A DOSE OF YOUR OWN MEDICINE!

THEREFORE, WE'VE WRITTEN ALL OUR THOUGHTS ABOUT YOU...
BETTY WILL GO FIRST...
YOUR BLOATED EGO IS SOMETIMES UNBEARABLE!
YOU RUN ME RAGGED LIKE SOME SORT OF SLAVE!

...NEVER STOPS LOOKING IN HER MIRROR...
...THINKS SHE CAN SING, AND SHE CAN! LIKE A WOUNDED HYENA, THAT IS!
...ONCE PAID ME A COMPLIMENT, THEN TOOK IT BACK!
...NEEDS TO CUT BACK ON THE PERFUME...

SOON...
AND LAST BUT NOT LEAST, YOU GRIT YOUR TEETH TOO MUCH,..
STOP! STOP! OKAY! I GET THE HINT!

I'VE LEARNED MY LESSON! CAN YOU ALL FORGIVE ME?!
I THINK YOU KIDS **SHOULD** FORGIVE AND FORGET!

YOU KIDS SHOULDN'T HAVE READ VERONICA'S DIARY, NO MATTER **WHAT** SHE WROTE!
AND VERONICA, YOU SHOULD **RESPECT** YOUR FRIENDS MORE!
HE'S RIGHT!
LET'S PUT ALL THIS BEHIND US!

SO...
IT'S TIME TO DITCH THIS BIG OL' MESS OF PAPER. **VOILA'!** MY NEW DIARY...

... MY **DIGITAL** DIARY!
I'LL KEEP THIS ON MY COMPUTER!
MY DIARY

I'LL JUST SAVE THIS ON MY HARD DRIVE.
NO BIG CLUMSY BOOK TO GET IN THE WRONG HANDS!

NOW, LET'S SEE... WHAT SHALL I WRITE ABOUT?
How about the onslaught I went through today at Pop's?
Those bozos ripped me apart! I'll show them when they least expect it!
IT'S GOOD TO BE BACK, DIARY!

NOBODY HINDERS MY RIGHT TO VOICE MY OPINION!
OH, HERE'S AN E-MAIL FROM REGGIE!
I'LL REPLY TO HIM BY ATTACHING THIS PICTURE OF A DONKEY!
I'LL JUST ATTACH IT LIKE SO...

... AND SEND...
WAIT! OH NO! I JUST ATTACHED MY DIARY FILE BY ACCIDENT!
IS THERE A CHANCE HE WON'T FORWARD THIS TO EVERYONE...?
YOU HAVE 85 NEW E-MAILS!
NO!
END

Betty and Veronica in "FIT TO BE TIRED"

Script: Mike Pellowski / Art: Dan DeCarlo / Letters: Bill Yoshida / Colors: Barry Grossman

MINUTES LATER...
LADIES, THE CONFERENCE CHEERLEADING CHAMPIONSHIPS ARE COMING UP SO LET'S WORK HARD TODAY!
COACH

LET'S START BY STRETCHING!
GET NICE AND LOOSE!
COACH

OOH!
GROAN!
A-YA!
OOF!

OKAY, NOW! PICK UP YOUR POM-POMS!
SOMETIMES I THINK POM-POMS ARE FOR DUM-DUMS!

WE'LL WORK ON OUR DANCE ROUTINE! REMEMBER TO SMILE!
COACH
CLICK

MOVE, GIRLS, MOVE! IN TIME! LOOK HAPPY! BIG SMILES!!

GRRRR... BIG SMILE! BIG SMILE!

PUFF
PUFF
PUFF
PUFF
MOVE, MOVE, MOVE!

NOW COME TOGETHER!
SMILE! SMILE! GOOD! OKAY! RELAX!

WHEW!

BACK TO WORK! LET'S PRACTICE TUMBLING!
ALREADY?

I'LL SPOT! LET'S GO!
I'LL START WITH SOME HANDSPRINGS, MS. GOODBODY!

ZOOM!
BOUNCE!
FLIP!
GOOD, BETTY! WAY TO GO, KUMI!! GREAT, MIDGE! HAPPY FACES, GIRLS!

STICK THOSE LANDINGS, GIRLS, AND SMILE!

VERY NICE, LADIES!

CATCH YOUR BREATH AND LET'S DO OUR CLOSING PYRAMID!
COACH
OKAY! PYRAMID TIME, GIRLS! EVERYONE, ON THE MAT!
TUT! TUT! PLEASE DON'T RUSH US!
GREAT! SUPER! KEEP SMILING! WONDERFUL!
OH! RIGHT! HAPPY! HAPPY! JOY! JOY!
R
IT'S GETTING LATE! THAT'S ENOUGH FOR TODAY! GOOD PRACTICE, GIRLS!
WHEW
THANKS!
PLOP!
PLOP!
FLOP!
5

AFTER THE GIRLS CHANGE...
THERE ARE THE GUYS!

HI, GIRLS! WANT TO GO OUT FOR A PIZZA?
AND THEN WE CAN GO TO AN ARCADE FOR A WHILE!

NOT REALLY! I'M GOING HOME! I'M EXHAUSTED!
ME, TOO! SORRY!

HUH? OH, SURE! NO PROBLEM! SOME OTHER TIME!
GREAT! SEE YA!

GEE, WHAT ARE THEY SO TIRED ABOUT? WE'RE THE ONES WHO HAD BASKETBALL PRACTICE!
I WONDER WHY THEY DIDN'T EVEN SMILE AT US?!
END

LOOK AT THAT COLLECTOR BUYING ALL THOSE CLOCKS! ALMOST ANY CLOCK HE COMES ACROSS!
THAT'S THE WAY IT GOES WHEN YOU'VE BEEN BITTEN BY THE COLLECTOR'S BUG!
RIVERDALE FLEA MARKET
COMIC BOOKS
COMIC BOOKS HALF PRICE SALE
Antique CLOTHING
Cheap
CHARLIE'S CLOCKS
SOLD
SCRIPT: GEORGE GLADIR
PENCILS: STAN GOLDBERG
INKS: RICH KOSLOWSKI
Betty in The COLLECTOR
CUKOO!! CUKOO!!
I THINK HE MUST BE A TAD CUCKOO HIMSELF!
OLD COINS & STAMPS
BOOKS and MAGAZINES
GOLD

YOU'RE RIGHT, BETTY!
THERE MUST BE SOMETHING WEIRD ABOUT COLLECTORS!
ANTIQU

I KNOW I'M RIGHT! COLLECTORS CAN NEVER BE SATISFIED WITH OWNING JUST *ONE* OF AN OBJECT!
LIKE THIS CUTE PENGUIN!

YOU'VE JUST GIVEN ME AN IDEA! WHY DON'T I WRITE ABOUT WEIRD COLLECTORS FOR THE SCHOOL PAPER?
WHY NOT? YOU HAVE MY EDITORIAL OKAY TO DO THE ARTICLE!

Jewelr
HI, GIRLS!
HI, ADAM!
WHAT BRINGS YOU TO THE FLEA MARKET?

SAME AS YOU TWO... JUST BROWSING!

Hmm... BETTY MUST BE INTO PENGUINS! *NOW* I KNOW WHAT TO GET HER FOR HER *BIRTHDAY*!
Sale

LOOK, ARCHIE! THERE'S YOUR RIVAL, ADAM!
HE'S NOT MY RIVAL! BETTY CLEARLY PREFERS ME TO ADAM!
HEY! YOU'RE BUYING UP ALL MY PENGUINS!
THEY'RE FOR MY GIRL-FRIEND!
FOR HIS GIRL-FRIEND? I DIDN'T KNOW BETTY LIKED PENGUINS!
FUNNY LITTLE ANIMALS
I CAN'T LET HIM OUTDO ME!
TOUGH LUCK!
HE'S BOUGHT UP EVERY PENGUIN HERE!
SO?! THERE ARE OTHER FLEA MARKETS!
I'LL HAVE NO TROUBLE FINDING A BIG ASSORTMENT OF THOSE FUNNY-LOOKING BIRDS IN TUXEDOS!
LATER...
SO HOW DO YOU LIKE THEM APPLES? ER... I MEAN, THEM PENGUINS?!
I AM IMPRESSED!
ARCHIE, YOU'VE BOUGHT ENOUGH PENGUINS TODAY TO LET BETTY OPEN UP HER OWN PENGUIN STORE!

NATURALLY, I'M NOT GOING TO LET ADAM OUTDO ME!
I'D BETTER RUSH OFF TO BETTY'S BE-FORE ADAM!

I'LL JUST LEAVE 'EM ON HER DOORSTEP!
... AND RING HER BELL!
DING DONG

? THERE'S NOBODY HERE!
JUST A BOX WITH MY NAME ON IT!
BETTY COOPER

SIS, LOOK AT ALL OF THESE PENGUINS ARCHIE GAVE ME! ...EVEN MORE THAN ADAM JUST GAVE ME!

BETTY, I DIDN'T KNOW YOU WERE INTO PENGUINS!
I'M NOT!
...EVEN THOUGH THE BOYS MUST THINK SO!

SO ARE YOU GOING TO GET RID OF THEM?
NEVER! THESE GUYS ARE MORE THAN PENGUINS! THEY'RE SYMBOLS OF THE BOYS' DEEP AFFECTION FOR ME!

THERE'S THE DOOR-BELL!
IT MUST BE NANCY. SHE PHONED TO SAY SHE WAS COMING OVER!
DING DONG

I FINISHED THAT ARTICLE ABOUT COLLECTORS!
GREAT! I'LL PUT IT IN THE NEXT EDITION OF OUR SCHOOL PAPER!

BETTY! WHAT ON EARTH ARE YOU DOING WITH ALL THESE PENGUINS?

I THOUGHT YOU SAID THAT COLLECTORS ARE WEIRDOS!
YES!

EXCEPT IF THEY COLLECT PENGUINS!
?!
END

Betty and Veronica in "COZY CAMPGROUND"

Script: George Gladir / Pencils: Jeff Shultz / Inks: Al Milgrom / Letters: Bill Yoshida / Colors: Barry Grossman

WE'VE GOT SEVERAL TENTS PITCHED... JUST CHOOSE WHICH ONE YOU'D LIKE TO SLEEP IN!

OR, IF YOU LIKE, YOU CAN SLEEP UNDER THE STARS!
WHAT STARS?

THERE! THE ONES PAINTED ON THE CEILING!
OH, WOW! THEY GLOW IN THE DARK!

SHOULD WE CHANGE INTO OUR JAMMIES NOW?
I'VE GOT A BETTER IDEA!

HEY! CHANGE INTO THESE!
SWIMSUITS?
2

EVERYBODY READY? LET'S HEAD FOR THE OL' SWIMMIN' HOLE!
DON'T YOU MEAN THE LODGE INDOOR POOL?

NO... I MEAN THE SWIMMIN' HOLE!
WAY COOL!

ALL THESE TREES AND BUSHES MAKE IT LOOK LIKE WE'RE OUTDOORS!
THE OUTDOORS DOESN'T HAVE EVENLY HEATED WATER AND AIR!
ESPECIALLY NOT NOW!

HELP YOURSELF TO THE PICNIC BUFFET! WE'VE GOT AN INDOOR GRILL THAT CAN COOK ANYTHING YOU LIKE-- BURGERS, HOT DOGS, CHICKEN, RIBS!

RON'S DONE THE IMPOSSIBLE! SHE'S MADE SUMMER IN THE MIDDLE OF WINTER!
EVEN BETTER! THERE ARE NO MOSQUITOES!

WHEW! I'VE HAD ENOUGH WATER FUN!
WHAT NEXT, RON?

LET'S CHANGE INTO OUR PAJAMAS AND GATHER 'ROUND THE CAMPFIRE BACK AT THE CAMPSITE!

WE CAN TOAST MARSHMALLOWS AND MAKE S'MORES!
HOW ABOUT TELLING GHOST STORIES?
U.S.A.

...AND SHE WAS NEVER THE SAME AGAIN!
EEEEW!!

THAT WAS WEIRD!!
NANCY, YOU'RE TOO GOOD AT TELLING SCARY STORIES!
IT COMES FROM BEING A BIG MONSTER MOVIE FAN!

GIRLS... ISN'T IT TIME TO TURN IN?
AFTER THAT?
I'D BE TOO AFRAID TO SLEEP!
4

THIS HAS BEEN SO MUCH FUN!
ESPECIALLY SINCE THE BOYS DIDN'T CRASH IT LIKE THEY USUALLY DO!

LISTEN! RON HAS A TAPE OF ANIMAL NOISES PLAYING!
GROOAR!
I CAN HEAR A BEAR GROWLING!

GREAT SOUND EFFECT, RON!
HOOOOOW!
B-B-B-BUT... I DIDN'T ARRANGE FOR ANY!

Y-YOU MEAN IT'S A REAL MONSTER?
NANCY SHOULDN'T HAVE TOLD THOSE GHOST STORIES!
OH, SURE! BLAME ME!

HOW LONG BEFORE YOU THINK THEY FIGURE IT OUT, ARCH?
LONG ENOUGH FOR US TO FINISH OFF THE BUFFET! YOUR TURN, REG!
GOTCHA!
AWWOOO!!
SHUDDER! SHUDDER
The End

Betty and Veronica in The SHOPPER

Script: Mike Pellowski / Pencils: Jeff Shultz / Inks: Al Milgrom / Letters: Bill Yoshida / Colors: Barry Grossman

VERONICA, JUST HOW MUCH DO YOU ACTUALLY SPEND AT OUR MALL?
PER MINUTE? PER SECOND?

ETHEL, I THINK SHE JUST ANSWERED OUR QUESTION!

HERE! HELP ME CARRY SOME OF THESE, BETTY!
I STILL HAVE MORE SHOPPING TO DO!

I FIND SHOPPING A CHALLENGE! ALL OF MY TALENTS AND ALL MY WITS GO INTO SHOPPING!
NOT TO MENTION ALL OF YOUR MONEY!

SOMETIMES I LIKE TO GO SHOPPING WITHOUT MONEY!
"WITHOUT MONEY"?!

EEYUCK! THAT'S LIKE KISSING A MANNEQUIN!

SPEAKING OF MANNEQUINS, I SEE THAT BULLSTROMS IS INTRODUCING A NEW LINE!

PSST! IT'S MISS LODGE!
PASS IT ON-- MISS LODGE IS HERE!

SOUNDS LIKE THEY'RE ABOUT TO GIVE YOU THE RED CARPET TREATMENT!
NO!

HERE AT BULLSTROMS THEY ALWAYS GIVE ME THE BLUE CARPET TREATMENT!

VERONICA, THE SIGN SAYS THAT YOU CAN TAKE ONLY FIVE ITEMS TO THE DRESSING ROOM!
THAT'S FOR ORDINARY CUSTOMERS!
ONLY 5 ITEMS PERMITTED IN DRESSING ROOMS

AS A SUPER PREFERRED CUSTOMER I HAVE ACCESS TO MY VERY OWN DRESSING ROOM!
PRIVATE
MS LODGE

WHICH OF THE OUTFITS HAVE YOU DECIDED UPON, MISS LODGE?
ALL OF THEM, OF COURSE!

SOMETIMES THE HELP CAN ASK SUCH SILLY QUESTIONS!
SHE OBVIOUSLY MUST BE NEW HERE!

WILL THAT BE CASH OR CHARGE, MISS LODGE?
CHARGE, PLEASE!

WOW!
I DON'T LIKE TO PLAY FAVORITES WITH MY CREDIT CARDS! I LIKE TO USE THEM ALL!

GOOD GRIEF! I HOPE YOU LEFT SOMETHING AT THE STORE FOR THE OTHERS!
DADDY'S ATTEMPTS AT HUMOR CAN BE SO FEEBLE AT TIMES!

I'M JUST TRYING TO GIVE OUR ECONOMY A SHOT IN THE ARM!
IF YOU DON'T DRIVE ME TO BANKRUPTCY FIRST!
4

OH, THERE'S A MESSAGE ON MY ANSWERING MACHINE!

MISS LODGE, THIS IS THE MANAGER OVER AT CENTERVILLE MALL...

HOW COME YOU HAVEN'T VISITED OUR MALL THIS WEEK?

SO, DEAR GIRL, I'M CURIOUS! HOW DO YOU MANAGE TO RELAX AFTER AN EXHAUSTING DAY AT THE MALL?

BY WATCHING MY FAVORITE TV SHOW!
CLICK

... THE HOME SHOPPING SERVICE!
ONLY 39.50
END

Betty and Veronica in SNOWBALL Effect

Hmph! HAVING A SNOWBALL FIGHT WITH A SNOWMAN IS KIND OF BORING! HE DOESN'T PUT UP MUCH OF A FIGHT!

SCRIPT:	PENCILS:	INKS:	LETTERS:	COLORS:	EDITOR-IN-CHIEF:	PRESIDENT:
MIKE PELLOWSKI	JEFF SHULTZ	AL MILGROM	JACK MORELLI	BARRY GROSSMAN	VICTOR GORELICK	MIKE PELLERITO

HAHA! THANK GOODNESS WE'VE OUTGROWN THAT SILLY STAGE OF OUR LIVES!
MATURE ADULTS NEVER GET IN-VOLVED IN SNOW-BALL FIGHTS!

WHAP

HEY, YOU!!
HAHA! BULLSEYE! NOW THAT WAS A LOT MORE FUN!

COME HERE, YOU LITTLE WISEGUY!
YIKES!
EMERGENCY EXIT, STAGE LEFT! GET GOING, FEET!

OH, NO YOU DON'T! WHAT'S YOUR NAME, JUNIOR?
GULP!
IT'S JOEY JENKINS!

DON'T YOU KNOW IT'S WRONG TO CLOBBER UNSUSPECTING PEOPLE WITH SNOWBALLS?
I'M... I'M SORRY!

THAT WAS A VERY NASTY THING TO DO!
I'M SORRY! I WON'T DO IT AGAIN!

IT'S JUST THAT I WAS TIRED OF PITCHING SNOWBALLS AT THAT OLD SNOWMAN! I WANTED TO SEE IF I COULD HIT A MOVING TARGET!

WELL... WE'LL FORGET ABOUT WHAT YOU DID THIS TIME!
JUST DON'T TRY ANYTHING LIKE THAT AGAIN!

I THINK WE HANDLED THAT QUITE WELL!
SO DO I!

WAP
UGH!
WOP
OOF!

NYAH! NYAH!
SUCKERS! YOU WON'T CATCH ME AGAIN!
GRRR!

AND FROM NOW ON, EVERY TIME YOU WALK PAST THIS VACANT LOT, BE ON THE LOOKOUT FOR A SNEAK ATTACK FROM JOEY JENKINS --
THE SNOWBALL SNIPER!

heh-heh! BYE, BYE, GIRLS! SEE YOU SOON!
ZOOM

THAT LITTLE MONSTER NEEDS TO BE TAUGHT A LESSON! WE'RE NOT AVOIDING THIS LOT! IT'S ON OUR USUAL ROUTE!
I HAVE A WAY WE CAN EVEN THE SCORE! REGGIE PULLED THIS STUNT ON US WHEN WE WERE SMALL!

WHAT DO WE HAVE TO DO?
FIRST WE HAVE TO BUILD UP AND THEN HOLLOW OUT JOEY'S SNOWMAN TARGET!

THE NEXT DAY WHEN JOEY ARRIVES AT THE LOT...
THOSE TWO GIRLS SHOULD BE PASSING BY ANYTIME NOW. THEY USUALLY SHOW UP HERE ABOUT THIS TIME!

HEY! SOMEONE MADE MY OLD SNOWMAN A LOT BIGGER AND BUILT ANOTHER ONE OVER THERE! I WONDER WHO DID THAT?

I CAN'T WORRY ABOUT THAT! IT'S ALMOST TIME FOR *TARGET PRACTICE!* BOY, WILL THOSE GIRLS BE SURPRISED WHEN I POP UP FROM BEHIND MY SNOW FORT AND BOMBARD THEM!

ATTENTION, JOEY JENKINS! IT'S PAYBACK TIME!!
ARRGH!!
THE SNOW-PEOPLE ARE MOVING!!

FIRE AT WILL, RON!
OKAY! BUT I THOUGHT HIS NAME WAS JOEY, NOT WILL!
YEOW!

WAP
SPLATT

ENOUGH! TRUCE!! HOLD YOUR FIRE! I GIVE UP! I'LL NEVER --AND I MEAN NEVER THROW SNOWBALLS AT YOU TWO AGAIN!!

GOOD! AND REMEMBER-- EVEN SNOWMEN CAN FIGHT BACK IF THEY HAVE TO!

AND SO CAN SNOW-GIRLS!!
GULP! SO I FOUND OUT!
END

Script & Art: Holly G! / Letters: Vickie Williams / Colors: Barry Grossman

WAIT, DO YOU MEAN THE SHOW WHERE YOU HAVE TO OUTLAST EVERYONE ELSE ON AN ISLAND TO WIN A MILLION DOLLARS?
YOU'D BE THE *FIRST* ONE VOTED OFF...

...FOR TRYING TO MAKE EVERYONE YOUR SERVANTS!
BIFF!
IF I PROMISE TO *PAY* THEM GOOD MONEY, WHY NOT?

NO, ACTUALLY, I WAS TALKING ABOUT THAT CLASSIC TV SHOW!
"GULLIBLE'S ISLAND?
CLICK

YEAH! HAVE YOU EVER THOUGHT ABOUT WHO *YOU'D* WANT TO BE STRANDED WITH ON AN ISLAND?
Hmmm?

MY MAID, A CELL PHONE, AND A GOOD MANICURE KIT.
I SAID, "*WHO*", NOT "*WHAT*"! TWO THINGS ON YOUR LIST AREN'T HUMAN!

SOO-- WHO WOULD *YOU* WANT TO BE STRANDED WITH... NEED I ASK?
YOU GOT IT! *ARCHIE*!

AH! BUT COULD ARCHIE BE TRUSTED TO FIND A WAY TO SURVIVE ON THAT DESOLATE PIECE OF REAL ESTATE?
I DUNNO--?!

BUT IF NOT, IT SURE WOULD BE A GREAT WAY TO GO!
YOU CAN HAVE IT THEN!

THERE'S NOT MUCH CHANCE OF GETTING STRANDED ON A DESERT ISLAND IN THIS WEATHER!
THANK GOODNESS I DROVE HERE! BRRR

VERONICA, ARE YOU STILL GOING OUT TOMORROW NIGHT WITH ARCHIE?
YES, DADDYKINS, WHY?

A BIG STORM IS SUPPOSED TO MOVE IN BY LATE TOMORROW NIGHT!
I SHOULD BE HOME IN BED BEFORE THAT, DADDY!

BUT--!
THAT MOVIE WENT ON LONGER THAN I THOUGHT!
WE BETTER SKIP OUR POST MOVIE TRIP TO POP'S!
3

WE WOULD CHOOSE A MOVIE THEATRE MILES FROM HOME ON THE NIGHT OF THE BIG STORM!
YOU'RE TELLING ME! I'M BARELY CRAWLING ALONG!

WHUMP!
WHA-WHAT HAPPENED?!?
WE HIT A SNOW BANK!

BAWL!
WE'RE STRANDED! WE'RE DOOMED!
CALM DOWN, RON. WE'LL BE ALL RIGHT!

DO WE HAVE ANY FOOD?
NO!
BLANKETS?
NO!
WATER?
NO!
MATCHES?
WE'RE DOOMED!

MY TOES, NOSE AND FINGERS ARE FROZEN! THIS IS THE END!
WE'VE ONLY BEEN STUCK FIVE MINUTES.

THEY'LL FIND OUR COLD, FROZEN BODIES IN THE SPRING! WE'RE DOOMED!
WHY ARE YOU PANICKING?

YOU'VE GOT A CELL PHONE!
THAT'S RIGHT! I'LL CALL FOR HELP!

DON'T BOTHER! I'M RIGHT HERE!
BETTY!
HOW'D YOU FIND US?
KNOCK KNOCK

IT WASN'T HARD CONSIDERING YOU'RE ONLY SIX FEET FROM THE LODGE DRIVEWAY!
OH.

WASN'T I RIGHT? THE ONLY THING THAT COULD'VE SAVED US WAS MY CELL PHONE! ARCHIE DIDN'T HAVE A THING THAT WOULD KEEP US ALIVE!
OH, I DON'T KNOW...
MUNCH MUNCH

I'D STILL RATHER BE STRANDED ON A DESERT ISLAND WITH ARCHIE RATHER THAN A CELL PHONE.
TO BE PERFECTLY HONEST WITH YOU...

...SO WOULD I!
end

Betty's Diary "TRUE REVIEW"

Script: Frank Doyle / Pencils: Doug Crane / Inks: Rudy Lapick / Letters: Bill Yoshida / Colors: Barry Grossman

BETTY, YOU'RE GOING TO REVIEW IT? THAT'S GREAT!!
YES... BUT I'VE GOT TO BE OBJECTIVE!
SCHOOL NEWS
NO PER

AND GIVE IT MY HONEST REVIEW!
OF COURSE! THAT'S WHAT I EXPECT YOU TO DO!

THE DAY OF THE PLAY...
LADIES AND GENTLEMEN!! ARCHIE ANDREWS PRODUCTIONS PRESENTS AN ORIGINAL PLAY ENTITLED, "CRIME ISN'T VERY NICE"!

EEEEEK!
INSPECTOR! WHAT WAS THAT?
IT SOUNDED LIKE "C-SHARP," DR. FLOTSAM!
HA HA HA!

DR. FLOTSAM ... THE LATEST VICTIM CLAIMS THAT FOUR LARGE, ARMED MEN STOLE EVERYTHING SHE OWNED ... I'M HAVING A HARD TIME BUYING YOUR THEORY THAT SHE SIMPLY MISPLACED HER FORTUNE!
HO HO HO!!

DUH-H-H... HOW DID YOU KNOW I WAS THE CRIMINAL?
SIMPLE! EXCEPT FOR DR. FLOTSAM AND MYSELF, YOU'RE THE ONLY OTHER MEMBER OF THE CAST!
CLIK!
HO HO!
HA HA!
HEE HEE HA!

THAT WAS THE ABSOLUTE PITS!! I CAN HARDLY WAIT FOR YOUR REVIEW TO SEE HOW YOU ROAST THAT TURKEY...THAT IS, UNLESS YOU WIMP OUT AND LIE!

THAT NIGHT...
...IF I TURN THIS REVIEW IN, ARCHIE WILL NEVER SPEAK TO ME AGAIN!

THAT WAS THE THIRTEENTH DRAFT! EACH ONE SOUNDS WORSE THAN THE LAST!
FLUMP!

THERE MUST BE SOME WAY I CAN WRITE IT HONESTLY WITHOUT IT SOUNDING TOO BAD!

THE DAY THE PAPER COMES OUT:
HEY, BETTY! THANKS FOR THE GREAT REVIEW! I'M GOING TO PUT IT IN MY SCRAPBOOK!
GREAT REVIEW?
BLUE & GOLD

HA! I KNEW YOU'D CAVE IN AND WIMP OUT!
OH, REALLY?!! THEN READ WHAT I WROTE!
BLUE & GOLD

"I've seen many, many plays in my time, but none quite like this one..."

YOU HAVE TO ADMIT THAT'S CERTAINLY TRUE! READ ON!

"The characters and situations are totally unique! The author did not borrow any ideas from any other playwright!"
BLUE & GOLD

SO, WHERE HAVE YOU EVER SEEN A PLAY IN WHICH AN INUIT ROCK STAR IS ATTACKED WITH A RUBBER CHICKEN BY AN INDEPENDENTLY WEALTHY SUPERMARKET CHECK-OUT GIRL...

...AT A U.S. NAVY DRY DOCK IN MONTANA?
OKAY, I'LL GIVE YOU THAT, BUT THEN YOU GO ON...

"...This is one play the audience is going to tell their friends about!"
IT'S HAPPENING ALREADY...
4

I OVERHEARD REGGIE SAYING...
I GOTTA TELL MY FRIENDS AT THE COMMUNITY THEATRE ABOUT THIS! THEY'LL CRACK UP LAUGHING!
R

OKAY, THEN, WHAT ABOUT THIS...?

"Of all the mysteries I have ever seen, this one kept me guessing the most."
THAT'S TRUE!!

IT WAS SO MIXED UP, I COULDN'T MAKE HEADS OR TAILS OUT OF IT!! CAN'T ARGUE WITH THAT!
HMMMM...!

BETTY, I JUST READ YOUR REVIEW, AND I THINK YOU HAVE A GREAT FUTURE AS A WRITER...

...OF ADS FOR USED CAR LOTS! HA-HA-HA-HA-!
END

Script: George Gladir / Pencils: Dan DeCarlo / Inks: Jimmy DeCarlo / Letters: Bill Yoshida / Colors: Barry Grossman

VERONICA, RIDES AROUND IN A FLASHY SPORTS CAR!
OH, IT'S JUST A LITTLE SOMETHING DADDY GAVE ME TO GET AROUND IN!
VL

TO ENTERTAIN HER DATES, VERONICA HAS A FUN ROOM THAT COMBINES ALL THE FEATURES OF A MOVIE THEATER, A VIDEO ARCADE, AND SODA SHOP!
WOW, A TALKING POPCORN MACHINE!
WOULD YOU CARE FOR EXTRA BUTTER ?
R

AND YOU ASK WHAT DO I HAVE TO COMPETE AGAINST HER ?
R

WELL, I'VE A WARDROBE THAT CONSISTS MOSTLY OF EMPTY HANGERS AND NOT-SO-EMPTY MOTHS!

WHEN IT COMES TO WHEELS, I RELY ON THE FAMILY CAR–THAT IS, *WHEN* I CAN BORROW IT!

OTHERWISE, I HAVE TO DEPEND ON WHAT-EVER WHEELS I CAN GET MY HANDS ON!

TO ENTERTAIN MY DATES, I CAN COUNT ON AN OLD T.V.!

BUT SOMETIMES THE OLD T.V. GIVES ME AS MUCH COMPETITION AS VERONICA!

BUT ALL THOSE QUALITIES OF MINE DON'T COUNT FOR BEANS WHEN I'M DEALING WITH AN UNSCRUPULOUS, TRICKY-VICKY LIKE VERONICA!
SCREEEEEE

QUICK!!! HOP IN, ARCHIE! IT'S AN EMERGENCY!

UH, YOU'LL HAVE TO EXCUSE ME, BETTY!

WHAT'S THE EMERGENCY, VERONICA?
ROAR

GETTING YOU AWAY FROM, BETTY!

HER PARTIES ATTRACT BOYS FROM NEAR...

FROM FAR...

AND FROM FAROUT!

SO HOW DOES A SIMPLE GIRL LIKE ME COMPETE AGAINST THOSE TREMENDOUS ODDS ?

I DO IT WITH A TRAIT THAT I HAVEN'T MENTIONED YET!
EXCUSE ME!
SORRY!
LET ME THROUGH!

BETTY!!
HI, ARCHIE!

C'MON! LET'S YOU AND I DITCH THIS CROWD!
AMEN!

I DO IT WITH OLD-FASHIONED PERSISTENCE!
THE END

Script: Barbara Slate / Pencils: Stan Goldberg / Inks: John Lowe / Letters: Bill Yoshida / Colors: Barry Grossman

?
BUS STOP

THAT POOR GIRL DOESN'T HAVE A COAT AT ALL!
BUS STOP

AND HERE I'VE BEEN FEELING SORRY FOR MYSELF BECAUSE I'VE GOT AN *OLD* COAT!

HERE YOU GO, FRIEND! TAKE MY COAT BEFORE YOU CATCH YOUR DEATH OF COLD!
? ?
BEST BOO

OH, REALLY?!
SURE! I'VE BEEN MEANING TO GET A NEW COAT, ANYWAY!

GEE... *THANKS!*
YOU'RE WELCOME!
BEST BOOKS
BUS STOP

WOW! NOW I'M *REALLY* FREEZING!

I'LL DUCK INTO GRUMBLES AND LOOK AT THEIR COATS!
GRUMBLES

SLEEVELESS DRESSES, SHORTS?

BATHING SUITS?
MAY I HELP YOU?

YES! WHERE ARE YOUR WINTER COATS?
IN STORAGE UNTIL NEXT YEAR!

WHAT?
OH, YES! WE'RE SHOWING OUR NEW *SPRING* LINES NOW!

BUT IT'S THE DEAD OF WINTER!
THAT'S RIGHT! THAT'S WHY WE'RE SHOWING *SPRING* CLOTHES!
SUPER T's SALE
$17

IF YOU WANT TO BUY A *WINTER COAT,* COME BACK IN LATE *SUMMER!*

THAT'S CRAZY! I'M GOING TO LACY'S!
IT'S THE SAME IN ALL THE STORES, DEARIE!
SUPER T'S SALE

WELL, THAT'S JUST GREAT!
GRUMBLES

NOW IT'S COLDER THAN EVER... AND I'VE GOT A LONG WALK HOME!
BEACH VACATION
FLY TAHITI
RIVERDALE TRAVEL
TAHITI
4

BOY, IT'S ABSOLUTELY FREEZING TODAY!
U.S. MAI

THIS OLD COAT OF MINE JUST ABOUT KEEPS THE COLD OUT!

OH, THERE'S BETTY! THE POOR GIRL DOESN'T HAVE A COAT AT ALL!
VIDEO WORLD
TOP TEN HITS

HERE YOU GO, FRIEND! TAKE MY COAT BEFORE YOU CATCH YOUR DEATH OF COLD!

UH... GEE, THANKS, RON!
YOU'RE WELCOME! I'VE BEEN MEANING TO GET A NEW COAT ANYWAY!
END

Veronica in SLIP-UP!

Script: Craig Boldman / Pencils: Jeff Shultz / Inks: Al Milgrom / Letters: Bill Yoshida / Colors: Barry Grossman

VERONICA, IT'S A SHEET OF ICE OUT THERE!
OH, DON'T BE A WORRYWART! IT'S NOT THAT...

B-B-BAD!
HUH?

HANG ON.!!
W-W-WHOA!

DON'T WORRY, DADDYKINS IS COMING... YEOW!!

GULP!
GULP!

IT'S NOT THAT SLIPPERY, HUH?
WELL, I GUESS IT IS A BIT SLICK!

GOODNESS! WHY IS THE DOOR OPEN? MY GOSH!

I'LL HAVE YOU OUT OF THERE AND THIS ICE CLEARED IN A MINUTE, SIR!
HURRY, SMITHERS!

MINUTES LATER...
BUT DADDY, I CAN'T MISS THIS LESSON! MY PERSONAL TRAINER WON'T LIKE IT!
YOU ARE NOT DRIVING IN THIS SLIPPERY WEATHER AND THAT'S FINAL!

THEN CAN SOMEONE DRIVE ME?
WHO? I'D HAVE TO RENT A SNOWPLOW TO GET YOU THERE SAFELY!

WELL...?
OKAY! OKAY! I GIVE UP!

LATER...
YO! DID SOMEONE HERE CALL TO HAVE THEIR DRIVEWAY PLOWED?
NO! I HIRED YOUR TRUCK TO DRIVE MY DAUGHTER TO HER LESSON!

HUMPH! HE MUST THINK THIS IS A TAXI SERVICE!
'BYE, DADDY! THANKS!

AND DON'T FORGET TO WAIT FOR HER! THERE'S A BIG TIP IN IT FOR YOU!
BOING! TIP?

YES, SIR! ACE TAXI PLOW COMPANY IS AT YOUR SERVICE, SIR!

I'LL TELL YOU WHERE TO GO!
YES, MISS! IT SURE IS A CRUMMY DAY TO GO OUT! THIS MUST BE AN IMPORTANT LESSON!
4

LATER STILL...
I'LL BE RIGHT HERE UNTIL YOU'RE FINISHED!
RIVERDALE

HI! I'M HERE FOR MY PRIVATE LESSON!
YES, MISS LODGE! GO RIGHT IN! YOUR TRAINER'S WAITING!

MINUTES LATER...
HI, RON! I'M AMAZED YOU MADE IT! ARE YOU ALL SET?
I'M READY TO GO, MR. MORGAN!

WELL, STEP OUT ONTO THE ICE AND LET'S GET STARTED!
I JUST LOVE FIGURE SKATING!
END

Script: **Bill Golliher** Pencils: **Fernando Ruiz** Inks: **Rudy Lapick** Letters: **Bill Yoshida** Colors: **Barry Grossman**
Editor-In-Chief: **Victor Gorelick** President: **Mike Pellerito** Publisher: **Jon Goldwater**

WHAT'S WRONG WITH GOING FOR A PHYSICAL?
I JUST DREAD ALL THAT POKING AND PRODDING AND THE COLD STETHOSCOPE!
THERE'S NOTHING TO WORRY ABOUT!
I'M SURE WE'LL BOTH GET A CLEAN BILL OF HEALTH AND GET SENT ON OUR WAY!
#1 DAD
AND SO...
ANDREWS.!!
THAT'S HIM!
WHICH ONE PLEASE?!

LET'S SEE...FRED!
WHEW! IT LOOKS LIKE I BOUGHT A FEW MINUTES!

SOON...
ARCHIE ANDREWS!
GULP! T-T-THAT'S ME!!

FANCY MEETING YOU HERE! DAD!

YOU TWO WILL BE OFF TO THE EXAMINATION ROOMS NEXT, BUT WE NEED TO CHECK YOUR VITAL STATISTICS FIRST!

LET'S SEE...
WHAT A CUTIE! I REALLY LUCKED OUT!

MY, YOUR HEART RATE IS VERY RAPID!
HELEN, THE DOCTOR NEEDS YOU IN THE LAB!

SURE THING! MADGE, WILL YOU TAKE OVER?
I'D LOVE TO!

HMMPH! YOUR HEART RATE SEEMS NORMAL TO ME!
I'M NOT SURPRISED!
3

SOON...
OKAY, FRED ANDREWS, YOU ARE IN EXAM ROOM THREE! ARCHIE, YOU'RE IN EXAM ROOM FOUR!
GREAT!
SEE YA SOON!
3
FIFTEEN MINUTES LATER...
SIGH! THIS WAITING IS THE WORST PART!
YOU SAID IT, PAL!
EEEK! A TALKING SKELETON!!
SORRY, ARCHIE, IT'S JUST ME!
DR. MEYERS?!
THOSE VENTRILOQUISM LESSONS I TOOK REALLY PAY OFF SOMETIMES!
I JUST FINISHED UP WITH YOUR FATHER HERE! HE'S DOING GREAT! I HOPE YOU'RE IN HALF THE SHAPE HE'S IN!
WHAT CAN I SAY? I GUESS I OWE THE CHANGE TO MY DIET AND EXERCISE REGIMEN!

YOUR OLD MAN HAS THE VITAL STATISTICS OF A YOUNG ADULT!
WAIT UNTIL MARY HEARS I'M AS FIT AS A FIDDLE!
WHOA! LOOK AT THIS ARCHIE! YOUR BLOOD PRESSURE IS HIGH! NOT TO MENTION YOUR CHOLESTEROL!
REALLY?
WE MAY HAVE TO TALK ABOUT SOME LIFESTYLE CHANGES
HUH?
TSK! TSK!
AND THIS INDICATES YOU PACKED ON FIFTEEN POUNDS SINCE YOUR LAST OFFICE VISIT!
I'VE GOT SOME EXTRA CHANGE IN MY POCKET, BUT THAT IS RIDICULOUS!
UH-OH! WE DO HAVE A PROBLEM!
WHAT IS IT, DOC?
THE NURSES PUT THE WRONG PAPER WORK IN YOUR FOLDERS!
YOUR FILES WERE MIXED UP!

THEN I'M THE ONE WHO'S FIT AS A FIDDLE!
EXACTLY! YOUR FATHER AND I ON THE OTHER HAND NEED TO HAVE A LITTLE TALK!
ULP!
THAT EVENING...
YOU'RE RIGHT, DAD! THAT PHYSICAL WASN'T SO BAD!
IT'S GREAT TO KNOW YOUR BODY'S IN TUNE!
I WON'T MIND GOING AT ALL NEXT YEAR!
HERE'S YOUR SALAD WITH LITE DRESSING, FRED!
HMMPH!
BY THE WAY, THE DOCTOR'S OFFICE CALLED! THEY SCHEDULED A FOLLOW UP APPOINTMENT FOR YOU IN TWO MONTHS!
HUH?
I DON'T HAVE TO GO, DO I? HUH?
BOY, THIS SOUNDS FAMILIAR!
The End

Archie IN The BIG THAW
YOU STILL HERE, CARROT TOP? I THOUGHT YOU HAD A DATE HOURS AGO!
POP'S SPECIALS TODAY
SPLORTCH!!
POP'S
MENU
SCRIPT: KATHLEEN WEBB
PENCILS: STAN GOLDBERG
INKS: BOB SMITH

THAT SODA YOU'RE WEARING HAS GOT TO BE COLD!
omigosh!!

I TOTALLY FORGOT I HAD A DATE WITH VERONICA TONIGHT!
THE OPERATIVE WORD, PAL, IS "HAD"!
POP'S

HE'LL BE LUCKY SHE DOESN'T BOIL HIM IN OIL!!
OR FRY HIS HIDE!
GREAT! NOW I'M EVEN HUNGRIER!

SHE'S-- GONNA-- KILL-- ME!!

BRRR! IF THIS COLD WEATHER DOESN'T DO IT FIRST!
LODGE

I'M SORRY, MASTER ANDREWS! MISS LODGE IS NOT AT HOME TO YOU!

SLAM

BRRR! SO MUCH FOR THE COLD WEATHER DOING ME IN!

THE NEXT DAY...
FROZE YOU OUT, HUH? WELL, YOU CAN'T SAY YOU DIDN'T DESERVE IT!
SHE'LL PROBABLY NEVER FORGIVE ME!!

HERE'S YOUR CHANCE TO FIND OUT!
VERONICA, BABY! IT WAS ALL A BIG MISTAKE! I--

HMPH!

WOW! WAS THAT ICY!
BRRR! N-NO KIDDING!

I'LL KEEP TRYING, THOUGH! SHE'S BOUND TO THAW OUT SOONER OR LATER!

HOWEVER...
HMPH!

...ARCHIE SOON FEELS...
P-PLEASE LET ME EXPLAIN!
HMPH!

...COLD ALL OVER!
HMPH!
B-BUT!
CRACKLE

NOW THAT'S AN ICY LOOK!
TALK ABOUT GIVING SOMEONE THE COLD SHOULDER!
NOK
NOK

OH, POOR ARCHIEKINS! HERE, LET YOUR LITTLE BETTYKINS WARM YOU UP!

SMOOCH!
CRACK

WOW! THANKS BETTY-- I WAS ALMOST A GONER!
YOU ALWAYS HAVE A WARM PLACE IN MY HEART, ARCHIE!

I'LL DO THE SPRING THAW AROUND HERE, BLONDIE!!
HUH?!

BESIDES, YOUR LITTLE PECK HARDLY DEFROSTED HIS CHILBLAINS!!
SMOOCH

OH, YEAH? I THINK I HELPED TOAST HIS TOES!
YOU BARELY REGISTERED ON HIS THER-MOMETER!

I'LL GET HIM BOIL-ING!! SMACK!
SMOOCH!
HOLD IT!!
HAH! MY LIPS WILL LIGHT HIS FIRE!! SWOCK!
SMERP!
SMACK!

WHAT I THINK YOU DID IS OVERDO IT! JUST LIKE ALWAYS!!
OOPS!
MAYBE WE SHOULD GET SOME ICE?
WAY AHEAD OF YOU!
BRRR! THAT'S TWO GIRLS WHO DON'T KNOW THEIR OWN STRENGTH!
END

Archie IN
SNOW WOE
DID YOU BOYS SEE TODAY'S PAPER?
THEY'RE RUNNING A PHOTO CONTEST... WINNER COPS THE $500 PRIZE!
YEAH, WE'VE SEEN IT! THAT'S WHY CHUCK AND I HAVE BROUGHT ALONG OUR CAMERAS!
RIVERDALE LEDGER
BIG $500 WINTER PHOTO CONTEST
POP
Menu
SCRIPT: GEORGE GLADIR
PENCILS: STAN GOLDBERG
INKS: BOB SMITH

WANNA JOIN US, JUG?
NO WAY AM I GONNA GO TRAMPIN' THROUGH THAT SNOW! WHEN I'M DONE HERE, I'M HEADING HOME WHERE IT'S NICE AND WARM!

POOR JUG! NOTHING VENTURED, NOTHING GAINED!

HMMM! I HAVE A GREAT IDEA FOR A WINTER GAG PHOTO!
WHAT?

I'LL GO GET MY MOTHER TO HELP ME POSE FOR IT... I'LL HAVE HER PRETEND SHE'S ASKING ME TO SHOVEL OUR WALKWAY.

THAT'S GREAT, MRS. ANDREWS!
THIS PICTURE SHOULD BE A WINNER!

THANKS, MA! WE SURE APPRECIATE YOUR HELP!
WAIT! WHERE DO YOU THINK YOU'RE GOING? I REALLY WANT YOU TO SHOVEL OUR SIDEWALK!

YUK! YUK! I THINK THIS SNAP IS EVEN BETTER!
HAR, HAR. YOU ARE SOOOO FUNNY!

LOOK! MATT'S TRYING TO START HIS OLD SNOW-MOBILE!
VROOM
MIND IF WE GET ON AND YOU TAKE OUR PICTURE?
OKAY... BUT THIS BABY ISN'T GOING ANYWHERE. I'M HAVING PROBLEMS WITH THE ENGINE!
SPUTT KLUNKLUNK SPUT
UH-OH! IT'S ACTING UP REAL BAD!
VROOM
NOK NOK
KA-BOOM
WOW! THIS SHOULD MAKE FOR ONE GREAT SHOT!
MAN! ARE WE LUCKY THIS HAPPENED TO US!
CLICK AWAY, MATT!

RIVERDALE BANK
HEY! THAT BIG SIGN SHOULD MAKE A GREAT WINTER PHOTO!
CURRENT TEMPERATURE
0
DEGREES

IT DOESN'T EVEN NEED A CAPTION! THE BIG FAT ZERO TELLS IT ALL!
CURRENT TEMPERATURE
0
DEGREES

MAN! IT IS REALLY COLD!
I'M ALL FOR WRAPPING IT UP.
I AGREE.

YOUR TEETH ARE CHATTERING AND YOUR LIPS ARE BLUE!
REALLY? SO NOW TAKE A CLOSE-UP OF ME!

I'LL TITLE THE PHOTO "I DIDN'T GET THESE LIPS FROM EATING BLUEBERRIES!"

SINCE WE COLLABORATED ON ALL THESE PICTURES, WHY DON'T WE SHARE THE PRIZE IF WE WIN?
GOOD IDEA!

ONE WEEK LATER...
I GUESS YOU BOYS HEARD ABOUT THE WINTER PHOTO CONTEST.
NO, POP! WHO WON?
POP'S MENU

NONE OTHER THAN JUGHEAD JONES!
BUT HE SAID HE WANTED NOTHING TO DO WITH THE COLD!... AND THAT HE WAS GOING STRAIGHT HOME WHERE IT WAS WARM!

SO HOW COULD HE POSSIBLY WIN?!

THAT'S HOW!
RIVERDALE LEDGER
FORSYTHE JONES WINS WINTER PHOTO CONTEST
WINNING ENTRY: "LET IT SNOW"
FOOD CHANNEL
END

Archie in "A Boy's Best Friend"

WELL, I KNOW THE COLD WEATHER'S REALLY ARRIVED WHEN I SEE *THAT* COAT!

RIGHT, POP! THIS IS MY FRIGID WEATHER UNIFORM! HAVEN'T HAD THIS ON SINCE THE SPRING THAW!

Script: Mike Pellowski / Pencils: Bob Bolling / Letters: Bill Yoshida / Colors: Barry Grossman

SAY! IT HAS TURNED COLD, HASN'T IT? MY FINGERS ARE FREEZING ALREADY!

PUT THEM IN MY POCKETS, LOVE BUG! THEY'RE LINED AND REAL WARM!
WHY, THANK YOU, SIR! I--- I---

AHA!
HEY! A LIPSTICK! WAS THAT IN MY POCKET?

OOH! OOH! DON'T PLAY INNOCENT WITH ME, YOU-YOU BLUEBEARD!
HEY, LOOK, PUMPKIN! I AM INNOCENT! THIS IS THE FIRST TIME I HAD THE COAT ON SINCE LAST WINTER!

WHAT DIFFERENCE DOES *THAT* MAKE? IT'S STILL *YOUR* COAT!
MAYBE IT'S *YOUR* LIPSTICK?

NOT MINE, AND NOT ANY OF THE GIRLS I KNOW! YOU'VE GOT A *SECRET LOVE*!
NO!

YES! AND UNTIL YOU'RE READY FOR A FULL CONFESSION, YOU AND I ARE THROUGH!
CUPCAKE! YOU CAN'T DO THIS TO ME!
DO WHAT?

SHE FOUND THIS LIPSTICK IN MY POCKET! WHO WEARS THAT SHADE?
NO ONE *WE* KNOW!

YOU'VE GOT A SECRET LOVE! SO OUR CROWD ISN'T GOOD ENOUGH FOR YOU ANYMORE, EH?
GLEEP!

NO! NO! I'M INNOCENT UNTIL PROVEN GUILTY!
DON'T SWEET TALK ME, ARCHIE ANDREWS!
HEY! WHAT'S GOING ON?
I NEVER SAW BETTY MAD AT YOU, ARCH!

RONNIE FOUND THIS LIPSTICK IN MY POCKET AND NOW EVERYBODY ACCUSES ME OF SOME SORT OF HANKY PANKY WITH A SECRET LOVE!

NOT EVERYBODY, ARCH! -- WE JUST HEARD ABOUT IT!
BUT NOW THAT WE'VE HEARD ABOUT IT! ---

I THINK HE'S UP TO SOME SORT OF HANKY PANKY WITH A SECRET LOVE!
YOU TOOK THE WORDS RIGHT OUT OF MY MOUTH!

ACTUALLY, I GOT THEM FROM ARCH!
HE TURNS A NEAT PHRASE!
SHEESH!

KNOW WHAT YOU ARE VERONICA? YOU'RE MAD, GIRL! YOU'RE DELIVERING HIM INTO THE HANDS OF THIS MYSTERY WOMAN!
IS THAT THE LODGE WAY? NO! IN NO WAY IS THAT THE LODGE WAY! GO FIGHT FOR YOUR MAN!
YOU! YOU TWO-TIMING WRETCH! STAND STILL! YOU'RE NOT DEALING WITH SOME QUITTER!
HUH?
SMOOCH!
LET'S SEE YOUR MYSTERY GIRL TOP THAT! I'M READY TO MEET AND BEAT ALL COMPETITION!
BY GOLLY! YOU'RE RIGHT, RON!
COME HERE, YOU CHEATING MALE, YOU!

?
D-UH!
CLUNK!

MARY! YOUR MISSING LIPSTICK! IT WAS IN ARCHIE'S COAT!
OF COURSE!

I THREW THAT ON WHEN I HAD TO RUN OUT IN THE BACK YARD FOR SOMETHING LAST WEEK!

I GUESS I LEFT IT IN THE POCKET BY MISTAKE! I'M SORRY, ARCHIE! I HOPE IT DIDN'T CAUSE YOU ANY TROUBLE!

YOU JUST CAUSE ALL THE TROUBLE OF THAT KIND THAT YOU CAN, MOM! I THRIVE ON IT, YOU MYSTERY WOMAN, YOU!
?
?
End

Script: Mike Pellowski / Pencils: Howard Bender / Inks: Jon D' Agostino / Letters: Bill Yoshida / Colors: Barry Grossman

SO, I GUESS NOW YOU'RE GOING TO LEARN HOW TO DO SNOWBOARD STUNTS!
FIRST THINGS *FIRST*, PAL!

KILLER SNOWBOARD GE
FIRST YOU HAVE TO *LOOK* THE PART!

MENS
S M L XL
JACKETS
...WITH THE RIGHT JACKET...
THE RIGHT PANTS...

HEADGEAR
CAN'T FORGET TO GET THE RIGHT HAT...
NOR A PAIR OF ULTRA COOL SUNGLASSES!

BUT THE BOOTS ARE *MOST IMPORTANT* OF ALL!
FOR SHOCK ABSORBTION, AND MAKING SHARP TURNS...RIGHT?

WRONG!
...FOR CATCHING THE EYES OF ADMIRING FEMALES!

NOW I'M READY TO HIT THE HALF PIPE!
WON'T YOU ALSO NEED A SNOWBOARD?

GLAD YOU REMINDED ME!
CAN'T SNOWBOARD WITHOUT A SNOW-BOARD! HEH! HEH!
SNOW

NOW WATCH ME DO A 720!
UH, DON'T YOU THINK YOU SHOULD FIRST TAKE LESSONS?

NAH! I ALREADY KNOW HOW FROM WATCHING THE PROS ON TV!
...AND FROM READING SNOW-BOARD MAGAZINES!

BESIDES, I KNOW HOW TO SKATEBOARD!
... THE SAME SKILLS ARE INVOLVED IN BOTH SPORTS... I THINK!

MAYBE YOU SHOULD FIRST WARM UP!
AN EXCELLENT SUGGESTION!
...THAT'S WHAT ALL THE PROS DO!

I'LL FIRST ATTEMPT A SIMPLE 360!
THAT'S JUST ONE COMPLETE SPIN!

HOW COME YOU'RE HESITATING?
WAITING FOR THE RIGHT MOMENT!

YOU MEAN THE RIGHT WIND FACTOR?
NO!... THE RIGHT AUDIENCE!

AND HERE THEY COME!
THEY'VE OBVIOUSLY NOTICED MY SELF-CONFIDENT ATTITUDE!
WHO'S THE DWEEB, MEGHAN?
DUNNO! NEVER SEEN THE CHARACTER BEFORE!

HERE GOES THE MASTER!

YIIIIIII!!!

I CAN'T BEAR TO LOOK!
KRASH!

POOR, POOR ARCHIE!

LATER...
WHAT HAPPENED?
YOU MEAN WHAT DIDN'T HAPPEN?

BUT, YOU DID GET YOUR FONDEST WISH!
WHAT?

TO BE SURROUNDED BY MANY FEMALES!
SHADDUP!!
ANDREWS
END

Script: George Gladir / Pencils: Stan Goldberg / Inks: John Lowe / Letters: Bill Yoshida / Colors: Barry Grossman

GEE, IT'S TOASTY WARM IN HERE!
I KNOW! I WAS CHILLY SO I TURNED UP THE THERMOSTAT JUST A TINY BIT!

MARY, WE AGREED TO KEEP THE THERMOSTAT AS LOW AS POSSIBLE TO CONSERVE FUEL!
SORRY, FRED! I'LL TURN IT BACK DOWN!

I'D BETTER CHECK THE FUEL TANK TO SEE HOW MUCH OIL WE HAVE!

ARRUGH!!
UH-OH! THAT DOESN'T SOUND GOOD!

I KNEW IT! I KNEW IT! WE NEED ANOTHER OIL DELIVERY ALREADY!
CHILL OUT, POP! DON'T GET SO HOT HEADED OVER HEATING OIL!

I CAN'T HELP IT! THE COST OF HEATING OIL IS **SKY HIGH!**
GULP!

VIC'S FUEL COMPANY
SO LONG, FRED! SEE YOU SOON!
I HOPE NOT TOO SOON, VIC! I CAN'T AFFORD IT!

LOOK AT THIS BILL! THAT DOES IT! WE HAVE TO USE LESS OIL!
I HAVE AN IDEA, FRED!

WE CAN WEAR EXTRA CLOTHING INSIDE! I'LL GET OUT SOME SWEATERS!
I HAVE AN IDEA, TOO!

WE CAN USE THE FIREPLACE MORE! IT'LL HELP HEAT THE HOUSE!
THAT'S GOOD THINKING, ARCHIE!

IN FACT, I'LL GO OUT RIGHT NOW AND BRING IN SOME FIREWOOD!

CUTTING DOWN THAT OLD DEAD OAK AND CHOPPING IT UP WAS A JOB WORTH DOING!

AFTER ALL, FIREWOOD DOESN'T GROW ON TREES... OH!... WAIT A MINUTE! IT DOES!

WEEKS LATER...
AH, IT'S REALLY COZY IN HERE!
SITTING IN FRONT OF THE FIREPLACE IS SO COMFORTING!

ENJOY THE FIREPLACE WHILE YOU CAN, MOM! THAT'S THE LAST OF OUR FIREWOOD!

YOU MEAN ALL THAT FIREWOOD WE CUT IS GONE ALREADY?
YUP! IT JUST WENT UP IN SMOKE, POP!
4

NOW WHAT, FRED? ARE WE GOING TO ADJUST THE THERMOSTAT?
NO WAY! FUEL OIL STILL COSTS AN ARM AND A LEG!

WE'LL JUST HAVE SOME FIREWOOD DELIVERED!
OKAY! I'LL PLACE THE CALL!

THE NEXT DAY...
HI, ARCHIE! I SEE THEY DELIVERED THE FIREWOOD, THAT SHOULD HOLD US FOR A WHILE!
YOU'RE RIGHT THERE, POP, AND THIS PAPER I'M HOLDING IS THE BILL! CHECK IT OUT!

EGAD! I HAD NO IDEA THE PRICE OF FIREWOOD WAS THIS HIGH!

DON'T GET SO STEAMED UP, POP! WHEN IT COMES TO HEATING A HOME IN WINTER, I GUESS YOU JUST CAN'T WIN!
The End

VEN STUDENTS GO HOME SVENSON GOES TO WORK TO CLEAN UP WHOLE SCHOOL FOR NEXT DAY!
LOTS OF WORK! BIG YOB! BY YIMINY!
RIVERDALE'S HIGH SCHOOL CUSTODIAN
MR. SVENSON
HELP WANTED

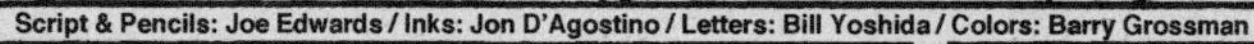
Script & Pencils: Joe Edwards / Inks: Jon D'Agostino / Letters: Bill Yoshida / Colors: Barry Grossman

NEXT MORNING -
MR. SVENSON NEVER EVEN TOUCHED THIS ROOM! COULD IT BE AN OVERSIGHT?
THIS IS THE FOURTH OVERSIGHT I'VE FOUND TODAY! I'VE HAD IT!

MR. SVENSON AND I ARE GOING TO HAVE A LITTLE TALK!
1

I DO BETTER YOB IF I HAD ASSISTANT, MR. VEDDERBEE!
WELL, ONE WAS REQUESTED, IN NEXT YEAR'S SCHOOL BUDGET!

IN THE MEANTIME, I'M SURE WITH A LITTLE EXTRA EFFORT, YOU CAN GET THE JOB DONE!
ULP! I-I TRY HARDER!

I JUST HEARD ABOUT MR. SVENSON! MAYBE WE CAN HELP HIM AND KEEP THE SCHOOL CLEANER!
WAIT! I'VE GOT AN IDEA!

WELL, DILTON? THEY DON'T CALL YOU THE "BRAIN" FOR NOTHING! WHAT IS IT?

I'VE BEEN WORKING ON A SCIENCE PROJECT THAT I'D LIKE TO TEST, AND MAYBE IT'LL DO THE TRICK!

A ROBOT? THAT TEENY TING VILL HELP ME CLEAN WHOLE SCHOOL?
YOU BET, MR. SVENSON! THEY CAN BUILD CARS, WHY NOT OTHER JOBS?
2

MR. JIFFY WILL BE OUR SECRET! WHAT WOULD YOU LIKE HIM TO DO FOR YOU? A TEST!
OKAY! LET'S SEE MR. YIFFY MOP FLOORS!

ZIP
SHLOP SLOP

BY YIMINY! IT DO A GOOD SPIC AND SPAN YOB!
GOOD! HE'S PROGRAMMED TO FOLLOW YOUR ORDERS!

A WEEK LATER –
HEH! HEH! I'VE GOT LOTS OF FREE TIME NOW! WATCH TV WHILE MR. YIFFY CLEANS SCHOOL!

SNAP!
I CALL GIRLFRIEND OLGA TO GO DANCING!

YOU NEVER WANTED TO GO DANCING BEFORE, YOU WERE SO TIRED! HOW COME?
VELL, OLGA! I GOT A NEW LITTLE HELPER! HEH! HEH!
3

BY YIMINY! GOT PLENTY OF ENERGY NOW! I COULD DANCE ALL NIGHT!
?
?
OOH! TOO MUCH DANCING!

DON'T GET UP! I SEE YOU MUST HAVE BEEN WORKING HARD!
?

MR. VEDDERBEE TINKS I VORK HARD FROM CLEANING SCHOOL!
RING

I CALLED YOU TO REMIND YOU TO COME EARLY! WE HAVE TO PRACTICE FOR THE BIG DANCE CONTEST!

OLGA VERY ANGRY WHEN I'M LATE! I SPEED UP MR. YIFFY SO I CAN FINISH EARLY!

HI, MR. SVENSON! HOW ARE THINGS WORKING OUT WITH MR. JIFFY?

YUMPIN' YIMINY!! SOMETHING IS WRONG! HE'S GOING CRAZY!
CHLUKA

CHUKKA
CHUGG
WHRRRRRRRR
RRRRRRRR

RUN!! IT'S OUT OF CONTROL!!
YIPE!! THE CIRCUITS ARE OVERLOADED!
CHUKA
CHUKA

CHULKA
CHUKA
ZIP!
CRASH

GULP! IT'LL TAKE ME MONTHS TO PUT ALL THIS JUNK BACK TOGETHER!

I TINK YOU FORGET ABOUT IT! ROBOT DO TOO GOOD A YOB! ONE DAY IT MIGHT REPLACE SVENSON!

I NOTICED HOW EXHAUSTED YOU WERE YESTERDAY, SO WE'RE GETTING *SOMEONE* TO DO YOUR JOB!
ULP! H-HERE IT COMES- FIRED!

... WHILE YOU GO ON A WEEK'S *VACATION*! YOU'VE DONE SUCH AN OUTSTANDING JOB, YOU DESERVE IT!
?

SVENSON! WE WON THE DANCE CONTEST! AREN'T YOU ENJOYING YOUR VACATION? WHY DO YOU LOOK SO TIRED?
DANCE
6

I'M *TIRED THINKING* ABOUT *ALL* THE *VORK* VEN I GET BACK TO SCHOOL!
END

Archie in "PARTING GESTURE"

Script: George Gladir / Pencils: Stan Goldberg / Inks: Chic Stone / Letters: Bill Yoshida / Colors: Barry Grossman

TRYING TO CONVINCE HER TO STAY HERE WITH US IS SELFISH ON OUR PART!
OKAY! LET'S BE SELFISH!

WE MUST FACE FACTS! WHAT'S GOOD FOR US IS NOT NECESSARILY GOOD FOR HER!
TRUE! RIGHT ON! ABSOLUTELY!

WHAT THE MAN SAYS IS TRUE! WE'VE GOT TO LET HER GO!
YOU HEARTLESS FIEND! HOW CAN YOU SAY THAT?
WE NEED OUR MISS GRUNDY!

LOOK, I FEEL BADLY! I'M CRYIN' ON THE INSIDE!
--AND ALMOST ON THE OUTSIDE, TOO!

BUT WE'VE GOT TO THINK OF WHAT'S GOOD FOR MISS GRUNDY!
OKAY!

THEN YOU'VE GOT TO GET HER BACK FOR SURE!
HUH?
WHAT DO YOU MEAN?

SHE'S GOING TO A PRIVATE SCHOOL!
I'M RICH! I'VE BEEN IN PRIVATE SCHOOL! I KNOW!

SHE'LL BE MISERABLE IN THOSE SNOB PALACES ONLY MONEY COUNTS!
SHE WON'T RULE THE STUDENTS! THEY'LL RULE HER!

OH, NOT OUR MISS GRUNDY! SHE WON'T STAND FOR THAT!
THEN SHE'LL GET BOUNCED QUICK!

---AND SHE'LL BE TOO EMBARRASSED TO COME BACK HERE!
WELL, IT'S HER DECISION! RIGHT?

YOU'RE GOING UP TO YOUR NEW SCHOOL, MISS GRUNDY?
YES, ARCHIE! I SIGN THE FINAL CONTRACT TODAY!

HOW ABOUT LETTING ME DRIVE YOU UP? I'D LIKE TO SEE THE PLACE!
I'D LOVE IT!
3

NICE LOOKING PLACE.!
LOOK AROUND, ARCHIE.! I WON'T BE LONG.!

WELL, NOW TO FIND OUT IF VERONICA IS RIGHT.!
LET'S SEE WHO RUNS WHO.!

ULP! THIS IS NOT GONNA BE PAINLESS.!
OUT OF MY WAY, DUMBULB.!

WHY, YOU GRUBBY LITTLE PEASANT.! HOW DARE YOU PUT YOUR DIRTY HANDS ON MY PERSON ?
BLAT!

WHAM!

OH, NO.!!
ZOK!
SOK!
WHAP!

STOP THAT! I DEMAND THAT YOU STOP IMMEDIATELY!
GRRRR!

MISS GRUNDY! NEVER, NEVER LAY HANDS ON ONE OF OUR STUDENTS! OH DEAR ME! NOT EVER!!

THE ONE THING YOU MUST LEARN IMMEDIATELY IS THAT THESE ARE NOTHING LIKE THE STUDENTS YOU'VE BEEN ACCUSTOMED TO!
THEY'RE NOT?
LEGGO!

WE EXIST ONLY BY THE GENEROSITY OF THEIR PARENTS!
WAIT'LL MY DAD HEARS HOW I'VE BEEN MANHANDLED BY A-A---TEACHER!

YOU LITTLE DICKENS, YOU COULD HAVE TAKEN HIM WITH ONE HAND, AND YOU KNOW IT!
COULD I?
SMACK!

WHAT A SACRIFICE! HE OPENED MY EYES BY GETTING ONE OF HIS CLOSED!
THAT'S OUR ARCHIE!
END.

MR. WEATHERBEE in "WEATHERBEE FOR MAYOR?"

Script & Pencils: Joe Edwards / Inks: Chic Stone / Letters: Bill Yoshida / Colors: Barry Grossman

THE MAYOR WANTS TO BUY A LIMO FOR CITY BUSINESS... AND THE MONEY HAS TO COME FROM SOMEWHERE!
SO HE'S TAKING IT OUT OF THE SCHOOL BUDGET! UNBELIEV-ABLE!
I KNOW HOW MUCH YOUR STUDENTS MEAN TO YOU, WALDO! BUT IF YOU REALLY WISH TO HELP THEM...
...YOU'LL RUN FOR MAYOR OF RIVERDALE AND RESTORE THE BUDGET! WELL?
BY JOVE! I'LL DO IT!!
BAMM!

AND SO---
RIVERDALE'S DAILY
WEATHERBEE THROWS HAT IN RING!

I THINK THE BEE WOULD MAKE A GREAT *MAYOR*!!
IF I WERE OLD ENOUGH, HE'D GET MY *VOTE*!
SUNDAES!
$4.00

THERE ARE PLENTY OF WAYS TO *HELP* THE BEE BESIDES *VOTING*...!
I'M FLAT BROKE! POLITICAL DONATIONS ARE DEFINITELY *OUT*!

I'M NOT TALKING DONATIONS, JUG! WE CAN VOLUNTEER AS *CAMPAIGN WORKERS*!
THAT'S A WONDERFUL *IDEA*! LET'S GO SIGN UP RIGHT NOW!

YEAH! IF THE BEE GETS *ELECTED*, WE CAN BREAK IN A BRAND NEW PRINCIPAL!! HOO-*HAH*!
REGGIE! THAT'S NOT THE REASON WE'RE DOING THIS!
CAMPAIGN HEADQUARTER
WEATHERBEE FOR MAYOR

WEATHERBEE FOR MAYOR
I *KNOW*, BUT I CAN STILL THINK OF FRINGE BENEFITS, CAN'T I ?!!

THIS IS BETTY COOPER! PLEASE VOTE FOR MR. WEATHERBEE ON ELECTION DAY!
WEATHERBEE FOR MAYOR

WOULD YOU CARE TO CONTRIBUTE TO MR. WEATHERBEE'S CAMPAIGN?
HERE'S A CHECK FOR $1,000!

HOPE I'VE SLAPPED UP ENOUGH *POSTERS*!

ELECT THE BEE!

WEATHERBEE FOR MAYOR!
WEATHERBEE FOR MAYOR!
WEATHERBEE FOR MAYOR!

RIVERDALE MALL
THESE *HANDBILLS* SHOULD DELIVER PLENTY OF VOTES!
WEATHERBEE FOR MAYOR

HI, MR. HOWITZER! ER, WHY ARE YOU SMILING? YOU FEEL ALL RIGHT?
I'M SMILING FOR TWO REASONS, ARCHIE!
MR. HOWITZ

FIRST, YOU KIDS ARE DOING A WONDERFUL JOB GETTING WEATHERBEE ELECTED!
AND THE OTHER REASON?

SECOND, ONCE HE'S MAYOR... THE SCHOOL BOARD WILL APPOINT ME HIS REPLACEMENT!!
G-GULP! NO--! A RETIRED DRILL SERGEANT AS OUR NEXT PRINCIPAL! IT'S A :SHUDDER: NIGHTMARE!!!

MEANWHILE, AT THE MAYOR'S OFFICE...
MAYOR HONEYWELL!! YOUR POLLSTER IS HERE!
BY ALL MEANS, SEND HIM IN!
MAYOR HONEYWELL

IT LOOKS BAD! WEATHERBEE IS GAINING IN THE POLLS!
BUT HOW CAN THIS BE?!

HE'S SOMEHOW MOBILIZED A STUDENT ARMY! THEY'RE GIVING THE CAMPAIGN A DECISIVE EDGE...!
I'D BETTER MAKE A DEAL WITH HIM...BE-FORE I LOSE THE ELECTION!

AND SO---
MR. WEATHERBEE! WHAT WOULD IT TAKE FOR YOU TO WITHDRAW FROM THE RACE?
HURUMPH! AS YOU KNOW, THE SCHOOL BUDGET HAS BEEN NEGLECTED FOR YEARS!
MAYOR HONEY

IT ISN'T ENOUGH TO RESTORE THE CUTS! I WANT THE ENTIRE SCHOOL BUDGET INCREASED!

YOU DRIVE A HARD BARGAIN, WEATHERBEE, BUT IT'S A DEAL...
LOOKS LIKE WE BOTH WIN! YOU STAY MAYOR...AND I STAY PRINCIPAL OF RIVERDALE HIGH!

SEVERAL DAYS LATER---
ARCHIE, WHY ARE YOU MILINGERING IN THE HALLS?
THANK GOODNESS WE'VE GOT THE BEE BACK! HIS VOICE IS MUSIC TO MY EARS...!!
The End

Archie in The LITTLE DRIP

Script & Pencils: Dick Malmgren / Inks: Jon D'Agostino / Letters: Bill Yoshida / Colors: Barry Grossman

I HATE TO ADMIT IT, BUT I'M A GENUIS!

SPLAT!

HEY, POP! MY BEDROOM HAS A COUPLE OF DRIPS IN IT!
A COUPLE?

I DIDN'T KNOW JUGHEAD WAS SLEEPING OVER WITH YOU!
VERY FUNNY!

I'M TALKING ABOUT LEAKS IN THE ROOF! I CAN'T SLEEP WITH WATER DRIPPING ON MY HEAD!

I DON'T THINK I COULD MYSELF, SON! I'LL SOLVE THE PROBLEM FOR YOU!
GREAT, I HAVE TO GET SOME SLEEP!

HERE, TAKE MY UMBRELLA TO BED WITH YOU!
GOOD GRIEF!

NOW HOW DO YOU EXPECT ME TO FALL ASLEEP WITH WATER DRIPPING ON AN UMBRELLA?

WHY, I'LL BE UP ALL NIGHT!
WELL, I CAN'T GO UP ON THE ROOF NOW, SON! I'D GET ALL WET!

I'LL DO IT TOMORROW WHEN THE RAIN STOPS! GOOD NIGHT, SON!
?

BUT THIS IS THE TIME TO FIND THE LEAK, POP! YOU CAN'T FIND IT WHEN IT ISN'T RAINING!
YOU KNOW, YOU'RE RIGHT, SON!

THERE'S SOME EXTRA SHINGLES IN THE GARAGE, SON!
3

(GRUMBLE!) WHEN I BUY A HOUSE IT'S GOING TO HAVE A CONCRETE ROOF!
BANG!
BANG!
BANG!
BANG!

ARCHIE! WILL YOU STOP WITH THE HAMMERING? YOU'RE KEEPING US AWAKE!
BANG!
BANG!
BANG!

I'M TRYING TO STOP THE LEAK!
SO HAMMER QUIETLY!

OH, WELL, I THINK I FIXED IT, ANYWAY!

NOW MAYBE I CAN GET SOME SLEEP!

DRIP!
SPLAT!
DRIP!
SPLAT!

THAT DOES IT! I'M NOT GOING TO BE UP ALL NIGHT FOR SOME DUMB RAIN!

JUGHEAD, DOES YOUR HOUSE HAVE A LEAKY ROOF?
NO, ARCHIE! WHY?

AT LEAST I'LL GET A FEW HOURS' SLEEP AT JUGHEAD'S!
POW!
POP!
CHUG!

MY MOM FIXED UP THE COUCH FOR YOU, ARCH!
YOU'RE A TRUE PAL, JUG! I'M BUSHED!

OH, BY THE WAY, MY MOM SAYS SHE HOPES THE DRIPPY FAUCET IN THE KITCHEN DOESN'T BOTHER YOU!
DRIP!
DRIP!
DRIP!
DRIP!
DRIP!
END

Script: Kathleen Webb / Pencils: Stan Goldberg / Inks: John Lowe / Letters: Bill Yoshida / Colors: Barry Grossman

HI, ARCHIE! WANNA COME OVER AND SHARE MY FIREPLACE?
I'D LOVE TO- BUT FIRST...
...CAN YOU TELL ME THE NAME OF THAT FANCY ITALIAN RESTAURANT REGGIE TOOK YOU TO LAST WEEK?
SURE! ALBERTO'S PASTA PALACE!
THANKS! VERONICA WAS HUNGRY FOR ITALIAN FOOD, AND I COULDN'T REMEMBER THE NAME OF THE PLACE!
VERONICA?
ER...UH...YEAH! SHE AND I HAVE A DATE TONIGHT! ER...GOTTA GO, THANKS AGAIN FOR HELPING ME!
GR...R..R...
YOU'RE SO NOT WELCOME!!
WHAM!
(SIGH) OH WELL, THERE'S STILL THE FIREPLACE, THE BOOK, THE HOT CHOCOLATE AND THE COOKIES!
BURP! THANKS, BETTY! THAT HIT THE SPOT!
2

YOU MEAN... IT WASN'T FOR ME?
NOT ORIGINALLY, DAD...

GOSH, I'M SORRY, PUMPKIN! LISTEN, YOU SIT THERE AND I'LL MAKE YOU A NEW CUP OF CHOCOLATE AND MORE COOKIES!
THANKS!

LOOKS LIKE THE BOOK AND THE FIREPLACE ARE MY ONLY COMPANIONS FOR THE TIME BEING!
BETTY! PHONE! IT'S ADAM!

HEY, ADAM! WOULD YOU LIKE TO SNUGGLE UP IN FRONT OF THE FIRE WITH ME?
SOUNDS GREAT, BETTY!

I HAVE TO STOP BY MY COUSIN'S PLACE FIRST! THEN I'LL BE OVER!
I'LL BE LOOKING FORWARD TO IT!

GUESS I WON'T NEED THE BOOK NOW! AND I'LL TELL DAD NOT TO BRING THAT HOT CHOCOLATE, EITHER! I'LL MAKE MORE FOR ADAM AND ME!

IT'S JUST AS WELL! YOUR MOTHER DRANK THE CUP I POURED FOR YOU!
SORRY!

LOOKS LIKE WE'RE OUT OF INSTANT HOT CHOCOLATE! GUESS I'LL MAKE SOME COCOA FROM SCRATCH!
HOT CHOCOLATE

DADDY, WHAT HAPPENED TO ALL THE COOKIES?
YOUR MOTHER HELPED FINISH THOSE OFF, TOO!
GUILTY AS CHARGED!
COOKIES

I'VE GOT A QUICK BROWNIE MIX! I'LL WHIP THEM UP TO GO WITH THE COCOA!
EGGS

THE FIRE'S LOW! BETTER ADD A FEW LOGS!

THERE! NOW EVERYTHING'S READY FOR A PERFECT EVENING FOR ADAM AND ME!
BRRING

SORRY, BETTY! I WON'T BE COMING OVER! THERE ARE RELATIVES VISITING MY COUSIN THAT I HAVEN'T SEEN IN A LONG TIME!
I UNDERSTAND, ADAM...

(SNIFF) A WARM FIRE ON A RAINY NIGHT... HOMEMADE COCOA AND BROWNIES... AND ONLY A BOOK TO SHARE THEM WITH ...!
BING BONG!

ARCHIE! BUT-YOU'RE DRENCHED!
HI, BETTY! DOES YOUR EARLIER OFFER STILL STAND?

HALF WAY TO ALBERTO'S PASTA PALACE, I HAD A FLAT! AND MY SPARE'S NO GOOD! RON CALLED REGGIE AND BAILED ON ME BEFORE I COULD GET EITHER TIRE FIXED!

I SHOULDA COME HERE IN THE FIRST PLACE!
IT'S OKAY, ARCHIE!

WITH YOU HERE NOW, I HAVE ALL THE INGREDIENTS FOR MY WONDERFUL EVENING!
END

Archie in "WHY ME?"

Script & Pencils: Dick Malmgren / Inks: Henry Scarpelli / Letters: Bill Yoshida / Colors: Barry Grossman

I WASN'T AWARE YOU WERE TALKING TO THE CLASS!
HOW COULD YOU BE AWARE WHEN YOU YAK AWAY LIKE SHE WASN'T IN THE CLASSROOM? YOUR PROBLEM IS THAT YOU DON'T EVEN THINK!

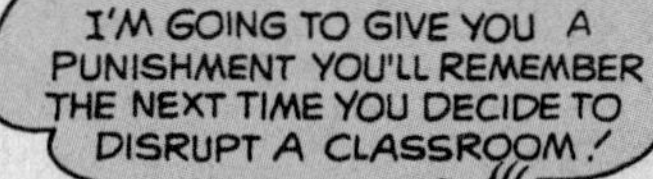
I'M GOING TO GIVE YOU A PUNISHMENT YOU'LL REMEMBER THE NEXT TIME YOU DECIDE TO DISRUPT A CLASSROOM!

WE HAVE TO NIP THIS THING AT THE BUD, MISS GRUNDY!
HE'S ALWAYS ACTING SO INNOCENT!

I'LL PUT A STOP TO THIS NONSENSE ONCE AND FOR ALL!
BUT WHAT DID I DO?

SEEING THAT MR. SVENSON ISN'T HERE TODAY, I WANT YOU TO SWEEP THE HALLWAY!

WHAT HALLWAY?
THIS HALLWAY! NOW GET TO IT!

AND SWEEP IT DOWN GOOD! I DON'T WANT TO SEE A SPECK OF DIRT LEFT ON THIS FLOOR!
?

WHEW!
I GUESS THAT DOES IT, MR. WEATHERBEE!

OH, NO, IT DOESN'T, ARCHIE! HOLD IT RIGHT THERE!

WHAT ABOUT THIS PILE OF TRASH OVER HERE?
WHAT TRASH? I DON'T SEE ANY TRASH!

SOMETIMES I THINK YOU ACT STUPID ON PURPOSE!
3

THERE! THAT TRASH! NOW DO YOU SEE IT!?

MAYBE YOU'RE BEING A LITTLE ROUGH ON HIM, MR. WEATHERBEE!
YOU THINK SO?
MAYBE YOU'RE RIGHT!

WHAT SHOULD I DO WITH THIS, MR. WEATHERBEE?
PUT IT IN THE BASKET!

WHAT BASKET?

GET HIM BACK TO CLASS! I CAN'T TAKE ANY MORE OF HIM! WHAT DID I DO TO BE PUNISHED LIKE THIS?
WHAT'S WITH HIM? DIDN'T I CLEAN THE HALL GOOD ENOUGH?
YOU WOULDN'T UNDERSTAND!
END

MISTER WEATHERBEE in "TRAP FLAP"

GOOD OLD JUG! HE ALWAYS KNOWS THE RIGHT THING TO WEAR!
SIX MONTHS OUT OF DATE!
BANK OF RIVER
Jughead in KNEES FREEZE!
NICE COAT, JUG!
THANKS SO MUCH!
HANDSOME-LOOKING SCARF!
THE HAT IS QUITE BECOMING!
SCRIPT: CRAIG BOLDMAN
PENCILS, INKS, LETTERS & COLORS: REX W. LINDSEY
EDITOR-IN-CHIEF: VICTOR GORELICK
PRESIDENT: MIKE PELLERITO

EVEN THE GLOVES HAVE THEIR GOOD POINTS!
AND THE BOOTS! NO COMPLAINTS ABOUT THE BOOTS!
WELL, THAT ABOUT COVERS IT THEN! GLAD MY ENSEMBLE MEETS WITH YOUR APPROVAL!
NOT SO FAST!
THERE IS THAT LITTLE NAGGING POINT WORTH MENTIONING!
YANK!
THE SHORTS?
THE SHORTS?
GOOD EYE, YOU TWO! I WAS INDEED REFERRING TO JUG'S SHORT PANTS!
ISN'T IT A LITTLE CHILLY FOR THOSE?
ONE WOULD THINK, BUT NO!
2

WHO COMPLAINS ABOUT THEIR KNEES BEING COLD?

YOU HEAR GRIPES ABOUT COLD EARS, COLD FINGERS, COLD TOES...

CHATTERING TEETH, JACK FROST NIPPING AT NOSES... BUT BARELY A MENTION OF CHILLY KNEES!

SO LET 'EM BREATHE, I SAY! THE BRISK WINTER AIR IS HEALTHY FOR 'EM!
TRANSIT

JUGGIE, YOU'RE A FASHION DISASTER, BUT A NUTTY FASHION DISASTER!
WHAT SAY YOU, DILT?

SIMPLE COMMON SENSE DICTATES THAT ONE BUNDLE UP IN FRIGID WEATHER!

EEK!
YOU YELPED?
I DIDN'T SEE THE PATCH OF ICE OVER MY SHOPPING BAGS!
I'LL HELP YOU UP!
AREN'T YOU GALLANT!
MY BUDDIES ARE WADDLING TO THE RESCUE TOO, IN THEIR POUNDS OF WINTER WEAR!
YOU OKAY, JENNY?
NO THANKS TO YOU!
J.G. NICKELS
SORRY I'M LATE! I TOOK A SPILL...
POPS

LUCKILY, THAT CUTIE JUGHEAD HELPED ME UP AND GATHERED MY PACKAGES!

DID I JUST CALL JUGHEAD CUTIE?
WE ALL HEARD YOU!

WELL, MAYBE WITH GOOD REASON! THE WAY HE'S DRESSED, AT LEAST YOU CAN TELL THERE'S A HUMAN BEING IN THERE!

LOOK AT THE REST OF THOSE OVERSTUFFED MATTRESSES! IT'S BEEN WEEKS SINCE WE'VE SEEN WHAT A GUY LOOKS LIKE!
POP'S BURGERS
RIVER

WELL, I'VE NEVER THOUGHT OF JUGHEAD IN TERMS OF SEX APPEAL...

BUT WHEN YOU PUT IT THAT WAY, I GUESS HE DOES START TO LOOK A LITTLE BETTER!

HEY, JUGGIE!
ARCH, AM I SEEING WHAT I'M SEEING OR HAVE I GOT A TOUCH OF SNOW-BLINDNESS?
LATER...
WELL, I'LL BE!
I THINK THIS WEATHER IS MORE SEVERE THAN JUGHEAD THOUGHT!
HAS IT GOTTEN TO HIS KNEES?

NO, TO THE OTHER GUYS' BRAINS!
END

SCRIPT: MIKE PELLOWSKI PENCILS: HENRY SCARPELLI INKS: BOB SMITH
LETTERS: JACK MORELLI COLORS: BARRY GROSSMAN

HAVEN'T YOU LOOKED OUTSIDE? IT'S SNOWING! SCHOOL IS CANCELLED! TODAY IS A SNOW DAY!
SCH-SCHOOL IS CANCELLED? SNOW DAY?!
YAHOOIE!
TEE-HEE! CALM DOWN AND EAT YOUR BREAK-FAST!

AFTER I EAT, I'LL TRUDGE OVER TO ARCHIE'S HOUSE! TOGETHER WE'LL FIGURE OUT HOW BEST TO ENJOY THIS BONUS DAY OFF!
I DOUBT IF YOU'LL BE ABLE TO DO THAT, SON!

WHAT DO YOU MEAN, DAD? WHAT ARE YOU STILL DOING HERE? WHY HAVEN'T YOU LEFT FOR WORK?

THIS SNOW STORM HAS PARALYZED TRAFFIC! NOTHING IS MOVING, INCLUDING ME! THE CAR IS STUCK IN THE GARAGE!
GOSH, POP! CAN'T OUR SNOWBLOWER HANDLE THE JOB?

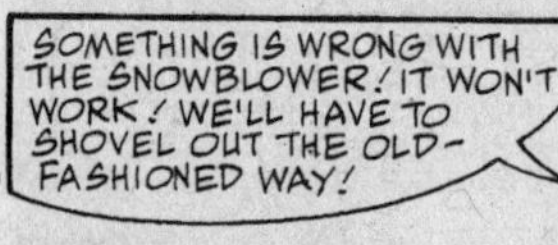
SOMETHING IS WRONG WITH THE SNOWBLOWER! IT WON'T WORK! WE'LL HAVE TO SHOVEL OUT THE OLD-FASHIONED WAY!

NOT ONLY WON'T YOU BE ABLE TO HANG OUT WITH ARCHIE TODAY, IT SOUNDS LIKE YOU'LL ALSO BE IN FOR A HARD DAY'S WORK, JUGHEAD!
OH, WELL!

THAT'S THE WAY IT GOES, MOM! BUT A SNOW DAY IS STILL A DAY I CAN RELISH!
THAT'S THE RIGHT ATTITUDE, SON! SHOVELING SNOW IS JUST A COLD HARD FACT OF WINTER!

SPEAKING OF COLD FACTS, I HAVE ANOTHER ONE FOR YOU!

OUR FUEL TANK IS LOW ON OIL! WE'RE DUE FOR A DELIVERY TODAY!
YES, SO?

BECAUSE OF THE STORM, THE OIL GUY CAN'T COME OUT. THE STORM MIGHT GET WORSE, SO WE HAVE TO CONSERVE OIL JUST TO BE ON THE SAFE SIDE!

I TURNED THE HEAT DOWN LOW UNTIL WE CAN GET A DELIVERY. WE WON'T FREEZE, BUT IT MIGHT GET A BIT CHILLY IN HERE!
WE'LL BE OKAY! WE CAN WEAR SWEATERS, AND KEEP THE FIREPLACE BURNING!

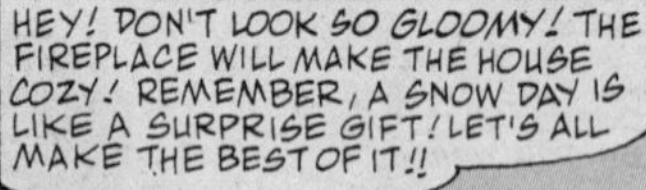
HEY! DON'T LOOK SO GLOOMY! THE FIREPLACE WILL MAKE THE HOUSE COZY! REMEMBER, A SNOW DAY IS LIKE A SURPRISE GIFT! LET'S ALL MAKE THE BEST OF IT!!

COME ON, DAD! LET'S START TO SHOVEL!

JUGHEAD SURE IS CHEERFUL ABOUT ALL THIS!
I GUESS HE JUST LOVES SNOW DAYS, DESPITE THE TROUBLE!

LATER...
WHEW! THAT WAS HARD WORK! AND THE WAY IT'S STILL SNOWING, WE'LL HAVE TO DO IT ALL AGAIN!
IN THAT CASE, WE HAVE TO FILL UP OUR FUEL TANKS! MOM, WHAT'S FOR LUNCH?

I MADE SOME CHICKEN SOUP! AND SOME PB AND J SAND-WICHES!
THAT SOUNDS FINE, MOM, BUT I WAS HOPING TO HAVE A REALLY BIG LUNCH!

I'M SORRY, JUGHEAD, I PLANNED ON GOING GROCERY SHOPPING AFTER BREAKFAST! WE'RE OUT OF EVERYTHING FROM FROZEN PIZZA AND HAMBURGERS TO SNACK ITEMS!

WE MIGHT BE OUT OUT YOUR FAVORITE FOODS FOR A DAY OR TWO!
UGH!! NO, NO, NO!
Hmph!!
IT BETTER STOP SNOWING! ONE STUPID SNOW DAY LIKE THIS IS ABOUT ALL I CAN TAKE!
END

Jughead in GOING TO THE DOGS

Script: George Gladir / Pencils: Tim Kennedy / Inks: Pat Kennedy / Letters: Bill Yoshida / Colors: Barry Grossman

LOOK! HOT DOG IS GETTING ON YOUR RED SNOWBOARD!

WOW! LOOK AT HIM GO!

I WOULDN'T BELIEVE IT IF I DIDN'T SEE IT!
MY HOT DOG IS A REAL HOT DOGGER!

I WAS LOADING MY CAMCORDER WHEN YOUR DOG DID THAT STUNT!
PAT! PAT!

DO YOU THINK HE CAN REPEAT IT FOR ME?
WHY NOT? LET'S GO UP THE HILL!
2

PAL, I CAN GET BIG BUCKS FOR A VIDEO OF THAT STUNT!
I'LL GIVE YOU HALF WHEN I SELL IT!
KEEP THOSE BURGERS COMIN', POP!

COME ON, PAL!
LET'S SEE YOU DO IT AGAIN!

HOT DOG! PLEASE!
SCRATCH SCRATCH

YAWN!
HOT DOG!!

BUDDY, I CAN'T WAIT ALL DAY!
GOT AN IDEA! BE RIGHT BACK!
Z Z Z

A LITTLE INDUCEMENT SHOULD DO THE TRICK!
SNACK SHOP

YES, MY FRIEND! ALL THESE HOT DOGS ARE YOURS!

...BUT FIRST YOU HAVE TO PERFORM THE SNOWBOARD STUNT!

YAWN!

THAT FAKER!
HIS STUNT WAS JUST A ONE-TIME FLUKE!
WAIT! I KNOW HE CAN DO IT AGAIN!
Z Z Z Z

SIGH! I EVEN HAD VISIONS OF HOT DOG HAVING A MOVIE CAREER!

HEY!
YANK!

HOT DOG! COME BACK WITH THOSE HOT DOGS!

CHOMP! CHOMP! CHOMP!

JUG, I'VE A GREAT TITLE FOR HIS FIRST MOVIE!
..."IT'S A DOG-EAT-DOG-WORLD"!
BURP!
?
End

Script: George Gladir / Pencils: Bill Vigoda / Letters: Bill Yoshida / Colors: Barry Grossman

WH...WHAT'S THIS?
SSSSSSSSS
FREE! FREE AT LAST!
WHO ARE YOU?
I'M A GENIE! AND YOU ARE MY MASTER!
BUT, YOU'RE A GIRL!

AND, WHAT'S THE MATTER WITH GIRLS?
ARE YOU PUTTING ME ON? GENIE'S ARE BIG HUSKY MEN WITH METAL ARM BANDS!

MAKE A WISH, MASTER! ASK ME FOR SOMETHING! ANYTHING AT ALL!
2

OKAY, THEN I'D LIKE SOME FOOD!
HMM... LET'S SEE WHAT I CAN COME UP WITH!

I'VE GOT IT!
POOF!

THERE YOU ARE MASTER! EAT TO YOUR HEART'S CONTENT!
WHAT? THIS IS JUST CRACKERS, LETTUCE AND SKIMMED MILK!

OF COURSE! I'M ON A DIET! YOU CAN'T EXPECT ME TO THINK OF FATTENING FOOD!

BAH! JUST MY LUCK TO GET A GENIE WHO'S ON A DIET! I'M GOING HOME!

WAIT, MASTER! SUPPOSE I GET YOU MONEY! YOU CAN BUY WHATEVER YOU DESIRE!

AH! NOW YOU'RE TALKING LIKE A REAL BONAFIDE GENIE!

I'LL START OFF WITH 500 DOLLARS!
GREAT!
POOF!

YAHOO! I'M RICH! I'LL NEVER GO HUNGRY AGAIN!

HEY! WHAT THE !! THIS IS CONFEDERATE MONEY!
WHAT DO YOU EXPECT? IT'S THE ONLY MONEY I KNOW!

AFTER ALL .. THE LAST TIME I WAS OUT OF THE BOTTLE WAS DURING THE CIVIL WAR!

BAH! THIS STUFF NEVER HAPPENED TO ALADDIN!
WAIT, MASTER!
4

FORGET IT, KID! WHY DON'T YOU GO BACK TO YOUR BOTTLE?
OH, NO MASTER!

DON'T MAKE ME GO BACK IN THE BOTTLE!! SOB! GIVE ME ONE MORE CHANCE!

YOU DON'T KNOW WHAT IT'S LIKE TO BE STUCK IN A BOTTLE FOR HUNDREDS OF YEARS WITH NO ONE TO TALK TO! SOB!
SOB!
SOB!
SOB!
SOB!

BOY! I'LL BET I'M THE FIRST FELLOW IN HISTORY TO GET STUCK WITH A CRYING GENIE!

OKAY! I'LL GIVE YOU ONE MORE CHANCE!

OH, THANK YOU MASTER! THANK YOU! SOB!
YEESH! TALK ABOUT OVER-ACTING!

OKAY, GENIE! I WANT ONE SUPER-SIZED, JUMBO HAMBURGER!
ONE SUPER BURGER WITH ONIONS AND KETCHUP COMING UP!

POOF!

WOW! WHO WOULD EVER BELIEVE THIS?

HEY YOU! WHAT ARE YOU DOING? STOP THAT THIS INSTANT!
LIBRARIAN

HOW DARE YOU TRY TO EAT OUR LIBRARY BOOK?
CHOMP
CHOMP
QUIET

RIVERDALE LIBRARY
MAYBE I SHOULD STICK TO WESTERN STORIES SO I WON'T GET SO EMOTIONALLY INVOLVED!
THE END

Jughead in BIRTHDAY GIRL

Script: Frank Doyle / Art: Harry Lucey / Letters: Bill Yoshida / Colors: Carlos Antunes

MISS GRUNDY, ARCH!--- SHE ACTED KIND OF STRANGE!
YOU MEAN SHE WASN'T HER USUAL GRUMPY SELF?

SHE SEEMED SORT OF DEPRESSED!
MAYBE YOU'RE IN ONE OF HER CLASSES TODAY! THAT WOULD DEPRESS ANYBODY!

THERE'S A TIME AND PLACE FOR WISECRACKS, REGGIE! THIS IS NEITHER!
MAN! TALK ABOUT GRUMPY!

JUGHEAD! WHAT ARE YOU UP TO?

N-NOTHING, MR. WEATHERBEE! I'M WORRIED ABOUT MISS GRUNDY! SHE'S ACTING SORT OF DEPRESSED!

MAYBE SHE HAS YOU IN ONE OF HER CLASSES TODAY! THAT WOULD DEPRESS ANYBODY!
YUK! YUK!

HMM! ASIDE FROM BEING DEEP IN THOUGHT, I SEE NOTHING WRONG!

COME ALONG, MY BOY! I THINK YOU'VE BEEN BUILDING THIS UP IN YOUR IMAGINATION!

SNIFF!

YOU WERE RIGHT! I DO BELIEVE SHE'S *CRYING*!
WE'VE GOT TO *DO* SOMETHING!

PEOPLE HAVE A RIGHT TO THEIR PRIVACY, JUGHEAD! SHE MIGHT RESENT OUR INTERFERENCE!
THEN WE'RE NOT GOING TO *DO* ANYTHING, SIR?

THAT'S RIGHT! WE'RE NOT GOING TO DO *ANYTHING*!
3

LOOK, JUG, FORGET IT! MR. WEATHERBEE IS RIGHT!
IT'S NOBODY'S BUSINESS BUT MISS GRUNDY'S AND WE SHOULDN'T INTRUDE!
RIGHT!

YOU BOTH FEEL THE SAME AS ARCHIE AND "THE BEE"?
OF COURSE!

NO WISECRACKS, JUG, BUT I ALSO THINK PEOPLE SHOULD BE LEFT ALONE IN THEIR GRIEF!
YEAH?

SHE'S A GROWN WOMAN!
SHE'S HAD PROBLEMS BEFORE AND LICKED THEM!
NO ONE APPRECIATES A "DO-GOODER"!
SHE HAS A RIGHT TO HER PRIVACY!

NO!! SHE ALSO HAS A RIGHT TO HAVE SOMEBODY CONCERNED ABOUT HER!

HOW DO I KNOW I CAN'T HELP IF I DON'T ASK? MAYBE I'M DOIN' THE WRONG THING BUT, BY GOSH, I'M GOING TO DO SOMETHING!

COUGH! COUGH!

I'M SORRY, MISS GRUNDY! I WAS TOLD TO LEAVE YOU ALONE! ---BUT I CAN'T!

IT'S NONE OF MY BUSINESS, BUT SOMETHING'S BOTHERING YOU AND I WANT TO HELP!
I DO APPRECIATE THAT, JUGHEAD!

--- BUT DON'T YOU WORRY ABOUT ME! I WAS JUST INDULGING IN A LITTLE SELF PITY BECAUSE I'M GROWING OLD!
5

(SIGH!) ANOTHER BIRTHDAY TOMORROW AND I'D LIKE TO FORGET IT!

NOW IF YOU'LL FORGET IT --- I'LL FORGET IT! IS IT A DEAL?
SURE! SURE! IT'S A DEAL, MISS GRUNDY!

I HAVE NO INTENTION OF KEEPING MY WORD! --- AND I'M NOT ONE BIT ASHAMED!

WELL, YOU POKED THAT OVERSIZED NOSE IN! WHAT HAP---
TURN IT OFF! YOU'RE TALKING WHEN YOU SHOULD BE LISTENIN'!

ROOM 212! TEN MINUTES! BE THERE! DON'T GIVE ME ANY FLACK! MOVE OUT!!
(GULP!) Y-YESS'R!
CHEE!

R-ROOM 212?
Y-YES, SIR!
GO!!

PASS THE WORD ALONG! I WANT THAT ROOM FILLED!--- AND I MEAN NOW!
EEP!
WHAT GOT INTO HIM?

MISS GRUNDY!--- YOU DIG? --- TOMORROW'S HER BIRTHDAY AND SHE'S FEELING OLD AND UNWANTED! WELL, I WON'T HAVE IT! NOW YOU GET OUT THERE AND SHOW HER EXACTLY HOW WANTED SHE IS!--- OKAY?
?
212
YEAH!
COUNT ME IN!
ME, TOO!
YES!

IT ISN'T FITTING FOR A PRINCIPAL, BUT WOW! I WONDER IF HE'D GIVE HALF-TIME PEP TALKS TO THE FOOTBALL TEAM?
GO, GO, GO!
GRUNDY ALL THE WAY!
"USELESS?" "OVER THE HILL?" NOT MISS GRUNDY! NO WAY!

NEXT DAY
"P-PARIS NIGHT" PERFUME? "PASSION?"... SINFUL SURRENDER?"---GOOD GRIEF! WHAT DO THEY THINK I AM?
I THINK WHAT THEY'RE TRYING TO SAY IS THAT YOU'RE A GREAT GAL WHO'S A LONG WAY FROM BEING "OVER THE HILL!"

YESTERDAY I DREADED THIS BIRTHDAY! TODAY IT'S THE MOST WONDERFUL THING THAT EVER HAPPENED TO ME!

EEYOW!
THOSE GREAT KIDS! THEY MAKE ME FEEL SO YOUNG!
CLICK!

JUG, HOW COME A WOMAN HATER LIKE YOU WAS THE ONLY ONE WHO KNEW HOW TO HANDLE THE SITUATION?
YEAH! HOW'D YOU LEARN SO MUCH ABOUT FEMALES?
WHO KNOWS ABOUT FEMALES? I ONLY KNOW ABOUT FRIENDSHIP!
END.

DIPSY
DOODLES

NO
PICNICKING
ALLOWED
ON BEACH

Jughead in SNORE CORPS

Mr. Lodge in "MIDNIGHT MADNESS"

(YAWN) I BELIEVE I'LL TURN IN, SMITHERS! LOCK UP BEFORE YOU RETIRE!

BUT, SIR! MISS VERONICA IS NOT AT HOME!

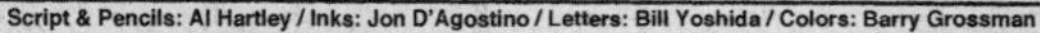
Script & Pencils: Al Hartley / Inks: Jon D'Agostino / Letters: Bill Yoshida / Colors: Barry Grossman

ARCHIE! IT'S GOT TO BE ARCHIE! HOW MANY TIMES HAVE I WARNED THAT BLOCKHEAD?

"GET HER HOME ON TIME", I TELL HIM! I ALWAYS TELL HIM THAT! DON'T I ALWAYS TELL HIM THAT, SMITHERS?
YOU ALWAYS TELL HIM THAT, SIR!

BRRING!
GOOD GRIEF! IT'S AFTER TWELVE!

HE'S IN BED, LODGE! WHERE ELSE WOULD HE BE AT THIS HOUR?
YES!
ALL RIGHT, I'LL CHECK!

(GRUMBLE) HIM AND THAT SCATTERBRAINED SNOB OF A DAUGHTER!

ALWAYS BLAMING MY NICE, DEPENDABLE BOY FOR ALL HIS TROUBLES!
2

OF COURSE HE'S IN BED!
WHERE ELSE WOULD HE...

GAK!

GONE! HIS BED HASN'T BEEN SLEPT IN!

MARY! THEY DID IT! THEY MUST HAVE RUN OFF TOGETHER! THEY'RE BOTH GONE!

I HEARD THAT, ANDREWS! WHAT HAS YOUR YOUNG MONSTER DONE WITH MY SWEET, LITTLE BABY GIRL?
OH, NO! NOT ARCHIE! BETTER SHE SHOULD BE STOLEN BY GYPSIES!
3

SOME PLACE HE'S HOLDING HER AGAINST HER WILL! I'LL SHAKE THAT ANDREWS UNTIL HE TELLS... UH... TELLS...

EGAD!

ALL RIGHT, LODGE! WHERE HAS YOUR DAUGHTER GOT MY LITTLE BOY? WHERE? WHERE?

LOOK! LOOK THERE!
OH! NO.!!

YOUR FORTUNE-HUNTING PLAYBOY HAS ELOPED! ELOPED I SAY, WITH MY LITTLE GIRL!!
I KNEW SHE'D TURN HIS HEAD WITH HER MADCAP, JET-SET MANNERS!!
4

MY INNOCENT LITTLE BABY!
"INNOCENT"?... SHE WAS BORN A WOMAN OF THE WORLD!

MY POOR, GULLIBLE GUY! SHE LED HIM AROUND BY THE NOSE!
WHY, YOU...

WATCH WHO YOU'RE PUSH...
OOPS!

EEP! I KNOCKED OVER A PAINT CAN!

PAINT CAN? OMIGOSH!
OOH! PAINT!

ARCHIE AND JUGHEAD!
THEY STARTED TO PAINT YOUR HOUSE TODAY!
5

ULP! THEY WERE GOING TO BUNK IN THE ROOM OVER MY GARAGE SO THEY COULD GET AN EARLY START IN THE MORNING!

I REMEMBER NOW! ARCHIE TOLD ME BUT I FORGOT!
SIR!

I FOUND THIS NOTE ON THE HALL TABLE!

VERONICA DIDN'T LIKE THE SMELL OF THE PAINT! SHE'S SLEEPING AT BETTY'S HOUSE!

THE BOYS IN THE NIGHT CLOTHES LOOK SHOOK! ANYTHING HAPPEN I SHOULD KNOW ABOUT?
NO! PRETTY COMMON STATE OF AFFAIRS! THEY'RE PARENTS OF TEEN-AGERS!
DINER
The End

Script: Mike Pellowski / Pencils: Tim Kennedy / Inks: Pat Kennedy / Letters: Bill Yoshida / Colors: Barry Grossman

DOES IT TAKE AWAY FROM THE CARD'S VALUE WHEN IT'S BENT LIKE THAT?
'FRAID SO, BETTY!

I THINK I STILL HAVE SOME OL' BASEBALL CARDS IN THE ATTIC!
YOU DO, GRAN'PA?

AND YOU'RE WELCOME TO HAVE 'EM ALL... BABE BOOTH, JIMMY FLAX, LOU MERIT...
WOW! THEY'RE ALL HALL OF FAMERS!

WHEN WOULD YOU LIKE TO DROP OVER TO MY PLACE, ARCHIE?

HOW 'BOUT RIGHT NOW, GRAN'PA?

HI, GRAN'MA!
I'M GOING UP TO THE ATTIC TO GIVE ARCHIE MY OLD BASEBALL CARDS!

THEY'RE HERE SOMEWHERE!
I FEEL LIKE AN ARCHAEOLOGIST ABOUT TO UNCOVER SOME ANCIENT EGYPTIAN TREASURES!
2

AHHH! AND HERE'S THE SHOE BOX I KEPT 'EM IN!

THEY'RE ALL MOLDY... GUESS THE RAIN GOT AT THEM!
GULP!

THEY ALL HAVE CREASES ... AND SOME OF THE CORNERS ARE MISSING!
WE KIDS USED TO FLIP 'EM AND HAVE ALL KINDS OF FUN WITH THEM!

BUT I HAVE A FEW CARDS THAT I DIDN'T FLIP!
YOU DO?

I PUT 'EM ON THE SPOKES OF MY BIKE TO MAKE GREAT NOISES!

BETTY, I COULD CRY!... IT'S SACRILEGIOUS WHAT HAPPENED TO THESE CARDS!

I HATE TO SAY IT, ARCHIE... BUT A LITTLE GIRL WOULD PROBABLY HAVE TAKEN BETTER CARE OF THOSE CARDS!
I STILL HAVE MY OLD POSTCARD COLLECTION... AND IT'S **WELL PRESERVED!**
SEE WHAT I MEAN?

I ALSO COLLECTED CARDS OF HANDSOME MOVIE ACTORS... AND HANDSOME BASEBALL PLAYERS!

GRANDMA! D-DID YOU JUST SAY "**HANDSOME BASEBALL PLAYERS?**"
YES, AND YOU'RE WELCOME TO HAVE 'EM ALL ARCHIE!

I EVEN HAD THE **GREAT** BABE BOOTH!
WITHOUT DOUBT THE GREATEST HOME RUN HITTER OF HIS TIME!

BUT I TRADED HIM FOR THREE OF THAT HANDSOME TEX VANN!

HEY, NO MATTER! ANYTHING GRANDMA COLLECTED, CONSIDERING HER AGE, HAS TO BE VERY VALUABLE!

OH, WOW! AND THEY'RE ALL IN MINT CONDITION!

I LOVE YOU, GRANDMA!
SMACK!

AND I LOVE YOU, GRANDPA! EVEN IF YOU WERE CARELESS WITH YOUR CARDS!
SMACK!

DAD! LOOK AT WHAT GRANDMA JUST GAVE ME!
HER OLD BASEBALL CARDS!

SON, THESE CARDS ARE PRICELESS! I HOPE YOU TAKE GOOD CARE OF 'EM!

I'M GOING TO TAKE THE VERY BEST OF CARE, DAD!

I'M GIVING THEM TO A "LITTLE GIRL" TO HOLD ONTO FOR SAFEKEEPING!
?
END

Script & Pencils: Joe Edwards / Inks: Jon D'Agostino / Letters: Bill Yoshida / Colors: Barry Grossman

NOTICE HOW THE MAGNIFYING GLASS CONCENTRATES THE SUN'S RAYS ON THE SCHOOL MODEL!
RIVERDALE HIGH SCHOOL

NOTICE HOW QUICKLY THE INSIDE TEMPERATURE GOES UP!
RIVERDALE HIGH SCHOOL

NOTICE HOW THE ROOF CATCHES FIRE!

IT'S A GOOD THING I DECIDED TO SCREEN THESE ENTRIES!

SOLAR ENERGY IS MORE COMPLICATED THAN SOME STUDENTS REALIZE!
SSSSS

NOW DILTON'S ENTRY IS SOMETHING ELSE!
INDEED IT IS!
WINDPOWERED DYNAMO STATION

NOW WHAT?
DOUBLE DESK
ENERGY
SAVER
A. ANDREWS

AHEM!
TAP
TAP

OH, HI! THIS IS *ANOTHER* OF MY CONTEST ENTRIES!
WHAT'S THE PURPOSE OF HAVING STUDENTS SIT SO CLOSE TOGETHER?

HUDDLING FOR WARMTH ALLOWS THE SCHOOL TO TURN DOWN THE THERMOSTAT!

I'M AFRAID THE DISTRACTIONS WOULD FAR OUTWEIGH ANY SAVING IN ENERGY!
DO YOU THINK SO?

I *KNOW* SO!

SHUCKS!
THE BOY MEANS WELL, BUT HIS IDEAS ARE SO IMPRACTICAL!

SOME OF THESE OTHER IDEAS ARE DEFINITELY INGENIOUS!
BATTERY-POWERED HEATING SYSTEM

I JUST THOUGHT OF ANOTHER IDEA, SIR!
HAVE FOOTBALL PLAYERS WEAR FLASHLIGHTS!
?

THAT WAY WE COULD DO AWAY WITH STADIUM LIGHTS FOR NIGHT GAMES!
CLICK

WE COULD EVEN PUT A LIGHT ON THE FOOTBALL!
THAT'S WHAT I'D CALL A LIGHT-HEADED IDEA!

ARCHIE! PEOPLE ARE NOT GOING TO COME TO A GAME TO SEE A BUNCH OF FLASHLIGHTS GROPING IN THE DARK!

GEE! I DIDN'T THINK OF THAT!

ARCHIE! I'M GOING TO HAVE TO ASK YOU TO WITHDRAW ALL OF YOUR ENTRIES!

I GUESS YOU'RE RIGHT, SIR!

I MAY AS WELL GO STRAIGHT HOME!
SUIT YOURSELF!

THE DISTRICT SUPERINTENDENT'S CAR JUST PULLED IN!
5

WELCOME, MR. HASSLE!
ARE YOU READY TO PICK OUR CONTEST WINNER, SIR?

I'VE ALREADY PICKED THE FIRST PRIZE WINNER!
YOU DID?

I'M AWARDING THE TROPHY TO THIS BOY!
ARCHIE! WHY ARCHIE?

JUST LOOK AT ALL THE 'GAS GUZZLING CARS IN YOUR STUDENTS' PARKING LOT!

BY SKATING TO AND FROM SCHOOL---
THIS LAD HAS COME UP WITH THE MOST BRILLIANT ENERGY CONSERVING IDEA OF ALL!
END

Script & Pencils: Bob Bolling / Inks: Bob Smith / Letters: Bill Yoshida / Colors: Barry Grossman

LET ME GUESS... WAS IT MR. STONE, SUPERINTENDENT OF SCHOOLS?
GOOD-GUESS, AND DO YOU KNOW WHAT?

HE'S COMING HERE!
MISS GRUNDY, YOU'RE UNCANNY! HE'LL BE HERE RIGHT AFTER LUNCH FOR A ROUTINE INSPECTION!

MY PROBLEM RIGHT NOW IS ALL THAT SNOW ON THE FRONT WALK! ...YOU KNOW HOW MR. STONE HATES THAT SORT OF THING!

LATER...
YOU MEAN YOU WANT REG AND ME TO SHOVEL OFF THE FRONT WALK BEFORE MR. STONE GETS HERE?
RIGHT! THESE ARE OUR ONLY TWO SHOVELS AND I KNOW I CAN RELY ON BOTH OF YOU!

TAKE YOUR TIME... JUST AS LONG AS YOU'RE FINISHED BY THE END OF LUNCH PERIOD.
GROAN!
CHEER UP, ARCH, WE'RE GETTING OUT OF GEOMETRY!

HOLY TOLEDO! WE'LL NEVER GET THIS SHOVELED OUT IN TIME!
HEY! WAIT! WHAT'S SNOW FOR ANYWAY BUT A-
RIVERDALE HIGH

SNOW-BALL FIGHT!
UH, OH! I CAN SEE ANOTHER ONE OF YOUR FLAKY IDEAS COMIN' UP!

LISTEN! AT LUNCH PERIOD WE'LL HAVE A BIG SNOWBALL FIGHT USING *ONLY THE SNOW ON THE WALK!* 30 KIDS ON EACH SIDE AND WE'LL HAVE THE GIRLS REFEREE!... THIS WALK WILL BE CLEAN IN NO TIME!
WELL, THROWIN' SNOW IS BETTER THAN SHOVELING IT!

LUNCH TIME -
ON YOUR MARK! GET SET -
RIVERDALE HIGH
BANG!

WHAT'S THE HURRY!
I JUST LOOKED OUT THE WINDOW! THERE'S A FIERCE SNOWBALL FIGHT OUT FRONT! STUDENTS KNOW SNOWBALLING IS FORBIDDEN!

CALM DOWN! CAN'T YOU SEE THEY'RE CLEARING OFF THE WALK?! IT WAS ARCHIE'S IDEA!
EEP! YOU'RE RIGHT... BUT STILL I MUST STOP IT!

CEASE FIRE! CEASE FIRE, I SAY!
WALK'S ALL CLEARED, MR WEATHERBEE!
GOOD TIMING, KIDS! IT'S THE END OF LUNCH PERIOD!
LET'S GO!

OH, ARCHIE, MAY I SPEAK TO YOU FOR A MOMENT?

THAT WAS A GOOD IDEA OF YOURS, BUT, HARUMPH! I NEVER WOULD HAVE APPROVED! YOUR INTENTIONS WERE GOOD BUT YOUR FORM WAS BAD!
MY FORM?

WHEN I WAS A BOY WE PACKED THEM SMALL AND HARD FOR ACCURACY... LIKE THIS!

SEE THE HOLE IN THAT TREE?!
GEE! YEAH! ARE YOU GOING TO

JUST WATCH!
OOPS! A WILD ONE!
SPLAT!

ACK! MR. STONE!
WEATHERBEE!? IS THAT YOU?!?

WHERE ARE MY GLASSES? I CAN'T SEE A THING WITH-OUT MY GLASSES!

LATER...
-SO I FOUND HIS GLASSES AND CALMED HIM DOWN... HE STILL ISN'T SURE WHO HIT HIM WITH A SNOWBALL... I TOLD HIM YOU HAD TO-ER- "RUSH OFF"!
WHERE'S MR. STONE NOW?
ATHLETIC EQUIPMENT STORAGE LOCKER

HE LEFT A COUPLE OF HOURS AGO... IT TOOK ME THAT LONG TO FIND YOU!
THEN IT'S SAFE TO COME OUT!

THANK YOU, ARCHIE! THANK YOU!
GEE, MR. WEATHERBEE, YOU MUST'VE BEEN COLD AND LONELY FOR THE LAST TWO HOURS HIDING DOWN HERE BEHIND OUR TACKLING DUMMY!

(SIGH!) MAYBE SO, BUT I WAS IN THE RIGHT COMPANY!
END.

Script: Frank Doyle / Pencils: Stan Goldberg / Inks: Jon D'Agostino / Letters: Bill Yoshida / Colors: Barry Grossman

I'M ON NIGHT DUTY NEXT WEEK! I'LL BE CHECKING THIS PLACE REGULARLY!
GREAT! THAT'S ALL I NEED!

THIS BUSINESS WILL GO DOWN THE TUBES FAST IF THAT FUZZ STARTS HANGIN' AROUND!

I LIKE OFFICER RYAN! HE'S A GOOD POLICE-MAN!
ONE OF THE BEST!

AND HE'S RIGHT! THAT PLACE IS BAD NEWS!
IT GETS A WILD, ROUGH CROWD!

NEXT DAY:
HAH! THEY FINALLY CAUGHT ONE OF THEM WITH HIS HAND IN THE TILL!
ONE OF WHO?

CROOKED COPS! THEY CAUGHT THIS ONE ACCEPTING A BRIBE!
LET'S SEE!
2

THIS IS NUTS! A CASE OF WINE IN OFFICER RYAN'S GARAGE---DELIVERED BY AN EMPLOYEE OF THE CROWN LOUNGE!
HOW ABOUT THAT, HUH ?
BANA

THE OWNER OF THE CROWN SAYS THAT WAS RYAN'S PRICE FOR NOT HARASSING HIS CUSTOMERS!
THAT'S AN OUTRIGHT LIE!

OFFICER RYAN WOULD NEVER ACCEPT A BRIBE!
HAH! OPEN YOUR EYES!
BURGE
TUN

EVERYBODY'S GOT HIS PRICE!
NO WAY! THERE ARE STILL HONEST PEOPLE IN THE WORLD!

IT'S OUR DUTY TO REPORT THE CONVERSATION WE OVERHEARD!
OF COURSE!

THE PAPER SAID RYAN WAS SUSPENDED, PENDING INVESTIGATION!
WE'LL GO SEE HIS SUPERIOR OFFICER!

- AND YOU HEARD THAT CONVERSATION BETWEEN OFFICER RYAN AND THIS FELLOW, SLADE ?
WE SURE DID!
CAPT. HASKIN

WOULD YOU SWEAR TO THAT IN COURT, IF IT CAME TO THAT ?
ABSOLUTELY!

LET'S GO SEE MR. SLADE!

ALL RIGHT! TELL MR. SLADE WHAT YOU REMEMBER OF THE CONVERSATION BETWEEN HIM AND OFFICER RYAN!
YES, SIR!

HAH! SO WHO'S GONNA BELIEVE A COUPLE OF CRAZY KIDS ? IT'S THEIR WORD AGAINST MINE!

ORDINARILY THAT WOULD BE TRUE - --- IF I HADN'T HAPPENED TO BE CARRYING MY PORTABLE TAPE RECORDER---
GULP!
4

D-DID SHE SAY, "TAPE"?
SHE SAID "TAPE!"

OKAY! OKAY! SO THE WINE WAS MY OWN IDEA!
I WAS JUST TRYIN' TUH GET THE GUY OFF MY BACK!

COME ALONG, SLADE! WE'RE GOING TO HAVE A LITTLE PRESS CONFERENCE AND CLEAR OFFICER RYAN'S NAME!
P.D

I WANT TO THANK YOU TWO! YOU'RE GOOD CITIZENS!
I WISH THERE WERE MORE LIKE YOU!

IT WAS A VERY LUCKY THING FOR US THAT YOU HAPPENED TO HAVE THAT TAPE RECORDER WITH YOU!
R

SHE'S A GREAT KIDDER, CAPTAIN! SHE DOESN'T HAVE A TAPE RECORDER!
SO SUE ME!
END

MR. WEATHERBEE in "PROMISES PROMISES"

Doyle / DeCarlo / Lapick / Yoshida / Grossman

I DON'T MEAN TO BE RUDE, BUT FROM YOUR APPEARANCE, YOU LOOK LIKE YOU NEVER DID!
I CAN'T HELP IT, MISS GRUNDY! I WAS HERE WORKING UNTIL TWO O'CLOCK IN THE MORNING!
YAWN!

THEN BY THE TIME I GOT HOME AND INTO BED IT WAS ALMOST THREE THIRTY! (YAWN!)

AND RIGHT NOW I DON'T FEEL IN ANY SHAPE TO DO ANYTHING!

OH, NO! LOOK AT THE MESS I MADE OF MY OFFICE!
WELL, AT LEAST IT LOOKS WORKED IN!
2

WOULD YOU GET THE JANITOR AND TELL HIM TO COME UP HERE AND CLEAN UP MY OFFICE ?

I WOULD IF I COULD, BUT HE'S BEEN OUT ON SICK LEAVE WITH A BAD BACK!

OH, THAT'S JUST GREAT! WHAT AM I GOING TO DO NOW? I'M TOO EXHAUSTED TO EVEN MOVE MY LITTLE FINGER!
I'LL ASK ONE OF THE STUDENTS IF THEY WANT TO VOLUNTEER FOR A CLEAN-UP JOB!

THANK YOU, MISS GRUNDY! I DON'T KNOW WHAT I'D DO WITHOUT YOU!
THAT'S TRUE!

OKAY, MR. WEATHERBEE! WHAT DO YOU WANT ME TO DO FIRST?
HUH?

ARCHIE! OH, NO! NOW WHY DID SHE SEND YOU?
BECAUSE I WAS THE ONLY ONE WHO VOLUNTEERED! DOESN'T THAT MAKE YOU HAPPY?
WHERE DO I START?

JUST CLEAN UP THIS MESS, BECAUSE I'M GOING TO GRAB A LITTLE SHUT-EYE! I'M BUSHED!

RIGHT ON, MR. WEATHERBEE! IT'S AS GOOD AS DONE!
AND DON'T YOU WORRY ABOUT ME DOING ANYTHING WRONG, BECAUSE I WON'T! I PROMISE!

SUGAR! --- SUGAR! --- SUGAR! YOU ARE MY CANDY GIRL...

DUM DEE DUM DUM!

RING!

THE PRESIDENT OF THE BOARD OF EDUCATION IS ON THE PHONE, MR. WEATHERBEE!
GOOD GRIEF! I'M HALF ASLEEP!

SHOULD I TELL HIM YOU'RE HERE BUT YOU'RE SLEEPING?
NO! NO! ARCHIE! I'M NOT HERE!

THEN WHERE ARE YOU?
I DON'T KNOW! TELL HIM ANYWHERE, BUT I'M NOT HERE!

HE'S HOME SLEEPING!!
AT LEAST, WHEN ARCHIE IS ALL DONE GETTING ME FIRED, I'LL HAVE PLENTY OF TIME TO SLEEP!
The END

YOU GIRLS DECLARED LAST WEEK "FIGHT GLOBAL WARMING WEEK".
...SO HOW DID IT GO?
WELL, THE OTHER DAY ARCHIE AND I AGREED TO GO ON A "FIGHT GLOBAL WARMING DATE"!
Betty in
THE BIG BATTLE
POP'S MENU
SCRIPT: GLADIR • PENCILS: GOLDBERG • INKS: LOWE
HONK HONK
THAT MUST BE ARCHIE IN HIS OLD GAS GUZZLER!
SO MUCH FOR YOUR ENERGY-SAVING DATE!
YOU'RE WRONG, DADDY! ABSOLUTELY NO GAS IS INVOLVED IN OUR SNOW-BOARD OUTING!
HONK

"POOR ARCHIE KEPT HITTING MORE THAN THE *SLOPES!*"

WHEW! TIME OUT FOR HOT CHOCOLATE!

I AGREE!

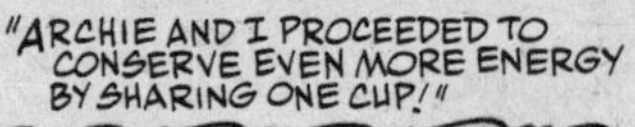

AND HOW'D IT GO WITH *YOU*, NANCY?
CHUCK AND I ALSO HAD A "FIGHT GLOBAL WARMING" DATE!

"INSTEAD OF USING A CAR WE *JOGGED* TO THE PARK TO PLAY A LITTLE BASKETBALL!"

WHO WON?
I FIGURE I DID!
POP'S

"IT ISN'T OFTEN THAT I CAN DRAG CHUCK AWAY FROM HIS DRAWING BOARD!"
R
R

I MAY ALSO BE A BIG WINNER IN ANOTHER WAY!
HOW SO?
OP'S

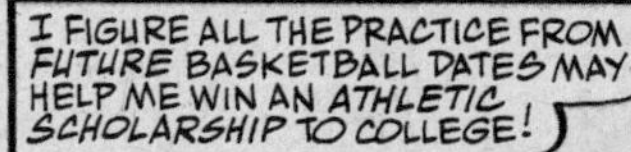
I FIGURE ALL THE PRACTICE FROM *FUTURE* BASKETBALL DATES MAY HELP ME WIN AN *ATHLETIC SCHOLARSHIP* TO COLLEGE!

AND HOW DID IT GO WITH YOU, MIDGE?
WELL, WHILE IT WASN'T MY INTENTION... REGGIE AND I MAN-AGED TO HAVE A VERY ENERGY-CONSERVING DATE...
"...I DID NOTHING BUT SIT AND LISTEN TO HIM BOAST ABOUT HIS MANY ATHLETIC ACHIEVEMENTS!"
BLAH BLAH BLAH
yawn!
BUT WE MISSED A BIG OPPORTUNITY TO CONSERVE EVEN MORE ENERGY!
HOW SO?
IF ONLY WIND TURBINES WERE THERE... HIS HOT AIR WOULD HAVE CREATED A LOT OF POWER!
SO WHICH OF US IS ENTITLED TO THE "FIGHT GLOBAL WARMING" TROPHY?
WE STILL HAVEN'T HEARD FROM RON!
HA! FAT CHANCE OF HER WINNING!
WE ALL KNOW HOW EXTRAVAGANT AND WASTEFUL VERONICA CAN BE!
AND HERE SHE COMES NOW!
POP'S
4

SO RONNIE, HOW DID "FIGHT GLOBAL WARMING" WEEK GO WITH YOU?
I'M GLAD YOU ASKED!

MY DATE AND I SAVED OODLES OF ENERGY BY SWIMMING IN OUR GIANT POOL!
HOW DO YOU FIGURE?

"THE POOL'S SOLAR PANELS NOT ONLY PROVIDED ENOUGH HEAT FOR THE POOL... BUT THE EXCESS ENERGY CAUSED OUR ELECTRIC METERS TO ACTUALLY RUN BACKWARDS!"

AND... oh, YES! I'VE JUST ABOUT CONVINCED FATHER HE CAN MAKE MORE MONEY BY PRODUCING ENVIRONMENTALLY-SOUND PRODUCTS!

BUT I WASN'T CONTENT TO STOP THERE... SO LAST WEEKEND I FOCUSED ON RECYCLING!

"I CLEANED OUT MY WARDROBE AND DONATED ENOUGH CLOTHES TO OUTFIT SEVERAL OF OUR LOCAL GIRLS IN STYLE!"
VERONICA'S CLOSET

I HAVE TO GO! HERE COMES MY DATE FOR TONIGHT!
IN THAT GAS-GUZZLING SPORTS CAR?
Ah..! BUT LATELY I'VE INSISTED THAT ALL MY DATES HAVE HI-TECH CARS THAT RUN ON LOW CARBON BIOFUELS!
IAN'S CAR RUNS ON EITHER CORN HUSKS OR BANANA SKINS... I FORGET JUST WHICH...!
Uh, VERONICA... I THINK IT'S UNANIMOUS! YOU WIN THE "FIGHT GLOBAL WARMING" TROPHY!
POP'S
IT JUST GOES TO SHOW YOU... IT TAKES ALL KINDS TO FIGHT GLOBAL WARMING!
FOR SURE! FOR SURE!
END

Betty and Veronica
Jacuzzi Cuties

Script: Kathleen Webb / Pencils: Doug Crane / Inks: Rudy Lapick / Letters: Bill Yoshida / Colors: Barry Grossman

BUT ALL I WANT TO DO IS DRINK COFFEE, NOT MANUFACTURE IT!
Celestial Coffee

THEN THIS IS THE MODEL YOU REALLY WANT! FEWER OPTIONS BUT ALSO LOWER PRICE!
WHY, THANK YOU, DEAR!
SALE
EZ COFFEE

YOU'LL NEVER BE SUCCESSFUL IN BUSINESS THAT WAY, BETTY!
REMEMBER, THE HIGHER THE MARK-UP, THE BIGGER THE PROFIT!
ISN'T IT MORE IMPORTANT TO CARE FOR THE CUSTOMER, RONNIE?
WIGS
10 Year Warranty
BETTY

OH, WHAT DO THEY KNOW? YOUR JOB IS TO MAKE MONEY FOR THE COMPANY!
YOU SIMPLY SHOW THE POOR DEARS WHAT'S BEST!

I'LL SHOW YOU BY TAKING CARE OF THE NEXT CUSTOMER! OH, ARCHIE! HOW MAY I HELP YOU?
IT FIGURES!

I DON'T NEED ANY...
WELL, IN THAT CASE, MISS, I COULD USE YOUR HELP OVER HERE! LIKE RIGHT NOW!
GULP!

I'VE BEEN HERE FOR SEVERAL MINUTES AND NOT ONE PERSON HAS ASKED ME IF I NEED ANY ASSISTANCE!

I... I...
I THINK OUR TRAINEE NEEDS A BREAK!
MA'AM, I'M AWFULLY SORRY FOR ANY INCONVENIENCE...

I JUST WANTED TO KNOW IF THIS BREADMAKER MAKES FRENCH BREAD!
THEY ALL DO, MA'AM! THEY JUST DIFFER IN THE AMOUNT THEY MAKE!
BREAD BAKER

THANK YOU! YOU'VE BEEN SUCH A HELP, BETTY, THAT I'M GOING TO TELL YOUR MANAGER WHAT A GOOD JOB YOU'RE DOING!
WHY, THANK YOU! PLEASE COME AGAIN!
BETTY

SEE, RONNIE? THAT LADY WASN'T SO...
...RONNIE?!
WHAT'S THAT LINE ABOUT NICE GIRLS FINISHING LAST...?

OUTSIDE THE STORE...
IT'S A GOOD THING YOU SHOWED UP, ARCHIE!
I COULD USE A RIDE HOME!
BUT BETTY AND I HAD A DATE!
ART'S APPLI

I'M SURE SHE WON'T MIND! BESIDES, THE POOR DEAR HAS TO WORK...

"...UNTIL THE STORE CLOSES TONIGHT!
I MAY NOT BE ABLE TO MAKE MY DATE...
BUT THERE'S ALWAYS ITEMS TO RESTOCK AND SHELVES TO STRAIGHTEN UP!

THERE! THAT'S ABOUT IT!
ANOTHER EVENING AT MALL-MART COMES TO AN END!
SALE
IF I'M LUCKY I MIGHT BE ABLE TO CATCH THE BUS!

ELSEWHERE...
HERE YOU ARE, RONNIE! HOME SWEET HOME!
THE LODGE COMPOUND
THAT WAS FAST!

WELL, IF I HURRY, I CAN STILL CATCH THE MOVIE AT THE THEATER!
THERE'S A BETTER ONE ON TV, ARCHIE! WHY DON'T YOU COME IN AND WATCH IT WITH ME!
MAIN HOUSE
RECEPTION AREA
POOLS 1-4
VERONICA'S COTTAGE
PLANETARIUM

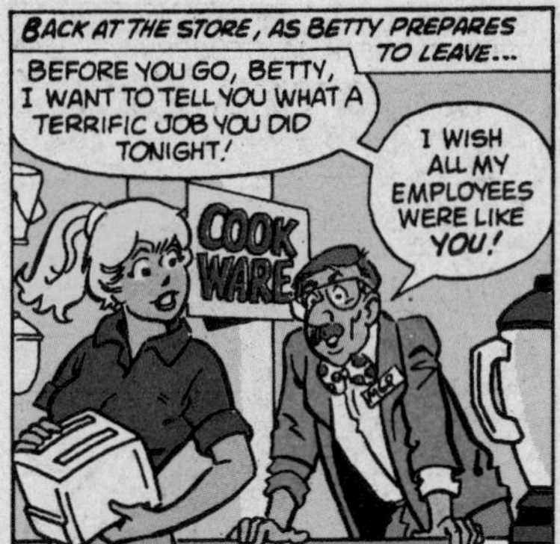
BACK AT THE STORE, AS BETTY PREPARES TO LEAVE...
BEFORE YOU GO, BETTY, I WANT TO TELL YOU WHAT A TERRIFIC JOB YOU DID TONIGHT!
I WISH ALL MY EMPLOYEES WERE LIKE YOU!
COOK WARE

AS A MATTER OF FACT, ONE OF YOUR CUSTOMERS FILLED OUT THE " CUSTOMER SATISFACTION FORM " COMMENTING ON WHAT A GREAT JOB YOU DID!

KEEP UP THE GOOD WORK, BETTY! GOOD NIGHT!
GOOD NIGHT, SIR!
SO WHY DO I FEEL SO BLUE THEN?

BETWEEN SCHOOL AND THIS JOB, MY SOCIAL LIFE IS SUCH A VOID! ... ON TOP OF THAT, RONNIE SPENDS MY TIME WITH ARCHIE!
WHAT DID I DO TO DESERVE THIS?!
APPLI

ARCHIE!!
WHAT ARE YOU DOING HERE?
THERE'S A SPECIAL LATE FEATURE AT THE DISCOUNT CINEMA...
SHOES

AND IF WE HURRY, THERE'S STILL TIME TO CATCH THE SHOW!
ARCHIE AND A MOVIE! NOW, THAT'S A BARGAIN!
The End

Betty and Veronica
in "ROLE MODELS"
SCHOOL ZONE
WOMEN'S STUDIES PROGRAM 101
IN OUR WOMEN'S STUDY CLASS WE'VE LOOKED AT STRONG, INDEPENDENT WOMEN THROUGHOUT HISTORY!
QUEEN ELIZABETH
CLEOPATRA
SUSAN B. ANTHONY

TODAY IS OUR ANNUAL DRESS UP DAY PRESENTATION OF THE INDEPENDENT WOMAN YOU MOST ADMIRE!
PELLOWSKI
BOLLING
SMITH

SOME OF YOU ARE DRESSED AS WOMEN I RECOGNIZE... OTHERS I CAN ONLY GUESS THE IDENTITIES OF!

BUT THAT'S ENOUGH FROM ME! NOW LET'S HEAR ABOUT THE WOMEN *YOU* ADMIRE! VERONICA, YOU GO FIRST!
YES, MS. GRUNDY!

I'M DRESSED AS JACKIE KENNEDY, THE FAMOUS FIRST LADY OF THE 1960'S!
SHE WAS QUITE A WOMAN!

I ADMIRE HER BECAUSE SHE WAS BEAUTIFUL, INTELLIGENT, BRAVE *AND* FASHIONABLE!

GREAT CHOICE, VERONICA! NOW HOW ABOUT YOU, NANCY?
CLAP!
CLAP!
CLAP!
CLAP!

I PICKED ROSA PARKS, THE COURAGEOUS WOMAN WHO HELPED START THE CIVIL RIGHTS MOVEMENT!
ANOTHER TERRIFIC CHOICE!
TELL US ABOUT HER, NANCY!

ROSA PARKS DEFIED AN UNFAIR LAW IN THE SOUTH... SHE REFUSED TO GIVE UP HER SEAT ON A BUS AND MOVE TO THE BACK!
CLAP!
CLAP!
CLAP!
CLAP!
THANK YOU, NANCY! OKAY, MIDGE, IT'S YOUR TURN! I THINK I CAN GUESS WHO YOU ARE!
REALLY?

I'M ONE OF THE GREATEST GOLFERS OF ALL TIME! I WAS ALSO A TRACK STAR AND GOOD AT ALL SPORTS!
WOOOSH!
YOU HAVE TO BE BABE DIDRIKSON, AM I RIGHT?

YES, BABE WAS ONE OF THE WORLD'S FIRST GREAT FEMALE ATHLETES!

BABE DIDRIKSON ALONG WITH OTHER EARLY FEMALE SPORTS STARS HELPED TO POPULARIZE ATHLETICS FOR AMERICAN GIRLS!

YOUR PRESENTATION WAS A REAL HIT, MIDGE! NOW LET'S HEAR FROM SOME OF THE OTHER GIRLS!

ONE BY ONE, GIRLS IN THE CLASS TALK ABOUT INDEPENDENT WOMEN THEY ADMIRE...
I CAME DRESSED AS CLARA BARTON, THE FOUNDER OF THE RED CROSS!

I REALLY ADMIRE MADAM MARIE CURIE THE NOTED SCIENTIST!
CLAP!
CLAP!
CLAP!

I THINK DOROTHY PARKER THE FAMOUS FEMALE WRITER, WAS WAY AHEAD OF HER TIME!

OKAY, BETTY, YOU'RE CLEARED FOR TAKE OFF! LET'S HEAR WHAT YOU HAVE TO SAY!
RIGHT, MS. GRUNDY!

PSST! BETTY I LOVE YOUR PANTS AND WIG!
THANKS, ETHEL!

I DRESSED AS PILOT AMELIA EARHART, THE FIRST WOMAN TO CROSS THE ATLANTIC OCEAN IN A AIRPLANE!
LOCKHEED ELECTRA PACIFIC FLIGHT
ISN'T SHE THE FOCUS OF AN UNSOLVED MYSTERY?

THAT'S CORRECT, VERONICA! NO ONE KNOWS WHAT BECAME OF AMELIA EARHART AFTER THE PLANE SHE WAS FLYING CRASHED SOME-WHERE IN THE PACIFIC!

HOWEVER, IT'S NO MYSTERY THAT THE LAST PERSON WE HAVE TO HEAR FROM IS ETHEL! WHO ARE YOU DRESSED UP AS, ETHEL?
GEE! CAN'T YOU TELL?

NO, ETHEL! I REALLY DON'T HAVE A CLUE!
WELL, I'M SOMEONE WHO HAS BEEN AN INSPIRATION TO ALL OF US FOR MANY YEARS!

THIS STRONG, INDEPENDENT WOMEN IS A TERRIFIC ROLE MODEL... SHE'S AN ADVISOR, A COACH, AN EDUCATOR AND A FRIEND!

I'M YOU, MS. GRUNDY! YOU'RE THE WOMAN I ADMIRE THE MOST!
GULP!
LET'S HEAR IT FOR ETHEL'S CHOICE!
YEAH! YOU GO, GIRL!
THANK YOU VERY MUCH, LADIES! I'M TRULY HONORED!
YAY!
YA-HOO!
CLAP!
CLAP!
HOO-RAY!

IT'S NICE TO RECOGNIZE GREAT WOMEN OF THE PAST, BUT IT'S MORE COMFORTING TO KNOW THAT THESE ARE THE INDEPENDENT WOMEN OF THE FUTURE!
THE END

Script: George Gladir / Pencils: Stan Goldberg / Inks: Henry Scarpelli / Letters: Bill Yoshida / Colors: Barry Grossman

GOSH! IT LOOKS LIKE ARCHIE!
YES, DADDY'S TOY PEOPLE DID IT AT MY REQUEST!

I THINK MY VIRTUAL BOYFRIEND WANTS A SNACK!
...I'LL FEED HIM SOME PIZZA!
PEEP! PEEP!

I THINK HE'D PREFER CHOCOLATE CHIP COOKIES!
BETTY!! WHOSE VIRTUAL BOYFRIEND IS THIS?

WHAT ELSE CAN YOU MAKE HIM DO?
GO ON DATES... WITH ME, OF COURSE!

I JUST TRAINED HIM TO DO HOMEWORK!
...THAT WAS MOST DIFFICULT!
WOW! JUST LIKE THE REAL THING!

I HAVE A STUDY PERIOD COMING UP!
AND I HAVE MY CHEM CLASS!
SEE YOU!
STUDY HALL

STUDY HALL

I HEAR MUSIC! WHAT HAVE YOU GOT VIRTUAL ARCHIE DOING?
DANCING!

BETTY, I THOUGHT YOU HAD CHEM THIS PERIOD?
I MANAGED TO HAVE MYSELF EXCUSED!

BETTY, WEREN'T YOU SUPPOSED TO REPORT TO NURSE THOMPSON?
UH, I'M ON MY WAY, MR. FLUTESNOOT!

3 P.M....
VERONICA! VERONICA!
STUDENT PARKING
COME ON! I'LL GIVE YOU A LIFT!

WHILE YOU'RE DRIVING, CAN I PLAY WITH YOUR VIRTUAL BOYFRIEND?
NO WAY!

I HAVE HIM DOING HIS CHORES!
HE CAN'T BE INTERRUPTED, OR HE'LL NEVER GET BACK TO THEM!

GOODNIGHT, DADDY!
GOODNIGHT, DEAR!

YES, SMITHERS?
IT'S MISS COOPER! SHE SAYS SHE ABSOLUTELY HAS TO SEE YOU!

PUH-LEESE LET ME PLAY WITH VIRTUAL ARCHIE...FOR JUST A FEW MINUTES!
SORRY! YOU'RE A TAD LATE, BETTY!

I JUST GAVE HIM A VIRTUAL GOOD NIGHT KISS!
SEE? HE'S SOUND ASLEEP!

THIS TOY SHOULD BE ON THE MARKET IN A FEW MORE MONTHS!
THEN YOU CAN PLAY WITH ONE TO YOUR HEART'S CONTENT!

SIGH! I UNDERSTAND!

BETTY HAS BEEN PESTERING ME FOR DAYS TO PLAY WITH MY VIRTUAL BOYFRIEND!
LOOKS LIKE YOUR FATHER'S TOY WILL BE A HUGE SUCCESS!

GOOD NEWS, LADIES!
I'M HOLDING AN IMPORTANT CONFERENCE IN DENVER THIS WEEK!
WHY DON'T YOU TWO COME ALONG FOR SOME SKIING?

BUT WHAT ABOUT MY VIRTUAL BOYFRIEND? I'M SUPPOSED TO TAKE CARE OF IT!
SO FIND A FRIEND TO DO THE CHORE FOR YOU!

BETTY! HOW'D YOU LIKE TO BORROW MY VIRTUAL BOYFRIEND FOR THE WEEKEND?
OH, WOW! WOULD I EVER!!

YOU AND I HAVE A LOT TO GO OVER...

...FOR EXAMPLE, WHICH BUTTONS TO PRESS, WHEN TO PRESS THEM...

OH, BY THE WAY, HOW SOON CAN YOU GET HERE?
I'M ALREADY HERE!!

I CAN'T BELIEVE IT, MOTHER! I'VE MY VERY OWN VIRTUAL ARCHIE FOR AN ENTIRE WEEK-END!
RING-G!!

BETTY! I'M OVER AT POP'S!
I HAVEN'T SEEN YOU IN A WHILE... I MISS YOU!

...HOW'D YOU LIKE TO GET TOGETHER...
SORRY, ARCHIE! I'LL BE EXTREMELY BUSY!
THEN THIS WEEKEND, MAYBE?

CLICK CLICK CLICK

GOOD GRIEF! I JUST TURNED DOWN THE REAL ARCHIE!
...FOR THIS VIRTUAL ARCHIE!

ARCHIE!! ARCHIE!!
?
POP'S CHOCKLIT SHOPPE
SPECIAL
END

Betty and Veronica IN "The SNOW MUST GO ON"

Script: George Gladir / Pencils Jeff Shultz / Inks: Al Milgrom / Letters: Bill Yoshida / Colors: Barry Grossman

SAY HELLO TO EVERYONE! GOTTA GO!!
WHY WOULD BETTY MAKE A SILLY OL' SNOWMAN WHEN SHE COULD BE WITH ME?

WOW! IT'S BEAUTIFUL! AND THIS SNOW IS PERFECTO FOR MAKING A SNOWMAN!

GOOD ROLLING...

GREAT PACKING!!

AND SOON...
TA-DAH!!

HMM... THERE'S SOMETHING MISSING!
2

I KNOW! A SNOW WOMAN!

ONE HOUR LATER...
AND SOME SNOW CHILDREN!
WOW! THIS IS THE PERFECT BACKDROP FOR MY "STAN THE WEATHERMAN" SIX O'CLOCK SPOT!

MEANWHILE...
LET IT SNOW... LET IT SNOW... LET IT SNOW!
I REALLY MISS BETTY, MIDGE, BUT SHE HURT MY FEELINGS WHEN SHE CHOSE TO BUILD A SNOWMAN INSTEAD OF OF BEING WITH ME!
MAYBE SHE JUST NEEDED A LITTLE "ALONE" TIME, RONNIE!

ALONE TIME? FROM ME? MAYBE YOU'RE RIGHT, MIDGE...

IT MUST BE VERY DIFFICULT FOR HER TO HAVE ME AS A BEST FRIEND!

AFTER ALL, BETTY IS ALWAYS IN THE SHADOW, WHILE I'M ALWAYS IN THE SPOTLIGHT...

I LOOKED FABULOUS AT THE "SNOW FLAKE BALL" WHILE BETTY HAD ON LAST YEAR'S DRESS!
AND I WAS THE ONE WHO TOOK THE CARRIAGE RIDE WITH ARCHIE, NOT BETTY!
AND WHEN I SKIED "LOOK OUT" MOUNTAIN, MY HAIR FLOWED MAGNIFICENTLY IN THE WIND WHILE POOR BETTY WAS WEARING A BOR-ING PONYTAIL...
RONNIE! WHERE ARE YOU GOING SO FAST?
TO SAVE MY BEST FRIEND!
BETTY NEEDS TO KNOW THAT SHE IS SPECIAL JUST THE WAY SHE IS!
4

SHE NEEDS TO UNDERSTAND THAT UNDERNEATH MY DESIGNER CLOTHES, LAVISH VACATIONS, AND SERVANTS JUMPING AT MY EVERY WHIM...

WE ARE *EXACTLY ALIKE*!!
LODGE

AND I KNOW JUST WHAT TO DO TO PROVE IT!

LAST YEAR'S PANTS!
A RIPPED JACKET!

AND I'LL USE THIS GEL THAT WILL MAKE MY HAIR ALL STICKY!
TRU GOO

NOW MY HAIR WILL DEFINITELY NOT BLOW IN THE WIND!

AND SOON...
I AM "STAN THE WEATHERMAN," AND HERE WE ARE, LIVE AT BETTY COOPER'S HOUSE! WHAT INSPIRED YOU TO MAKE ALL THESE SNOW PEOPLE?
I LOVE THE SNOW AND I'VE ALWAYS LOVED SCULPTURE!
BETTY IS SO TALENTED!
WHAT A WONDERFUL ARTIST!
SHE'S BEAUTIFUL, TOO!

NOW LET'S GET A SHOT OF A LOCAL ADMIRER!
YIKES! I'M GOING TO BE ON TELEVISION LOOKING LIKE THIS?!

AND WHAT DO YOU THINK OF RIVERDALE'S SHINING STAR?
DON'T GET ME STARTED!
End

Betty IN... CITIES and their NICKNAMES

SEE IF YOU CAN MATCH THE NAMES OF THESE CITIES TO THEIR NICKNAMES!

1 - CHICAGO	A - THE CITY OF ANGELS
2 - PHILADELPHIA	B - THE ETERNAL CITY
3 - NEW YORK	C - THE CITY OF LIGHTS
4 - ROME	D - THE WINDY CITY
5 - LOS ANGELES	E - THE CITY OF BROTHERLY LOVE
6 - PARIS	F - BRIDE OF THE SEA
7 - VENICE	G - THE BIG APPLE

ANSWERS: 1-D 2-E 3-G 4-B 5-A 6-C 7-F

Betty and Veronica IN BOWLED OVER!

Script: Frank Doyle / Pencils: Doug Crane / Inks: Rudy Lapick / Letters: Bill Yoshida / Colors: Barry Grossman

HI, EVERYBODY! COLD ENOUGH FOR YOU?
REAL SHARP QUESTION, ARCHIE!

I THINK THE FROST HAS SEEPED THROUGH YOUR FOREHEAD!
COLDER THAN REGGIE'S HEART!
I USED THAT ALREADY, JUG!

SLAM!
ANOTHER CHILLED CHILD SEEKING REFUGE?

HELLO, YOU FROSTED FLAKES! WHAT'S NEW?

BETTY! ARE YOU MAD? THAT'S NO WAY TO DRESS FOR THIS WEATHER!

I'M JUST FINE, RON! DON'T BE A NAG!
WELL, EXCU-U-U-SE ME!

WHERE'S THAT GREAT SWEATER OF YOURS, BETS?
ARCHIE! GET OFF MY BACK!

HOW I DRESS IS MY BUSINESS! YOU'RE NOT MY MOM!
WOW! TOUCHY!!

I'LL HAVE A HOT CHOCOLATE, POPS!
LET'S GO, JUG!
GOOD IDEA!

IT WAS GETTING COLDER IN THERE THAN IT IS OUT HERE!
POP'S
CHOCK'L
SHOP
BETTY'S NOT USUALLY THAT GROUCHY!

HEY! THAT KID!!
WHAT ABOUT HIM?

HE'S WEARING BETTY'S SWEATER!! HEY! KID! STOP!!

COME BACK HERE, YOU LITTLE TWERP!
EEE-PP!

I'LL CUT HIM OFF AT THE PASS, PARD'NER!

HAH! GOTCHA! NOW, LET'S SEE WHAT THIS IS ALL ABOUT!
LET ME GO!

WHERE DID YOU GET THAT SWEATER ?
YOU CAN'T HAVE IT! IT'S MINE!

I DON'T WANT TO STEAL IT, ... I JUST WANT TO KNOW HOW YOU GOT IT!
I WAS COLD, SEE? SHIVERIN', LIKE!

I DON'T HAVE NO WARM CLOTHES, ON ACCOUNT OF MY DAD AIN'T GOT NO JOB!
GET ON WITH IT!! SPIT IT OUT!

THIS NICE LADY COME ALONG AN' SEEN ME! SHE FELT SORRY FOR ME, I GUESS!
BETTY!
IT FIGURES!

SHE TOOK OFF HER SWEATER AN' PUT IT ON ME!
OKAY, KID! SORRY IF WE SCARED YOU!

HOW ABOUT THAT BETTY ?!
WHEN THEY MADE HER, THEY BROKE THE MOLD!

AN UNSELFISH GESTURE LIKE THAT MAKES A GUY THINK!
I'LL SAY!

THE WORLD IS FULL OF "HAVES" AND "HAVE NOTS"!
AND WE'RE LUCKY TO BE AMONG THE "HAVES"!
5

COUPLE OF HOT CHOCOLATES, POPS!
THE HOTTER, THE BETTER!

WHAT'S GOING ON? IS THERE A PRIZE FOR THE FIRST ONE WHO GETS PNEUMONIA?

ALL PART OF THE MACHO IMAGE, POP!
YEAH! THAT'S IT!!

TOUGHEN UP THE OL' BODY! JUG AND I ARE GOING TO BE HARD AS NAILS!
SURE YOU ARE!!

THE WORLD SHOULD BE FULL OF SUCH HARD, TOUGH CHARACTERS!
POP'S SUPER!
MON, WED, FRI
$3.85
INSTANT WHIP
Hot Chokl'it
END

Betty and Veronica in "SLOW BURN, QUICK FREEZE"

Script: Frank Doyle / Pencils: Dan DeCarlo / Inks: Jimmy DeCarlo / Letters: Bill Yoshida / Colors: Barry Grossman

HE JUST HAS TO SNAP HIS FINGERS AND YOU COME RUNNING!
OOH! DID YOU HEAR A SNAP?

CONTROL YOURSELF! DON'T EVER LET ONE OF THEM GET TO YOU LIKE ---

---AIEEEE!
WHAT? WHAT? WHAT?

THAT FABULOUS MIKE MACHO! OOOH! HE'S SUCH A DREAM!

HE IS CUTE, ISN'T HE?
"CUTE?" WOW! THAT'S THE UNDERSTATEMENT OF THE YEAR!

HE WORKS AT MEYERS DRUG STORE!
EEEEEE! I'D BUY HIM A CHAIN OF DRUG STORES!
2

BUT THAT'S STILL NO EXCUSE FOR MAKING A FOOL OF YOURSELF OVER A BOY!
SIGH! I GUESS I JUST DON'T HAVE YOUR SELF-CONTROL!

WELL, IT'S ALMOST TIME FOR DINNER! BE SEEING YOU, BETTY!
'NIGHT, RON!

EEE! THAT MIKE! I'VE *GOT* TO ADD HIM TO MY COLLECTION!

MEYERS DRUG STORE? HOW LATE ARE YOU OPEN? AND DO YOU DELIVER?

WE CLOSE AT TEN TONIGHT! BUT WE ONLY DELIVER UNTIL EIGHT, WHEN OUR DELIVERY BOY GOES OFF!
PRESCRIPTI

YOU'RE SHREWD, RONNIE, GIRL! SO HE FINISHES AT EIGHT!
THAT'S A NICE TIME FOR A DATE!
3

LATER:
TSK! I'M OUT OF HAIR SPRAY! I'D BETTER GO GET SOME!

BE RIGHT BACK, MOM! UNLESS I MEET SOME OF THE KIDS AND HANG OUT FOR AWHILE!
ALL RIGHT, DEAR!

CALL IF YOU'RE GOING TO BE LATE!
RIGHT!

BRRR! COLD NIGHT! A GOOD TIME TO BE INDOORS!

HOPE I DON'T FREEZE BEFORE I CAN PULL OFF THIS LITTLE "ACCIDENTAL" MEETING!
MEYE
PHARMA

OMIGOSH! *BETTY!* SHE MUSTN'T KNOW I'M HANGING AROUND TO MEET A *BOY!*
ME
PHAR

RONNIE! WHY ARE YOU STANDING OUT HERE IN THE STREET IN THIS BITTER COLD?
BECAUSE IT'S WINTER TIME, DUMMY!

IT'S HARD TO STAND IN THE STREET IN WARMTH AND COMFORT AT THIS TIME OF YEAR!
I DIDN'T MEAN---

WHEN IT'S WINTER, THE TEMPERATURE DROPS! WHEN THE TEMPERATURE DROPS, IT DOESN'T GET HOT-- IT GETS *COLD!*

NOW, HAVE YOU GOT ANY MORE NOSY QUESTIONS?
JUST ONE!

WHY ARE YOU BITING MY HEAD OFF?
STOP TRYING TO WORM INFORMATION OUT OF ME! IT'S NONE OF YOUR BUSINESS!

SOMETIMES A PERSON DOESN'T FEEL LIKE TALKING! SOMETIMES A PERSON LIKES TO BE ALONE!
OKAY! OKAY!

WHOOOEE.! IT'S LIKE I STEPPED ON A TIGER'S TAIL.!
WHAT'S THAT, BETTY?

VERONICA, MIKE.! SHE'S OUTSIDE.! AND WHAT A FOUL MOOD.!!

TERRIBLE TEMPER.! I'M EVEN AFRAID TO PASS HER AGAIN.!
YOU COULD GO OUT THE BACK WAY.!

YOU COME OUT AROUND THE CORNER.! I'M DONE HERE.! C'MON, I'LL SHOW YOU THE WAY.!
FINE.! I'LL NEED SOME HAIR SPRAY FIRST.!

WHAT'S KEEPING BETTY? I CAN'T HAVE HER HANGING AROUND WHILE I'M MAKING A BIG PLAY FOR MIKE.!
MEYERS PHARMACY
PIZZA?
I'D LOVE IT.!
The END

Script: Bob Bolling / Pencils: Stan Goldberg / Inks: Rudy Lapick / Letters: Bill Yoshida / Colors: Barry Grossman

HOW DO I KNOW IT'S GOING TO BE A GREAT DAY?... BECAUSE I'M WEARING MY LUCKY HAT!

AM I DOING ALL RIGHT? ...THANKS FOR HOLDING ME UP, GUYS!
YOU'RE DOING JUST FINE, MISS LODGE!
GOOD GRIEF! AN ACADEMY AWARD PERFORMANCE!!!

HMMPH! WHO NEEDS A SKI INSTRUCTOR ANYWAY?!... I ALREADY KNOW HOW TO SKI... A LITTLE!

WE SUGGEST THAT ALL BEGINNERS TAKE THAT TRAIL DOWN!
LODGE

BA BOOM!
WHAT'S THAT?!
BLASTING ON THE WEST SLOPE... IT'S A SAFETY PRECAUTION!

IT PREVENTS THE SNOW FROM BUILDING UP TO THE POINT WHERE IT MAY CAUSE AN AVALANCHE!
...ONCE IT SETTLES DOWN OVER THERE, WE'LL OPEN THAT SLOPE AGAIN TO SKIERS!

THE BLAST CAUSES A SERIES OF SMALL SLIDES, FRIGHTENING INNUMERABLE HARES AND SQUIRRELS, THREE MOOSE AND A PARTRIDGE IN A PINE TREE...

... WHILE UNCOVERING ONE HIBERNATING URSUS ARCTOS...

THE BAFFLED BRUIN LOPES OVER THE SLOPE...
YAW-W-W-N-N

ULP!

URRRK!...
I'M OUT OF CONTROL!

PHEW!
WHUMF!
THINGS CAN ONLY GET WORSE! THERE GOES MY LUCKY HAT!
SNAP!
THIS COMES AS NO SURPRISE...

THUD!
WHUMPH!

OOOWW! MY LEG! I CAN'T GET UP! gro-o-an!

...B... BROKEN?!
'FRAID SO, MISS COOPER!

WE'LL HAVE TO PUT IT IN A CAST!
THE TIMBERLAND LODGE HAS THE FINEST IN MEDICAL FACILITIES!
I KNOW! I KNOW!

I COME OUT AFTER LUNCH... AND NO INSTRUCTORS! ...WHAT GIVES?
THEY'RE ALL IN THE MAIN HALL LISTENING TO YOUR FRIEND BETTY TELL HOW SHE SNOW-BALLED DOWN THE SOUTH SLOPE WITH A BROWN BEAR AND BROKE A BONE!

BETTY?! BROWN BEAR?! BROKEN BONE!
MAIN HALL

I LOST MY LUCKY HAT, BUT THINGS DIDN'T TURN OUT TOO BADLY AFTER ALL!
SHE'LL RECEIVE THE UTMOST IN ATTENTION HERE AT TIMBERLAND!
6
END
...NO, I THINK I LIKE IT BETTER ON THE BACK OF YOUR HEAD...

Script: Kathleen Webb / Pencils: Dan DeCarlo / Inks: Allison Flood / Letters: Bill Yoshida / Colors: Barry Grossman

I WISH I COULD! THE ONLY DECISION I EVER GET TO MAKE IS WHETHER I NEED NEW SHOE-LACES FOR MY SNEAKERS!

YOU PROBABLY NEED NEW SNEAKERS FOR YOUR SHOELACES!
VERY FUNNY!

STILL, IT'S TRUE---ALL I'VE GOT ARE A FEW MEASLY ARTICLES OF CLOTHING TO CHOOSE FROM!
AND MEASLY THEY ARE, TOO!

YOU HAVE A WHOLE SMORGASBORD OF FASHIONABLE DELIGHTS!
!

SAY, WHY NOT?
WHY NOT WHAT?
SNAP!

WHY DON'T YOU TAKE MY WARDROBE FOR A WHILE, AND I'LL TAKE YOURS?
D-DO YOU MEAN THAT?
2

ARE YOU SURE YOU WON'T GET BORED WITH MINE, THOUGH?
I'M ALREADY BORED WITH MINE!

ANYTHING WOULD BE A REFRESHING CHANGE!
BUT HOW ARE WE GOING TO MOVE ALL YOUR CLOTHES TO MY HOUSE?

WE WON'T! WE'LL JUST TRADE BEDROOMS INSTEAD!
HUH?

YOU MOVE INTO MY ROOM, AND I'LL MOVE INTO YOURS!
OH! OKAY!

FIRST LET'S MAKE SURE IT'S OKAY WITH THE MAMAS AND THE PAPAS!
THAT GOES WITHOUT SAYING!

DADDYKINS, MEET YOUR NEW DAUGHTER!
HOPEFULLY SHE WON'T COST ME AS MUCH FOR CLOTHING AS YOU DO!

I'LL CALL MY PARENTS AND ARRANGE THINGS WITH THEM!
THIS WILL SAVE ME A BUNDLE! I SHOULD'VE THOUGHT OF IT YEARS AGO!
OH, DADDY!
WHAT'S WRONG?
YOUR DAUGHTER HAS DECIDED TO BE GREEDY AND VERONICA IS GOING TO BE IMPOVERISHED!
HUH?
I'LL EXPLAIN LATER!
HI, FOLKS! JUST TREAT ME LIKE ONE OF THE FAMILY!
I'M DINING OUT THIS EVENING BUT TOMORROW MORNING PLEASE GIVE ME A NINE O'CLOCK WAKE-UP CALL WITH BREAKFAST IN BED!
JUST ONE OF THE FAMILY, EH?
AHHH --- HOW MARVELOUS! SIMPLE AND SKIMPY! NOW I CAN BE READY FOR ANYTHING!
RIVER
WOW!
NOW I CAN REALLY IMPRESS ARCHIE ON OUR DATE TONIGHT!
4

BUT... WHICH DRESS SHOULD I REALLY IMPRESS HIM IN?

REGGIE IS HERE TO TAKE YOU OUT, VERONICA!
GOOD! I TOLD HIM TO PICK ME UP HERE!

I'M READY!
YOU INTEND TO GO TO THE COUNTRY CLUB BALL LIKE THAT? IT'S NOT FORMAL ENOUGH!

WHAT DO YOU THINK I RENTED THIS MONKEY SUIT FOR, ANYWAY?!
(MOAN) THIS IS THE MOST FORMAL DRESS I COULD FIND!

AND, BACK WITH BETTY!
ARCHIE IS HERE, BETTY!
OH, UMM---TELL HIM I'LL BE DOWN SOON...
KNOCK
KNOCK

I HOPE!
R-RINGGG
KFL

BETTY! BETTY! MY NEW FORMAL! I'VE GOT TO HAVE IT FOR TONIGHT!
(SIGH) YOU'RE WELCOME TO IT, RON!

HAVING LOTS OF CLOTHES ISN'T AS MUCH FUN AS I THOUGHT IT WOULD BE!
TELL ME ABOUT IT!

HAVING VERY LITTLE TO CHOOSE FROM ISN'T MUCH FUN EITHER!
LET'S TRADE BACK BEFORE IT GETS TOO LATE!

THE GREAT EXPERIMENT FAILED?
YEP! VERONICA CAN'T SURVIVE WITHOUT HER PLENTY!

... AND BETTY CAN'T SURVIVE WITH IT!
IT'S NICE TO KNOW SHE ISN'T AS GREEDY AS WE THOUGHT!

YOU KNOW WHAT? I THINK I'VE DECIDED THAT HAVING A LITTLE IS MORE THAN ENOUGH!
END

Veronica in FORGIVE & FORGET?

I'M *REALLY, REALLY* SORRY I'M SO LATE, RON!

STOP RIGHT THERE, ARCHIE ANDREWS! TEN MINUTES IS LATE! FORTY MINUTES IS HISTORY! AND THAT'S WHAT YOU ARE... HISTORY!

B-BUT I FORGOT ALL ABOUT...

OH! YOU FORGOT, HUH? WELL, *FORGET* YOU, BUSTER!

PLEASE, LET ME EXPLAIN!

NO! I NEVER WANT TO SEE YOUR FACE AGAIN!

Script & Pencils: Dan Parent / Ink: Rich Koslowski / Letters: Bill Yoshida / Colors: Barry Grossman

GLOOM!
BOOK NO
WE'RE THROUGH! I DON'T WANT TO THINK ABOUT YOU! I DON'T WANT TO BE REMINDED YOU EXIST! GOODBYE!

HA! THE LATE MR. ARCHIE ANDREWS! WHO NEEDS HIM?

MOMMY! CAN I HAVE THIS ORANGE BALL?
NO, DEAR! PUT IT BACK!
TIM'S TOYS

HMMM... THAT ORANGE BALL SORT OF REMINDS ME OF YOU-KNOW-WHO!

GASP!
YOU KNOW YOU DIDN'T MEAN WHAT YOU SAID!

I-I MUST BE COMING DOWN WITH SOMETHING! SUDDENLY I FEEL REALLY STRANGE!

ARCHIE GOT ME SO UPSET I'M SEEING AND HEARING THINGS!
STEP RIGHT UP, FOLKS! WATCH THE SUPERJUICER AT WORK!

WHEN YOU HAVE A BUSY SCHEDULE TO JUGGLE, YOU DON'T HAVE THE TIME TO SQUEEZE ORANGES!

WATCH HOW FAST THE SUPERJUICER MAKES ORANGE JUICE!
ORANGES?
SALE

FORGIVE ME!
FORGIVE ME!
UGH!
FORGIVE ME!

MY MIND MUST BE PLAYING TRICKS ON ME FOR A REASON! MAYBE I WAS TOO HARSH WITH ARCHIE!

HOLD ON TIGHT TO YOUR BALLOON, JIMMY!
YES, MOM!

YOU KNOW YOU JUST CAN'T FORGET ABOUT ME!
GAH!

THE PROBLEM COULD BE FOOD! I'M STARVING! HUNGER DOES ODD THINGS TO PEOPLE!

I'LL STOP IMAGINING THINGS!
FOOD COURT
IMP

DON'T YOU DARE!
Orange Sun
IMPORTS

Orange Sun
IMPORTS
GULP!
FOOD COURT

WHEW! I'M HERE AT LAST!
CAN I HELP YOU MISS?

YES! ONE SMALL CHEESE PIZZA WITH EXTRA SAUCE!
COMING RIGHT UP!

HUH? OH NO! NOT AGAIN!
IS ANYTHING WRONG, MISS?

I'M NOT SURE! I MAY BE LOSING MY APPETITE... OR MY MIND!

JOIN THE CLUB! I LOST SOMEONE I CARE VERY MUCH ABOUT!
A-ARCHIE?
IZZA

CAN'T YOU FORGIVE ME, RON? I'LL NEVER BE LATE AGAIN! I PROMISE!
WELL, I GUESS I CAN THIS LAST TIME!

NO HARD FEELINGS! BUT DON'T EVER KEEP ME WAITING IN THE FUTURE!
WHEW! I WON'T!
SMACK!

YOUR PIZZA IS READY, MISS!
THANKS! JOIN ME FOR LUNCH, ARCHIE!
PIZZA

WHAT MADE YOU CHANGE YOUR MIND ABOUT ME, RON?
LET'S JUST SAY THERE'S SOMETHING ABOUT YOU THAT'S UNFORGETTABLE!
THE End

VERONICA HAS A SIMPLE BASIC PHILOSOPHY THAT WORKS MOST OF THE TIME!
FIND OUT WHAT IT IS BY CHANGING THE LETTERS TO THE NEXT ONE OF THE ALPHABET!

(A=B, B=C, C=D, D=E, E=F, F=G, G=H, H=I, ETC.)

LNRS RLHKDR
ZQD RSZQSDC
AX ZMNSGDQ
RLHKD!

MOST SMILES ARE STARTED BY ANOTHER SMILE!

Veronica SLEEK AND SLINKY!!

Script: **John Workman** Pencils: **Rex Lindsey** Inks: **Rich Koslowski** Letters: **Vickie Williams** Colors: **Barry Grossman**
Editor-In-Chief: **Victor Gorelick** President: **Mike Pellerito** Publisher: **Jon Goldwater**

DON'T WORRY, RONNIE! MY BOOK SAYS THAT THERE ARE NO POISONOUS SNAKES IN THIS AREA!
YEAH? WHAT IF IT'S A REALLY WEIRD CREATURE THAT ESCAPED FROM A LAB EXPERIMENT?
JUGGIE--SOMETIMES I THINK YOU ARE A REALLY WEIRD CREATURE THAT ESCAPED FROM A LAB EXPERIMENT!
NOW... BE NICE, YOU TWO!
JUGHEAD...OH, PLEASE FORGIVE MY LACK OF RESPECT FOR YOUR EMINENT SELF! I AM SO ASHAMED!
AND I, MY FRIEND, CAN OFFER NOTHING BUT CONTRITION FOR MY INANE REMARKS!
I AM A WRETCH!
EEEUWWW! NOW THEY'RE FAKING BEING KIND!
WILL NOTHING SAVE US FROM THIS HOKEY SENTIMENTALITY?
CRACK!
THAT'LL DO THE TRICK!
IT'S STARTING TO RAIN! WE NEED TO FIND SHELTER!
LOOK... A CABIN!
WE'RE IN LUCK! LET'S RUN!

HELLO? ANYBODY HOME?
KNOCK! KNOCK!

UH... HELLO?
CREAK!

THERE'S NO ONE HERE!
WHAT A DELIGHTFUL, LITTLE CABIN!

AS LONG AS IT'S OUT OF THE RAIN AND SAFE FROM LIGHTNING, I'M HAPPY!
I'D BE HAPPIER IF WE COULD FIND SOME FOOD!

WHAT'S WRONG, ARCHIE? YOU SEEM WORRIED!
I DON'T KNOW... SOMETHING'S NOT QUITE RIGHT!

HEY, AN OLD RADIO! IF IT STILL WORKS, MAYBE WE CAN LISTEN TO SOME MUSIC!
LADIES AND GENTLEMEN! ...THIS IS THE END OF THE SECOND WORLD WAR!
CLICK!

THE WAR IS OVER!
SECOND WORLD WAR? I'VE HEARD OF RERUNS, BUT THIS IS RIDICULOUS!
YOU PROBABLY HAVE IT ON SOME KIND OF HISTORY STATION, JUGHEAD!

WOW! LOOK AT THIS NEWS-PAPER! IT'S FROM 1945, BUT IT LOOKS BRAND NEW!
CHRONICLE
WAR OVER
LOOK AROUND... EVERYTHING HERE IS OLD, BUT IT LOOKS NEW!
I'M BEGINNING TO WONDER IF THIS PLACE IS... HAUNTED!
COME ON, ARCH...
GHOSTS DON'T HANG AROUND LITTLE CABINS! THEY HAUNT MANSIONS AND CASTLES...
AND, DO YOU SEE ANY GHOSTS? I DON'T SEE ANY GHOSTS...
WELL...,
COME ON OUT, GHOSTS! SHOW YOURSELF! JUGHEAD JONES DARES YOU!
CREAK!
UH...THE DOOR'S OPEN, GUYS...!
MAYBE WE SHOULD GO NOW!
AND IT'S STOPPED RAINING!
LET'S DEFINITELY GO... NOW!

HA HA! GHOSTS... HAUNTING A LITTLE CABIN! YOU KILL ME, ARCH!
'COURSE THEN I'D BE A GHOST, AN' I'D HAVE TO HAUNT A PIZZA SHOP...OR A HAMBURGER JOINT, OR...
JUGHEAD!
SORRY, GIVE ME ANY SUBJECT TO TALK ABOUT...EVEN GHOSTS... AND I START THINKING OF FOOD!
HEH!
AND THEN, THE NEXT DAY AS THE FOUR FRIENDS ARE ON THEIR WAY TO THE LAKE...
LOOK, ARCHIE... IT'S YOUR MANSION OF TERRORS!
HMM... WE SHOULD SEE IF ANYONE'S HOME...TO THANK THEM FOR OUR KEEPING DRY IN IT!
UH...THE DOOR'S OPEN, ARCH!
I... GULP! NOTICED THAT, JUG!
HOLY COW! IT'S ALL DIFFERENT IN HERE NOW!
YEAH, BUT IT STILL LOOKS SORT OF OLD!
HEY... AN OLD TV! LET'S SEE WHAT'S ON!
CLICK!

FANS AROUND THE WORLD ARE SADDENED BY THE RUMORS OF THE BREAKUP OF THE MUSICAL GROUP KNOWN AS THE BEATLES!
NEWS 9
THE BEATLES!?!
BUT... THEY BROKE UP YEARS AGO!
YEAH, BUT PEOPLE ARE STILL LISTENING TO THEIR STUFF!
HEY! LOOK AT THIS!
IT'S FROM 1969... BUT THE PAPER ISN'T EVEN YELLOWED FROM AGE!
PEACE
CHRONICLE
MAN ON THE MOON!
AAAIIIIIIEEE!
VROOM!
YOU KNOW, ARCH... YOUR GHOST THEORY MAY NOT BE TOO FAR FETCHED!
HMM...
NO, JUGHEAD...
...THERE HAS TO BE A LOGICAL EXPLANATION!... AND WE'RE GOING TO FIND OUT WHAT IT IS!
WE ARE?
I WAS AFRAID OF THAT!
CONTINUED-

Archie & FRIENDS

FUN HOUSE! PART TWO

AH, LODGE! WE WERE JUST TELLING THAT YOUNG MAN ABOUT MARNIE MILSON!
WELL, SHE WAS INVITED TO THIS PARTY, BUT SHE'S NOT HERE!
"NOT HERE"... YOU MEAN SHE'S...
SHE'S IN NEW YORK-- WORKING HARD FOR THE BIG MEDIA COMPANY SHE RUNS!
HER SECRETARY CALLED... SAID MARNIE SENDS HER REGRETS!
I'M GLAD SHE'S DOING SO WELL! SHE WAS THE POOREST OF OUR LITTLE GROUP... GROWING UP WITH HER PARENTS IN THAT SMALL CABIN!
DID YOU HEAR THAT, JUGHEAD? THAT'S THE ANSWER! THE GHOST THAT'S HAUNTING THAT CABIN MUST BE MARNIE MILSON!
HUH?
YEAH! SOME SECRETARY CALLS AND SAYS THAT POOR OL' MARNIE CAN'T BE HERE! BUT THE TRUTH IS...
THE TRUTH IS, ARCHIE ANDREWS, THAT YOU HAVE AN OVERACTIVE IMAGINATION!
WE'LL SEE ABOUT THAT! TOMORROW, WE'LL GO BACK TO THAT CABIN AND..
NO, THANKS! BETTY AND I ARE GOING TO SWIM AND GET SOME SUN! YOU AND JUGGIE CAN HUNT GHOSTS!
PLOP!
MOAN!
8

THE NEXT MORNING FINDS ARCHIE AND JUGHEAD WALKING ON A TREE-LINED PATH HEADING TOWARD THE MYSTERIOUS CABIN...
I TELL YOU, JUG... IT HAS TO BE THE GHOST OF MARNIE MILSON...
BUT, ARCHIE...
MARNIE MILSON IS LIVING A GREAT LIFE IN NEW YORK...
UH... WELL...
WELL...MAYBE THE CABIN IS BEING HAUNTED BY THE GHOSTS OF HER PARENTS!
GULP!
ARCHIE... IT'S CHANGED AGAIN!
YEAH, BUT IT STILL HAS THAT OLD LOOK!
MARNIE MILSON! WE'RE HERE TO HELP YOU! ARE YOU HERE?
ARCH... M-MAYBE SHE DOESN'T WANT TO BE BOTHERED!
!
?
PING!
KER-WHUMP!

WHAT IS IT?
A NEWSPAPER FROM ≡GULP≡ 1989!
CHRONICLE
FREEDOM SWEEPS U.S.S.R. & EASTERN EUROPE

CLICK!

...REPORTING FROM WEST GERMANY WHERE PEOPLE ARE TEARING DOWN THE BERLIN WALL!
BERLIN

Y'KNOW, ARCH, I DIDN'T EAT NEARLY ENOUGH FOR BREAKFAST!
YEAH, ME, TOO! WHY DON'T WE GO MAKE SOME MORE TOAST?!
KA-THUMP! WHUMP!

I EAT MINE WITH LOTS OF BUTTER AND JELLY!

AND BACK AT THE LODGE LODGE...
ARCHIE! JUGGIE! WHAT'S UP?
ALL THE HAIRS ON THE BACK OF MY NECK!
TELL ME THE TRUTH! HAS MY HAIR TURNED WHITE?

DON'T BE SILLY! WHILE YOU TWO WERE OUT IN THE MORNING FOG, WE'VE BEEN FINDING ANSWERS!
YEAH? WELL, NOW ARCHIE AND I HAVE A WHOLE DIFFERENT BATCH OF QUESTIONS!

HERE, ARCHIE... VERONICA TOLD ME ABOUT YOUR THEORY... THERE'S SOMEONE YOU NEED TO TALK TO... MARNIE MILSON!
!

UH... H-HELLO, MISS MILSON! AHH... HOW ARE YOUR PARENTS?

MY PARENTS ARE FINE, MR. ANDREWS! THEY'RE VACATIONING IN THE SOUTH OF FRANCE! WHY DO YOU ASK?
MILSON
MEDIA IN

WELL... WE WERE... UH... VISITING YOUR CABIN THE OTHER DAY AND...

WHAT? BUT THAT CAN'T BE POSSIBLE! YOU SEE...

WH-WHAT DID YOU JUST SAY?
WHAT?

TH-THANK YOU, MISS MILSON! GOOD-BYE!

WELL, FOLKS... LET'S TAKE A LITTLE WALK OUT TO THE CABIN!
?

BUT WHY, ARCHIE? DIDN'T MARNIE MILSON CONVINCE YOU HOW SILLY THIS "GHOST" STUFF REALLY IS?
JUST THE OPPOSITE, RONNIE! I NOW KNOW THE TRUE IDENTITY OF THE CABIN GHOST!

THERE'S THE CABIN! NOW, I WANT YOU TO LOOK AT IT... REALLY LOOK AT IT!
BUT, ARCHIE...
WH-WHAT'S HAPPENING?
WOW!
B-BUT THIS CAN'T BE!
MARNIE WILSON TOLD ME THAT SHE HAD A WONDERFUL LIFE GROWING UP IN THE CABIN... THERE ARE NO GHOSTS IN THE CABIN!
IT WAS STRUCK BY LIGHTNING AND BURNED DOWN LAST WINTER! THE GHOST IS THE CABIN!
WHY, I BELIEVE YOU'RE RIGHT, ARCHIE!
OF COURSE HE IS, DADDY...! NOT ALL GHOSTS ARE SCARY OR MEAN! SOME JUST WANT TO RE-LIVE HAPPY TIMES!
YOU KNOW... MARNIE MILSON SHOULD REBUILD... TURN THE CABIN INTO SOMETHING THAT MAKES PEOPLE HAPPY!
HOW ABOUT A HAMBURGER JOINT?
JUGHEAD!
SORRY! THIS HAS ALL BEEN SO WEIRD... IT MAKES ME HUNGRY JUST TO THINK ABOUT IT!
THE End

TODAY, CLASS, I WANT TO HEAR YOUR COMPOSITIONS ON MEDIEVAL TIMES!
MOOSE, WE'LL START WITH YOU!
THIS SHOULD SET MEDIEVAL TIMES BACK 5,000 MORE YEARS!
Moose IN "DOING RESEARCH"
Pellowski / T. Kennedy / M. DeCarlo / Yoshida / Grossman
DUH-H... IN THOSE OLDEN-TIME DAYS, KNIGHTS HAD TO CARRY FIRE EXTINGUISHERS BECAUSE THERE WERE SO MANY DRAGONS, AND THEY HAD NO TV, SO THEY LISTENED TO CDS!
YEAH, THEY LISTENED TO HEAVY METAL AS WELL AS WORE IT! HA-HA!
REGGIE, PLEASE! MOOSE, ADMIT IT! YOU DIDN'T DO ANY RESEARCH, DID YOU?

DUH-H... NO, MA'AM!
MOOSE, I HATE TO GIVE YOU AN "F", SO I'LL GIVE YOU ONE MORE CHANCE...

WRITE A COMPOSITION ON DINOSAURS THAT SHOWS ME YOU RESEARCHED IT AND I'LL GIVE YOU A PASSING GRADE!
DUH-H...GEE, THANKS, MISS GRUNDY!

LATER...
HOW'S IT COMING?
DUH-H...GET OUT OF HERE. THIS PRE-HYSTERICAL STUFF IS HARD ENOUGH TO LEARN...
PUBLIC LIBRARY
PRE-HISTORIC TIMES

WITHOUT YOU RAGGIN' ON ME!
MOOSE, I'M HURT! YOU MISJUDGE ME! I WANT TO HELP!

DUH-H... NOTHIN' DOIN'! YOU JUST WANT TO PLAY A DIRTY TRICK ON ME!
NO, MOOSE! HONEST! I CAN REALLY HELP YOU!
BOOK TALK

IT JUST SO HAPPENS THAT MY COUSIN NED IS MAKING A MOVIE ABOUT DINOSAURS JUST OUTSIDE OF TOWN AS A COLLEGE FILM PROJECT!

AND I FIGURE IF YOU COULD GO AND EXPERIENCE THE AMBIANCE OF PRE-HISTORIC TIMES, IT WOULD GIVE YOU A GRASP OF ITS INDIGENOUS ENVIRONMENT!
DUH-H... HUH?

IF YOU COULD SEE WHAT THE WORLD OF THE DINOSAURS WAS LIKE, FIRST HAND, YOU COULD WRITE ABOUT IT INTELLIGENTLY!
DUH-H... YEAH THAT'D BE COOL!

I'LL GIVE MY COUSIN A CALL AND TELL HIM TO EXPECT YOU!
DUH-H... GEE, THANKS, REGGIE! HOW CAN I EVER REPAY YOU?

JUST DON'T TELL ANYONE I DID ANY-THING NICE FOR YOU! THEY'D THINK I WENT SOFT IN THE HEAD OR SOMETHING!
DUH-H...OKAY!

IF ANYBODY ASKS, I'LL TELL THEM YOU'RE A REAL NASTY GUY!
THANKS, MOOSE, I APPRECIATE IT!

OH, WOW! DID I ACTUALLY DO SOME-THING NICE FOR SOMEBODY? MAYBE I AM GOING SOFT IN THE HEAD!
REGGIE, GET A GRIP!

LATER...
DHH-H... HELLO, I'M MOOSE!
OH, YES, COUSIN REGGIE'S FRIEND! WELCOME TO OUR FILM SITE!
B

DUH-H... OH, WOW! LOOK AT THAT BIG DINOSAUR!
OH, YES! THAT'S OUR TYRANNOSAURUS REX!

DUH...H... LET ME WRITE THIS DOWN! HOW MANY "R'S" IN "WRECKS ?"
ONE! THIS BIG GUY WAS CONSTRUCTED BY THE SPECIAL EFFECTS CLASS!

ITS SKIN IS MADE OF LATEX AND IT'S DRIVEN BY THREE ELECTRIC MOTORS!
DUH-H... GEE!

WE USE THESE EIGHT-INCH-HIGH MODELS FOR THE BATTLE SCENE!
DUH-H... WOW!

AND WE USE THESE STYROFOAM BOULDERS SO THAT OUR TIME TRAVELERS DON'T GET HURT IN OUR "LANDSLIDES!"
DUH-H.. GEE!

THE NEXT DAY...
MOOSE, ARE YOU READY TO READ YOUR COMPOSITION?
DUH-H... YES, MA'AM!

DUH-H... DINOSAURS HAD SKIN MADE OF LATEX AND WERE DRIVEN BY THREE ELECTRIC MOTORS! ONLY THE EIGHT-INCH TALL ONES USED TO FIGHT, AND BOULDERS IN THOSE DAYS WERE MADE OF STY-RO-FOAM...

MOOSE, THAT'S THE MOST ABSURD COLLECTION OF INANE BALDERDASH I'VE EVER HEARD!
DUH-H... THANK YOU!

AND I'M GOING TO GIVE YOU AN "F!"
DUH-H AN "F?"
UH-OH!

DUH-H... MAKE A FOOL OUT OF ME WILL YOU?
B-BUT, MOOSE I REALLY WANTED TO... HELP!
THERE GOES MOOSE CHASING REGGIE AGAIN!
YES, WHY CAN'T REGGIE EVER STOP BEING A WISE GUY AND BE NICE TO MOOSE FOR A CHANGE?
END

Script & Pencils: Dick Malmgren / Inks: Rudy Lapick / Letters: Bill Yoshida / Colors: Barry Grossman

MAN! I DO LIKE THIS JACKET! IMAGINE HIM WANTING TO GIVE IT TO ME! MAYBE I'VE MISJUDGED OL' REG!

THAT'S NOT LIKE YOU, REGGIE!
HOW CAN YOU SAY THAT, RON?

OF COURSE IT'S LIKE ME TO RIP OFF OL' ARCH!
RIP OFF?

HA! THE ZIPPER WON'T WORK ON THAT JACKET! IT'S USELESS!

NOW THAT'S THE REGGIE I KNOW AND UNDERSTAND!
HYUK! YUK!

HAH! I WISH I COULD SEE HIS FACE WHEN HE FINDS OUT HE'S BEEN HAD!
YOU'RE INCORRIGIBLE!
2

ARCHIE, YOU GULLIBLE GOONEY BIRD! HE DID IT TO YOU AGAIN!

I SHOULD HAVE SUSPECTED SOME FOUL PLAY WHEN HE CALLED ME A LIFELONG FRIEND!

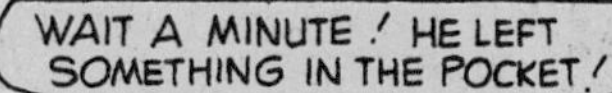
WAIT A MINUTE! HE LEFT SOMETHING IN THE POCKET!

A KEY! BIG DEAL! MAYBE I CAN USE THE KEYRING AT LEAST!

BUT THE CROOK ISN'T GETTING THIS BACK! I DON'T OWE HIM ANY FAVORS!

I'LL PUT MY HOUSE KEY ON THE RING! I MIGHT AS WELL GET SOMETHING FOR MY FIVE BUCKS!

HOURS LATER...
WHA...? SOMEBODY'S TOSSING PEBBLES AT MY WINDOW!
PING!
RATTLE!

PSST! COME DOWN AND OPEN THE DOOR, ARCH!

LISTEN, BUDDY! I LEFT MY HOUSE KEY IN THAT JACKET I GAVE YOU!
SOLD ME-- FOR FIVE DOLLARS!

MY FOLKS ARE AWAY, AND I'M LOCKED OUT!
SORRY, LIFELONG FRIEND, WE DON'T RENT ROOMS!

THERE'S A NICE MOTEL ABOUT A MILE OUT OF TOWN!
DON'T BE A WISE GUY!

JUST GIVE ME THE KEY THAT'S IN THE JACKET POCKET!
WHICH JACKET? THE ONE WITH THE FAULTY ZIPPER?
4

GEE, OL' BUDDY, I'M AFRAID THAT'S A SET! THAT'S THE WAY I BOUGHT THEM!
WHAT DO YOU MEAN?

YOU WANT THE KEY, YOU BUY THE JACKET!
GRRR! OKAY! OKAY! HERE'S YOUR FIVE BUCKS BACK!

YOU HAVEN'T HEARD OF INFLATION? THE PRICE IS TEN!
ACK!

MY! CAN THAT BE THE GENTLE PITTER PATTER OF RAIN? HOW NICE!

WRONG KEY! THE LITTLE BLISTER CHANGED KEYS ON ME! I'M OUT FIVE BUCKS! I'VE STILL GOT THE LOUSY JACKET, AND I'M TIRED AND WET! NOT ONE OF MY BETTER DAYS!
END

Archie in "SNOWBALL EFFECT"

Gladir / Goldberg / Scarpelli / Yoshida / Grossman

SNOW MAKES DRIVING TREACHEROUS! IT'S MESSY!
SURRENDER, YOU ROGUES!
NEVER!

HUH?!
CHARGE!!!

GOTCHA!
HARR! HARR!
SPLAT!
HA! MISSED!
WHAP!

KIDS! THEY DON'T KNOW WHAT SNOW IS REALLY ALL ABOUT!
YES! VICTORY!

TRUE, BUT THOSE SNOWBALL FIGHTS WE HAD IN THE OLD DAYS WERE CLASSICS!
YEAH... I GUESS!

HA! GOT YA', MANTLE!

HEY! SNOW ANGELS! REMEMBER?
HOW COULD I FORGET?
HEE! HEE!
HA! HA!

HUMPH! LOOK AT THIS FROZEN GLOP!
ICKY, WET, SLUSHY STUFF!

SNOW! WHAT'S IT GOOD FOR?

SAY...
SURE!
WHY NOT?
LET'S DO IT!

ENEMY IN SIGHT!
PREPARE TO FIRE!
SNOW ANGELS!!
4

IF IT KEEPS SNOWING, I'LL HAVE TO SHOVEL MY WALK AGAIN!
YUK! WINTER! WHAT'S IT GOOD FOR?
SLOSH
SCRUNCH
HUH?
YA-HOO!
HOORAY!
HA! HA!
HUMPH! KIDS! THEY DON'T KNOW WHAT SNOW IS REALLY ALL ABOUT!
OR DO THEY?...
END

Script: Craig Boldman / Art: Rex Lindsey / Letters: Vickie Williams / Colors: Barry Grossman

ZZZZZ
RIP!
EEK!
SOMEONE HELP ME!
DUH! THIS LOOKS LIKE A JOB FOR MIGHTY MOOSE!
CRASH!

NOW, WHERE CAN I CHANGE INTO MY SUPER COSTUME ?
CRASH!
CINEM

OH, WELL,...ANY PORT IN A STORM!
TR

INTO THE HEAP GOES AN ORDINARY GUY...
A-1

RATTLE!
RATTLE!
RUMBLE!
SLAM!
A-1 TRASH

... OUT FLIES MIGHTY MOOSE TO THE RESCUE!
M

SNIFF! SNIFF! PHEW! TALK ABOUT A STRONG ODOR!
SAVE ME, MIGHTY MOOSE!
GIVE THIS OVERSIZED FROG-FACE YOUR FAMOUS ONE-TWO PUNCH!
CINE

WHY DOES HE CALL IT HIS ONE-TWO PUNCH?
BECAUSE THAT'S AS HIGH AS HE CAN COUNT!

TAKE THIS, AND THAT!

EYEOW! I'M FALLING!
URP!

DON'T WORRY! I'LL CATCH YOU!

THANKS FOR SAVING ME, BUT... P.U.! YOU NEED A BATH!

I'LL WASH UP LATER! RIGHT NOW I HAVE A MONSTER TO MASH!
GO GET HIM, MIGHTY MOOSE!
OKAY, FROG-BOY, LET'S GO FOR A SPIN!
SNIFF!
PHEW!
AROUND AND AROUND WE GO, WHERE THE MONSTER STOPS, NOBODY KNOWS!
ZIP!
SWISH!
DUH! SO LONG, GOON! SAY HELLO TO THE MAN IN THE MOON!
ZOOM!
NOW TO LAND NEAR MY FAITHFUL FANS!
OH, MIGHTY MOOSE, YOU'RE MY HERO!
BUT, HE STILL STINKS!
PHONE
CIN

THUNK!
HEH! HEH! I GUESS I HAVE TO EASE UP ON MY LANDINGS A LITTLE!
OH, MIGHTY MOOSE, I COULD JUST KISS YOU!
PHEW!
BUT NOT UNTIL YOU TAKE A SHOWER!
POOF!
OKAY! OKAY! I CAN'T HELP IT IF I SMELL LIKE GARBAGE!
HUH?
MOOSE, WHAT IN THE WORLD WAS THAT SILLY OUT-BURST ALL ABOUT?
HA! HA! HA! HO! HO!
NOTHING, MIDGE! I WAS JUST TRASH TALKING IN MY SLEEP!
DID YOU HEAR WHAT MOOSE SAID? NOW, THAT WAS SUPER FUNNY!
THE End

Jughead in THE LOLLIPOP KID
GEE, COACH! IT'S A BEAUTY! OUR OWN PROFESSIONAL SIZE POOL TABLE!
IT'S A GAME OF SKILL AND SCIENCE! AND OTHER SCHOOLS ARE PUTTING THEM IN!
COACH
Script: Frank Doyle
Art & Letters: Samm Schwartz
Colors: Barry Grossman
WILL OUR SCHOOL HAVE A TEAM?
SURE! IT'LL ADD TO OUR LIST OF GAMES!
I'M GOING OUT FOR THAT TEAM! I LOVE TO SHOOT POOL!
HAH!
1

I'LL SPOT YOU A RACK OF BALLS AND WHIP YOU LIKE A BOWL OF CREAM!
WELL, IT LOOKS LIKE OUR COMPETITION HAS STARTED! WHY DON'T YOU TWO SET UP A MATCH?
HOW ABOUT TOMORROW AFTER CLASS?
YOU'RE ON!
THAT'LL GIVE ME TIME TO GATHER AN AUDIENCE TO WATCH ME HUMILIATE YOU!
BIG TALK!
JUG, HE IS SOMEWHAT OF A POOL SHARK!
COOL IT! I'M GOING INTO TRAINING!
YOU'VE GOT ONE DAY! HE'S GOING TO BEAT THE SOX OFF YOU!
TROUBLE WITH YOU, ARCH, IS YOU'VE GOT NO FAITH!
2

NEXT DAY...
BEFORE I MASSACRE YON PIGEON, I MUST INSIST ON ABSOLUTE SILENCE! SAVE YOUR APPLAUSE FOR LATER!
KNOCK OFF THE CHATTER AND PLAY POOL!
JUGHEAD GETS TO BREAK!
THINK HE CAN BEAT "JAWS?"
I HATE TO SAY IT... NO!
MAKE YOUR PLAY, SUCKER! IT'LL BE YOUR LAST ONE!
OH, YOU SCATTERED THEM REAL SWEET! NOW WATCH ME RUN THE TABLE!

SLURP

?
SLURP!
SLURRRP!
SHLLPP!

WHAT'S THAT?
WHAT'S IT LOOK LIKE? SLURP!

IT'S THE MARK OF A GREAT SPORTS FIGURE!
WHAT?

AREN'T THE BASEBALL GREATS ALWAYS CHOMPIN' ON SOMETHING TO KEEP THEIR MOUTHS FROM DRYING UP?
YEAH! GUM!

I DON'T LIKE GUM!
COACH?
HE'S GOT A VALID POINT!

ARRGH! I GOT SO UPSET I MISSED!

NOT BAD! I RAN OFF SEVEN BEFORE I MISSED!
STEP ASIDE, CHUMP, AND I'LL SHOW YOU HOW TO SHOOT POOL!

I'LL TAKE IT REAL EASY THIS TIME!

YECCH!
LET GO OF MY LOLLY!

WHY DON'T YOU KEEP THAT... YEEOWTCH!
HOPE YOU DIDN'T GET POOL CHALK ON IT!

SLURP
SLURP
ACK! MISSED AGAIN!

JUG LOOKS SILLY WITH THAT LOLLIPOP!
MAYBE SO, BUT HE IS WINNING!

CONCENTRATE! CONCENTRATE! DON'T LET HIM...

SLURP!
RIP!

YAAAGH!

YOU KNOW, I'VE GOT A HUNCH THAT CHARACTER'S GOING TO BRING THE POOL TROPHY TO RIVERDALE!
ALL HAIL THE LOLLIPOP KID!
END

Script: Mike Pellowski / Pencils: Stan Goldberg / Inks: Mike Esposito / Letters: Bill Yoshida / Colors: Barry Grossman

HE'S SIMMERED DOWN TO HIS NEFARIOUS CHORTLE!
IF YOU MEAN EVIL, VICIOUS, I WISH YOU'D SAY SO!

I SUGGEST WE WAIT HERE UNTIL WE FIND OUT WHAT HE'S UP TO!
"NO GOOD" IS WHAT HE'S UP TO! YOU CAN COUNT ON IT!

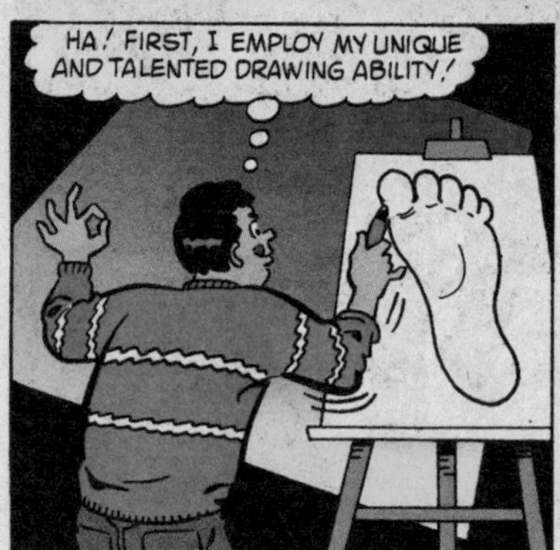
HA! FIRST, I EMPLOY MY UNIQUE AND TALENTED DRAWING ABILITY!

- AND DEPICT TWO LARGE, OUTSIZED BARE FEET, WHICH I WILL TRANSFER TO A CHUNK OF RUBBER AND CUT OUT!
SLICE!
SNIP!

GLUE THESE TO AN OLD PAIR OF SHOES AND -- (BY GOSH, YOU'RE A GIGANTIC GENIUS, MANTLE!)
SLAP!
GLUE

VOILA! THE TRACK OF THE ELUSIVE ABOMINABLE SNOWMAN!
2

I'LL CARRY THESE UNDER MY ARM UNTIL I GET NEAR THE WILDERNESS TRAIL IN SIMS PARK!

MY, MY! HE'S TURNING HIMSELF INTO THE MONSTER HE'S *ALWAYS* BEEN!
OH! INDEED HE DO! HE *DO* THAT ALL RIGHT!

– AND THERE HE GOES, TO BAIT HIS TRAP!
HE GETS MORE CHILDISH EVERY DAY!

YOU REALIZE HE'S SETTING US UP TO MAKE FOOLS OF OURSELVES!
OF COURSE! IT'S HIS LIFE'S WORK!

WELL, THERE GOES THE ABOMINABLE SNOWMAN, LEADING US UP THE WILDERNESS TRAIL!
IT'S THE ABOMINABLE *SOMETHING*, THAT'S FOR SURE!
CLUMP!
CLUMP!
PLOP!
SQUISH!
WILDERNESS TRAIL

I HATE TO DISAPPOINT THE POOR SLOB! HE WORKS SO HARD AT HIS CHOSEN CAREER!
IT WOULD BE A SHAME, WOULDN'T IT?
HMM! YOU RECALL LAST YEAR'S HORROR PLAY BY THE DRAMA CLASS?
- "THE SINISTER SNOWMAN OF SIBERIA"? -A REAL WEIRDIE!
SURE! WE STILL HAVE THAT MONSTER COSTUME! IT'S IN MOTHBALLS RIGHT NOW!
WE'D LIKE TO BORROW IT, CLYDE!
DRAMA CLUB H.Q.
BE CAREFUL OF IT! THAT THING DIDN'T COME CHEAP!
PHEW! IT IS PUNGENT, ISN'T IT?
LET'S HOPE IT AIRS OUT BY THE TIME WE GET TO THE PARK!
HEY, THERE ARE LITTLE STILTS BUILT INSIDE THE LEGS!
A MONSTERS GOT TO BE NOT ONLY UGLY, BUT BIG AND UGLY!
4

HYUK! THAT OUGHT TO BE ENOUGH TO FOOL THOSE TWO TURKEYS! TOP OF THIS HILL, I'LL STEP OFF ONTO THE PAVEMENT, AND...
W-WHAT THE H-HECK?!
R-ROAR!!
GRRROWL!!
SCREECH!!
IT'S THE REAL S-SNOW-MAN! -AND HE SURE IS ABOMINABLE!
RRRR!-D-DA-DA--?
GAK! N-NO! I'M NOT YOUR DA-DA! I'M A FAKE!! SEE?
THE FEET! THEY'RE NOT MINE! J-JUST HUNKS OF RUBBER!!
5

L-LOOK! N-NORMAL EVERYDAY FEET!!
HOLD THAT POSE, REG!

ACK!!
FLASH!

I SEE REGGIE HAS BEEN TRYING TO OUTWIT JUGHEAD AGAIN!
MADE THE PAPER, DID HE?

(SIGH!) IT'S GOING TO TAKE HIM A LONG TIME TO LIVE THIS ONE DOWN!
BLUE AND GOLD
RIVERDALE HIGH NEWS
MANTLE BARES FEET TO FIEND IN SIMS PARK

HA! HEY, REG! WHO'S YOUR HAIRY FRIEND?
WAY TO GO, HUNTER MAN!!
WHAT'S WITH THE BARE TOOTSIES, PAL?
A NEW METHOD OF TAMING FEROCIOUS BEASTS!
HYUK! W-WHO WAS THE MOST ABOMINABLE?
END

Script: Frank Doyle / Art & Letters: Samm Schwartz / Colors: Barry Grossman

LET ME PUT IT THIS WAY! I CAN'T FORCE YOU TO WEAR A TIE! HOWEVER, IF YOU DON'T, YOU AND YOUR GRANDCHILDREN WILL BE IN THE SAME GRADE BY THE TIME YOU'RE OUT OF DETENTION!

NEXT DAY:

NO SENSE WRINKLING OUR JACKETS UNTIL IT'S TIME FOR THE PICTURE!
IT'S THE TIE I'D LIKE TO GET RID OF!
JONES, FORSYTHE P., REPORTING FOR INSPECTION, SIR!
RAISE THE SHADE SO I CAN GET A GOOD LOOK AT YOU!
RATTLE! RATTLE YIPE!
SILLY THING CAUGHT IN THE ROLLER! A GUY COULD GET KILLED WEARING A TIE!
LET'S NOT OVERDO IT!
CLUNK
3

LOOK AT THAT! YOU NEARLY PULLED THE SHADE BRACKET OUT OF THE WALL!
HAND ME THE SCREW-DRIVER! IT'S IN THE TOP DRAWER OF MY DESK!
ACK!
GO! GO TO CLASS! GO MAKE LIFE MISERABLE FOR MISS GRUNDY!
YOU'RE LATE! SIT DOWN AND GET TO WORK! AND STRAIGHTEN YOUR TIE!
4

MISS GRUNDY, MY PENCIL BROKE!
LET'S NOT PANIC! GO SHARPEN IT!
TIES! BAH! I'D LIKE TO GET MY HANDS ON THE GUY WHO INVENTED TIES!
GRIND! GRIND!
ARE YOU STILL COMPLAINING?

I INSISTED HE WEAR A TIE FOR THE CLASS PICTURE!
IT'S ONLY RIGHT!

IT'S EASY FOR HER TO SAY! WOMEN DON'T WEAR THE SILLY THINGS!
GRIND GRIND

UH-OH!

ER...MISTER WEATHERBEE...

NICE TRY, BUT NO CIGAR! I'VE GOT A SPARE TIE IN MY OFFICE! **MOVE IT!**

THAT'S MORE LIKE IT! CLOSE THE DOOR AND GET BACK TO CLASS!

SLAM!
GRAK!

SIGH! IT *DOES* ADD A TOUCH OF VARIETY, I GUESS!
R
END

SUNNY
CLOUDY
RAIN
T-STORM
SNOW
Jughead
WEATHER BEATEN
BY USING WEATHER SATELLITES AND COMPUTERS...
Script: Frank Doyle / Art & Letters: Samm Schwartz / Colors: Barry Grossman
...WE ARE NOW ABLE TO PREDICT THE WEATHER WITH 80% ACCURACY!
ACCORDING TO THE LATEST DATA, TOMORROW WILL BE RAINY WITH A HIGH IN THE LOW FIFTIES!
NOT ACCORDING TO JUGHEAD!
L

JUGHEAD? JUGHEAD PREDICTS WEATHER?
HE'S BEEN WRITING A WEATHER COLUMN FOR THE SCHOOL PAPER!
RING!

HE PREDICTS THE WEATHER FOR A WHOLE MONTH!
RIDICULOUS!

SO FAR, HE'S BEEN RIGHT EVERY DAY THIS WEEK!
SHEER DUMB LUCK!

ACCORDING TO ALL THE SCIENTIFIC DATA AVAILABLE TO THE LOCAL WEATHER BUREAU IT'S GOING TO RAIN LIKE CRAZY TOMORROW!

NEXT DAY
AM I THE ONLY ONE WITH AN UMBRELLA?

JUGHEAD WAS RIGHT, MISTER FLUTESNOOT!
BAH! A LUCKY GUESS!
2

ACCORDING TO THE LATEST WEATHER INFORMATION WE CAN LOOK FORWARD TO A SUNNY DAY TOMORROW!
JUGGIE SAYS IT'LL RAIN!

NEXT DAY
JUGHEAD SAID IT WOULD RAIN! YOU SHOULD HAVE LISTENED!
I DON'T CARE TO DISCUSS IT!
SQUISH
SQUISH

HOW? HOW? HOW?
HOW DOES HE DO IT?

THIS CAN'T CONTINUE! HE'S GOT TO MAKE A MISTAKE!
LET'S SEE WHAT HIS FORECAST IS FOR TOMORROW!
BLUE AND

HA! HE PREDICTS A HIGH TOMORROW IN THE 90'S! THE RECORD HIGH FOR THAT DATE IS 53°! THIS SHOULD BE GOOD!

NATURALLY
DIDN'T YOU READ THE..
AH, SHUDDUP!

THE NEXT DAY
YOU SHOULD HAVE WORN YOUR STORM GEAR! JUGHEAD SAID IT WOULD SNOW!

DON'T FORGET TO WEAR SUN GLASSES TOMORROW! IT'LL BE BRIGHT AND SUNNY ACCORDING TO JUGHEAD!
I'VE GOT TO FIND OUT HOW HE DOES IT!

AAARGH!
JUGHEAD! JUGHEAD! JUGHEAD!
THAT'S ALL I HEAR... JUGHEAD!

JUGHEAD! I'D LIKE A WORD WITH YOU! A FEW WORDS IN FACT!
AS MANY AS YOU WANT, SIR!

YOU SEEM TO HAVE COME UP WITH AN ACCURATE WAY OF PREDICTING WEATHER!
IT DOES SEEM TO WORK!

JUGHEAD, M'BOY, AS FELLOW WEATHER SCIENTISTS, IT IS INCUMBENT UPON US TO SHARE IN OUR METHODS!
I'M A SCIENTIST?
NOT ONLY MUST WE SHARE OUR SECRETS BUT IT COULD MEAN AN "A" IN SCIENCE CLASS FOR YOU!
"A"? DID YOU SAY "A"?
LOUD AND CLEAR!
FOLLOW ME!
I'M ABOUT TO MAKE MY PREDICTIONS FOR NEXT MONTH! PAY CLOSE ATTENTION!
I CAN'T WAIT!
FAIR
SNOW
SUN
CLOUDY
RAIN
5 10 20 30 40 50 60 70 80 90 100 -5 0
THE FORECAST FOR THE FIRST IS FAIR WITH A TEMPERATURE OF...
END

HOW DO YOU LIKE YOUR NEW HOUSE, JUG?
GREAT! KINDA STRANGE TO THINK THAT A NEW FAMILY IS LIVING IN THE OLD PLACE THOUGH...
HIP
Jughead
THE HOUSE THAT JUG BUILT
Boldman
Lindsey
Yoshida
ESPECIALLY WHEN I'D GOTTEN IT FIXED UP JUST THE WAY I WANTED IT!
AT THE SAME TIME...
WE SURE ARE LUCKY, DEAR! A GREAT NEW TOWN... NICE NEW HOUSE...
BUT MOST OF ALL...
RIVERDALE
1

THE MOST WELL-BEHAVED, DEPENDABLE SON TWO PARENTS COULD ASK FOR!
YOU SAID IT!
THIS END UP
A REAL SELF-STARTER! HELPFUL! INDUSTRIOUS!
QUITE A LAD IS OUR FILBERT!
WHEW! GOOD NIGHT, FOLKS!
HITTING THE SACK SO SOON?
CAN'T WAIT TO GET MY FIRST NIGHT'S SLEEP IN OUR NEW HOUSE!
Swifty MOVERS CO.
EARLY START TOMORROW! THERE'S A LOT OF WORK TO DO AROUND HERE!
OKAY, MOM!
SNIFF! SNIFF! ?
WHAT'S THAT SMELL? DIDN'T NOTICE IT BEFORE! SNIFF SNIFF
SOMEONE'S BEEN COOKING IN THIS ROOM!
TICK!

IT'S NOT ONE SMELL! IT'S LOTS AN' LOTS! IT PERMEATES THE WALLPAPER!
WHOEVER HAD THIS ROOM BEFORE WAS QUITE AN EATER!

SNIFF! AND HE HAD GREAT TASTE AS WELL! I'M GETTING KINDA HUNGRY!

4:00 A.M.
NO USE! I CAN'T SLEEP!
YUM YUM!

5:00 A.M.
MMM!

IN THE MORN...
LOTS OF WORK TO DO, SON! YOU CAN PUT THE GARAGE IN ORDER!
YAWN OKAY, MOM!

I'M DOG-TIRED! I LOST TOO MUCH SLEEP THINKING OF FOOD!
THAT LATE-NIGHT SNACK HIT THE SPOT THOUGH!
3

I COULD GO FOR A NAP RIGHT NOW!
WHAT'S THIS? A TRAP DOOR!
ROXANN'S CRACKERS
MOVERS

WOW! SLEEPING BAG! SOMEONE HAD A LITTLE HIDEAWAY!

THIS IS THE LIFE! AND LOOK!
CHIPS
COMICS

A STASH OF SNACKS! THE FORMER OCCUPANT SURE HAD THE RIGHT IDEA!
CRUNCH! SLURP!

WHERE'S FILBERT?
I DON'T KNOW! BUT I HEAR A FAINT CRUNCHING NOISE!
HOPE IT'S NOT MICE!

FILBERT! WHERE A-ARE YOU?
WHAT THE... HIDDEN PANEL!

WELL NOW! ISN'T THIS COZY!

SO...
WELCOME TO RIVERDALE! HOW DO YOU LIKE YOUR NEW HOUSE?
IT'S HAUNTED!! THAT'S HOW!
SINCE WE MOVED IN I ONLY SEE MY SON AT MEAL TIMES! WHEN THERE ARE CHORES TO BE DONE, HE VANISHES!
WHAT DOES YOUR HUSBAND SAY?
WHAT HUSBAND?! HE EVAPORATES TOO! GRRR!
I WONDER IF THE GUY IN MY ROOM IS ANYTHING LIKE ME?
I DOUBT IT, JUG! YOU'RE ONE OF A KIND!
WHAT A GREAT LITTLE SPOT TO ENJOY THE GAME IN PERFECT PRIVACY!
IT'S DOWNRIGHT EERIE, I TELL YOU!
ZZZZZZ ZZZ
THE END
COMICS

Jughead
THE SLEEPER
JUGHEAD, I DEMAND TO SPEAK TO ONE OF YOUR PARENTS ABOUT YOUR APPETITE! YOU'VE EMPTIED MY REFRIGERATOR THREE TIMES THIS WEEK!

ER.. I'M SORRY, MR. LODGE... ER.. BUT MY DAD'S ASLEEP!
Z-Z-Z
Z-Z!

IN THAT CASE, LET ME TALK TO YOUR MOTHER! SHE'S ONE OF YOUR PARENTS!
POOR WOMAN!

ER.. THEY'RE BOTH ASLEEP... AND I CAN PROVE IT!

END

Jughead WHIFF SNIFF

JUGHEAD
LOOK UP, DOWN, FORWARD, BACKWARD AND DIAGONALLY TO FIND NINE THINGS I SAW DURING MY WALK TO SCHOOL! CHECK THEM OFF BELOW AS YOU FIND THEM!! HERE'S A HINT FOR YOU... THEY ALL START WITH AN "S" --LIKE ON MY SWEATER! SEE YA!!
S H D T E E R T S
O C O G S A F T W
T S H R U B S E E
K N F O A I R K A
L O N R O S A W T
A A O Y N L Y O E
W I C O F E O K R
E C E W G E N C S
D L O L D T J N I
I N E N N H O N V
S N O W D R I F T
"S" FIND LIST!!
SNOWFLAKE · SIDEWALK · SHRUBS
SWEATERS · STREET · SCHOOL
SKY · SNOWDRIFT · SLEET

BY LEANING FORWARD, I CAN GET GOOD ACTION PICS OF THE STUNTS!
SNOW BOARDING CONTEST
Jughead
"GAFF LAFF"

OOPS!
BLAM!

DID JUGHEAD GET HIS PICTURES?
NO!

--- BUT HE GOT SECOND PLACE!
END

Script: Frank Doyle / Pencils: Harry Lucey / Inks & Letters: Marty Epp / Colors: Barry Grossman

SHE PROMISED A BIG SURPRISE TO WHICHEVER ONE IS FLEETER OF FOOT!

IT'S PROBABLY A KISS...OR EVEN A DATE AT HER EXCLUSIVE COUNTRY CLUB!

WELL, I'M NOT ONE TO DULL THE COMPETITIVE SPIRIT!

HAVE AT IT!
FOUR!
THREE!
TWO!
ONE!

BLAST OFF!

WHUMP!

HMM! LOOKS LIKE YOU BOTH GOT HUNG UP!

ALLOW *ME!*

HEY, THERE, ARCH, OL' BOY!

WHAT'S YOUR HURRY ?
JUG! LET GO!!

THAT WAS REGGIE YOU WERE RUNNING WITH! SURELY YOU'D RATHER BE WITH ME!

FLIP
OOPS!

THAT CRAZY JUGHEAD! OF ALL THE TIMES TO,...

ARCHIE!
WHUP!

BETTY! NOT NOW!
DON'T STRUGGLE SO, LOVER DOLL!
KISS!

YOU'RE MAKING A LOSER OUT OF ME!
THEN STICK WITH ME! WE'RE TWO OF A KIND!

WHOOPS!
TOSS

(SIGH!) WHY DO THEY ALWAYS RESIST ME ?

YIKES! HE'S OUT OF SIGHT!

I'LL TAKE THE SHORTCUT!

IT'S MY ONLY CHANCE TO...

WHAP!

(GROAN!) NO SIGN OF HIM! HE MUST BE IN ALREADY!

YOU'RE TOO LATE MASTER ARCHIE!... MASTER REGGIE HAS WON THE CONTEST!
WHAT WAS THE SURPRISE, SMITHERS?

THE SURPRISE IS THAT MISS VERONICA IS AWAY FOR THE WEEKEND!
TH--THAT'S ALL?

OH, NO! SINCE MASTER REGGIE WON, HE GETS THE PRIVILEGE OF DOING MISS VERONICA'S HOMEWORK!

CONGRATULATIONS, FLEET FOOT! I'M NO POOR SPORT!
GET LOST!
The End

Archie
IN
TROUBLE by the FOOT!
HIYA, MR. LODGE!
KRUNCH
SCRIPT: CRAIG BOLDMAN
PENCILS: STAN GOLDBERG
INKS: BOB SMITH
OOPS! COMIN' THROUGH AGAIN!
CLOMP
HEH! HEH! FORGOT MY DRINK!
TROMP

ARCHIE, YOU'VE MADE ME VERY HAPPY TODAY!
HOW DID I DO THAT, MR. LODGE!?

BY DECIDING NOT TO WEAR YOUR MOUNTAIN-EERING CRAMPONS!!!
I WAS ONLY BORN WITH TEN TOES, AND YOU'VE SMASHED ABOUT A DOZEN OF THEM!

WHEN I'M NOT STUMBLING OVER YOUR BIG TEENAGE FEET, YOU'RE STOMPING ON MINE!

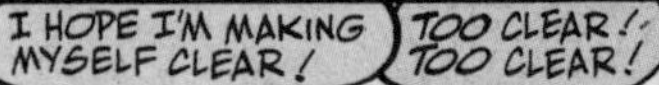
I HOPE I'M MAKING MYSELF CLEAR!
TOO CLEAR! TOO CLEAR!

I DON'T MAKE THE SAME MISTAKE TWICE. I'M KEEPING MY FEET FAR AWAY FROM HIS!
2

WHOOPS!

YOU REALLY DO HAVE A CASE OF THE CLUMSY FEET!
BUT AT LEAST I'M OVER HERE AND HE'S OVER THERE!

YEAH, BUT-!
JUSTLE

TIP

YOW!!
SMASH

FLIP

EEK!!
LOOK OUT!!
GRAB
LEAP
SPLOOSH
TEETER
whew!
MERCY!
CLATTER
WHAT'S ALL THIS RACKET I--
BONK
CHUNK

DADDYKINS!!
WHAT'S HAPPENING?!
SOMEBODY'S JUST LUCKY IT WENT BETWEEN MY TOES!
TUG

WOW! I WISH I'D SEEN THAT!
BELIEVE ME! IT WASN'T PRETTY!

I'VE GOT TO WATCH MY STEP. MY FEET HAVE CAUSED MR. LODGE ENOUGH GRIEF FOR ONE DAY!
THEY'RE ABOUT TO CAUSE MORE!

YOU'RE ABOUT TO TRACK MUD ALL OVER HIS PRICEY CARPETING!
WOW! GOOD CATCH, JUG!

I'LL JUST SET THEM ASIDE, SAFELY OUT OF HARM'S WAY!

UH-OH! THERE GOES CLODHOPPER AGAIN!
PROBABLY WAITING FOR ME TO LOWER MY GUARD SO HE CAN RIDE ROUGHSHOD OVER MY TOOTSIES!
I'M MUCH TOO SMART FOR HIM! I'LL JUST TAKE THE LONG WAY AROUND!
WHOOPS!
BLOMP
BLOMP
I HAD A CHANCE WHEN IT WAS JUST HIM! NOW THE THREE OF YOU ARE GANGING UP ON ME!!
END

Archie AND THE GANG in "TRAIL TRAVAIL"

Script: George Gladir / Pencils: Dick Malmgren / Inks: Jon D'Agostino / Letters: Bill Yoshida / Colors: Barry Grossman

UH, OH! YOU BETTER SCOOT, ARCHIE! DADDY LOOKS PRETTY ANGRY!
I DIDN'T MEAN TO SPLATTER HIM! IT MUST BE THIS LOOSE POWDER!

IT'S A GOOD THING HE LEFT!
DADDY, DON'T GET YOURSELF WORKED UP! ARCHIE MEANT NO HARM!
VA-ROOM!

LATER---
AHH! CROSS-COUNTRY SKIING IS THE WAY TO GO! NATURE IN THE RAW --- MILES AWAY FROM CIVILIZATION!

THIS IS FUN! I DON'T THINK WE'VE EVER BEEN SO DEEP IN THE FOREST!
WHEW! I'M EXHAUSTED! LET'S TAKE A BREAK!

VRROOM!
OH, NO! IT CAN'T BE!
2

BY FOLLOWING YOUR TRAIL, I FOUND YOU!
WELL, YOU CAN UNFIND US, YOUNG MAN!
PUTT! PUTT! PUTT!

HOW DARE YOU BRING THAT NOISY, POLLUTING MACHINE INTO THIS PRISTINE FOREST?
IT'S NOT THAT BAD, MR. LODGE!
PUTT! PUTT! PUTT!

BUT IF THAT'S THE WAY YOU FEEL ABOUT IT, I CAN TAKE A HINT!
GOOD! TAKE IT AND GO!
PUTT! PUTT!

DADDY, YOU WERE VERY HARSH WITH ARCHIE!
I'M SORRY, BUT THAT'S THE WAY I FEEL ABOUT THOSE NOISY, ROTTEN-SMELLING MACHINES!

OWW!!!
WHAT IS IT?

MY ANKLE! I THINK I SPRAINED IT!
GOOD HEAVENS!

WE'RE MILES AWAY FROM ANY LIVING SOUL! WHAT ARE WE GOING TO DO?
MAYBE WE COULD BUILD A STRETCHER AND CARRY HER!

NO! WE WOULDN'T GET VERY FAR IN THIS SOFT SNOW!
FORTUNATELY, I BROUGHT ALONG A FLARE GUN!

I JUST HOPE SOME FOREST RANGER SEES IT!

LOOK! IT'S ARCHIE AGAIN!
VRRROOM!

I'M SORRY, BUT I THOUGHT I SAW AN EMERGENCY FLARE GO OFF AROUND HERE!
YOU DID!

VERONICA IS HURT! YOU CAN BRING HER TO THE FIRST-AID STATION!
WILL DO!

WE WERE LUCKY ARCHIE SAW THAT EMERGENCY FLARE!

WE GOT HERE AS SOON AS WE COULD! HOW ARE YOU, DEAR?
JUST FINE, MOTHER---THANKS TO ARCHIE AND HIS SNOWMOBILE! THEY GOT ME HERE REAL QUICK!
FIRST AID STATIC

ARCHIE, TO CELEBRATE THIS HAPPY OCCASION, I'M INVITING YOU TO MY CHALET TONIGHT!
GEE! THANKS, SIR!

SMITHERS, I WANT YOU TO PREPARE A ROYAL FEAST FOR TONIGHT!

THE DINNER WILL BE IN HONOR OF THE TWO THINGS I ADMIRE THE MOST!
WHAT'S THAT, SIR?

ARCHIE AND HIS INFERNAL SNOWMOBILE!
?
END

Archie in PAYBACK TIME

PELLOWSKI\BOLLING\MILGROM

BUT IT'S SATURDAY AND I DON'T HAVE TO DRIVE TO WORK!
AND YOU BOUGHT A NEW SNOW BLOWER ON SALE, SO YOU DON'T HAVE TO WORRY ABOUT SHOVELING WITH YOUR BAD BACK!

THAT NEW SNOW BLOWER MEANS NO MORE BACK-ACHES, AND NO HIRING KIDS TO HELP ARCHIE SHOVEL!

NOW WHEN I LOOK OUTSIDE, ALL I SEE IS BEAUTIFUL SNOW WITH NO AGGRAVATION!
WHAT DO YOU SEE, ARCHIE?
$ KA-CHING!!
I SEE DOLLAR SIGNS!!

NOT ONLY WILL WE SAVE ENERGY AND MONEY, POP, I'LL ALSO MAKE EXTRA CASH!
WHAT DO YOU MEAN, ARCHIE?

WITH OUR SNOW BLOWER, I CAN HIRE MYSELF OUT TO CLEAR SNOW FOR PEOPLE ALL OVER THE NEIGHBORHOOD!

OKAY, BUT DO OUR DRIVEWAY FIRST! I HAVE TO GO TO THE GROCERY STORE!
SURE, MOM! NO PROBLEM!
KLIK

MINUTES LATER...
DO YOU NEED ANY HELP, SON?
NO, POP! THE BLOWER MAKES THE JOB EASY AND YOU HAVE TO BE CAREFUL WITH YOUR BACK!
WHRRRR
WHOOSH

HEY, ARCHIE! WOULD YOU LIKE TO MAKE A FAST THIRTY BUCKS?
DOING WHAT, MR. SMITH?
WHOOSH
WHRRR

CLEARING MY DRIVEWAY! I HAVE A MEETING IN TOWN AND I HAVE TO GET OUT! THE JOB HAS TO BE DONE RIGHT AWAY!
OKAY, SIR! IT'S A DEAL!
WHRRR

I CAN'T TURN MY BACK ON A QUICK PROFIT! I'LL FINISH OUR HOUSE AFTER I MAKE SOME COLD CASH!
WHRRRRRRRR
WOOSH

CLEARING MR. SMITH'S DRIVEWAY WILL BE EASY MONEY!
WHOOSH
SMITH

IN A WHILE...
NICE JOB, ARCHIE! HERE'S YOUR PAY!
HEY, ARCHIE! CAN YOU DO MY DRIVEWAY REAL QUICK? I HAVE AN APPOINTMENT!
SMITH

IF YOU DO IT THIS INSTANT, I'LL PAY YOU AN EXTRA TEN BUCKS!
WOW! I'LL BE RIGHT OVER!

ONE THING LEADS TO ANOTHER AND ARCHIE GOES FROM JOB TO JOB...
I SURE MADE A LOT OF MONEY TODAY! UH-OH! I LOST TRACK OF TIME... I'D BETTER GET HOME AND FINISH OUR HOUSE!

WHEN ARCHIE ARRIVES HOME...
HUH?
THANK YOU, BOYS! YOU DID A FINE JOB!
ANDREWS

HEY, MOM! WHY DID YOU HIRE PEOPLE TO SHOVEL SNOW WHEN WE HAVE A SNOW BLOWER?
BECAUSE I NEEDED TO GO TO THE STORE, ARCHIE, AND YOU WEREN'T AROUND!

I WAS WORKING AND MADE LOTS OF MONEY! BUT I'M HERE NOW!
THAT'S GOOD! YOUR TIMING IS PERFECT!

YOU CAN PAY THE BOYS FOR THE WORK YOU SHOULD HAVE DONE!
GULP!
END

Archie in The FINISH LINE

Script & Pencils: Dick Malmgren / Inks: Jon D'Agostino / Letters: Bill Yoshida / Colors: Barry Grossman

ULP! I THOUGHT IT WAS SODA OR SOME-THING! IT'S POISON!
ONLY IF YOU *DRINK* IT!

SO WHAT ARE YOU DOING WITH VARNISH ?
I'M LEARNING A NEW TRADE!

KILLING YOUR FRIENDS ?
NO, GOOFUS! FINISHING FURNITURE!
RIVE ALE

THE SHOP TEACHER, MR. KROSSKUT, HAS BEEN SHOWING ME THE FINE POINTS!
SOUNDS DULL!

IT'S VERY SATISFYING TO TAKE A BEAT UP PIECE OF FURNITURE AND RESTORE ITS ORIGINAL BEAUTY!
SOUNDS REAL NOBLE!

NOW LET'S HAVE THE *REAL* REASON!
HEH! THE LITTLE GREY CELLS ARE IN THERE CHURNING!
2

THE SCHOOL'S GOT A WHOLE MESS OF FURNITURE THAT NEEDS REFINISHING!

DESK CHAIRS, LAB TABLES! LOTS OF THINGS!
A-HA! I'M STARTING TO GET THE PICTURE!

YOU'RE GONNA DO THE JOB AND BECOME WEATHERBEE'S FAIR-HAIRED BOY!
W-ELL, HE *MIGHT* SHOW A LITTLE APPRECIATION!

ESPECIALLY WHEN HE SHOWS THE SCHOOL BOARD HOW MUCH MONEY HE SAVED BY NOT CALLING IN A PROFESSIONAL!

IT MAY BE A LOT OF WORK, BUT IT'LL PAY OFF IN THE END!
I'LL SAY ONE THING FOR YOU YOU NEVER STOP TRYING!
3

THAT GUYS GOT MORE SCHEMES THAN AN ALLEY CAT HAS FLEAS!

DUH! JUG! YUH SEEN ARCH?
THAT DEPENDS, MOOSE! ARE YOU FRIENDLY OR OTHERWISE?

FRIENDLY! HE DONE ME A GOOD TURN AND I OWE HIM A FAVOR!
IN THAT CASE, I'LL TELL YOU!

HE'S DOWN IN THE BASEMENT STOREROOM WITH A BUNCH OF FURNITURE!
FURNITURE?

A LOT OF BEAT UP STUFF THAT NEEDS FINISHING!--- HE'S TRYING TO GET IN GOOD WITH THE BEE AGAIN!

DUH! THAT'S GREAT! THEN I CAN HELP HIM AND PAY HIM BACK FOR THE FAVOR HE DONE ME!
YOU KNOW HOW TO FINISH FURNITURE?
4

LEAVE IT TUH ME! I'M A EXPERT!
?

HEY, ARCH! I THOUGHT YOU WERE DOWNSTAIRS!
HAD TO PICK UP SOME SANDPAPER IN THE SHOP!
SHOP NEWS

DID YOU SEE MOOSE? HE WAS ON HIS WAY TO HELP YOU!
HELP ME WHAT?

FINISH THAT FURNITURE! HE SAID HE'S AN EXPERT!
?

DUH! ANY TIME YUH WANT ANY FURNITURE FINISHED, PAL, JES' CALL ON OL' MOOSE!
AND ANOTHER SHREWD ANDREWS SCHEME BITES THE DUST!
CRUNCH!
END

Archie in "CALL OF THE WILD"

Script: Mike Pellowski / Pencils: Stan Goldberg / Inks: Jimmy DeCarlo / Letters: Bill Yoshida / Colors: Barry Grossman

DUTY CALLS, LOVEBUG! I'LL SEE YOU LATER!
RIGHT, ARCHIE!

I WONDER WHY MR. WEATHERBEE WANTS HIM?
WHO SAYS HE DOES?

I THOUGHT YOU DID!
I SAID HE WAS NEEDED AT THE OFFICE!

-- BY ME!
HUH?
HEE! HEE!

HE WAS WITH YOU, AND I WANTED TO BE WITH YOU!
-- ALONE!

SO I NEEDED HIM ELSEWHERE!
GIGGLE! YOU DEVIL, YOU!
2

TIME PASSES--
YOU SENT ME ON A WILD GOOSE CHASE.!!
SO I DID!

DID YOU CATCH ANY WILD GEESE?
MMMPH!

SHE DIDN'T HAVE TO THINK IT WAS SO FUNNY!
ARCHIE!

I HAVE TO SELECT A BOY AND A GIRL TO REPRESENT THE SCHOOL ON A TRIP TO THE STATE CAPITAL!
GEE, THAT'D BE GREAT!

WHO WOULD YOU SUGGEST?
BOY! I'D LIKE TO GO MYSELF, BUT--

IN ALL HONESTY I'D SAY REGGIE AND VERONICA DESERVE THE HONOR!
YOU WOULD?

ALL RIGHT! I'LL RELY ON YOUR JUDGMENT, ARCHIE!
ASK THEM TO COME TO MY OFFICE, WILL YOU?
SURE, SIR!

THE BEE WANTS US? HA! YOU'VE GOT TO BE KIDDING!
YOU HAVE NO ORIGINALITY, ARCHIE! THAT'S REGGIE'S GAG!

JUG, DO ME A FAVOR! ASK RON AND REGGIE TO GO TO MR. WEATHERBEE'S OFFICE!
OKAY, ARCH!

NOW HE'S TRYING IT WITH HIS BEST FRIEND!
GET LOST, DUMMY!

WELL, I TRIED!
HE CALLED ME A DUMMY!

THEY WON'T COME, SIR! THEY JUST LAUGH AND SAY, "GET LOST!"
WHAT?
NCIPAL

REGGIE AND VERONICA ? YES, SIR! I'LL ASK THEM TO COME TO YOUR OFFICE!

IS HE STILL SENDING MESSENGERS WITH THAT SAME DUMB REQUEST ?
TELL HIM TO KNOCK IT OFF! IT'S GETTING TIRESOME!

TELL HIM IF THE BEE WANTS TO SEE US, HE KNOWS WHERE TO FIND US!

THE "BEE" KNOWS WHERE TO FIND YOU, ALL RIGHT!
IT'S CALLED THE "DETENTION" ROOM!
ULP!

TOO BAD REGGIE AND RONNIE MISSED OUT ON THIS TRIP TO THE STATE CAPITAL!
YES! I CAN'T UNDERSTAND WHAT MADE THEM ACT SO STUPIDLY!
END

Jughead
The SUBSTITUTE
OH, BOY! OH, BLISS!
ARCHIE'S OUT OF TOWN AND ALL'S RIGHT WITH THE WORLD!
ZIP!
Boldman / Lindsey / Koslowski / Yoshida / Grossman
SMITHERS, TAKE THE GOOD ARTWORK OUT OF STORAGE! WE CAN ENJOY IT WHILE THE CLUMSY CALAMITY IS GONE!
AT ONCE, SIR!
EEK!
WHAT ARE YOU DOING HERE?
SAVING ARCHIE'S PLACE!
CHOMP!
1

BEG PARDON?
BETWEEN YOU AND ME, SIR, WE KNOW VERONICA WOULD NEVER DATE ANOTHER WHILE ARCHIE'S GONE!

OH, NOOO! CERTAINLY NOT!
SO ARCH FIGURED, AS LONG AS RONNIE'S GOING TO BE FAITHFUL...

SOMEBODY OUGHT TO BE ON HAND TO ADMIRE HER!
I SEE!

AND YOU DON'T MIND KEEPING TABS ON MY DAUGHTER FOR YOUR SUSPICIOUS FRIEND?

I NEVER MIND COMING HERE, MR. LODGE! HERE'S WHERE THE FOOD IS!
EGAD!

JUST THINK OF ME AS FILLING IN FOR GOOD OL' ARCH!
YOU MEAN FILLING IN THAT HOLE IN YOUR STOMACH!
2

Jughead
The SUBSTITUTE
OH, BOY! OH, BLISS!
ARCHIE'S OUT OF TOWN AND ALL'S RIGHT WITH THE WORLD!
ZIP!
Boldman / Lindsey / Koslowski / Yoshida / Grossman
SMITHERS, TAKE THE GOOD ARTWORK OUT OF STORAGE! WE CAN ENJOY IT WHILE THE CLUMSY CALAMITY IS GONE!
AT ONCE, SIR!
EEK!
WHAT ARE YOU DOING HERE?
SAVING ARCHIE'S PLACE!
CHOMP!
1

BEG PARDON?
BETWEEN YOU AND ME, SIR, WE KNOW VERONICA WOULD NEVER DATE ANOTHER WHILE ARCHIE'S GONE!

OH, NOOO! CERTAINLY NOT!
SO ARCH FIGURED, AS LONG AS RONNIE'S GOING TO BE FAITHFUL...

SOMEBODY OUGHT TO BE ON HAND TO ADMIRE HER!
I SEE!

AND YOU DON'T MIND KEEPING TABS ON MY DAUGHTER FOR YOUR SUSPICIOUS FRIEND?

I NEVER MIND COMING HERE, MR. LODGE! HERE'S WHERE THE FOOD IS!
EGAD!

JUST THINK OF ME AS FILLING IN FOR GOOD OL' ARCH!
YOU MEAN FILLING IN THAT HOLE IN YOUR STOMACH!
2

OH, WELL, A WEEK'S GROCERY BILL IS NOTHING COMPARED TO ARCHIE'S USUAL TALLY FOR BREAKFAST!
THESE BEAUTIES RARELY SEE THE LIGHT OF DAY!
?
DADDY, WHY IS THE SUIT OF ARMOR MISSING ITS GAUNTLETS?
HMM! I JUST WONDER!
EXPLAIN!
I'M BAKING COOKIES! YOU CAN'T FIND AN OVEN MITT IN THIS JOINT!
THOSE THINGS AREN'T TOYS! THEY'RE EXPENSIVE! HAND THEM...
3

AAAAA!
HOT!
FSSST!
OW!
OW!
OW!
YIPES!
TOK!
GEE, I THINK ARCHIE GETS A BUM RAP! SEEMS LIKE PEOPLE ARE PRETTY RECKLESS AROUND HERE EVEN WHEN HE'S GONE!
CRASH!
BAM!
THUD!
SMITHERS, I CHANGED MY MIND! GATHER UP THE OBJECTS D'ART! THEY'RE GOING BACK IN THE VAULT!
YES, SIR!
THAT KNOTHEAD IS TOO ADEPT AT FILLING IN FOR THE DIMBULB!
JUGGIE, TAKE THOSE OFF! YOU'LL DO MORE DAMAGE!
HELP ME! THOSE KNIGHTS HAD SMALL HANDS!
4

NOW WHAT'S THE *NITWIT*...
UGH!

KLONK!
DADDY?

NO SIR, THE *ART*!

WHEW!
SHOVE!
THUMP!

JUGGIE, GRAB THE *ART*!

GOT IT!!
SCREECH!

BUT HEY! WHERE'D THEY GO?
SMASH!
DO I WANT TO REGAIN CONSCIOUSNESS, SMITHERS?
NO, SIR!
CARD FROM RONNIE?
NO, IT'S FROM HER DAD!
WHAT'S IT SAY?

"WISH YOU WERE HERE--INSTEAD OF JUGHEAD!"
?
THE END

Script: George Gladir / Art & Letters: Samm Schwartz / Colors: Barry Grossman

WHAT'S THAT STRANGE LOOK IN HIS EYES?

THE HAT CHANGED HIS WHOLE PERSON-ALITY! LOOK AT THAT WALK!

WHAT'S HE UP TO? HE DOESN'T DANCE!
I HOPE HE'S NOT GOING TO SING!

LET'S GO, LITTLE MISSY! THAT GOOD OLD, DOWN HOME, COUNTRY MUSIC MAKES A FELLA WANT TO KICK UP HIS HEELS!

JEST CALL ME 'TEX!'
CAN'T WE STOP? MY FEET ARE WRECKS, TEX!
STOMP
TROMP

DON'T LET HIM HURT ME ANYMORE!
NOW IT'S YOUR TURN, MAH LITTLE PRAIRIE FLOWER!
OH, NO!

AH'M A DANCIN' FOOL!
THAT'S THE TRUEST THING YOU EVER SAID!
STOMP! CLUNK!

OKAY, SUNDANCE, TIME TO MOSEY BACK TO THE CORRAL!
HEY! DON'T LEAVE ME HATLESS!
TRY THIS ON FOR SIZE, SHERLOCK!
HAH! SHERLOCK JONES! THE DEFECTIVE DETECTIVE!
UH, OH! THERE'S THAT LOOK AGAIN!
HMM! VERY INTERESTING! YES! VERY INTERESTING INDEED!
HUH?
THAT LIPSTICK STAIN ON YOUR COLLAR! IT'S NEITHER BETTY'S OR VERONICA'S SHADE! SOME NEW YOUNG LADY CATCH YOUR EYE?
AND I SEE BY THIS THREAD THAT YOU'VE BEEN ENJOYING MIDGE'S COMPANY WHILE MOOSE IS AWAY!
ENOUGH WITH THE KOOKY HATS! YOUR ORIGINAL PERSON-ALITY WAS BAD ENOUGH!
NILL
ROCKY R
RASPBER

HEY! COME ON, GUYS! I FEEL NAKED WITHOUT A HAT!

NOT TO WORRY! I WAS SAVING THIS HAT FOR MY MAD-HATTER PARTY!
IT'S THE LATEST FAD IN CALIFOR-NIA!

DON'T YOU JUST LOVE IT?
THAT HAT IS JUGHEAD! WEIRD AND OUT OF THIS WORLD!

MONDAY ROLLS AROUND
WE'VE GOT TO GET THESE REPORTS OUT TODAY, MISS PHLIPS!
OFFICE

OFFICE

HELP ME WITH THE SOUP, PLEASE!

EE-EE

JUGHEAD IS A WALKING DISASTER AREA WITH THAT HAT!
WE'VE **GOT** TO GET IT AWAY FROM HIM!
CHEMIS

JUGGIE, WE'D LIKE YOU TO SWITCH BACK TO YOUR OLD HAT! PLEASE?
WHAT'LL YOU GIVE ME IF I DO?

ZIP

NOW YOU KNOW WHY I CALL IT MY LUCKY HAT!
HE **ALWAYS** WINS!..YOU'VE GOT TO TAKE YOUR HAT OFF TO HIM!
END

Script: Rod Ollerenshaw / Pencils: Nate Butler / Inks: Tom Moore / Letters: Bill Yoshida / Colors: Barry Grossman

NOTHING COULD EVER CHANGE THAT!
ETHEL ONLY PROVES THAT WOMEN ARE TROUBLE!

OH, I WOULDN'T SAY THAT EXACTLY!
NOW DON'T GO ALL MOONY-EYED ON ME AND PHASE OUT!
SCREECH!

"MOONY-EYED?"
YEAH! THAT'S THE RIDICULOUS LOOK YOU GET WHEN YOU SEE SOME FEMALE PASS BY!
YOUR BRAIN GOES ON OVERLOAD AND YOU BECOME INSENSIBLE!
BUT IT'S SUCH A NICE WAY TO GO!

FORGET IT! I WANT ALL MY FACULTIES AT FULL CAPACITY!
WHAT FOR? ALL YOU EVER DO IS EAT AND SLEEP!
REST AREA

RIGHT! FULLY AWARE AND ALERT FOR THE FINER THINGS IN LIFE!
GIRLS ARE THE FINER THINGS IN LIFE!
PIG OUT!
JOE ENGLISH BAND
2

HAH! THAT'S A LAUGH AND A HALF!
COME ON NOW, JUG!

WHAT'S WRONG WITH GIRLS?
WHAT'S WRONG? WHAT'S WRONG?!

I ASKED YOU FIRST!
WHAT'S RIGHT WITH GIRLS, THAT'S WHAT I WANNA KNOW!?

YOU BEND OVER BACKWARD FOR THEIR EVERY WHIM AND COMMAND--

---AND IN RETURN YOU GET NOTHING FOR YOUR TROUBLES!
GOOD NIGHT!
YAWN
OH, JUGGIE, DEAR-- WAIT UP!
Jones
U.S. MAIL

HERE'S THAT APPLE PIE I PROMISED TO BAKE FOR YOU FOR TAKING CARE OF MY CAT!
ARCH

NOTHING IN RETURN, EH?
THAT WAS AN UNUSUAL CIRCUMSTANCE!

BESIDES, SHE OWED IT TO ME! IF I HADN'T HELPED HER OUT IN THE FIRST PLACE, SHE'D NEVER---
HI, ARCHIE! HI, JUGHEAD!
BEEP! BEEP!

JUGHEAD, HERE'RE TWO TICKETS TO THE INTERNATIONAL FOOD FESTIVAL AT THE ARENA TOMORROW NIGHT!

DADDY GOT THEM FREE BUT CAN'T USE THEM! I ASKED IF I COULD GIVE THEM TO YOU! I HAVE TO WATCH MY FIGURE!
TH-TH-THANKS!

YOU'RE WELCOME!
TONIGHT AT EIGHT, ARCHIEKINS?
BUT OF COURSE, LOVEBUG!
ZOOM

MY, MY! AND YOU DIDN'T EVEN DO VERONICA ANY FAVORS TO GET THOSE!
GOOD FRIENDS KEEP THEIR MOUTHS CLOSED!
POP'S

BESIDES, IT STILL DOESN'T CHANGE MY OPINION! WOMEN ARE SELFISH, SELF-CENTERED---
YOO-HOO! JUGGIE!

HI, PAM!
HULLO!
DILTON TOLD ME YOU WANTED TO READ THAT NEW BEST-SELLER BUT COULDN'T FIND A COPY!
POP'S

HERE! YOU CAN READ MY COPY! KEEP IT AS LONG AS YOU LIKE!
MY, MY! HARDBOUND EDITION, TOO!

WOMEN ARE SELFISH, HUH?
SO FAR, EVERY LAST FEMALE YOU'VE MET HAS DISPROVED THAT THEORY!
Cola

BOY! I WISH I WAS GETTING HALF THE ATTENTION YOU'RE GETTING!
YOU CAN HAVE IT!
POP'S
ARCH

OH, JUGHEAD---PLEASE TAKE THIS BOX OF CANDY FOR ME! REGGIE GAVE IT TO ME, AND MOOSE WILL KILL HIM IF HE FINDS OUT!

CHOCOLATES

THANKS!
MY PLEASURE! BUT DEFINITELY!
POP'S

THIS HAS GOT TO CHANGE YOUR VIEWS ABOUT WOMEN NOW, JUG!
WE-ELL, MAYBE SOMETIMES THEY'RE NOT ALL THAT TROUBLESOME--
D-UHH!
CHOCK

I SAW MY MIDGE GIVIN' YOU CANDY!!
N-N-N-NO, M-M-MOOSE! IT'S NOT WHAT YOU THINK!

WOMAN-HATER, NOTHIN'! YOU'VE JUST BEEN FAKIN' IT SO'S YOU CAN MAKE TIME WITH MY MIDGE!
MOOSE--- NOOO!!

POW

I'VE SAID IT BEFORE AND I'LL SAY IT AGAIN!
GIRLS ARE NOTHING BUT TROUBLE!
POP'S
END.

WELCOME TO "CUPID INCORPORATED"! ROMANCE IS OUR BUSINESS!
FOR A SMALL FEE WE HELP GUYS IMPRESS THEIR GIRL-FRIENDS!
HI! MY NAME IS ROGER! YOU TWO GUYS SOUND EXACTLY LIKE WHAT I'M LOOKING FOR!
CUPID INCORPORATED
INC.
INC.
Jughead in "STUPID CUPID"
Gladir / Stone / Lapick / Yoshida / Grossman
SAY NO MORE, ROGER!
JUST TAKE YOUR GIRL SKIING ALONG THE OLD BALDY TRAIL AND WE'LL DO THE REST!
INC.
YOU CAN RELY ON ME AND MY PARTNER CAUSE WE'RE OLD PROS!
ACTUALLY, HE'S OUR VERY FIRST CLIENT!
1

OH, ROGER! IT'S *SO ROMANTIC* UP HERE - JUST THE TWO OF US!
YOU HAVEN'T SEEN ANY-THING YET!

THEY'LL BE HERE ANY MINUTE, ARCHIE! ARE YOU ALMOST FINISHED?
JUST ABOUT!
RO

HEY! I THOUGHT ROGER SAID HIS GIRLFRIEND'S NAME IS JILL!
NO, JUG! I'M POSITIVE HE SAID IT WAS JULIE!
ROGER
LOVES
JULI

HERE THEY COME!
LET'S GET OUT OF SIGHT!
INC.

OH, HOW NICE! YOU HAD A HEART MADE OUT OF SNOW!

ROGER LOVES... *JULIE?!*
THAT'S THE NAME OF YOUR *OLD* GIRLFRIEND!
ROGER
LOVES
ULIE

YOU DID THIS DELIBERATELY TO HUMILIATE ME, YOU... OAF!
CALM DOWN, JULIE, UH, I MEAN JILL!

LOOK, JUG! ROGER IS WAVING AT US! HE MUST HAVE LIKED OUR HEART!

BUT WAIT TILL HE SEES WHAT WE HAVE IN STORE FOR HIM NEXT!
INC.

CUPID INCORPORATED AT YOUR SERVICE! PLEASE BE SEATED!
OH, ROGER! YOU HAD THEM BUILD US A CAMPFIRE! *HOW WONDERFUL!*

AND THE CAMPFIRE IS JUST THE BEGINNING, MADEMOISELLE!
OH, LOOK! NOW THEY'RE BRINGING US A PICNIC BASKET!

WOULD YOU TWO LIKE SOME HOT COCOA?
YES, INDEED!

OOPS!
EEOWW!!

YOU CLUMSY CLOD! LOOK WHAT YOU DID TO MY NEW SWEATER!

UH, HAVE SOME CHOCOLATE CHIP COOKIES!
CHOCOLATE CHIP COOKIES!

YUM! YUM! CHOCOLATE CHIP COOKIES, MY ABSOLUTE FAVORITE!

GOOD GRIEF! WHAT IS THAT HORRIBLE NOISE?
ROAR
ROAR
ROAR

VROOM!
VROOM!

DIDN'T YOU CLOWNS READ OUR NOTICE? WE'RE RUNNING A RACE ON THIS TRAIL TODAY!
SOB! MY OUTFIT IS RUINED!
RACE OFFICIA

CALM DOWN, ROGER! ACCIDENTS CAN HAPPEN!
AND ONE IS ABOUT TO HAPPEN TO YOU TWO!

LOOK, RONNIE! THERE'S ARCHIE AND JUG WITH THEIR FIRST CLIENT!
SOMETHING TELLS ME HE'S ALSO THEIR LAST CLIENT!
END

Script: Frank Doyle / Pencils: Dan DeCarlo Jr. / Inks: Jimmy DeCarlo / Letters: Bill Yoshida / Colors: Barry Grossman

AND WHAT MAKES HIM SO OBNOXIOUS ?

HE'S WELL BUILT, HANDSOME, AND PROBABLY CAN CHARM THE BIRDS FROM THE TREES!

YOU'RE NOT WORRIED ABOUT THE BIRDS IN THE **TREES**!
OH ?

YOU'RE WORRIED ABOUT THE BIRD IN THE **HOUSE**!
NAMELY, **VERONICA**!

SIGH! YOU SPEAK WITH STRAIGHT TONGUE, OH GREAT TRAIL BROTHER!

OH BROTHER, IS RIGHT! HERE COMES HUBIE HIMSELF-UNLESS I MISS MY GUESS!

HI, GUYS! THIS IS HUBERT VON WARTENDYKE, MY HOUSEGUEST!

HI!
YOU DON'T MISS YOUR GUESS!

HI! VERONICA HAS TOLD ME ALL ABOUT YOU!
THAT WASN'T VERY NICE OF HER!

TO TELL YOU THE TRUTH, I DIDN'T LISTEN TOO CLOSELY!
I WAS TOO INTENT ON TEACHING HER THE FACTS OF LIFE!

THE BIRDS AND BEES JAZZ?
VERY AMUSING!
OF COURSE NOT!

HOW TO CARE FOR ONESELF! HOW TO PRESERVE THE MUSCLE TONE!
VERONICA?

SHE'S GOT THE GREATEST LOOKING MUSCLE TONE ANYONE EVER SAW!

I MEAN... YOU'RE TALKING ABOUT MUSCLE TONE... YOU'RE TALKING ABOUT VERONICA!
THANK YOU, ARCHIEKINS!

NONSENSE! DO YOU KNOW SHE EATS --- UGH... FRIED FOODS?
NO?

SHE EATS WRONG! SHE SLEEPS WRONG! SHE SUFFERS FROM LACK OF EXERCISE!

I TRIED TO TEACH HER ABOUT PUSH-UPS!
YOU'VE GOT TO DO PUSH-UPS!

BRISK CALISTHENICS ARE A MUST, AS A WARM-UP, PRIOR TO YOUR DAILY FIVE MILE JOG!
4

COME, VERONICA! WE'LL DO AN EASY TWO OR THREE MILES, UNTIL YOU GET IN CONDITION!
SIGH! I'LL BE RIGHT WITH YOU, HUBIE!

THINK OF SOMETHING! THIS INFURIATING BORE IS GOING TO DESTROY ME COMPLETELY!
?

Y-YOU DON'T CARE FOR HIM?
I DETEST HIM! SAVE ME!

HOW ABOUT THAT?

HOW CAN SHE POSSIBLY DETEST A NICE GUY LIKE HUBIE BABY?
END

JUST WHEN YOU THOUGHT IT WAS SAFE TO BE A LITTER-BUG—

HERE'S MORE OF... PROFESSOR JUGHEAD'S "LOONEY LAWS"

A LAW IN A MIDWESTERN STATE SAYS THAT ANYONE INJURED BY A MOB MAY RECOVER FROM THE COUNTY GOVERNMENT A SUM NOT TO EXCEED FIVE HUNDRED DOLLARS!

AN OLD NEW YORK CITY LAW MAINTAINS YOU CAN'T SHOOT RABBITS FROM THE REAR OF A THIRD AVENUE STREETCAR -- WHILE THE VEHICLE IS IN MOTION!

A STATE IN NEW ENGLAND MAKES IT ILLEGAL TO EXCESSIVELY EAT AT FUNERALS!

IN A CERTAIN STATE IN THE DEEP SOUTH, IT IS AGAINST THE LAW TO PREDICT THE FUTURE BY READING THE BUMPS ON A PERSON'S HEAD!

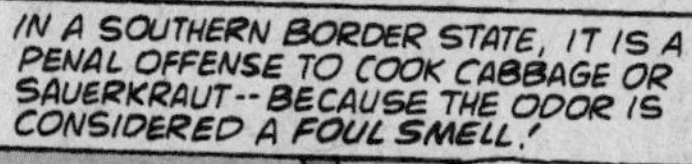

IN A LARGE SOUTHWESTERN STATE, IT IS AGAINST THE LAW TO OWN A COPY OF THE ENCYCLOPEDIA BRITANNICA--SINCE IT CONTAINS A FORMULA FOR LIQUOR!

END

Jughead the ABC's of JUG

J IS FOR *JOYOUS!* JUGHEAD JUST GOT HIS *ALLOWANCE!*

YAHOO!

U IS FOR *UNUSUAL!* NO ONE HAS AN *APPETITE* LIKE JUG!

CRUNCH! SLURP! CHOMP!

G IS FOR A *GOOD SNOOZE* AFTER ALL THAT *CHOW!*

ZZZ BURP! ZZZ

OR G IS FOR A ***GRATEFUL*** HOT DOG, 'CAUSE JUG DIDN'T FORGET ABOUT HIM!

DOGGIE TREATS

Archie
HENRY SCARPELLI
CRAIG BOLDMAN
THIS DELIVERY IS TO THE LODGE RESIDENCE! YOU KNOW WHERE THAT IS?
PIZZA
OH, SURE!
I'VE BEEN THROWN OUT OF THERE LOTS OF TIMES!

ARCHIE! I DIDN'T KNOW YOU WERE DELIVERING PIZZAS!
I WANTED TO SURPRISE YOU!

AS LONG AS YOU'RE HERE, YOU MIGHT AS WELL COME IN AND STAY AWHILE!

I'D LOVE TO, BUT I CAN'T! I STILL HAVE A DELIVERY TO MAKE!

OH, COME IN AND RELAX! I'LL HAVE MY CHAUFFEUR MAKE YOUR DELIVERY!
PSST! HEY, DAD! HAVE YOU GOT A FEW MORE BUCKS?
I GAVE YOU MONEY FOR THE PIZZA!
SPORTS
RIVERDALE

SOMEHOW A TWO-DOLLAR TIP DOESN'T SEEM LIKE ENOUGH!

Jughead
in
HEAT TREAT
BRRR! IT'S TEN BELOW!

LET'S CUT OUT TO WHERE WE CAN KEEP WARM!

WHERE ?
JUST FOLLOW ME!

RIGHT OVER YONDER!

VISIT Sunny FLORIDA
The End

Script & Pencils: Fernando Ruiz / Inks: Al Nickerson / Letters: Bill Yoshida / Colors: Barry Grossman

THAT'S ODD! I WONDER WHAT'S UP WITH HER?

WHAT'S THIS?
BETTY MUST'VE DROPPED IT!
U.S MAIL

PUBLISHER'S CLEARING HOME MY ITALIAN PUMPS! IT'S A *PARTY INVITATION* ALONG WITH AN ENVELOPE ADDRESSED TO JUGHEAD!

...BUT WHY WAS SHE ACTING SO MYSTERIOUS ABOUT THE WHOLE THING?
HI, RONNIE!

OH, HI, ARCHIE!
I'LL JUST PUT THIS AWAY FOR A LITTLE FURTHER INVESTIGATION!

LATER...
SO SHE'S HAVING A PARTY NEXT FRIDAY NIGHT WHILE HER PARENTS ARE OUT OF TOWN, YET SHE DIDIN'T MENTION A WORD TO ME ABOUT IT!
SLAM!
2

SURELY SHE'S MAILING ME ONE TOO, BUT THEN WHY WAS SHE SO SECRETIVE?!
HEY IT'S A PARTY!

I'LL GIVE IT A FEW DAYS BEFORE I GET TOO PARANOID!

HMMPH! IT'S BEEN FOUR DAYS AND STILL NO INVITATION!
SORRY, M'AM! I JUST DELIVER THEM!
US MAIL

AND SO...
SO, BETTY! WHAT ARE YOU DOING NEXT FRIDAY NIGHT?
NEXT FRIDAY NIGHT? UH... I'M DOING MY HAIR!

DOING YOUR HAIR?! NOW THAT'S WHAT I CALL ADVANCE PLANNING!
GOT TO KEEP THOSE FOLLICLES HEALTHY! OOPS! I'M LATE! GOT TO RUN!

HMM! I'VE GOT IT! I'LL THROW A BIGGER PARTY THE SAME NIGHT AND INVITE EVERYONE BUT HER!
?

DAYS LATER...
IT'S THE R.S.V.P. DATE FOR MY PARTY! AND NO ONE'S CALLED AT ALL!

RING!
AH-HA! MAYBE I SPOKE TOO SOON!

HI, VERONICA! IT'S ME, JUGHEAD! ARE YOU HAVING FOOD AT THIS PARTY?!
OF COURSE! ALL KINDS!
COUNT ME IN!

UH-OH! HERE'S JUGHEAD'S INVITATION TO BETTY'S PARTY! I FORGOT TO MAIL IT!
AT LEAST THIS WAY SOMEONE'S COMING TO MY PARTY!
HEY! IT'S A PARTY!

PARTY NIGHT...
SO WHERE IS MY BEST FRIEND JUGHEAD? HE'S LATE!
RING!
COLA

JUGHEAD, WHERE ARE YOU?!
I FOUND OUT ABOUT THIS BIG PARTY AT BETTY'S! BUT AFTER I CLEAR OUT HER SNACKS I'M COMING OVER TO YOUR PLACE!

I'M FLATTERED! BUT DON'T BOTHER, YOU IMBECILE!
SLAM!

THAT DOES IT! I'M GOING OVER THERE TO GIVE MY FRIENDS A PIECE OF MY MIND AND PART OF MY BUFFET!

VERONICA?! THIS IS A SURPRISE!
ISN'T IT THOUGH?! YOU WIN! SO I BROUGHT SOME FOOD TO YOUR PARTY!

TAKE THAT!!
HEY! DON'T WASTE THOSE PIES!

DON'T WORRY! HERE'S ONE FOR YOU, PAL!
MPHL!

SURPRISE, VERONICA!
WHAT'S THIS?!

HAVEN'T YOU FIGURED IT OUT YET ?! THIS IS A SURPRISE PARTY FOR *YOU!*
ME ?! BUT I THOUGHT YOU WERE HAVING A PARTY BECAUSE YOUR PARENTS ARE AWAY!

I PUT THAT ON THE INVITATION SO YOU WOULDN'T SUSPECT ANYTHING!
THEN I DROPPED IT ON PURPOSE AND GOT JUG TO PLAY ALONG FIGURING YOU'D GET TICKED AND CRASH MY... I MEAN *YOUR* PARTY!

BUT WHAT'S THE OCCASION ? IT'S NOT MY BIRTHDAY!
YOU REALLY DON'T KNOW?!

I COULDN'T FORGET! IT'S THE ANNIVERSARY OF THE DAY YOU *MOVED* HERE TO *RIVERDALE* AND WE BECAME FRIENDS!
HERE! HERE!

! SNIFF ! YOU'VE GOT TO BE THE *SWEETEST* FRIEND A GIRL COULD HAVE!
ACTUALLY, I THINK *I AM!*
SLURP!
The End

ACROSS THE TREACHEROUS SHOALS OF WHITE SHARK REEF AND INTO THE MURKY WATERS OF DEAD MAN'S BAY SLIDES THE SINISTER SHIP OF ***BLACK BLECH***, MOST DREADED BUCCANEER OF THE ***SPANISH MAIN!*** ON DECK, A SCENE OF HORROR AND UNBELIEVABLE ROTTENNESS IS TAKING PLACE AS THIS SCOURGE OF THE SEVEN SEAS PLOTS TO ADD TO HIS HOARD OF---

Pirate Gold

PART I

Script: Frank Doyle / Pencils: Stan Goldberg / Inks: Jon D'Agostino / Letters: Bill Yoshida / Colors: Barry Grossman

CAPTAIN TRUEBLUE! YOU MUST SAVE ME! MY FATHER, SIR JASON SNOBNOSTRIL WILL REWARD YOU HANDSOMELY!
WHAT IS YOUR PRICE, YOU CUR?

YOU COMMAND THE GARRISON HERE ON SPARKEEL ISLE!
YOU BET YOUR BIPPY! I'M IN CHARGE OF THE WHOLE SHOOTIN' MATCH!

I WANT THE GOLD BARS THAT ARE STORED IN THE GOVERNMENT STOREHOUSE!
AND IF I REFUSE?

I TOSS HER TO THE SHARKS!
HEH! HEH!
SHE'D PREFER THAT TO *YOU*, BLACK BLECH!
HEY, LET *ME* DECIDE THAT, HUH?
2

I CANNOT ALLOW YOU TO HARM THIS FAIR DAMSEL! YOU SHALL HAVE YOUR GOLD!
LOWER THE LONGBOAT!

ER- THE LONGBOAT IS STOVE IN, BLACK BLECH!
WE GOTTA USE THE SHORT BOAT!
SO WE'LL MAKE MORE TRIPS!

ONWARD TO SPARKEEL ISLE, AND A FORTUNE IN GOLD!
TOAD, MY FAITHFUL FLUNKY, WE'RE IN BIG TROUBLE!
"WE?"

IF THE GUARDS GIVE US ANY TROUBLE, YOU'LL BE THE FIRST TO GO!
THERE'S ONLY ONE GUARD ON DUTY!

BUT HE'S A DEDICATED OLD TIMER WHO'D DIE BEFORE HE GAVE UP THE GOLD!
MAYBE WE CAN ARRANGE THAT!
3

SHIVER MY TIMBERS.! IT'S THAT SWINE OF A PIRATE, BLACK BLECH.!
GIVE HIM THE GOLD, DEDICATED OLDTIMER.!

HE'S HOLDING SIR JASON'S DAUGHTER FOR RANSOM.!
THEN ALL THAT GOLD WILL BELONG TO HIM?

I'M AFRAID SO.!
WAL, I GOT SOMETHIN' TUH SAY ABOUT THAT.!
WHAT?

KIN I JOIN UP WITH YER CREW, YER SWINESHIP, SIR?
FLIP!
NOW THERE'S A SENSIBLE MAN.!

COME, LEAVE US GENTLEMANLY TYPES SWIG A FLAGON OF RUM WHILST THESE SWABS LOAD UP THE LOOT.!
MIGHT AS WELL.! BETRAYING YOUR TRUST IS THIRSTY WORK.!
FILTHY
4

FILTHY FERNANDEZ! HOW'S BUSINESS IN THE LOWEST DIVE ON THE SPANISH MAIN?
BLACK BLECH, YOU OLD WHARF RAT!

I'LL SEND THE WENCH OVER TO TAKE YER ORDER!

WHAT'LL YEZ HAVE, MATEY?
WHAT A CHARMING CHILD! WHAT IS YOUR NAME, DEAR?

"WENCH" IS THE NAME, GUV'NOR! "ANNIE WENCH!" WHUT'S YOURS?
CAPTAIN TERENCE TRUEBLUE!

SHE MEANS, "WHAT DO YOU WANT TO DRINK," YOU DUMMY!
OH!

BLIMEY! 'E'S A REAL SWELL, THAT ONE IS! TOO GOOD FOR THE LIKES OF ME, THOUGH!
5

THAT BLACK BLECH IS A SMART ONE! WE BREAKS OUR BACKS, LOOTIN' AN' PLUNDERIN' AN' FER WHAT?

HE GETS A FORTUNE IN GOLD JUST HANDED TO HIM!
FER TURNIN' LOOSE THAT RICH FEMALE!

HAR! TRUEBLUE WILL SAVE THE GAL, BUT HE'LL HANG FER GIVIN' AWAY THE GOLD!

"HANG?" THAT BEAUTIFUL GENT? WHAT A AWFUL WASTE!

'E'S WORTH TEN OF ME, 'E IS! I GOTTA SAVE HIM, NO MATTER WHUT HAPPENS TUH ME!
THY FERNANDEZ
CONTINUED

PIRATE
GOLD
PART II
MOMENTS LATER A SKIFF GLIDES SILENTLY THROUGH THE STILL WATERS OF DEAD MAN'S BAY! A HOODED FIGURE PROPELS IT EXPERTLY TOWARD THE SINISTER SHIP, SHROUD IN MIST, THAT SWINGS AT ANCHOR OFF SPARKEEL ISLE ---

DROPPING LIGHTLY ONTO THE DECK, THE FIGURE CROUCHES-- LISTENS-- AND MOVES TOWARD THE MAST --

ONLY TO FIND-- NOTHING!
GASP! SHE'S GONE! SHE MUST BE LOCKED UP BELOW!
7

THE CREW, BUSY LOADING GOLD, OFFER NO DANGER--
IF I KNOW THAT SWINE, BLACK BLECH, 'E'LL 'AVE 'ER IN 'IS CABIN!

AND-- SURE ENOUGH--
WHO ARE YOU, YOU CREATURE OF LOW DEGREE?

I COME TO RESCUE YOU, MUM!
ARE YOU MAD, GIRL?

NOW THAT HE'S GOT THE GOLD, BLACK BLECH IS WEALTHIER THAN MY DADDY!
AND, HE'S NOT BAD LOOKING!

BUT THEY'LL 'ANG THAT LOVERLY CAP'N TRUEBLUE!
PIFFLE! WHO CARES?

I'LL SHOW YER WHO CARES, ME FINE LADY! I CARES-- THAT'S WHO!!
OUCH! HOW DARE YOU?
WHUMP

BUT, AS THE TWO WOMEN APPEAR TOPSIDE--
UH-OH!
BLACK BLECH! SAVE ME FROM THIS SAVAGE CREATURE!
SEIZE HER, MEN!

'OW'S ABOUT WE DEEP-SIX THE WENCH, BLACK?
JUST TIE HER TO THE MAST FOR NOW!

THE GOLD'S ALL ABOARD! NOW HAVE A NIGHT ON THE TOWN, M'LADS! YOU DESERVE IT! TELL FILTHY FERNANDEZ TO PUT IT ON MY BILL!
H'RAY!

LET'S HEAR IT FER BLACK BLECH!
FER 'E'S A JOLLY GOOD FELLOW!

I BROUGHT THE BOAT BACK! WE KIN WEIGH ANCHOR, CAP'N TRUEBLUE!
VERY GOOD, TOAD!

'E'S NOT BLACK BLECH! 'E'S CAP'N TRUEBLUE!
CORRECT, MY DEAR! LET ME CUT YOU LOOSE!
FLIP

THIS IS NOW OUR SHIP, AND OUR GOLD!
'OW DID YOU DO IT?

BLACK BLECH AND HIS CREW ARE NOW STRANDED ON SPARKEEL ISLE!

HOW DID YOU MANAGE THAT SNEAKY SWITCH?
WITH THE HELP OF TOAD, AND FILTHY'S RUM!

BLACK BLECH IS KNOWN AS A HARD DRINKING PIRATE! EVEN FILTHY'S RUM WOULDN'T HIT HIM THAT HARD!

WHEN IT AIN'T TAKEN OUTTA THE BOTTLE, MA'AM, IT PACKS A GOOD WALLOP!
10

'OW ABOUT 'ER? SHE WANTED TO STAY WITH BLACK BLECH!

YES, I ASSUMED THAT! YOU'LL FIND HIM AT FILTHY'S PLACE, MISS!
I WANT TO GO WHERE THE GOLD GOES!

MAY I INSIST?
ULP! ALL RIGHT! I'M GOING! I'M GOING!
SWOOSH!

OOPS!
SPLASH!

SHE EXPECTED TO STEP INTO THE LONGBOAT – BUT IT WAS THE SHORT BOAT!
MISSED IT BY THAT MUCH!
HA! HA! UP ANCHOR, TOAD! LET'S GET THE SHOW ON THE ROAD!
OOH, AIN'T 'E THE HANDSOME DUDE, THOUGH?
END

Script: Kathleen Webb / Pencils: Stan Goldberg / Inks: John Lowe / Letters: Bill Yoshida / Colors: Barry Grossman

CHIP ON HIS SHOULDER!
YOU KNOW THIS MOVIE?
EVERYBODY KNOWS THIS MOVIE!
WELL, WHAT DO YOU KNOW? I THOUGHT I DISCOVERED IT!

WELL, OKAY, ENJOY IT! DON'T FORGET YOU PROMISED TO SET THE TABLE FOR DINNER!
I WILL!

HELLO, RICK!
IT'S SO ROMANTIC...

SO... RO...MANT...
ZZZZZZZ
RICK! PICK YOUR HEAD UP! IT'S ME! YOUR LONG-LOST LOVE!

YIKES! IT'S ARCHIE!

BETTY! YOU'VE COME BACK TO ME AT LAST!
HUH?

BETTY, YOU'RE THE GIRL OF MY DREAMS!
I THOUGHT VERONICA WAS THE GIRL OF YOUR DREAMS!

BUT THIS IS YOUR DREAM, BETTY! IN YOUR DREAM, YOU ARE THE GIRL OF MY DREAMS!
HUH?

I'M GETTING DIZZY! I'VE GOT TO GET OUT OF HERE!
BETTY, DON'T GO! COME BACK!
3

SIGH

JUG–YOU KNOW WHAT I WANT TO HEAR!

NO–NO, ARCHIE..
YOU PLAYED IT FOR HER, YOU CAN PLAY IT FOR ME!

PLAY IT, JUG! PLAY IT!!

I'M A LITTLE TEAPOT, SHORT AND STOUT...

HERE IS MY HANDLE HERE IS MY SPOUT...
THAT'S IT! MY FAVORITE SONG!

PLAY IT AGAIN, JUG!!

ARCHIE! HE'S PLAYING OUR SONG!
YES, MY LOVE!
COLA

ARCHIE, I'M AFRAID WE MUST NEVER SEE EACH OTHER AGAIN!
BUT WHY, MY DEAREST?
CHERRY FIZZ
MALT

BECAUSE THAT'S THE WAY IT WORKS IN THIS MOVIE!
OH!

WELL, AT LEAST WE'LL ALWAYS HAVE PARIS!

BUT WE'VE NEVER BEEN TO PARIS!
YOU'RE RIGHT!

WELL, AT LEAST WE'LL ALWAYS HAVE RIVERDALE!

HERE'S LOOKING AT YOU, KIDDO!
DON'T CALL ME KIDDO - I REALLY HATE IT!

WELL, I MUST GO NOW!
I'LL TAKE YOU TO THE AIRPORT!

NO - I'M NOT LEAVING TOWN!
SO, WHERE ARE YOU GOING?

I'M GOING TO SET THE TABLE FOR DINNER! I PROMISED MOM!

POP!
!?

DID YOU ENJOY SEEING THE MOVIE AGAIN, BETTY?
WELL...MAYBE I'VE SEEN IT ONE TIME TOO MANY!
END

Script: Craig Boldman / Pencils: Rex Lindsey / Inks & Letters: Jon D'Agostino / Colors: Barry Grossman

TELL HIM TO WAIT HERE FOR ME! I SAW THE CUTEST OUTFIT IN THE WINDOW AND...
... IT'LL GO PERFECTLY WITH A PAIR OF EARRINGS I HAVE!

MOMENTS LATER...
HUMPH! SOMETIMES I THINK MALLS WERE INVENTED FOR VERONICA!
WHY, MR. LODGE?
TWO PERUVIAN NUT MUNCHIE-WUNCHIES, PLEASE!

SHE SEEMS TO MAKE A CAREER OUT OF SHOPPING!
WELL, THIS JOB IS NOT GOING TO BE MY CAREER!

WITH COLLEGE EXPENSES BEING WHAT THEY ARE, THE MONEY I EARN WILL SURE HELP!

VERY COMMENDABLE! I'M GAINING A NEW RESPECT FOR YOU, ARCHIE!

DADDY! WAIT'LL YOU SEE WHAT I BOUGHT! I DIDN'T HAVE ENOUGH MONEY, SO I CHARGED IT!

IT'S TIME YOU LEARNED THE VALUE OF MONEY! ARCHIE DID! I WANT YOU TO GET A JOB!

ME WORK, DADDY?
YES! THAT'S THE WAY I'LL PAY FOR HALF OF THAT OUTFIT!
HERE WE GO AGAIN!

WHAT? YOU WANT ME TO HIRE YOU?
IT'S ONLY FAIR! YOU ARE RESPONSIBLE FOR DADDY'S NEW ATTITUDE!

NEXT DAY...
VERONICA, THIS IS YOUR FIRST DAY AND YOU'RE AN HOUR LATE!
I KNOW, BUT I HAD A TOUGH TIME DECIDING...

...WHICH NAIL POLISH GOES WITH MY UNIFORM!
YIPES!

GET STARTED BY DIPPING THE DONUTS INTO THIS MELTED **CHOCOLATE...**

WHO ME? THAT'S SUCH A **YICKY** JOB!
HEY, I'M **BOSS** AROUND HERE! YOU **DIP** THEM LIKE THIS!

OH, DEAR! YOU GOT A **SPOT** ON ME!
I'LL WIPE IT OFF WITH THIS TOWEL... **OOOPS!**
LOOK OUT!
SPLASH!

GET THE MOP OUT, VERONICA!
ARCHIE ANDREWS! DO YOU EXPECT **ME** TO USE A MOP?!
HUMPH! BOSSES SHOULDN'T HAVE GIRLFRIENDS!

I'LL WATCH THE **FRONT** OF THE **STAND** WHILE ARCHIE IS MOPPING UP!

HI, CUTIE!
HEY! YOU'RE NEW!
BOY! I SUDDENLY GOT A BIG HUNGER FOR DONUTS!

HEY, VERONICA, YOU'RE SUPPOSED TO BE WORKING!

LOOK, BUSTER! YELL AT HER LIKE THAT AGAIN AN' YOU'RE HISTORY!
YEAH... ANYTHING YOU SAY... HEH, HEH!

ARCHIE, WE NEED **MORE** DONUTS...
WHAT HAPPENED? THERE WAS A LOAD OF THEM!

THEY WERE ALL SOLD OUT TO MY NEW FRIENDS!

ONE DOZEN DONUTS!
I'LL TAKE TWO DOZEN!
FOUR FOR ME!

WE NEED MORE DONUTS, ARCH!
GULP! COMING, VERONICA!

FLOUR
THOSE GUYS HAVE BEEN EATING THEM FASTER THAN I CAN MAKE THEM!
POP!
HURRY, ARCHIE!
WHEW! I'M POOPED!
SALT
SUGAR

WHAT? YOU QUIT?
WHY, VERONICA?

BECAUSE I DON'T WANT TO WORK IN A PLACE WHERE THEY OVERWORK POOR ARCHIE!
WHA...?
END

Betty and Veronica
PATCHES PALS
HOT
HI!
Your Pal, Betty
THIS END UP
POW!
Love ya, Archie
VOTE
U.S.A.
HI!
REX W. LINDSEY

Veronica "Strike a Pose!"

VERONICA LOVES HER FASHION MAGAZINES! SEE WHICH ONES SHE READS BY ELIMINATING THE LETTERS WITH THE ODD NUMBERS, THEN UNSCRAMBLE THE REMAINING LETTERS TO DISCOVER THE TITLE!

Answers: ① VAGUE ② GLIMMER ③ FRESH ④ BABE

Betty's PET fashions

Dan DeCarlo

in "THAT'S RICH"

STORY: FRANK DOYLE - ART: DAN DECARLO
INK: JIM DECARLO - LETTER: BILL 'Y.' - COLOR: B. GROSSMAN

SARAH IS IN THE ROAD SHOW PRODUCTION OF "HOW RICH CAN YOU GET?"
AN ACTRESS! HOW INTERESTING!!
THAT WAS A HIT ON BROADWAY A FEW YEARS BACK, WASN'T IT?
YES, SIR! IT'S GREAT FUN TO DO!
I PLAY THE DAUGHTER OF A MAN SO WEALTHY THAT RICH TYCOONS BORROW FROM *HIM*!
NOW, THAT'S RICH!
THAT'S INTERESTING! WE WERE JUST DISCUSSING VERONICA LODGE AND···
MMPH! YES, I SEE THE SIMILARITY!

HER BRAGGING HAS BEEN GETTING OUT OF HAND! I WONDER IF---
HMM? IF IT WOULD GET RONNIE TO PUT A LID ON IT?

SARAH, COULD YOU GO INTO YOUR ACT WITHOUT A STAGE?
I DON'T SEE WHY NOT!

OH DEAR, YES! IT'S SO DIFFICULT TO FIND A GOOD PERSONAL MAID THESE DAYS!
PLEASE, RON!

RON! I WANT YOU TO MEET MY GOOD FRIEND, SARAH!
HI! WHERE ARE YOU FROM, SARAH?
PARIS!

OH, FRENCH!
---AND MADRID! ALSO LONDON, OF COURSE, OSLO AND BERLIN!

NATURALLY, THAT'S NOT COUNTING THE PENTHOUSE IN NEW YORK, THE VILLA ON THE COSTA DEL SOL, AND A SHACK IN ACAPULCO!
HMPH! RESTLESS LITTLE CREATURE, AREN'T YOU?

IT IS A NUISANCE! BUT WHEN ONE HAS ALL THESE HOMES, ONE SIMPLY MUST MAKE USE OF THEM!

DEAR OLD DADDY! HE COLLECTS ESTATES LIKE MOST PEOPLE COLLECT STAMPS!
HOW PERFECTLY DREADFUL FOR YOU!

HE USED TO COLLECT DIAMONDS, BUT GOOD HEAVENS - THE CLOSETS BEGAN OVERFLOWING WITH THE SILLY THINGS!

WHAT'VE YOU GOT THERE, A FEMALE REGGIE? I NEVER HEARD SUCH EXAGGERATING!!
"EXAGGERATING"? WHAT'S THAT?

PRETENDING TO BE RICHER THAN YOU ARE!

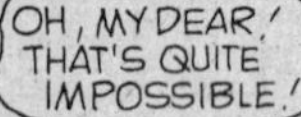

OH, MY DEAR! THAT'S QUITE IMPOSSIBLE!

THERE *IS* NO ONE RICHER THAN I AM!
HAH! DID YOU EVER HEAR OF THE LODGES?

THOSE QUAINT WOODSY TYPE CABINS?
MY UNCLE MIDAS HAS THOUSANDS OF THEM IN WILDERNESS AREAS ALL OVER THE WORLD!
UNCLE *MIDAS*?

FICTION! FABRICATIONS! NOBODY WAS EVER AS RICH AS YOU CLAIM TO BE!!!
OH, WE WEREN'T *ALWAYS* THIS RICH!

WHY, WHEN I WAS A BABY, MY DADDY ONLY HAD A MERE FOUR OR FIVE BILLION!
THAT DOES IT!

I WON'T LISTEN TO THAT AWFUL SNOB ANYMORE!! THERE OUGHT TO BE A LAW AGAINST SUCH OUTRAGEOUS BRAGGING!

MR. WEATHERBEE! MISS GRUNDY! DID YOU HEAR THE BOASTING OF THAT FRIEND OF BETTY'S?
WE HEARD, VERONICA!

WE AGREE WITH YOU! BRAGGING ABOUT ONE'S WEALTH IS IN VERY POOR TASTE!
YOU CAN SAY THAT AGAIN!
WE MIGHT, IF IT BECOMES NECESSARY!

MMPH! I OUGHT TO GET AN OSCAR FOR THAT PERFORMANCE!
WHY DON'T YOU HAVE YOUR UNCLE MIDAS BUY YOU ONE?
HOW CAN BETTY POSSIBLY HAVE A FRIEND LIKE THAT?
The END

Betty in "SNOW JOB"

PUFF! PUFF! MAYBE IT ISN'T TOO LATE!

DADDY, YOU CAN'T SHOVEL OUR DRIVEWAY!
AND WHY CAN'T I?

STATISTICS SHOW SHOVELLING SNOW IS MUCH TOO STRENUOUS FOR A MIDDLE-AGED MAN LIKE YOURSELF!
REALLY?

ARCHIE WAS HERE BEFORE! I THINK I'LL ASK HIM!
GOOD IDEA, DADDY!
WHAT A COINCIDENCE! HE'S DRIVING BY NOW!

I CHANGED MY MIND, ARCHIE! YOU CAN SHOVEL MY DRIVEWAY!
THANK YOU, MR. COOPER!

ARCHIE, BEFORE YOU START WHY DON'T I MAKE YOU SOME HOT COCOA?
THAT SOUNDS NEAT, BETTY!

THIS IS GOING TO BE OH, SO COZY, JUST THE TWO OF US!

GULP!

SO THAT'S WHY HE'S SO ANXIOUS TO SHOVEL SNOW!
---HE'S NEEDS THE MONEY TO DATE VERONICA!

DADDY, I'VE BEEN THINKING!
---IF YOU'RE HIRING SOMEONE TO SHOVEL SNOW, WOULDN'T IT BE FAIRER TO GIVE *ME* THE CHANCE TO MAKE MONEY?

I SUPPOSE YOU'RE RIGHT, BUT I ALREADY HIRED ARCHIE!
IT'S NOT TOO LATE TO CANCEL HIM! HE HASN'T STARTED YET!

YOU'RE NOT GOING TO MAKE YOUR DATE MONEY OFF MY FAMILY, ARCHIE!

I CAN'T UNDERSTAND YOUR DAD!
HE KEEPS CHANGING HIS MIND ABOUT HIRING ME!

I SAW YOU TALKING TO RONNIE! I GUESS YOU HAVE A DATE WITH HER TONIGHT!
NO! SHE STOPPED TO SAY GOOD-BYE! SHE'S LEAVING FOR THE BAHAMAS!

AS A MATTER OF FACT, I WAS HOPING TO ASK *YOU* OUT TONIGHT!

BUT SINCE I DON'T HAVE ANY MONEY I'LL HAVE TO WAIT TILL I PICK UP SOME WORK!

QUICK, DADDY! YOU'VE GOT TO REHIRE ARCHIE!
HIRE HIM! CANCEL HIM! REHIRE HIM! WHAT IS THIS?

I JUST BENT OVER TO PICK UP SOMETHING AND I THINK I PULLED A MUSCLE IN MY BACK!
4

DO YOU WANT ME TO TAKE YOU TO THE DOCTOR?
NO, IT'LL BE ALL RIGHT AS LONG AS I DON'T DO ANYTHING STRENUOUS LIKE SHOVELLING SNOW!
BUT YOU'VE GOT TO GO OUT AND GET ARCHIE BEFORE HE LEAVES!
YOU WON'T BELIEVE THIS BETTY, BUT YOUR DAD JUST REHIRED ME!
THE COCOA IS READY! COME ON IN!
WOULD YOU LIKE TO GO BOWLING TONIGHT?
OF COURSE!
THAT'S WHY I DIG YOU, BETTY!
... UNLIKE YOUR DAD, YOU MAKE UP YOUR MIND RIGHT AWAY!
?!
The End

THE Archies in "GROUP WHOOP"
WHY ISN'T THE LEADER OF YOUR GROUP HERE WITH YOU?
ARCHIE WAS DELAYED BY A DENTAL APPOINTMENT! BUT HE'LL BE HERE IN TIME FOR TONIGHT'S SHOW!
BETTY IS AN OPTIMIST! ARCHIE'S JALOPY WILL NEVER MAKE IT THROUGH THESE MOUNTAINS!
SV
REGISTRATION
SNOW VALLEY TALENT FESTIVAL
Script: George Gladir / Pencils: Dan DeCarlo Jr. / Inks: Jimmy DeCarlo / Letters: Bill Yoshida / Colors: Barry Grossman
SO FAR, SO GOOD! THE OL' BUGGY IS HOLDING ITS OWN!
YOU CAN'T GO BEYOND THIS POINT! AN AVALANCHE HAS WIPED OUT THE ROAD UP AHEAD!
GOOD GRIEF!

BUT I'VE GOT TO BE AT SNOW VALLEY TONIGHT!
HMMM!

THERE'S A SHORTCUT TO SNOW VALLEY!
---THE AERIAL TRAMWAY AT EAGLE POINT TAKES YOU STRAIGHT THERE!

BUT YOU'D BETTER TAKE THESE! YOU'LL NEED THEM!
GEE THANKS!

PUFF! PUFF! GETTING THESE SNOWSHOES WAS A REAL LUCKY BREAK!

OH NO!
AERIAL TRAMWAY OUT OF ORDER

MISTER, WHEN IS THIS TRAM GOING TO BE FIXED?
NOT FOR A COUPLE OF WEEKS!

BUT I'VE GOT TO GET TO SNOW VALLEY! IT'S AN EMERGENCY!
HMMM! MAYBE I CAN RADIO MY SUPPLY HELICOPTER!

I TOLD HIM IT WAS AN EMERGENCY! HE'S WILLING TO PICK YOU UP!

OUR ACT IS SUPPOSED TO GO ON IN THIRTY MINUTES, AND STILL NO ARCHIE!

LET'S HEAD FOR THE AUDITORIUM ANYWAY!
---HE MAY STILL SHOW UP IN TIME!
AUDITORIUM

THANKS AGAIN, MISTER!
X-13
YOU'RE WELCOME, YOUNG FELLA!

YOU MEAN TO SAY GETTING TO THE TALENT FESTIVAL IS YOUR IDEA OF AN EMERGENCY?
YES!
X13

AND FOR THIS I MADE A SPECIAL TRIP!
I APPRECIATE IT!
X-13

THIS IS THE ONLY PLACE I CAN LAND! THE SKI LIFT WILL TAKE YOU DOWN TO SNOW VALLEY!
THANKS AGAIN!
X-13

SORRY! THE SKI LIFT CLOSES DOWN EVERY NIGHT AT SEVEN!
BUT I'VE GOT TO GET DOWN TO SNOW VALLEY!
LIFT

CAN I BORROW THAT SLED?
BE MY GUEST!

BE SURE TO TURN LEFT AT THE BOTTOM OF THE CLIFF!
I WONDER WHAT SHE SAID!

BUT WE'RE EXPECTING OUR LEADER TO SHOW UP ANY SECOND!
SORRY! I CAN'T DELAY THE FESTIVAL ANY LONGER!
The Archies

CLEAR THE STAGE AND SET UP THE TRAMPOLINE FOR THE NEXT ACT!
DARN!

THE SNOW IS GETTING SO HEAVY I CAN'T SEE WHERE I'M---

YIPES!

KRASH

BOUNCE!

IT'S ARCHIE!!
PLOP!

ARCHIE, I CAN'T BELIEVE YOU'RE HERE!
NEITHER CAN I!

THE ARCHIES ARE READY TO RIP!

IT WAS WORTH WAITING FOR THIS GROUP! THEY'RE FANTASTIC!

CONGRATULATIONS! YOUR GROUP NOT ONLY WON THE FESTIVAL, BUT WE'RE BOOKING YOU FOR ANOTHER WEEK!
OH, WOW!

ONLY PLEASE DO ME ONE FAVOR!
WHAT'S THAT, SIR?

CUT OUT THAT TRICK ENTRANCE OF YOURS!
--- WE CAN'T AFFORD TO PUT IN A NEW SKYLIGHT FOR EVERY PERFORMANCE!
END.

Betty in "WHOLE LOTTA SHAKIN'"
WHEN WAS THE LAST ONE?
ONLY A FEW DAYS AGO! IT DIDN'T SHAKE US UP MUCH!
SCRIPT: KATHLEEN WEBB
PENCILS: STAN GOLDBERG
INKS: JOHN LOWE

GOSH, POLLY, YOU MAKE IT SOUND LIKE SAN FRANCISCO IS EARTHQUAKE CENTRAL!
THEY'RE NOT THAT FREQUENT, LITTLE SISTER!
WHAT WERE YOU AND POLLY CHATTING ABOUT?
CALIFORNIA'S MOST FAMOUS HOMEGROWN PRODUCT! EARTHQUAKES!

OH, YEAH! BACK IN THE SEVENTIES, EVERYONE WAS CONVINCED SAN FRANCISCO WAS GOING TO SLIDE RIGHT INTO THE OCEAN!

IT'S STILL A PRETTY RUMBLY PLACE TO LIVE!
POLLY SAYS THEY'RE NOT THAT COMMON!

WHAT A RELIEF TO KNOW I LIVE IN AN AREA THAT'S NOT PRONE TO MANY!

HEY, DILT! WHAT'S THE LATEST?
SCIENTISTS HAVE FOUND A FAULT LINE RUNNING UNDER RIVERDALE!
SCIENTIST JOURNAL

WHA-?
OH, YES! SOMEDAY WE COULD BE FACING A MAJOR EARTHQUAKE!
SCIENTIST JOURNAL

THANK **YOU** FOR THAT CHEERFUL NEWS!
HEY, AT LEAST THEY HAVEN'T FOUND A MAGMA POCKET UNDER THE TOWN YET!

GREAT! NOT ONLY DO I GET TO START WORRYING ABOUT EARTH-QUAKES IN RIVERDALE, BUT A MAJOR VOLCANIC ERUPTION AS WELL!

RRRRUMBLE!
WHA--- IT- IT'S *HAPPENED ALREADY!!*

BETTY?
YIKES!!!

IT'S NOT THAT I DON'T *LIKE* THIS, BUT WHAT'S THE OCCASION?
EARTHQUAKE! DON'T YOU *FEEL IT?!*

I FEEL THE GROUND SHAKING, YES!
WHERE CAN WE GO TO GET OUT OF HARM'S WAY?

WELL, SINCE THE GARBAGE TRUCK THAT CAUSED THE SHAKING IS GOING AWAY FROM US, I DON'T THINK WE NEED TO WORRY ABOUT IT!
OH!
RRUMBLE!
CITY REFUSE

YOU OKAY NOW?
YEAH, I THINK SO! I ...

BOOM!
EEK!!
ZIP!

BETTY, IT WAS ONLY A SONIC BOOM FROM A JET!
OH!

WHAT'S GOT YOU SO SKITTISH?
WELL, POLLY WAS TELLING ME ABOUT AN EARTHQUAKE SHE FELT IN SAN FRANCISCO...

...THEN DILTON TOLD ME A A MAJOR FAULT HAS BEEN FOUND UNDER RIVERDALE!
WHOSE FAULT?

YOU KNOW WHAT I MEAN! THE KIND THAT MAKES QUAKES!
DON'T LET IT SPOOK YOU, BETS!

IT'S PROBABLY A PRETTY REMOTE POSSIBILITY! AND EVEN SO, YOUR SISTER'S MANAGED TO LIVE THROUGH THEM!
Y-YEAH!

AND WHAT ABOUT NORIKO? HER GRANDPARENTS IN JAPAN HAVE LITTLE EARTHQUAKES ALL THE TIME!
IT'S NOT THE END OF THE WORLD!

YOU DON'T SEE ME FREAKIN' OUT OVER IT!
YOU'RE RIGHT, ARCHIE! I SHOULD TAKE IT IN STRIDE, LIKE YOU!
OMIGOSH!! IT HAPPENED!!

RIVERDALE ACTUALLY HAD AN EARTHQUAKE! I CAN'T BELIEVE IT!
WHEN?

ABOUT TWENTY MINUTES AGO! IT WASN'T MUCH! IT WOULD'VE FELT LIKE A BIG TRUCK GOING BY!
OMIGOSH! SO THAT GARBAGE TRUCK WASN'T THE ONLY THING MAKING THE GROUND MOVE, HUH, ARCHIE? ARCHIE?

I'D SAY HIS EARTHQUAKE PREPAREDNESS SKILLS DEFINITELY NEED SOME FINE TUNING!
NO, HE JUST FREAKS OUT AFTER THE QUAKE!
END

Betty and Veronica in "THE UNTOUCHABLE"

Script: Frank Doyle / Pencils: Dan DeCarlo / Inks: Jimmy DeCarlo / Letters: Bill Yoshida / Colors: Barry Grossman

MMPH! OH, BETTY! LIGHTEN UP! WHERE'S YOUR SENSE OF HUMOR?

SPLOOSH

AARGH

SOMEBODY'S GOING TO DIE!

NOBODY! NOBODY TAKES LIBERTIES WITH THE PERSON OF VERONICA LODGE! NOBODY!!

WHAT WAS THAT YOU WERE SAYING ABOUT A SENSE OF HUMOR, RONNIE?

PUT A LID ON IT, COOPER!!
EEP!

COME ON! EVERYBODY THROWS SNOWBALLS!
AT YOU, MAYBE!

BUT VERONICA LODGE IS SOMETHING ELSE AGAIN!

PEOPLE ARE NOT TO TAKE LIBERTIES WITH A LODGE! PARTICULARLY THIS ONE!

ON THE SOCIAL LADDER IN THIS TOWN I'M NUMBER ONE! AND NOBODY TREATS ME WITH DISRESPECT!

NOBODY! YOU DIG? NOBODY!!! IN THIS TOWN I GET RESPECT!!!
YIPE!

W-W-WHO WAS T-THAT?
I DON'T KNOW! BUT I KNOW ONE THING!

I'M SURE GONNA TREAT HER WITH RESPECT!
YOU BETCHA! FROM FOUR OR FIVE BLOCKS AWAY, IF POSSIBLE!
BRRR!

LATER:
ANOTHER DAY, ANOTHER DOLLAR!
THOUSAND, PERHAPS! MAYBE TEN THOUSAND! A DOLLAR? GOOD GRIEF!

WHAPPO
EEP!

ZAP
ACK!

OOF! THOSE MISERABLE MALES! IT'S AN AMBUSH!!!
OUCH!
POW
WAP

RUN, GIRLS! HEE, HEE! COVER UP!
OUR TURN WILL COME!

HA! THAT'S ALFIE! HE ALWAYS MISSES TO THE LEFT!
STAY LOW AND KEEP YOUR EYES PEELED!
I THINK WE'RE WEARING THEM DOWN!
SURE! THEIR ARMS ARE GETTING TIRED!
WHIZZZ
ZOOOM!
POW!

HUMPH!

SLAM
?

WAH

EVERBODY HATES ME!
WHAT MAKES YOU SAY THAT, SWEETHEART?

NOBODY WILL HIT ME WITH S-SNOWBALLS!
?
DON'T ASK ME, SIR! I'M JUST THE BUTLER!
THE END

Script: Kathleen Webb / Pencils: Stan Goldberg / Inks: John Lowe / Letters: Bill Yoshida / Colors: Barry Grossman

WHAT... WHAT AM I DOING BACKSTAGE?
GUESS YOU DON'T REMEMBER EVERYTHING, YET!

YOU WON A CONTEST TO MEET THE MEMBERS OF OUT OF SYNC!
OH, WOW! I-I FORGOT!

SURELY YOU REMEMBER MEETING THE REST OF US... BOBBY... JET... ALBERTO... AND FRED?
HI!
HEY, BETTY!
YO!

THE LAST THING I REMEMBER IS LYING DOWN ON THE COUCH FOR A NAP! I DON'T REMEMBER WINNING ANY CONTEST!

BESIDES, OUT OF SYNC ISN'T EVEN IN TOWN! THEY'RE TOURING ASIA RIGHT NOW!
TONIGHT ONLY
OUT OF SYNC

THIS HAS TO BE A DREAM! AND THERE'S ONLY ONE WAY TO FIND OUT!

IF THIS IS A DREAM, THEN I SHOULD BE ABLE TO DO ANYTHING I WANT!
HERE GOES!
SMOOCH! SMOOCH! SMOOCH! SMOOCH!
ZIP! ZIP!
ZOOM!

THERE! I JUST KISSED ALL FIVE BAND MEMBERS, AND NOBODY STOPPED ME!
SMOOCH!

WHOA! I JUST KISSED ALL THE GUYS IN OUT OF SYNC! IT HAS TO BE A DREAM!
THANKS FOR THE GOOD LUCK KISSES, BETTY! LET'S HEAD ONSTAGE, GUYS!

WE'LL BE BACK LATER FOR OUR AFTER CONCERT PARTY!
HEY! THIS IS A DREAM, RIGHT?

WHO SAYS I CAN'T GO OUT ON STAGE WITH THEM!
LET'S GO, GUYS! OUR PUBLIC IS WAITING!

LOVE YA LOVE YA...
ME! HUMBLE LITTLE BETTY COOPER! SINGING AND DANCING ON STAGE WITH OUT OF SYNC!
IF ONLY THIS DREAM WOULD COME TRUE!
BAYBEH!

LET'S HEAR IT FOR BETTY!
SHE HARMONIZES WITH US SO BEAUTIFULLY!
YAAAY! CLAP CLAP!

I'D LIKE TO SOLO ON THIS NEXT NUMBER, FUZZY!
YOU GO, GIRL!
WE ♥ OUT OF SYNC

OH, WOW! I HOPE THIS DREAM NEVER ENDS!
I'M HAVING SUCH A FANTASTIC TIME!
WHY... WHY O DID YOU LEAVE... COME BACK TO ME...

YOU HELPED MAKE THIS A MEMORABLE CONCERT, BETTY!
MAYBE WE OUGHT TO MAKE HER A MEMBER OF THE BAND, GUYS!

FOR OUR AFTER-CONCERT PARTY, WE'RE GOING TO THE BILTWELL HOTEL!
OH, WOW! THAT'S THE CLASSIEST PLACE IN TOWN!

YOU READY TO GO, BETTY?
YES! JUST LET ME GET MY...
FELLOWS, THERE'S BEEN A MISTAKE!

THE REAL CONTEST WINNER BROKE HER ANKLE AND COULDN'T MAKE IT!
BUT... WE THOUGHT BETTY WAS THE CONTEST WINNER!
SECURITY

SHE CAME BACKSTAGE WITH SOME RICH KID, A VERONICA LODGE!
WHEN BETTY TRIPPED AND KNOCKED HER-SELF OUT, WE PUT HER IN YOUR DRESSING ROOM TO RECOVER!
SECURITY

YOU...YOU MEAN... THIS WASN'T ALL A DREAM? THIS IS REALITY?
IS THAT THE EXCUSE YOU'VE GOT FOR LEAVING ME WAITING ALL THIS TIME?

SOME FRIEND YOU ARE! YOU HAVE ALL THE FUN WITH OUT OF SYNC, AND FORGET ME!
BUT...BUT...IF THIS ISN'T A DREAM...

...WHY CAN'T I REMEMBER WAKING UP ON THE COUCH BEFORE THE CONCERT STARTED?...
MAYBE BECAUSE YOU'RE STILL ASLEEP!

H-HUH? MOM! IT... IT REALLY WAS A DREAM!
SORRY TO SAY, YES!

IT MUST HAVE BEEN A DOOZY! YOU WERE SINGING IN YOUR SLEEP!
UH...YEAH! I GOT TO MEET THE MEMBERS OF OUT OF SYNC!

THAT WOULD BE A DREAM COME TRUE, WOULDN'T IT?
YEAH... HA HA... BUT IT'S NOT LIKELY TO HAPPEN IN MY LIFETIME!
BING
BANG

BETTY! YOU WON'T BELIEVE IT! OUT OF SYNC CAME OVER TO LODGE MANSION TO SEAL A RECORDING CONTRACT WITH DADDY'S MUSIC COMPANY, SO I BROUGHT THEM OVER TO MEET YOU AFTERWARDS!

APPARENTLY SHE DIDN'T BELIEVE IT!
THAT WOULD EXPLAIN WHY SHE'S OVER IN A CORNER PINCHING HERSELF!
End

SCRIPT:	ART & LETTERS:	COLORS:	EDITOR-IN-CHIEF:	PRESIDENT:
FRANK DOYLE	HARRY LUCEY	BARRY GROSSMAN	VICTOR GORELICK	MIKE PELLERITO

BOY! I LOVE CUTTING THAT FIRST FIGURE EIGHT OF THE SEASON!

HEY! WHAT'S UP?
THE POND IS FROZEN!

WHAT'D YOU EXPECT IT TO DO IN THIS WEATHER? -BOIL?

SKATING, LAME BRAIN! -SKATING!
SAY! YOU'RE RIGHT!

DID YOU CHECK WITH VERONICA?
I'M DOING IT NOW!

OH, BOY! -SKATING!
I'LL MEET YOU AT THE POND!
ROGER!

ER--WHAT DOES VERONICA SAY ABOUT IT?
2

JUST WHAT DO YOU MEAN BY THAT?
MAYBE SHE'LL WANT YOU TO DO SOMETHING ELSE!

WHEN I SEE HER I'LL **ASK** HER!
S-SURE, ARCH!

JEEPERS! YOU'D THINK I COULDN'T MAKE A MOVE WITHOUT RONNIE'S OKAY!
THE CHOK LIT SHOP
POP TATE-PROP.

HI, POP! SEEN MY GIRL?
NO, ARCHIE! -WHAT'S UP?

THE POND'S FROZEN!
WE'RE ALL GOING **SKATING**!
THAT'S NICE!

I'LL HAVE PLENTY OF HOT CHOCOLATE READY!
ENJOY YOURSELF!
THANKS, POP!

THAT IS- IF VERONICA SAYS IT'S ALL RIGHT FOR YOU TO GO!

SLAM!
F'GOODNESS SAKES! WHAT'S WRONG WITH **HIM**?

HENPECKED! JUST PLAIN OL' **HENPECKED!**

"DID YOU CHECK WITH VERONICA?"
"WHAT DOES VERONICA SAY?"

"IF VERONICA SAYS IT'S ALL RIGHT!"
WHAT AM I? A MAN OR A MOUSE?

I'M A **MAN!** **THAT'S** WHAT I AM!
THUMP THUMP!

I'M NOT GOING TO **ASK** HER IF **SHE** WANTS TO GO **SKATING!**

-I'M GOING TO **TELL** HER THAT **I'M** GOING!

WHAM! BANG! BAM!

COULD I LEND YOU A HAMMER? - I'D HATE TO SEE YOU BRUISE YOUR KNUCKLES!
MR. LODGE! I'D LIKE TO SEE YOUR DAUGHTER!

I'M AFRAID YOU CAN'T SEE VERONICA AT THIS MOMENT!
AND WHY NOT?

MOSTLY BECAUSE SHE ISN'T AT HOME!
OH!

IN THAT CASE, WILL YOU INFORM HER THAT I AM SKATING AT THE POND WHETHER SHE LIKES IT OR NOT?
GLADLY!

OH, ARCHIE! PERHAPS YOU'D PREFER TO TELL HER YOURSELF!

-SHE'S SKATING AT THE POND!
SLAM!

BOY, I REALLY MADE A FOOL OF MYSELF!

THERE'S THE GANG!
HI, ARCH!
ARCHIE! COME ON OVER!

NO, ARCHIEKINS! -NO SKATING!
COME AND GET WARM!
JUST AS SOON AS I DO A FEW TURNS!

I SAID I'M GOING SKATING AND THAT'S WHAT I'M GOING TO DO!
OH, DON'T BE SO THICK!

I AM NOT "THICK"!
I JUST DON'T LIKE BEING HENPECKED!

HAVE IT YOUR WAY, ARCHIEKINS! -YOU ARE NOT THICK!
6

---BUT NEITHER IS THE ICE!
THE END

Archie in "SNOW JOB"

Gladir / T. Kennedy / Selig / Yoshida / Grossman

GOOD THINKING, FRED! DURING THE LAST SNOW STORM WE RAN OUT OF MILK AND BREAD!
BLECH!!
REMIND ME NEVER TO EAT CEREAL AND SODA POP EVER AGAIN!
HUMPH! FOR LUNCH I'M HAVING A BALONEY ON GRAHAM CRACKER SANDWICH!

"AND IT TOOK HOURS TO SHOVEL THE WALK BECAUSE THE SNOW BLOWER NEEDED A NEW SPARK PLUG!"
OOF!!

"AND WE HAD NO ROCK SALT TO MELT THE ICE!"

BUT NOT THIS TIME! COME ON ARCHIE... WE'RE GOING SHOPPING!
I'M RIGHT BEHIND YOU, POP!

WHEN YOU COME BACK BRING IN SOME EXTRA FIREWOOD!
OKEY-DOKEY, MOM!

AT THE GROCERY STORE...
LOOK, POP! THEY'RE ALMOST OUT OF BREAD!
HURRY!! GRAB THAT LAST LOAF!
SALE

HEY, KID! HAND THAT OVER!
SORRY, MISTER! I WAS HERE FIRST! YO, POP! CATCH!
BLUNDER BREAD

NICE PASS, SON! RIGHT IN THE OL' BREADBASKET!

YOU SURE HAVE SOFT HANDS, POP! THE LOAF ISN'T CRUSHED ONE BIT!
THAT'S BECAUSE I USED TO BE A WIDE RECEIVER!
HUMPH! HE'S STILL WIDE!

MILK, BREAD, CANNED GOODS... HOW ABOUT SOME BEEF JERKY?
GOODNESS! DOESN'T THAT MAN KNOW IT'S NOT NICE TO CALL PEOPLE NAMES?

LATER...
THE GROCERIES ARE ALL PACKED! LET'S HEAD TO THE HARDWARE STORE!
HERB'S HARDWARE
OKAY, POP!
HA! HA! IT LOOKS LIKE AN ARMY OF SNOW SHOVELERS MARCHING OFF TO BATTLE!
SHOVELS 1/2 OFF
IT IS A WAR, SON... AND MOTHER NATURE STARTED IT! SO LET'S GET READY TO FIGHT BACK!
AYE, AYE, CAPTAIN!

I'LL GET ROCK SALT! YOU PICK OUT A SHOVEL!
A NEW SHOVEL? YES, SIR! I DIG!
SALE
ROCK SALT

IN A WHILE...
WHEN WE GET HOME I'LL DOUBLE CHECK THE SNOWBLOWER TO MAKE SURE IT'S IN PERFECT ORDER!
I'LL PUT NEW BATTERIES IN ALL OF THE FLASH-LIGHTS!

AT HOME...
WELL, MARY, WE'RE READY FOR THE WORST!
I GOT OUT YOUR BOOTS AND COLD WEATHER GEAR, FRED!
BEEF JERKY

WHEN THAT BLIZZARD HITS TOMORROW, THE ANDREWS CLAN WILL BE PREPARED!
YEAH! BRING IT ON, MOTHER NATURE! BRING IT ON!

THE NEXT DAY...
SO, POP, WHEN DO YOU THINK IT'LL START TO SNOW?
ANYTIME NOW! THE TEMPERATURE IS DROPPING!

(GULP!) HEY, GUYS! I HAVE GOOD NEWS AND BAD NEWS!

ACCORDING TO THE LATEST WEATHER UPDATE THAT SNOW STORM IS NOW GOING TO MISS US COMPLETELY!
UGH!!
END

Script & Pencils: Joe Edwards / Inks: Rudy Lapick / Letters: Bill Yoshida / Colors: Barry Grossman

AT HOME...
WELL, MARY, WE'RE READY FOR THE WORST!
I GOT OUT YOUR BOOTS AND COLD WEATHER GEAR, FRED!
BEEF JERKY

WHEN THAT BLIZZARD HITS TOMORROW, THE ANDREWS CLAN WILL BE PREPARED!
YEAH! BRING IT ON, MOTHER NATURE! BRING IT ON!

THE NEXT DAY...
SO, POP, WHEN DO YOU THINK IT'LL START TO SNOW?
ANYTIME NOW! THE TEMPERATURE IS DROPPING!

(GULP!) HEY, GUYS! I HAVE GOOD NEWS AND BAD NEWS!

ACCORDING TO THE LATEST WEATHER UPDATE THAT SNOW STORM IS NOW GOING TO MISS US COMPLETELY!
UGH!!
END

Script & Pencils: Joe Edwards / Inks: Rudy Lapick / Letters: Bill Yoshida / Colors: Barry Grossman

DO YOU REMEMBER THE SQUEAK I ASKED YOU TO FIX, MR. SVENSON?
YES, MR. VEDDERBEE... VHY?

WELL, THE SQUEAK IS BACK... AGAIN!
...AND I DON'T THINK YOU REPLACED THE...
SQUEEK

... WEAK SPRING...

CRASH

VHY NOT GET A NEW CHAIR?

WHAT? WHY SPEND THE TAXPAYER'S MONEY WHEN THIS CHAIR CAN STILL BE REPAIRED?

HURRY BACK WITH IT! THE SUPERINTENDENT IS COMING TODAY FOR AN INSPECTION!
SQUEAK

HUMPH! SVENSON FIX THIS... FIX THAT... PATCH THIS UP... THEY TINK I'M A MIRACLE VORKER BY YIMMINY!
STORE ROOM

I GO CHECK ALL OLD BROKEN CHAIRS IN BASEMENT FOR SPRING!

MMM... THIS SPRING IS MUCH VORSE THAN THE ONE ON VEDDERBEE'S CHAIR!

SVENSON, HOW IS MY CHAIR COMING ALONG?

NOT TOO GOOD! I CAN'T FIND ONE GOOD SPRING FROM OLD CHAIRS!

WELL, USE YOUR INGENUITY! AND HURRY! THE SUPERINTENDENT IS ON HIS WAY OVER!

I GOT GOOD INGENUITY IDEA VERE TO FIND A STRONG SPRING EVEN VEDDERBEE VILL LIKE!

I BETCHA FIND ONE IN HERE, BY YIMMINY!
AUTO JUNKYARD

AS SUPERINTENDENT OF SCHOOLS, I MUST CONGRATULATE YOU ON THE VARIOUS MONEY SAVING CUTS YOU'VE MADE IN RIVERDALE HIGH!

THANK YOU! BUT I'M JUST TRYING TO DO MY JOB! AHEM!

MR. VEDDERBEE, I FIXED YOUR CHAIR AND PUT IT IN YOUR OFFICE!
GREAT!

THIS GIVES ME AN OPPORTUNITY TO SHOW YOU ANOTHER MONEY SAVING EXAMPLE!

GOOD! I WOULD LIKE A PLACE TO WRITE UP MY REPORT! A MOST FAVORABLE ONE I MIGHT ADD!
MY OFFICE AND DESK IS AT YOUR DISPOSAL!
HERE, BE THE FIRST TO TEST... HEH! HEH!... THE REPAIRED CHAIR!
SPRING
DID YOU SEE SVENSON ANYWHERE?!
YES! HE SAID HE'S TAKING HIS VACATION IMMEDIATELY AND WON'T BE BACK TILL NEXT SPRING!
CUSTODIAN
OUT!
END.

HI, I'M OLD MAN WINTER ON MY SEASONAL CHECK UP OF RIVERDALE HIGH! IT'S THAT TIME WHEN SNOW FLIES AND SO DO THE TEMPERS!
ARCHIE! I WAITED ALL NIGHT FOR YOU TO CALL ME...
AW! KNOCK IT OFF, VERONICA!
HOLD IT, ARCHIE! YOU CAN'T TALK TO VERONICA THAT WAY!
Script & Pencils: Joe Edwards / Inks: Rudy Lapick / Letters: Bill Yoshida
BUTT OUT, BETTY!!!
?
Archie & the gang
WINTERRUPTIONS!
1

MMM... IT LOOKS LIKE SOMETHING IS ABOUT TO ERUPT IN MISS BEAZLY'S LUNCHROOM!
HEY! THAT'S THE LAST PUDDING! I WANT IT, JUG!
OKAY, MOOSE! I'LL TOSS YOU FOR IT!
OKAY! I GOT A COIN!
NO, RAISIN BRAIN! I MEAN I'M GOING TO TOSS YOU ON YOUR EAR!
HOLD IT! I WON'T HAVE ANY VIOLENCE IN MY LUNCHROOM OR I'LL BANG YOUR HEADS TOGETHER!!!
2

HMMM... THE WINTER DOLDRUMS ARE GETTING TO THE STUDENTS! I WONDER HOW THE TEACHERS ARE DOING?
HOW CAN I TEACH MY STUDENTS WITH THAT RACKET YOUR SCHOOL BAND IS MAKING?
YOU'RE TEACHING? HA!
AT LEAST I'M KEEPING THEM AWAKE!
LISTEN HERE, YOU DISCORD CHAMP!
HEY! KEEP IT DOWN TO A ROAR!
YOU STAY OUT OF THIS, BIG NOSE!
OH YEAH!
YEAH! WAIT'LL THE PRINCIPAL HEARS ABOUT THIS!
I HEARD IT...
...AND SO DID THE WHOLE SCHOOL!
3

I KNOW IT'S THE WINTER DOLDRUMS, BUT CUT IT OUT!
BACK IN SVEDEN VE HAVE A WAY...
HOW CAN I STOP EVERYBODY FROM JUMPING ON EVERYBODY ELSE?
YOU TAKE THE JUMPING OUT BY DRAINING THE ENERGY!
VHY NOT HAVE WHOLE SCHOOL IN A BIG SNOWBALL FIGHT LIKE IN SVEDEN?
MMM?
IT MIGHT JUST WORK!
I'LL TRY IT!
4

EVERYBODY IS INVITED TO A SNOWBALL FIGHT AFTER SCHOOL TODAY ON THE FRONT LAWN!
WOW!
WHAT A SMASHING IDEA!
BOY! THIS SURE LOOSENS UP THE TENSIONS!
SPLAT
WELL, WELL! THINGS ARE PICKING UP!
SVENSON WAS RIGHT! THEY'RE HAVING FUN! I'LL JOIN THEM!
SPLAT

HI! CAN I JOIN YOU?

YOU BET, MR. WEATHERBEE!

SPLAT!
ZIP!
SPLAT!
SPLAT!
ZIP!
SPLAT!
ZIP!

ACHOO!! MR. SVENSON! GET RID OF THAT SNOW IMMEDIATELY --DOWN TO EVERY LAST SNOWFLAKE!!

Y-YES, MR. VEDDERBEE! MAYBE IDEA VORKS BETTER IN SVEDEN!

ONE THING YOU CAN COUNT ON - I'LL BE BACK NEXT YEAR!
The End

Archie in "A CHIP OFF THE OLD BLOCK"

Script & Pencils: Dick Malmgren / Letters: Bill Yoshida / Colors: Barry Grossman

I THINK IT'S SUPER THAT YOU SPEND SO MUCH TIME TEACHING ME TO SKI! YOU HAVE SUCH PATIENCE!
IT'S MY PLEASURE!

ROME WASN'T BUILT IN A DAY, MY SWEET!
COULD YOU SPEED IT UP, REG? I'D LIKE SOME INSTRUCTIONS MYSELF!

OH, I DON'T THINK I'LL EVER GET THE HANG OF THIS, REG!
SURE YOU WILL!

JUST BE PATIENT, DOLL! WE'LL KEEP AT IT UNTIL YOU LEARN, EVEN IF IT TAKES ALL WINTER!
GIGGLE!

COME ON, REG! YOU'RE JUST STALLING TIME WITH RONNIE BECAUSE IT'S THE ONLY WAY YOU EVER GET TO HOLD HER IN YOUR ARMS!

OKAY! ARE YOU READY TO SPRING FOR SOME LESSONS?
THAT DEPENDS ON HOW MUCH!

25 BUCKS FOR THE SUREFIRE GUARANTEED MANTLE METHOD!
25 BUCKS?

YOU'RE JOKING! I'M NOT SPENDING THAT KIND OF BREAD FOR YOUR LESSONS! JUST GIVE ME 5 BUCKS WORTH AND I'LL TAKE IT FROM THERE!

OKAY! I'LL GIVE YOU 5 BUCKS WORTH! LET'S GET OVER ON THE SLOPES!
ONE LESSON IS ALL I'LL EVER NEED!

OKAY, NOW, KNEES FLEXED, SHOULDERS BACK!
I ALREADY KNOW THAT!

SHOW ME SOMETHING I NEED TO KNOW!
I'M TRYING TO SHOW YOU THE PROPER STANCE!

YOU MEAN YOU RIP THE GIRLS OFF 25 BUCKS FOR THIS DRIVEL? HEE! HEE!

HA! HA! HEE! WHY SHOULD ANY-ONE PAY YOU THAT MUCH MONEY?--- HEE! HEE! I MEAN WHAT FOR?

PERSONALIZED ATTENTION!!

HEY!

GEEP!

WHOOOA!
ZOOM!

FUMP!

THUNK!

AUGGGH!

SPLASH!

ON SECOND THOUGHT, I THINK I'LL TAKE THE FULL 25 DOLLAR MANTLE METHOD!
SMART MOVE!
CHIP!
CHIP!
CHIP!
END

Script: Mike Pellowski / Pencils: Doug Crane / Inks: Rudy Lapick / Letters: Rod Ollerenshaw / Colors: Barry Grossman

ENCLOSED IN A FORTUNE IN FURS, THIS EXQUISITE BODY IS TOASTY WARM!!
YOU KEEP THAT IN YOUR SCHOOL LOCKER, RON?

OF COURSE NOT, SILLY! I CALLED HOME, AND OUR CHAUFFEUR, JASON, DELIVERED IT!!
OH, FOR THE LIFE OF AN HEIRESS!

THEY OUGHT TO SEND US HOME! THIS PLACE IS UNHEALTHY!
THE HEAT'S BEEN OFF A LONG TIME!!

I'M GOING DOWN TO THE BASEMENT AND SEE HOW SVENSON IS DOING!
GOOD IDEA!!
CAUTION STAIRS ↓

SO, WHAT'S THE GOOD WORD, MR. SVENSON?
ISS NO GOOT VORD!!

FURNACE NO PUSH-UM-UP HEAT! SCHOOL ISS COLD LIKE FEETS OF A VELL DIGGER!!

MR. SVENSON! HAVING ANY LUCK WITH OUR RECALCITRANT FURNACE?
NO, MISTER VEDDERBEE!

... AN' DIS VON AREN'T VORKING EITHER!!

I CALL REPAIRMAN... HE PROMISE COME NEXT WEEK...

...MAYBE!
EGAD!!

THIS IS INTOLERABLE! THE BOARD OF HEALTH COULD CLOSE US DOWN!!
SOME GOOD MAY COME OF THIS YET!!

BUT, SERIOUSLY, WOULD YOU LIKE ME TO LOOK AT IT?
JUST AS SERIOUSLY, NO!!

I HAVE A KNACK! I'VE HAD SOME SUCCESS WITH MECHANICAL THINGS!

...VY NOT?!! GIFF BOY A CHANCE! SVENSON RUN OUT OF IDEAS!
NONSENSE!

JUGHEAD'S WORLD OF EXPERTISE BEGINS AND ENDS WITH FOOD!
NOT TRUE, SIR!

I FIXED OUR TV SET AND OUR DISHWASHER LAST WEEK WITH MY SPECIAL TOUCH!
SO TOUCH! GET US SOME *HEAT*!!

HEEEEE...YAH!
CHUNK!
CLANG!

GLIP!
CLUP!
KOFF!
WHEEEEEZZ!
BIP!
BIP!
BANG!

BY GAR! THE HEAT!! SHE COME ON!!

AN HOUR LATER...
THE HEAT--SHE COME ON TOO MUCH! NOW THE FURNACE NOT TURN OFF!!
CLANG!
HISSSSS!
HISSS!

HEY! THE HEAT'S UP!!
--MORE THAN WE NEED!!
JUGHEAD TURNED IT ON!!

MY! IT'S HOT IN HERE! HOW COME JUGHEAD IS GETTING THE HERO TREATMENT, CHIEF?
I HAVE NO IDEA! LET'S SEE!

GOOD GRIEF! --FROM ONE EXTREME TO THE OTHER!!
WAY TO GO, JUG!!
JUGHEAD! HE'S OUR MAN!!
THE END.

Script: George Gladir / Pencils: Stan Goldberg / Inks: Rudy Lapick / Letters: Bill Yoshida / Colors: Barry Grossman

WE NEED A BOLD, BRIGHT AND DYNAMIC PERSON!

SOMEONE WHO'S NOT AFRAID TO GO OUT THERE AND GET THE REAL STORY!

SOMEONE WHO INSTINCTIVELY KNOWS HOW TO BE IN THE RIGHT PLACE AT THE RIGHT TIME!

AND MR. WEATHERBEE TELLS ME YOU'RE THE ONE FOR THE JOB!
WOW!

YOU'LL REPORT TO ME AT ACTION NEWS AT 5:30!
I'LL BE THERE!
R

NOW TAKE THIS CAMERA AND "MAKE MAGIC"!
THANKS FOR THIS OPPORTUNITY!
ACTION NEWS

I'LL MAKE YOU PROUD YOU CHOSE ME, MR. WEATHERBEE!
I'M PROUD ALREADY!

WITH ARCHIE OUT OF MY HAIR, NOW I CAN GET MY WORK DONE!

AND SOON...
HMMM... A GOOD REPORTER HAS TO BE AT THE RIGHT PLACE AT THE RIGHT...
CHIRP
CHIRP
CHIRP
RIVERDALE HIGH SCHOOL

...TIME!
THAT LOOKS LIKE THE RARE BIRD THAT ESCAPED FROM THE ZOO!
CHIRP
CHIRP
ACTION NEWS TV

WOW! EVERYONE HAS BEEN LOOKING ALL OVER FOR THAT BIRD!
ACTION NEWS TV

TALK ABOUT TIM...
ACTION NEWS
RCHIE

...ING!
HEY! WHERE'D IT GO?

DARN! I MISSED IT!
NEWS
TV

I GUESS A GOOD REPORTER HAS TO BE QUICK, TOO!

WOW! THAT'S INCREDIBLE!
ACTION NEWS

I'VE NEVER SEEN ANYONE JUMP AND TWIRL AT THE SAME TIME!
RCHIE

THIS WILL BE PERFECT FOR THE YOUTH MARKET!
DING DONG!
ACTION NEWS TV
ICE CREAM
27 FLAVORS

YAY!
ICE CREAM!
HOORAY FOR ICE CREAM!

GEEZ! I ONLY GOT ABOUT 2 SECONDS!
HI, ARCHIE!

OH, HI, VERONICA!
WHY ARE YOU SO BUMMED OUT?

MR. WEATHERBEE CHOSE ME TO BE A TV REPORTER, BUT SO FAR I'VE GOT NOTHING TO REPORT!
TV?

TA-DAH! A STAR IS BORN!
?

ROLL TAPE, ARCHIE!
ER...SURE, RON!

HELLO! I AM VERONICA LODGE AND WELCOME TO SHOP TALK!

TODAY I BOUGHT A NEW PAIR OF SHOES...

...AND THEN I BOUGHT A DRESS, A SKIRT AND A NEW HAT!
RONNIE SURE LOOKS GREAT ON CAMERA!
6

BUT THIS ISN'T
EXACTLY NEWSWORTHY!

AREN'T I
AWESOME?
ER... THANKS, RON...
I THINK I GOT ALL
I NEED!

I'M GLAD I COULD
HELP, ARCHIE!

BUT WHEN YOU WANT
SHOP TALK PART II, YOU'LL
HAVE TO TALK TO MY
AGENT!
!

GEEZ... FINDING
A **GOOD** STORY IS A
LOT MORE DIFFICULT
THAN I THOUGHT
IT WOULD BE!
LODGE
ACTION NEWS
TV
TO BE
CONTINUED

MAYBE I DON'T HAVE WHAT IT TAKES TO BE A REPORTER!
BANK OF RIVERDALE
ACTION NEWS TV
2 JAIL
Archie
in "ACE REPORTER"
PART 2

AND IT'S ALMOST 5:30!

I BETTER GET THIS CAMERA BACK TO LIZA!
ZOOM!
ACTION NEWS

AND SOON...
A BAKE SALE?!
CHANGING THE SPEED LIMIT TO 25?
ACTION NEWS
TV STUDIO
COLA

IS THAT ALL THE NEWS YOU CAN COME UP WITH?

SORRY, LIZA!
THERE'S NOT MUCH NEWS HAPPENING AROUND TOWN!
THEN MAKE NEWS!

I NEED AN ACTION STORY AND IT CAN'T BE ABOUT CRUMMY COOKIES!
RIGHT AWAY, LIZA!
ACTION NEWS
ACTION NEWS TV

HELLO, ARCHIE! LET ME SEE WHAT YOU'VE GOT!
UH-OH!

IT'S REALLY *NOTHING*!
ACTION NEWS

BUT *COOKIES* CAN BE EXCITING IF ER... THEY TASTE GOOD!
CLICK

BLUE SKY?!

2 SECONDS OF JUMP ROPE WITH A BATON?!
MR. WEATHERBEE WILL BE SO DISAPPOINTED IN ME!
ACTION NEWS

AREN'T I AWESOME?
MORE LIKE BOR-ING!
OLA

I FEEL LIKE SUCH A FAILURE!

DYNAMITE!
CLICK!

ARCHIE! YOU CALL THIS NOTHING?
ARCHIE

YOU'RE CERTAINLY NOT AFRAID TO GO OUT THERE AND GET THE REAL STORY!
GEEZ... I DIDN'T KNOW "SHOPTALK...WITH VERONICA" COULD BE SO THRILLING!
ACTION
ACTION NEWS TV
ACTION NEWS TV

WE GOT OUR *LEAD* STORY!
MAYBE IT'S A GIRL THING!
ACTION NEWS
ARCH

GEE... I BETTER CALL RONNIE'S AGENT RIGHT AWAY FOR PART II!

3, 2, 1, *ACTION!*
GOOD EVENING! I'M CONNIE LUNG AND WELCOME TO ACTION NEWS!
ACTION NEWS TV

TONIGHT WE HAVE AN *EXCLUSIVE* ON THE BRAZEN BANK ROBBERY IN OUR USUALLY QUIET TOWN!

OUR ACE REPORTER *ARCHIE ANDREWS* WAS ON THE SCENE!
HE WAS?
ACTION NEWS
ARCHIE

ER... I WAS?
HE BRAVELY CAUGHT THE ROBBERS ON TAPE AS THEY WERE MAKING THEIR GETAWAY!

WITH THIS INCRIMINATING FOOTAGE, THE POLICE SHOULD HAVE NO PROBLEM CATCHING THE BAD GUYS!
2 JAIL

THIS IS CONNIE LUNG FROM ACTION NEWS WISHING YOU A GOOD EVENING!

THE NEXT DAY...
ARCHIE! MY HERO!
CONGRATULATIONS, MY BOY! I'M SO PROUD OF YOU!
THANK YOU, MR. WEATHERBEE!
GOOD SHOW, ARCH!

BUT TELL ME, ARCHIE, HOW DID YOU GET THAT STORY?
BEING A GOOD REPORTER IS ALL ABOUT BEING IN THE RIGHT PLACE AT THE RIGHT TIME!
AND FORGETTING TO TURN OFF YOUR CAMERA!
END

Archie IN CANDID COMMENT

Script: Frank Doyle / Art: Chic Stone / Letters: Bill Yoshida / Colors: Barry Grossman

HE'S GOT **HIMSELF**! THAT'S ALL SOME PEOPLE WANT!
AND THAT'S WHAT HE **DESERVES**!

HE DOESN'T KNOW WHAT HE'S BEEN MISSING! IT'S NOT RIGHT TO BE ALONE ALL THE TIME!

COME, BUDDY! YOU ARE GOING TO JOIN THE LAND OF THE LIVING!
LEGGO!

PEOPLE WHO NEED PEOPLE ARE THE LUCKIEST PEOPLE---
IN THE PIG'S EYE! THEY JUST CAN'T MAKE IT ON THEIR OWN!

I'M GOING TO INTRODUCE YOU TO THE JOYS OF FRIENDSHIP AND MINGLING AND ALL THAT GOOD STUFF!
YOU **CATCH** THINGS FROM PEOPLE! THEY'RE CONTAGIOUS-- FULL OF COLDS AND SNIFFLES AND-- AND BAD BREATH!
2

YOU'RE A LONELY MAN! YOU NEED COMPANIONSHIP!
I NEED TO STOP BEING MANHANDLED!

EVERYBODY WHO'S ANYBODY HANGS OUT HERE! COME ON! YOU DON'T KNOW WHAT YOU'RE MISSING!
THE HANGOUT
THE HANGOUT

YIPE! IT'S DANCING--- WITH GIRLS--- WITH EAR-BREAKING MUSIC! IT'S BEDLAM!!
YEAH! ISN'T IT GREAT?

HEY, ARCHIE BABY! YOU AND YOUR FRIEND JUMP IN! THE WATER'S FINE!
HEY! NO---

AWK!

EEEYAHOO! LET IT ALL HANG OUT, MAN!
WHOOPS!

ACK! I'LL BE TRAMPLED TO DEATH!
WHUMP!

SAY, WELCOME, STRANGER!

C-COULD YOU THROW ME TOWARD AN EXIT?

DIDN'T I TELL YOU IT'D BE FUN, JUG?
W-WHAT OTHER LIES DID YOU TELL ME?
ZOOM!

ARCH! THEY'RE GANGING UP ON ME!

THAT'S BECAUSE YOU'RE A NEW MAN, JUG! IT'S A KIND OF WELCOME! LIKE AN INITIATION!
PASS HIM ON!

HE'S LIGHT ON HIS FEET!
I HAVEN'T BEEN ON MY FEET SINCE I GOT HERE!

HE'S SLIPPERY, TOO! HOLD IT, JACKSON !!!---
EEP!

JUGHEAD ISLAND, BUDDY! AND THE BEACHES ARE MINED! SO BUG OFF!!
JUGHEAD ISLAND
NO TRESPASSING
END

"REMOTELY CONTROLLED"

Gladir / Goldberg / Milgrom / Yoshida / Grossman

LET ME TRY IT!
NO WAY! GO GET YOUR OWN!
HEY, BOYS! REMEMBER US?
SAVE YOUR BREATH, BETTY!
VIDEOLAND
SPOOK
TOP VIDEOS

BOYS! GIVE 'EM A NEW TOY AND THEY GO APE!
YEAH, THEY NEVER GROW UP!

OKAY, I'LL GET ONE OF MY OWN AND I'LL RACE YOU!
YOU'RE ON!

HEY, WHATCHA GOT, ARCH?
A REMOTE-CONTROL CAR! I'M GONNA RACE REGGIE!
HOBBY Shop

HEY-THAT'S A COOL IDEA! LET'S ALL GET ONE AND HAVE A RALLY AFTER SCHOOL!
DUH-H... YEAH!

LATER:
WHATCHA GOT IN THE BOX, JUG?
A REMOTE-CONTROL CAR! WANT TO SEE?

WHOOPS! TOO MUCH SPEED!
YIPE!
CLUNK!

I'M CONFISCATING THIS AND I'LL TAKE THAT REMOTE-CONTROL UNIT TOO, JUGHEAD!

YOU AND I HAVE A DATE IN THE PRINCIPAL'S OFFICE AFTER SCHOOL!

I CAN'T RACE TODAY, ARCH! MR. FLUTESNOOT REPORTED MY CAR AND I GOTTA SEE THE PRINCIPAL!
ME TOO, JUG! MISS HAGGLY GOT MINE!
TELL ME ABOUT IT! MISS GRUNDY TOOK MINE!
DUH-H... YEAH, AND MR. WEATHERBEE CAUGHT ME RACING MINE IN THE HALL!..
17

MAYBE IF WE APOLOGIZE TO MR. WEATHER-BEE AND APPEAL TO HIS BETTER NATURE, HE MIGHT GIVE US OUR CARS BACK!
MR. WEATHERBEE PRINCIPAL
MOOSE

IT'S A BIZARRE IDEA, BUT IT MIGHT JUST WORK!

MR. WEATHERBEE, THE GUYS AND I ARE SORRY FOR THE TROUBLE WE CAUSED...

AND IF YOU'LL GIVE US BACK OUR CARS, WE'LL NEVER DO IT AGAIN AND WE'LL BE WILLING TO DO ANYTHING TO MAKE UP FOR IT!
I'M SORRY, ARCHIE, BUT THE TEACHERS AND I AGREE...

...THAT YOU BOYS MUST BE TAUGHT A LESSON! SO THE CARS WILL REMAIN IN MY DESK THIS WEEKEND!
17

AND THEY WILL BE RETURNED TO YOU ON MONDAY AFTER SCHOOL!
BUT, SIR, WE WERE GOING TO RACE THEM TODAY!

YES, I KNOW, BUT MAYBE THIS WILL HELP YOU REMEMBER THAT SCHOOL IS NO PLACE FOR THIS SORT OF THING!

I GUESS WE'LL HAVE TO POSTPONE OUR "RALLY!"
WHAT A ROTTEN BREAK!

ARE THEY GONE?
THEY JUST LEFT THE PARKING LOT IN ARCHIE'S CAR!

I'VE BEEN WAITING ALL DAY FOR THIS!
GYM

GIVE IT UP, SIR! I'VE GOT THIS RACE IN THE BAG!
EAT MY DUST, FLUTESNOOT!
COME ON, SILVER RACER!
PUT THE HAMMER DOWN, RED PHANTOM!
END.

Archie "TEACH ME TONIGHT"

Script: Frank Doyle / Pencils: Dan DeCarlo Jr. / Inks: Jimmy DeCarlo / Letters: Bill Yoshida / Colors: Barry Grossman

I SAID IT IN ENGLISH, 'CAUSE YOU WOULDN'T UNDERSTAND IT IN FRENCH!
NO WEEKNIGHTS OUT UNTIL YOUR MARKS COME UP!
ACK!

M-MY SOCIAL LIFE!! I'LL BE RUINED!! POP! THAT'S NOT FAIR!!

TUT, TUT! DO NOT FRET, BELOVED FIRSTBORN!
"FAIR" IS DECIDED BY FATHERS--- NOT SONS!
EEP!

NEXT DAY-
NOT OUT AT ALL DURING THE WEEK?
THAT'S INHUMAN!
WHAT ARE YOU GOING TO DO?

FACE IT, ARCHIE! CRACK THE BOOKS AND GET THOSE FRENCH MARKS UP! IT'S THE ONLY WAY TO BECOME A FREE SOUL AGAIN!
SIGH! THAT'S EASY FOR YOU TO SAY!

BUT I'LL NEVER BE ABLE TO CONCENTRATE WHEN I'M THINKING OF YOU GUYS OUT THERE, LIVING THE GOOD LIFE!
IF I MIGHT MAKE A SUGGESTION?
2

HOW ABOUT TAPES, INSTEAD OF BOOKS?
YOU MIGHT FIND IT EASIER!
"TAPES"?

UNDER YOUR PILLOW - WHILE YOU'RE SLEEPING! LEARNING TAPES!
YOU CAN BUY THEM TO LEARN ANY LANGUAGE!
SON OF A GUN! I LIKE IT!

HMPH! YOU'LL FIND THEM VERY EXPENSIVE! I CAN DO BETTER! - AND AT NO COST TO YOU!
HOW?

VIDEO TAPES! I CAN MAKE THEM AT HOME FOR YOU!
LEARNING BY TV IS THE EASIEST WAY TO LEARN!

HEY, WOW! THAT'D BE GREAT!
I'LL START ON THEM RIGHT AWAY!
AND I HAVE A DELIGHTFUL FRENCH ACCENT!

GOLLY! YOU, TEACHING ME FRENCH! RIGHT ON MY OWN TV SET!
-AND NO COMMERCIALS!
3

WEEKS GO BY–
SOMETHING'S WRONG, MARY! HE HASN'T COMPLAINED ONCE ABOUT STAYING HOME NIGHTS!
HE'S A GOOD BOY, FRED!

AHA! I THOUGHT AS MUCH! HE'S SMUGGLED A TV SET INTO HIS ROOM!
NOW, FRED ---!

AHA! CAUGHT IN THE ACT!!
MAIS OUI, MON PAPA! CAUGHT IN THE ACT OF STUDYING FRENCH!
RIVERD

HOMEMADE VIDEO TAPES! LOOK! VERONICA LOANED ME THE WHOLE SETUP!

LE LIVRE --- THE BOOK!

LA TÊTE! - THE HEAD!

LA BOUCHE --- THE MOUTH!
WOW! WHAT A BOUCHE IT IS!

LE CIL --- THE EYELASH!
HOO HOO HOOO.!!
WINK

MARY! COME UP HERE!! ON THE DOUBLE!!

I WANT YOU TO SEE THIS.!! YOU'VE GOT TO SEE IT TO BELIEVE IT!
SOMETHING WRONG, FRED?

I ORDER HIM TO STAY HOME AND STUDY, AND LOOK WHAT HE COMES UP WITH!
LES JAMBES --- THE LEGS!

SHE'S---SHE'S FLIRTING WITH HIM IN A FOREIGN LANGUAGE!
MAGNIFIQUE!

GIGGLE! I THINK IT'S BOTH CUTE AND CLEVER!
WHAT?

I GOT A CALL FROM HIS FRENCH TEACHER TODAY!
THEY HAD A TEST!
AND?

ARCHIE GOT THE HIGHEST MARK IN THE CLASS!
H-HE DID?

WHO SAYS TV ISN'T EDUCATIONAL?
RON IS WORKING ON SOME SPANISH TAPES NOW!
EEP!
LE PIED - THE FOOT!
MAN! I CAN HARDLY WAIT!
END

Archie
HENRY SCARPELLI
CRAIG BOLDMAN
MY HOMEWORK IS CALLING TO ME...

I THINK I'LL ANSWER LATER!

DOING ANYTHING? YOU CAN HELP ME MOVE SOME BRICKS!
WELL, UH...
I'VE GOT SOME HOMEWORK!
WHEN YOU'RE DONE, LET ME KNOW!

SO...
HOW'S IT COMING?
IT'S A BIG STACK, DAD!

AND...
SOON?
THEY KEEP US SWAMPED, DAD!

WHAT'S THIS? YOU'RE TRYING TO GET ARCHIE TO MOVE SOME BRICKS?
NO...

...TO DO HIS HOMEWORK!

Archie

INDECISION REVISION

Script: George Gladir / Pencils: Stan Goldberg / Inks: Mike Esposito / Letters: Bill Yoshida / Colors: Barry Grossman

DR. DUGGY WUGGY, I HAVE NO OBJECTION TO YOUR DISPLAYING YOUR MEDICAL DEGREES IN OUR HOSPITAL!

BUT DID YOU ALSO HAVE TO PUT UP YOUR KINDER-GARTEN DIPLOMA?
DUGGY WUGGY
KINDERGARTEN

BUT KINDERGARTEN IS WHERE MY SURGICAL CAREER WAS FIRST LAUNCHED!
HOW SO?

ALL THE GIRLS IN MY CLASS SAID I WAS QUITE AN OPERATOR!

SPEAKING OF GIRLS - YOUR FRIENDS BETTINA AND COBINA DROPPED BY TO SAY HELLO!
HI, DUGGY!

OH, DOCTOR! I SCRATCHED MY FINGER ON MY LOCKER! KISS IT, AND MAKE IT BETTER!
2

THANK YOU! MY FINGER IS NOW CURED!
KISS!

I ALSO HURT MYSELF, DR. DUGGY!
AND WHERE IS YOUR BOO-BOO, BETTINA?

YOU CAN'T SEE THE SCRATCH, BUT IT'S RIGHT HERE ON MY LIP!

KISS!
SOME GIRLS JUST DON'T PLAY FAIR!

I'M THE ONE WHO REALLY LAUNCHED DR. DUGGY'S CAREER IN MEDICINE!
YOU DID?

WHEN WE WERE ONLY FIVE, WE PLAYED DOCTOR AND NURSE WITH MY BEN AND BERTHA DOLLS!
SEEMS LIKE ALMOST YESTERDAY ...AND IT WAS!
3

MY DEAR, I'LL HAVE YOU KNOW I WAS DR. DUGGY WUGGY'S *VERY FIRST* PATIENT!
YOU?!

SIGH! HE CURED ME OF A BROKEN HEART WHEN HE CONFESSED HIS LOVE FOR ME!
AND NOW *I'M* SICK!

YOU'RE WANTED IN SURGERY, DOCTOR!
CAN WE COME AND WATCH?
SURE!

LOOK! HE WASHED HIS HANDS, AND NOW HE'S PUTTING ON SURGICAL GLOVES!

THAT'S SO HE CAN PERFORM SURGERY IN A STERILIZED MANNER!
NOT REALLY!

IT'S SO I CAN HANDLE MY VALUABLE BASEBALL CARD COLLECTION WITHOUT SCUFFING IT!
4

FORCEPS!

FORCEPS!
PLUNK!

CLAMP!

CLAMP!
PLUNK!

PIZZA AND SODA!
PIZZA AND SODA!

THERE'S NO PEPPERONI ON MY PIZZA! WHAT KIND OF NURSE ARE YOU?
FORGIVE HER, DOCTOR! SHE'S NEW HERE!

OH, DUGGY! YOU WERE BRILLIANT!
SO BRILLIANT WE HAD TO WEAR EXTRA STRONG SUNGLASSES!

OHMIGOSH! LOOK WHO JUST ARRIVED AT THIS HOSPITAL!
WHO?! WHO?!

IT'S MY TWELVE-YEAR-OLD COUSIN, DOCTOR SKIPPY!
I AM THE NEW NUMBER ONE CHILD PRODIGY AT THIS HOSPITAL!
M.D.

SAYS WHO?
SAYS ME, DR. WUGGY! I CAN BLOW BIGGER BUBBLEGUM BUBBLES THAN YOU!
M.D.

THAT'S KID STUFF! THERE'S ONLY ONE WAY TO DECIDE WHICH OF US IS TOP DOG!

SEE THE SURGERY ROOM AT THE END OF THIS CORRIDOR, DOCTOR?
YEAH!

WELL, BZZZ! BZZZ! BZZZ!
YOU'RE ON!

SURGERY
FIRST ONE THERE IS THE REAL NUMERO UNO!
END

Script: Mike Pellowski / Pencils: Stan Goldberg / Inks: John Lowe / Letters: Bill Yoshida / Colors: Barry Grossman

BUT WILL YOUR FATHER BE OKAY WITH THAT?
OH, SURE!

BESIDES, DADDY WON'T EVEN BE HOME THIS SATURDAY NIGHT!
IT'S A DATE!

SO...
WELL, HERE I AM, TOOTS! AND I'VE COME FULLY EQUIPPED!
!?
POP CORN

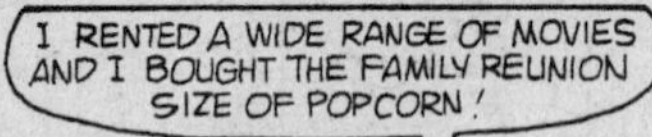
I RENTED A WIDE RANGE OF MOVIES AND I BOUGHT THE FAMILY REUNION SIZE OF POPCORN!

POP CORN

WHAT ARE YOU DOING, MOVING IN?
I JUST WANTED TO BE PREPARED!
ARCHIE

OKAY, I'LL ORDER A PIZZA, YOU CHOOSE A MOVIE!
2

YES, A LARGE SAUSAGE AND MUSHROOM...OH, JUST A MINUTE, THAT'S MY CALL WAITING! HOLD ON!

OH, HELLO DADDY! UH, HUH! EVERYTHING'S FINE! ARCHIE BROUGHT OVER SOME MOVIES!
SPACE STARS

DADDY, I'VE GOT THE PIZZA MAN ON HOLD, SO I'VE GOT TO GO... 'BYE! HELLO? YES, SEND IT TO LODGE RESIDENCE! 'BYE!

WHICH MOVIE DO YOU WANT TO WATCH..."SPACE STARS" OR "SLUGZ"?
YOU'VE GOT MAIL

I NEED TO CHECK MY E-MAIL, ARCHIE! JUST PUT ON WHICHEVER YOU WANT!

OHH, IT'S FROM ASHLEY! MY FRIEND IN ENGLAND!
I'LL PUT ON "SLUGZ"!

I'LL BE RIGHT THERE, ARCHIE! I JUST HAVE TO ANSWER HER!
GO AHEAD AND START THE MOVIE!

ASHLEY'S GOING TO BE STUDYING IN PARIS NEXT SEMESTER... WITH HER NEW BOY-FRIEND!
ACE PICTURES PRESENTS
SLUGZ
POP CORN

I'VE GOT TO LET SOME OF THE OTHER GIRLS KNOW ABOUT THIS!

WELL, HERE I AM... HOW'S THE MOVIE SO FAR?
WELL...

DING DONG!
OOPS! THERE'S THE DOORBELL!

HERE'S THE PIZZA!
GREAT! HURRY, THE GOOD PART IS JUST STARTING!

OH, THERE'S THE PHONE!
DON'T WAIT FOR ME...GO AHEAD AND EAT!
BRR-ING!

HELLO?
OH, HI, DADDY! YES, THE PIZZA JUST ARRIVED! WHAT? OKAY... WAIT, THAT'S THE OTHER LINE! 'BYE!
PIZZA
POP CORN

AMANDA! DID YOU GET MY E-MAIL ABOUT ASHLEY? YES, PARIS! ISN'T THAT SUPER?

EXCUSE ME, MISS, THERE IS A FAX FOR YOU!
I'VE GOT TO GO, AMANDA!

BE RIGHT BACK, ARCHIE! SAVE ME A SLICE!
PIZZA
LATER:
SORRY, IT TOOK LONGER THAN I THOUGHT! MEGAN FAXED ME A TON OF STUFF FROM THE NEW FASHION MAGAZINE!
WHAT HAPPENED TO THE MOVIE?
IT'S OVER, AND I FINISHED THE PIZZA! SORRY!
OH, I DIDN'T REALIZE HOW LATE IT'S BECOME! WELL, YOU CAN FILL ME IN ON THE MOVIE TOMORROW!
IT WAS REALLY GREAT SPENDING THIS EVENING ALONE WITH YOU, ARCHIE!
LET'S DO IT AGAIN SOON!
POP CORN
R
I'M SO-OO GLAD THAT I FINISHED THE PIZZA!
ARCHIE
END

Script: George Gladir / Pencils: Chic Stone / Inks: Rudy Lapick / Letters: Bill Yoshida / Colors: Barry Grossman

LATER, WHEN WE'RE BACK AT THE LODGE, I'LL SLIP INTO THE CAST!
RONNIE WILL THINK MY LEG IS BROKEN AND WAIT ON ME HAND AND FOOT!
NOT TO MENTION SMOTHER ME WITH KISSES!

NOW THAT'S WHAT I CALL A FUN-FILLED WEEKEND!
2

THAT WEEKEND -
RONNIE, WOULD YOU LIKE TO SKI THIS SLOPE WITH ME ?
SURE, ARCHIE!

THIS IS GREAT FUN!
IT SURE IS!

WHOOOOOOOOOOM
OH, ARCHIE!
WOMP!

ARE YOU HURT ?

I THINK MY LEG IS BROKEN!
YOU DO?

CAN YOU GET HELP, SWEET, SWEET RONNIE ?
SURE, MY BABY DOLL... YOU WAIT RIGHT HERE, SWEETHEART!
3

HURRY BACK, DEAR!
I WILL, BABYKINS!

SHE CALLED ME BABYKINS... WILL THERE EVER BE AN END TO THAT?

RONNIE, I... YIPE!

HELP!
HELP!
GRRRRRRRRR!!

GO AWAY!!! GO AWAY!!!

LATER...
SAY, RONNIE, HAVE YOU SEEN ARCHIE ?

I LEFT HIM ON THE SLOPES HOURS AGO! HE'S NOT BACK YET ?

OH, MY! WHAT HAVE I DONE ?

ARE YOU SURE HE WAS FAKING THAT FALL ? IT MIGHT HAVE BEEN FOR REAL!

WE'VE GOT TO GO OUT THERE AND GET HIM!

WHERE IS HE ? I LEFT HIM RIGHT HERE!
LOOK!!!!
5

zzZZZZ...
ARCHIE ANDREWS, YOU FAKER.!! WAKE UP AND GET DOWN OUT OF THAT TREE.!!

WHAT.!!!

ARE YOU ALL RIGHT ?!!
OH, ARCHIE! SPEAK TO US! SPEAK TO US!

CAN I GET YOU ANYTHING ELSE, MY BABYKINS ?
DO YOU WANT ANOTHER PILLOW, SWEET-UMS ?
SODA
END

Archie in "I'M POSITIVE"

Script & Pencils: Dick Malmgren / Inks: Jon D'Agostino / Letters: Bill Yoshida / Colors: Barry Grossman

I'M NEVER CHOSEN FOR SCHOOL SPORTS! I NEVER HAVE FUN LIKE YOU DO!
POW! POP!

HEY! COME ON, NOW! LOOK ON THE BRIGHT SIDE OF THINGS! WHERE'S YOUR POWER OF POSITIVE THINKING?
PING!

HOW CAN YOU THINK POSITIVELY, WHEN YOU'RE A LOSER?
-YOU, A LOSER? DON'T MAKE ME LAUGH!

WHY, YOU'RE THE SCHOOL GENIUS!
SURE, BUT YOU HAVE ALL THE FUN!
POP! POW!

THAT'S BECAUSE I DON'T LET THINGS GET ME DOWN!
POW!

OH, HECK! MY BEST TIRE!
OH WELL! WE'LL JUST HAVE TO WALK, DILTON! THESE THINGS WILL HAPPEN!

SEE, THE SECRET IS YOU CAN'T LET LITTLE THINGS GET YOU DOWN, THAT'S WHY I'M A WINNER!

IT'S ALL BECAUSE I THINK POSITIVE!
ARCHIE ANDREWS!

WE HAD A DATE LAST NIGHT AND YOU STOOD ME UP!
OH, GEE, I FORGOT ALL ABOUT IT, BETTY!

WELL FROM NOW ON, I'M FORGETTING ALL ABOUT YOU-- FOREVER!
GOOD-BYE!!

IT'S LIKE I SAID, THESE THINGS HAPPEN!
BUT I LOOK ON THE BRIGHTER SIDE!

THINGS ALWAYS SEEM TO WORK OUT FOR THE BEST!
SO THERE YOU ARE, DEADBEAT!

GIVE ME THE TEN BUCKS YOU OWE ME!
GEE! THAT'S ALL I HAVE ON ME, REG!

I DON'T CARE! I DIDN'T SAY THAT WHEN I LENT YOU THE MONEY! NOW FORK IT OVER!
GULP!

NOW YOU'RE DEPRESSED!
ME?--- NO WAY!
TEN

EVERY CLOUD HAS A SILVER LINING!
YOU HAVE TO THINK POSITIVE!

YOO-HOO! ARCHIE!
HI, DREAMBOAT!

I'M ALL SET TO GO TO THAT ROCK CONCERT WITH YOU TONIGHT!
OH, THAT?
4

SOMETHING CAME UP AND I CAN'T AFFORD THE ADMISSION PRICE, RON! WOULD YOU RATHER WATCH TV, INSTEAD?
?

NO WAY! I'M LOOKING FORWARD TO SEEING THIS ROCK GROUP! IF YOU CAN'T TAKE ME, REGGIE WILL!

I SHOULD HAVE ASKED HIM IN THE FIRST PLACE! YOU'RE ALWAYS BROKE!
BUT---

YOO-HOO! REGGIE! WAIT UP!

YOU'RE DEPRESSED NOW!
NEVER!

YOU HAVE TO THINK POSITIVE TO HAVE POSITIVE THINGS HAPPEN!

HOW DID YOU DO ON YOUR HOME-WORK ASSIGNMENT, ARCH ? ... DID YOU COMPLETE YOUR BOOK REPORT ?
?

OH, NO! I FORGOT ALL ABOUT IT!
YOU'RE GOING TO GET DETENTION AGAIN!

YOU HEARD WHAT MISS GRUNDY SAID!
GOOD GRIEF !!!

COME ON, ARCH! WHERE'S YOUR POWER OF POSITIVE THINKING ?
GROAN!

SOB! I'M POSITIVE I'M DEPRESSED!
WHY ME ?
WHY DO THESE THINGS ALWAYS HAPPEN TO ME ?
LET'S GET OUT OF HERE, DILTON! IT COULD BE CATCHING!
I'M POSITIVE!
END

Script: Mike Pellowski / Pencils: Stan Goldberg / Inks: Mike Esposito / Letters: Bill Yoshida / Colors: Barry Grossman

Y-YOU MEAN...?
SHE WON'T APPRECIATE IT! SHE EXPECTS YOU TO BE JUST AS GULLIBLE AS SHE IS!

BY GOLLY, YOU'RE RIGHT OF COURSE! MAN! YOU'RE A GOOD FRIEND, JUG!
YOU GOTTA LAY IT ON REAL THICK! - NOW, WHAT DID SHE PREDICT FOR YOU?
LODGE

NOTHIN' SPECTACULAR! SHE SAID I'M GOING TO MEET A TALL MAN!
SO GO BACK AND TELL HER YOU DID!
Arch

WOW! ARE YOU GOOD, LOVE-BUG! YOU'RE REALLY GOOD!!
YOU MEAN THE CARDS WERE RIGHT? YOU MET A TALL MAN?

-RAN INTO "STRETCH" MALONE!- RIGHT OUTSIDE YOUR GATE!!
I TOLD YOU SO! THESE CARDS ARE INFALLIBLE!!
SLAM!

THERE'S THE SIX OF SPADES, FOLLOWED BY THE... UH-OH!
"UH-OH"?
2

THEY DON'T TELL A HAPPY STORY *THIS* TIME! YOU'RE ABOUT TO HAVE AN ACCIDENT! PERHAPS A *FALL* OF SOME KIND...!!
GOSH! I'D BETTER WATCH MY STEP!

EEP! NOW HOW DO I FAKE A FALL WITH-OUT HURTING MYSELF TOO MUCH?

I GOTTA MAKE HER PREDICTION COME...
OOPS!!
TRIP!
Arch
SALT

EEYIPE!!!

WHAP!

OH! YOU POOR DEAR!! SEE? THE CARDS ARE *NEVER* WRONG!!

MAYBE YOU'LL BE LUCKIER THIS--UH-OH! - MORE SAD NEWS, DARLING!--YOU'RE GOING TO LOSE A FRIEND!
GEE, NONE OF THEM ARE EVEN SICK!

WAIT A MINUTE! "LOSE" COULD JUST MEAN "MISPLACE"!

HEY, ARCH! WANTA HANG OUT AT THE MALL FOR A WHILE?
SOUNDS GOOD TO ME, OL' BUDDY!

NOW, DO ME A FAVOR!-GET LOST!!--PLEASE!!
UH-OH! THE NOSTRADAMUS OF RIVERDALE SAID YOU WERE GONNA LOSE A FRIEND! RIGHT? SO LONG, PAL!
VIDEO
WORLD
SALE
TODAY
ICE
CRE

I SWEAR, RON! JUST LIKE YOU PREDICTED! I LOST MY BEST FRIEND, JUG, IN THE MALL!
THESE CARDS ARE UNCANNY, AREN'T THEY?

OH, ARCHIE! I LOVE YOU! YOU HAVE CONFIRMED MY BELIEF IN THESE INCREDIBLE CARDS!!
SHUCKS, SWEET-HEART! I ALWAYS KNEW YOU HAD TALENT!!
4

LATER!
WHAT'S THIS I HEAR ABOUT YOU FREAKING OUT ON FORTUNE TELLING?
BETTY, IT WORKS SO WELL, IT'S-- SCARY!

MY CARDS HAVE BEEN PREDICTING ARCHIE'S LIFE WITH UNBELIEVABLE ACCURACY!!
SO, MAKE A BELIEVER OUT OF ME!

OKAY! WE'LL LET MY MYSTERIOUS CARDS REVEAL WHAT FATE HAS IN STORE FOR YOU!
JUST DEAL ME A WINNING HAND!

UH-OH! ALL HEARTS TURNED UP! YOU'VE GOT A LOT OF LOVE COMING YOUR WAY, GIRL!
I COULD LIVE WITH THAT! DOES IT SAY WHO?

WELL, THE CARDS ONLY HAVE TWO COLORS! THE NEXT CARD WILL TELL US SOMETHING ABOUT HIS HAIR!

LET'S SEE--NO! THAT'S NOT RIGHT--I-ER-THINK WE HAVE TO DO TWO OUT OF THREE!
I SAW THAT! - THE SIX OF DIAMONDS!--HE'S A RED-HEAD!!

ARCHIE!! IT'S ARCHIE!! HE'S MAD ABOUT ME!! THE CARDS NEVER LIE!! YOU SAID THAT!!

BAH! CHILDISH NONSENSE!! SURELY YOU DIDN'T THINK I WAS SERIOUS, DID YOU?
SWIPE

RON! HOW AM I GOING TO DO ON MY MATH TEST? WHAT DID YOUR MAGIC CARDS TELL YOU?
HOW WOULD I KNOW? I GAVE UP THAT SILLY STUFF!

NOW I'M INTO PALM READING! LET ME SEE YOUR HAND!
GEE, AND JUST AS I WAS BEGINNING TO BELIEVE IN THOSE CARDS!

HMM! WHAT DO YOU KNOW? IT SAYS IF YOU PERSIST IN BELIEVING IN THOSE CARDS YOU HAVE A VERY, VERY SHORT LIFELINE!!
6
END

REGGIE & MOOSE "TICKED OFF!"

UH, OH! MOOSE IS AFTER REGGIE AGAIN! FIND OUT WHAT REGGIE WILL BE TAKING ONCE HE SEES MOOSE ON THE ATTACK! JUST USE THE DOTTED LETTERS TO FIND OUT!

Jughead
in..
"MUNCH MONEY"
I GOT A PART-TIME JOB AT THE FOOD CHANNEL!
THE TV STATION?
POP'S

YEAH! I RUN ERRANDS FOR THEM, AND AFTER EACH COOKING SHOW...
POP'S

I GET TO MUNCH ON WHAT THEY COOKED!
SOUNDS LIKE A GOOD IDEA!

WHAT'S THE PAY?
$20 A WEEK!

THAT'S NOT VERY MUCH!
I KNOW...

BUT IT WAS ALL I COULD AFFORD TO PAY THEM!
END

Betty and Veronica in Kiss & TELL!

Script & Pencils: **Dan Parent** Inks: **Jim Amash** Letters: **Teresa Davidson** Colors: **Barry Grossman**
Editor-In-Chief: **Victor Gorelick** President: **Mike Pellerito** Publisher: **Jon Goldwater**

REMEMBER, I GOT IT FROM A CLAIRVOYANT FRIEND OF MINE!
IT HAS SPECIAL POWERS!

OH, COME ON NOW, LILY!
FINE. DON'T BELIEVE ME.

BUT IF YOU KEEP IT ON LONG ENOUGH, VERONICA, YOU'LL FIND OUT!
Er--OKAY, AUNTIE!

WHAT A QUACK!
HIRAM! THAT'S MY SISTER!

I JUST DON'T BUY ALL THAT PSYCHIC MUMBO JUMBO!
BUT YOU HAVE TO ADMIT...

...THIS IS A BEAUTIFUL NECKLACE!
A RUBY KISS--HOW LOVELY!

WELL, IT'S LATE...
I GUESS IT'S TIME FOR BED!

GOOD NIGHT, MOM!
KISS!

FWOOM!
WHA?!

THAT WAS FREAKY!
WHAT JUST HAPPENED?

GOOD NIGHT, DEAR.
GOOD NIGHT, DADDY!

FWOMP!
Huh?

WOW! ANOTHER WEIRD MOMENT!
I'D BETTER GET SOME SLEEP!

LATER...
I CAN'T GET OVER THOSE WEIRD IMAGES...
THEY WERE MOM AND DAD-- YOUNG! AND THEY WERE KISSING SOMEONE!

THE NEXT MORNING...
HURRY, VERONICA! YOU'LL BE LATE FOR SCHOOL!

BYE, MOM!
KISS!

FWOMP!
OH NO! NOT AGAIN!
VERONICA? ARE YOU ALL RIGHT?
I HAD A WEIRD IMAGE WHEN I KISSED YOU!
IT WAS YOU--AS A YOUNG GIRL!
YOU WERE KISSING ANOTHER LITTLE BOY WITH BRIGHT RED HAIR!
DID HE HAVE A BASEBALL OUTFIT ON?
YES!
THAT WAS MY FIRST KISS-- ROBBIE JENKINS! AT AGE 13!
BUT HOW--?
Uh, I GUESS WE'LL HAVE TO FIGURE THIS OUT LATER--

I'VE GOT TO CALL AUNT LILY!
HELLO, AUNT LILY? THAT NECKLACE! PLEASE EXPLAIN IT TO ME!

FROM THE SOUNDS OF IT, YOU'VE ALREADY HAD A VISION.
YOU COULD SAY THAT!

IT'S A "FIRST KISS" NECKLACE...
...WHOEVER YOU KISS, YOU CAN SEE WHO THEIR FIRST KISS WAS!

REALLY?
OKAY... I NEED TO LOOK INTO THIS MORE...

I'LL SEE IF THIS REALLY WORKS...
ARCHIE, WHO WAS YOUR FIRST KISS?

WHY, I BELIEVE IT WAS YOU, SUGAR PLUM!
PUCKER UP.

KISS!
FWOMP!
WHOA!
LIAR! YOUR FIRST KISS WAS EVELYN EVERNEVER!

YOU KNOW? I THINK YOU'RE RIGHT...
BUT HOW DID YOU...?

NEVER MIND! ALL I KNOW IS THAT YOU WERE MY FIRST KISS...

...BUT YOU WON'T BE MY LAST!

BETTY, WHO WAS YOUR FIRST KISS?
ARCHIE, OF COURSE!

WELL, I'M NOT GOING TO KISS YOU TO FIND OUT!
?
DILTON! PUT THIS ON!
IT'S NOT REALLY MY STYLE, BUT OKAY...

KISS BETTY!
WHA...?

JUST A PECK ON THE CHEEK WILL DO!
OKAY.
KISS!

FWOMP!
WHAT DID YOU SEE?

I SAW LITTLE BETTY KISSING LITTLE ARCHIE!
Hmph!
?

NOW KISS ME!
ARCHIE, EAT YOUR HEART OUT!

QUICK! ON THE CHEEK!
KISS!

FWOMP!
WHAT DID YOU SEE?
I SAW YOU, LITTLE VERONICA, KISSING LITTLE JUGHEAD!
SAY THAT AGAIN?

I SAW YOU KISSING JUGHEAD!
?
WHAT?! THAT'S SICK!

EXACTLY WHAT IS GOING ON HERE?
JUGHEAD, COME HERE!

BETTY, PUT THIS ON!
NOW KISS JUGHEAD!

NO WAY!
IT'S EITHER HER OR *ME!*

WELL, THAT'S THE LESSER OF TWO EVILS, I GUESS.
SORRY, JUG. SHE'S TRYING TO PROVE SOME KIND OF POINT.

KISS!
FWOMP!

WHAT DID YOU SEE?
I SAW YOU AND JUGHEAD KISSING!

WHAT? OF ALL OF US IN THIS GROUP, *WE* ACTUALLY SHARED OUR FIRST KISS TOGETHER?!
OF COURSE! DON'T YOU REMEMBER? IT'S ONE OF THE DARKEST DAYS OF MY *LIFE!*

WE WERE IN THE SCHOOL PLAY OF "SLEEPING BEAUTY"!
I WAS THE PRINCE AND HAD TO KISS YOU!

OHMIGOSH! NOW I REMEMBER!
I MUST HAVE BLOCKED IT OUT! LIKE HOW PEOPLE BLOCK TRAUMAS FROM THEIR MINDS!

I ACTUALLY GOT SICK AFTER THAT KISS!
I CAN TOP THAT! I COULDN'T EAT FOR HOURS AFTER THAT!

I'M SO RELIEVED!
I NOW KNOW THAT YOU'VE ALWAYS REPULSED ME!

AND AS FAR AS I CAN TELL, YOU'LL REPULSE ME UNTIL THE DAY I DIE!
THANK YOU, JUGHEAD!
SOMEONE BETTER START EXPLAINING ALL THIS TO ME...

AFTER SCHOOL...
YOUR AUNT LILY EXPLAINED HER CRAZY NECKLACE TO ME!
HERE! PLEASE TAKE IT AWAY FROM ME!
Hmmm...

HIRAM? WHO WAS YOUR FIRST KISS?
I BELIEVE YOU WERE, MY DEAR!

KISS
FWOMP!
KISS
THAT'S FUNNY...

... BECAUSE I'M SEEING A YOUNG HIRAM...
... KISSING MY SISTER, LILY!

SMITHERS! HAVE YOU SEEN MR. LODGE?
?
Shhh!
End

Betty and Veronica in Royal FLUSH

Oh, I'M SO EXCITED! I MUST GET MY HAIR DONE--NAILS--NEW SHOES--DRESS--!
W-WHAT?!

A--A DUKE, PRINCE, AND A KING!?!

OMIGOSH! WHAT ON EARTH WILL I WEAR?

EVENTS LIKE THIS ARE ALWAYS SO FORMAL! I SUPPOSE I COULD WEAR MY PROM GOWN!

I'LL NEED NEW SHOES AND A PURSE--NEW MAKE-UP--MAYBE EARRINGS, TOO! I'D BETTER GET SHOPPING!

A FEW HOURS LATER...
WHAT A RELIEF I GOT ALL THIS STUFF ON SALE! NOW TO GET HOME AND SHAMPOO MY HAIR!

PLUS I HAVE TO DO MY NAILS, PUT ON MY MAKE-UP...
HI, BETTY!

WHAT DOES ONE SAY TO A KING, ANYWAY?
BETTY... YOO-HOO!

I MEAN, YOU CAN'T JUST WALK UP AND SAY ANYTHING!
YOU MEAN LIKE I CAN, 'CAUSE YOU'RE NOT LISTENING TO ME?

LIKE "NICE WEATHER WE'RE HAVING, YOUR MAJESTY!"
CONSIDERING IT LOOKS LIKE RAIN... I'LL HAVE TO DIS-AGREE!

YOU KNOW, I MAY WEAR A CROWN, BUT THERE'S NO NEED TO CALL ME "YOUR MAJESTY!"
JUGGIE!

WHAT'S GOT YOU SO LOST IN THOUGHT?
VERONICA'S INVITED ME TO A ROYAL BANQUET TONIGHT!

VERONICA SAYS THERE'LL BE A DUKE, A PRINCE AND A KING THERE!
BE SURE TO BRING DOG BISCUITS!

SAY WHAT?!
THE ANNUAL DOG LOVERS AWARDS BANQUET IS TONIGHT!

THEY'LL BE AWARDING TROPHIES TO THE BEST OF BREEDS! HOT DOG WASN'T INVITED BECAUSE OF HIS MIXED PEDIGREE!
D-DOG SHOW?!
snobs!

THAT'S THE ONLY BANQUET IN TOWN! AND BELIEVE ME... I KEEP UP ON ANYTHING THAT INVOLVES FOOD!
TH-THANKS, JUGGIE!

DOG SHOW! DOG SHOW! I CAN'T BELIEVE SHE GOT ME ALL EXCITED ABOUT A DOG SHOW!
Hmph! DON'T YOU LIKE DOGS?

STILL, I SHOULD DRESS UP A BIT, EVEN IF IT'S FOR A BUNCH OF DOGS!

SIX P.M. COMES...
THERE! NOTHING OVERLY FORMAL FOR A LOT OF MUTTS TO SLOBBER ON!
VERONICA'S HERE!

OH, BETTY! I CAN HARDLY WAIT UNTIL WE GET THERE!
ME EITHER, I GUESS!

HAVEN'T WE GOTTEN TO THE CONVENTION CENTER BY NOW--?
DIDN'T I TELL YOU? WE'RE HEADED TO THE AIRPORT!
AIRPORT

THE BANQUET'S IN NEW YORK AT ONE OF THE FINEST HOTELS THERE!
NEW YORK?

AND TO THINK JUGHEAD HAD ME CONVINCED THIS WOULD BE A DOG SHOW!!
NOW WHAT DO I DO WITH ALL THE DOG BISCUITS IN MY PURSE?
ISN'T THE PRINCE A HOTTIE? AND THE DUKE'S DOG HAS TAKEN TO YOU!
... AND THEN I SAID "KING ME!" SO THEY DID! THAT'S THE LAST TIME I PLAY CHECKERS WITH THE PRIME MINISTER!!
END

Betty and Veronica in "FEET FIRST"

Script: Frank Doyle / Pencils: Dan DeCarlo / Inks: Jimmy DeCarlo / Letters: Bill Yoshida / Colors: Barry Grossman

HI, BETTY! WHAT'S NEW?
RONNIE'S HAVING FOOT PROBLEMS!

SHE'S TAKEN HER PRECIOUS TOOTSIES TO A PODIATRIST!
THE FINEST IN THE COUNTRY?

AREN'T THEY ALWAYS?
BUT OF COURSE!

NEXT DAY-
SO HOW DID YOU AND THE DOC MAKE OUT PLAYING FOOTSIE?
MARVELOUSLY! IT ALWAYS PAYS TO GO FIRST CLASS!

HE MEASURED MY FEET FOR A PAIR OF VERY SPECIAL SHOES! HE SAYS FINE FEET LIKE MINE SHOULD NOT BE ABUSED BY ORDINARY SHOES!

WHAT WILL THESE SHOES LOOK LIKE?
I HAVEN'T THE FOGGIEST! BUT THEY'RE GOING TO BE TERRIBLY HEALTHY!

THEY'LL BE HAND MADE TO FIT ONLY THESE FEET! SOFT IMPORTED LEATHER! THEY SHOULD BE READY BY NEXT FRIDAY!
I'M DYING TO SEE THEM!
2

SO, HERE IT IS... NEXT FRIDAY!
DING DONG

HI, SMITHERS!
HOW DO, MISS BETTY?

BETTY! BETTY! THEY'RE HERE! I'M WEARING THEM!

HOW DO YOU LIKE THEM?
OMIGOSH!

THEY'RE SO INCREDIBLY SOFT AND COMFORTABLE! IT FEELS LIKE I'M BAREFOOT!
T-THAT'S NICE!

THEY COST A FORTUNE, OF COURSE! BUT I'M WORTH IT!
HEY, RONNIE! WHERE'D YOU GET THE GUNBOATS?

IGNORAMUS! HE DOESN'T KNOW QUALITY SHOES WHEN HE SEES THEM!
SURE! WHAT DOES HE KNOW FROM HEALTHY FEET?

ANOTHER SORORITY INITIATION, RON?
NERD!

MMPF! D-DID YOU SEE VERONICA'S SHOES?

STOP LAUGHING OR I'LL DECK YOU!!

YOU LIKE THEM, DON'T YOU, ARCHIE?
THEY LOOK VERY-ER-HEALTHY!

THAT'S IT! HEALTHY!
THEM'S HEALTHY SHOES, ALL RIGHT!
HEY! IF YOU GOT HAPPY FEET, WHO CARES WHAT YOU LOOK LIKE?

HUMPH! PEARLS BEFORE SWINE! WHAT DO THESE IDIOTS KNOW ABOUT QUALITY?

THERE GOES THE FREEDOM BELL! I'VE GOT TO SPLIT FOR HOME!
BRINNG!!
4 O'CLOCK AT POP'S, FOR THE DAILY GATHERING OF THE GANG!

4 P.M.
YOU'RE VERY PROMPT!
I WONDER IF RONNIE IS HERE!?

IF SHE'S NOT, I'LL BET THE WHOLE CONVERSATION IS ABOUT HER SHOES!
I DON'T KNOW IF I COULD PAY THAT PRICE FOR HAPPY FEET!

WELL, FOR GOODNESS SAKES! DON'T THOSE THINGS MAKE YOUR FEET HURT, RON?
SURE! BUT THEY MAKE THE REST OF ME FEEL GREAT!
The END

Script: Kathleen Webb / Pencils: Jeff Shultz / Inks: Al Milgrom / Letters: Bill Yoshida / Colors: Barry Grossman

IS THAT A NEW FAD?
NO! THEY'RE FROM ICELAND!

YOU'VE HEARD OF THAT OTHER ICELANDIC ROCK STAR!?
YEAH! "BORK" OR "FORK" OR "REKJAVIK" OR SOMETHING!

THESE GUYS ALSO HAIL FROM THAT NECK OF THE WOODS!
FROM THE LAND OF LONG WINTER NIGHTS AND LONGER UNDERWEAR, HUH?

THEY ARE KINDA CUTE!
AREN'T THEY? MY FAVORITE IS SJVET OR SVEN OR WHATEVER!

HOW DID YOU HEAR OF THEM?
ONE OF MY FRIENDS IN EUROPE E-MAILED ME ABOUT THEM! THEY'RE REALLY HOT OVER THERE!

I WENT TO THEIR WEBSITE AND LISTENED TO SOME MUSIC CLIPS! THAT'S WHEN I GOT HOOKED!
2

I'D LOVE TO SEE THEM IN CONCERT!
REMEMBER TO WEAR YOUR WARMEST FAKE FUR WHEN YOU DO!

NEXT DAY...
BETTY! BETTY! GREAT NEWS! DADDYKINS SAYS I CAN GO HEAR MY ICELANDIC BAND IN PERSON THIS WEEKEND!

AND THE BEST PART IS, YOU GET TO GO WITH ME! WE LEAVE TONIGHT AFTER SUPPER!

DON'T WORRY! YOUR PARENTS SAID IT WAS OKAY, AND SMITHERS IS COMING ALONG AS A CHAPERONE!
B-BUT-RON-!

SEE YOU LATER!
OHMIGOSH-I SUPPOSE THAT MEANS I'D BETTER GO PACK MY SUITCASE!

ICELAND! AND IN THE MIDDLE OF WINTER, TOO! I'D BETTER PACK MY WARMEST THINGS!

DON'T FORGET TO PACK YOUR SWIMSUIT, BETTY DEAR!
MY SWIMSUIT?

OH, WAIT! THAT'S RIGHT! ICELAND HAS LOTS OF GEYSERS AND HOT SPRINGS!

I BET PEOPLE GO SWIMMING IN THEM DURING WINTERTIME!

BETTER TAKE A WARM NIGHTIE, TOO, PLUS MY FUZZY BATHROBE AND SLIPPERS!

AND OF COURSE, I'M NOT GOING TO FORGET MY THICKEST WINTER UNDERWEAR!

GOOD THING I BOUGHT A NEW DOWN-FILLED JACKET BEFORE WINTER STARTED! I'LL NEED IT!
4

BETTY! VERONICA'S HERE TO TAKE YOU TO THE AIRPORT!
I'M READY, MOM!

DO YOU HAVE MUCH LUGGAGE TO CHECK IN?
JUST THE ONE BAG! I TRIED TO PACK LIGHT!

IT WASN'T EASY, CONSIDERING WHERE WE'RE GOING!
ME, EITHER! WHY, I BROUGHT TWELVE DIFFERENT SWIMSUITS ALONE!
?

BUT IT'S WORTH IT! WHO KNOWS? MAYBE WE'LL MEET ONE OF THE BAND MEMBERS OUT BY THE POOL, BASKING IN THE FLORIDA SUN!
FLORIDA?!
FLORIDA

YES! FLORIDA WILL BE THE ONLY STOP IN THE U.S. THIS SEASON!
I CAN'T UNDERSTAND IT, SEEING AS HOW THEY'RE SUCH A HOT BAND!
GATES 1-12

:SIGH: CONSIDERING WHAT'S IN MY SUITCASE, RON, THEY'RE NOT GOING TO BE THE ONLY HOT THING IN FLORIDA!
?
The END

Script: Mike Pellowski / Pencils: Jeff Shultz / Inks: Mike DeCarlo / Letters: Bill Yoshida / Colors: Barry Grossman

HOW I EVER GOT THIS STATUETTE OF A BIG-EYED, CRYING PUPPY, I'LL NEVER KNOW!
THINK HARD! MAYBE YOU'LL FIGURE IT OUT!

IT'S SO TACKY IT CRACKS ME UP!
HOLD IT IN, GIRL!

AFTER ALL, THE PROCEEDS ARE GOING TO CHARITY, SO DON'T MAKE A BIG DEAL OF IT!
WHAT GOODIES DID YOU BRING, BETTY?

UM, LET'S SEE ...
OH, THIS GARISH THING!

THIS AWFUL TIARA! IT MUST'VE BELONGED TO AN AUNT WHO WAS OLD AND OUT OF TOUCH!
ER-YES!
WELL, I NEVER!

I LENT THAT TIARA TO HER FOR A WEDDING SHE WAS GOING TO, FROM MY OWN PRIVATE COLLECTION!
2

IT'S SO GAUDY! I CAN'T IMAGINE ANYONE WANTING IT!
YEAH!
BOY, SHE PRETENDED TO LOVE IT WHEN I LENT IT TO HER!

AND SO...
HOW MUCH FOR THE PUPPY?
FIFTY CENTS! IF YOU'RE WILLING TO PAY THAT MUCH!

ENJOY IT, MA'AM! MAYBE THE PERSON YOU GIVE IT TO WILL APPRECIATE IT! ISN'T IT A SHAME WHEN PEOPLE FORGET ACTS OF GENEROSITY?
?
GOOD LUCK! MAY OTHERS NOT STAB YOU IN THE BACK!
WHAT'S HER PROBLEM?
PICKLED PEPPERS 10¢

IS SOMETHING THE MATTER, BETTY?
AS IF YOU CARE, VER...
EXCUSE ME!

WHAT'S THE PRICE ON THIS TIARA?
GOING TO A WILD COSTUME PARTY? HEE, HEE, HEE!

THAT TRASHY THING IS SO HILARIOUS I HATE TO SELL IT!
BUT IT'S YOURS FOR ONE DOLLAR!
ONE DOLLAR?
OF ALL THE NERVE! I SHOULD TELL BETTY WHOSE IT IS!
BUT I'M NOT GOING TO BE PETTY AT OUR CLASS FUNCTION!
RIVERDALE FLEA

THERE YOU GO, MA'AM! GET IT APPRAISED! YOU MAY BE SURPRISED!
YEAH! IT'S PROBABLY WORTH FIVE CENTS!
THAT'S NOT WHAT I MEANT, BETTY!
EXCUSE ME FOR LIVING!

IT'S JUST A TRAGEDY THAT SOME PEOPLE ARE SO FORGETFUL! AND DON'T KNOW GOOD JEWELRY AT THE SAME TIME!
WHAT ARE YOU GETTING AT?
HEY, GIRLS! THE MONEY'S GOING TO CHARITY, BUT YOU DON'T HAVE TO SELL YOUR PERSONAL POSSESSIONS!
HUH?

I SAW SOME LADY WITH THE PUPPY BETTY GAVE YOU FOR CHRISTMAS!
AND SOME OTHER LADY WITH THE TIARA VERONICA LENT YOU!

OH BETTY, I FEEL AWFUL!
VERONICA, CAN YOU EVER FORGIVE ME?

I'LL ALWAYS TREASURE EVERYTHING YOU GIVE ME FROM NOW ON!
AND ANYTHING YOU LEND ME WILL ALWAYS BE PRECIOUS, FRIEND O' MINE!
GEE, THERE'S ONE THING I'D LIKE TO BORROW FOR THE DANCE NEXT WEEK...

COULD YOU LEND ME ARCHIE?

I SHOULD'VE KNOWN! WHY YOU...
HE'S MINE, YOU...
NEXT THING YOU KNOW THEY'LL SELL ME FOR A BUCK!
The END

Archie's Girls Betty and Veronica®

A NEW HAIR-DO? CERTAINLY, BETTY! ARE YOU INTERESTED IN THE NEW **LOVER BOY**?

THERE'S ONLY ONE *LOVER BOY* I'M INTER-ESTED IN!

From the Vault of Archie Comics!

Ski Sick, Wrong Guest, Climb on My Hands, Dark Dilemma, Soda Jerk, Memories, Behavior Pattern, Lip Service, A Salty Tale, Wiser Adviser, On the Other Foot

Originally Printed in: *Betty & Veronica Vol. 1 #12, #15 (1954) and #16, #17 (1955)*

By Frank Doyle (Writer), Joe Edwards & Samm Schwartz (Writer, Artist & Letterer), Harry Lucey, George Frese & Bill Vigoda (Artists) and Terry Szenics (Inks & Letters)

It's 1954-55! This month's ARCHIE VAULT shifts focus to Archie's girls Betty and Veronica as we take a glance at the earliest works of *four* classic Archie artist masters: Harry Lucey, Samm Schwartz, Bill Vigoda and Joe Edwards! These four crackerjack artisans have chronicled the tales of Archie and his gaggle of pals for years -- so let's see how they fare when the gals are at the helm.

Archie's Girls BETTY AND VERONICA #12 and #15 (*c.1954*) gives us "SKI SICK," "WRONG GUEST," "CLIMB ON MY HANDS," "DARK DILEMMA," and "SODA JERK" while #16-#17 (*c.1955*) gives us "BEHAVIOR PATTERN," "LIP SERVICE," "A SALTY TALE," "WISER ADVISER," "ON THE OTHER FOOT," and "MEMORIES."

Thousands of men, women, teens and kids all over the country and in the armed forces read Archie Comics during this period and it's no wonder; the stories are great and the artists in their prime! We hope you enjoy this presentation of classic tales from Archie Comics' past! Take care, pals n' gals!

APPROVED
AN Archie MAGAZINE
READING

The following stories are reprinted here without alteration for historical reference.

SCRIPT: *FRANK DOYLE* PENCILS: *HARRY LUCEY* INKS & LETTERS: *TERRY SZENICS*

C'MON! WHAT DO WE DO FIRST?
YEAH! WE YEARN TO LEARN!
REGGIE, AS AN EXPERT WHAT IS YOUR ADVICE TO THESE NOVICES?

FELLOW EXPERT, IT IS MY CONSIDERED OPINION THAT THEY SHOULD STICK TO SOMETHING THEY CAN HANDLE... ...LIKE TIDDLEY WINKS!
C'MON, RONNIE! LET'S SHOW 'EM!

THEY DIDN'T HAVE TO GET SO HUFFY! LET 'EM STRUGGLE ALONG WITHOUT US!
HEY, ARCH! LOOK! A MOVIE TRUCK!

HI, MISTER! ARE YOU SHOOTING SOME SKI EXPERTS?
NO, BOYS! JUST GETTING SOME SHOTS OF THE OPENING OF THE SKIING SEASON FOR THE NEWSREEL!

HOW WOULD YOU LIKE SOME COMEDY SHOTS OF A COUPLE OF GALS ON THE BEGINNER'S SLOPE WHO ARE REAL NOVICES!
SUB NOVICES!
THAT MIGHT BE GOOD HUMAN INTEREST!

BUT I WAS GOING TO SHOOT THOSE TWO GIRLS ON THE CHAMPIONSHIP RUN!
NO! ARCH... IT CAN'T BE!
BUT IT IS!

BETTY, ARE YOU SURE YOU KNOW WHAT YOU'RE DOING! IT LOOKS AWFULLY STEEP!
SURE! I'VE BEEN READING A BOOK! ALL YOU'VE GOT TO DO IS KEEP YOUR FEET TOGETHER!

YI-I-I! THEY'RE GOING DOWN!
OF COURSE! DID YOU THINK THEY WERE GOING UP?

KNEES BENT... BODY FORWARD IN A CROUCH TO CUT DOWN WIND RESISTANCE!
BUT HOW DO YOU STOP?

I DIDN'T READ THAT PART!
BUT I BETTER TRY SOMETHING!

BETTY! NOT THAT WAY!! EEEEEEEEEP!

WHAM!

HA-A-ALP!

WOW! THIS IS TERRIFIC! NOW THEY'RE SKIING TANDEM!
--RIGHT INTO--
--A SNOW-BANK!

YI-I-I-I-I-I-I-I-I!!
WHUMP!!

BETTY!! ARE YOU ALL RIGHT?
I THINK SO! ...BUT YOU BETTER DO SOMETHING ABOUT VERONICA!

SHE'S ON THE OTHER END OF THESE SKIS!
BLUB

YOUNG LADY, THAT WAS THE GREATEST EXAMPLE OF TRICK SKIING I'VE EVER SEEN!
IT WAS?

AND REGGIE AND I WILL BE ONLY TOO GLAD TO TEACH YOU ALL WE KNOW ABOUT SKIING!
SURE! WE THINK YOU DESERVE TO HAVE THE BENEFIT OF OUR EXPERIENCE!
REALLY?

AS EXPERTS, IT IS OUR CONSIDERED OPINION THAT YOU SHOULD STICK TO SOMETHING YOU CAN HANDLE!
... LIKE TIDDLEY-WINKS!
4.

Betty
"WRONG GUEST"
HOW ABOUT IT, JUGGIE? A DINNER FIT FOR A KING! - THICK STEAKS, MUSHROOMS,- FRENCH FRIES,-CORN ON THE COB,-LUSCIOUS APPLE PIE,---
LET'S GO! LET'S HAVE AN EARLY DINNER-- --SHLURP-- ... BEFORE LUNCH!!
(GIGGLE) - SILLY! - YOU'LL JUST HAVE TO WAIT TILL THIS EVENING!
(PANT, PANT!) - H-HOW CAN I HELP? - I'LL BRING SOMETHING FOR THE FEAST!- IT'S ONLY RIGHT! - WHAT? - WHAT CAN I BRING?
by JOE EDWARDS

WHY NOTHING, JUGGIE DARLING! - JUST YOURSELF!
AND ARCHIE, OF COURSE!

GREAT! - SOME ARCHIE, EH? -
I'LL GET A HALF-DOZEN! - NO! - BETTER MAKE IT A DOZEN!
MIGHT AS WELL HAVE ENOUGH!- IT WON'T GO---

---ARCHIE???
IS THAT ASKING MUCH?

NO! - NOT MUCH, REALLY! - JUST THE IMPOSSIBLE! - YOU KNOW HE WON'T COME!
PROMISE HIM ANYTHING UNDER THE SUN, IF NECESSARY, - BUT, - NO ARCHIE, NO DINNER!

EVENING -
BETTY! THIS IS GREAT! JUST GREAT! - YOU'LL NEVER KNOW HOW MUCH I APPRECIATE THIS! - YOU'RE SOLID, KID! - SOLID!
WOW! - SUCH ENTHUSIASM! JUGGIE REALLY DID A JOB ON THIS BOY!
WHOOSH
MAN! - LOOK AT THOSE VITAMINS! - MMM! - WHAT A MEAL!!
LET'S EAT!
BETTY, YOU'RE WONDERFUL! - WHAT A MEAL!
BOY! WHAT A WIFE YOU'LL MAKE!
WELL! I'VE GOT TO BE GOING! - SO LONG NOW!
(SIGH!) HE SAID I'M WONDERFUL!
HE SAID WHAT A MEAL!
HE SAID, WHAT A WIFE I'LL MAKE!
HE SAID HE'S GOT TO BE GOING!
HE---
---HE'S GOT TO BE GOING??
SLAM!
W-WHAT DO YOU MEAN, "WHERE AM I GOING?" --D-DON'T YOU KNOW?
ZIP
JUG SAID IF I CAME TO DINNER YOU'D DO VERONICA'S HOMEWORK FOR HER SO SHE AND I COULD GO TO THE MOVIES!!
♪ JUGGIE!! - WHERE ARE YOU? - DINNER ISN'T OVER YET! ♫
♪ YOU'RE GOING TO GET YOUR JUST DESSERTS! ♫
THE END

BY GEORGE! THIS MOUNTAIN CLIMBING IS WONDERFUL EXERCISE!!
Archie's Girls
Betty and Veronica
"CLIMB ON MY HANDS"
WE SURE ARE HIGH!
DO YOU FOLKS MIND IF I GO BACK FOR MY STOMACH?
SAMM SCHWARTZ

COME ON KIDS! WE'RE ALMOST AT THE TOP!
NO THANKS! I'VE HAD ENOUGH!
ME TOO!

THEN STAY HERE AND TAKE MOVIES OF ME REACHING THE SUMMIT! IT WILL MAKE A TERRIFIC SEQUENCE!!
OKAY!

I MIGHT PRETEND TO SLIP, JUST TO MAKE IT LOOK MORE EXCITING!! DON'T STOP GRINDING THE CAMERA FOR AN INSTANT, BETTY!
I UNDERSTAND. LEAVE IT TO ME!

WHAT A CLIMB! I HOPE BETTY IS GETTING ALL THIS!!

OOPS! A LOOSE ROCK!!

OH BETTY!
DON'T WORRY! I'M GETTING IT!!

I'M NOT FOOLING! THIS IS FOR REAL!!

YOUR DAD CERTAINLY HAS A FLAIR FOR EXCITING TOUCHES, VERONICA!

BETTY, M-MAYBE HE'S **REALLY** IN TROUBLE!
DON'T BE SILLY! YOU HEARD WHAT HE SAID!

RRIP
HELP!

CHEE-EE! WHAT ACTION!!
DADDY? AREN'T YOU OVERDOING IT?

CRASH!

I GUESS THE JOKE'S ON YOUR DAD, RONNIE! HE FORGOT TO PUT **FILM** IN THE CAMERA!!
TELL HIM LATER, BETTY! RIGHT NOW IT HURTS WHEN HE LAUGHS!
END.

Archie's Girls
Betty and Veronica in "DARK DILEMMA!"
I WONDER WHAT KIND OF A SECRET VERONICA HAS, THAT SHE'S SCARED WILL BE FOUND OUT?
SECRET? SCARED? VERONICA'S GOT NOTHING TO BE SCARED ABOUT, JUG!

OH YEAH! THEN WHY IS SHE BEING BLACKMAILED?
B-B-BLACKMAI-- HA! HA! WHO TOLD YOU A GOOFY STORY LIKE THAT?

SHE DID HERSELF! AND THERE'S HER BLACKMAILER, NOW!
BETTY! HA! HA! ....JUG, YOU'VE REALLY FLIPPED!

YOU'RE SURE, YOU DON'T MIND LENDING ME THIS FUR-PIECE FOR TONIGHT RONNIE?
NOT AT ALL BETTY!

THANKS FOR THE FUR, RONNIE! I'LL SEND YOU ANOTHER BLACKMAIL LETTER!
BLACKMAIL LETTER! THEN IT'S TRUE!

GOLLY, SHE SURE IS BRAZEN ABOUT IT! POOR VERONICA!

RONNIE BABY, I KNOW ALL ABOUT BETTY AND HER.... ....HER BLACKMAIL! NOW DON'T WORRY ABOUT IT SUGAR.....
WHO'S WORRIED?

TEE, HEE! THAT'S THE FIRST TIME SHE EVER TRIED BLACKMAIL! HEE, HEE! WHAT'LL THAT BETTY THINK OF NEXT?

Archie *in*................ **"MEASURING FACTS!"**

Archie's Girls
Betty and Veronica
in
"SODA JERK"
WOW! LOOK AT ALL THAT MONEY! YOU'RE LOADED!
THIRTY.... THIRTY-FIVE... FORTY CENTS!
GEE! JUST ENOUGH FOR TWO SODAS, ARCHIE!
GEO FRESE

HEY! THAT'S RIGHT, BETTY! THIS IS JUST ENOUGH TO BUY SODAS FOR ME AND...
YES, ARCHIE..?
THUMP!
THUMP!

...VERONICA! I'LL HAVE TO FIND HER AND SEE IF SHE'S INTERESTED!
VERONICA! AGH-H-H..!

VERONICA IS ALL HE HAS ON HIS MIND! IF HE WAS TWINS, HE'D BE TWICE AS CRAZY OVER HER! SOB!
AW, ARCHIE LIKES YOU, TOO, BETTY...

HE'S JUST A LITTLE FORGETFUL, AT TIMES! I'LL SPEAK TO HIM, BETTY!
YOU WILL, JUGGY?

I DON'T USUALLY BUTT IN WHERE GIRLS ARE CONCERNED, BUT I'M GOING TO TELL ARCHIE HE OUGHT TO GIVE YOU A LITTLE MORE ATTENTION!
OH-H-H, JUGGY! YOU WILL?
HAVE YOU SEEN VERONICA AROUND? I CAN'T FIND HER ANYWHERE!
I'VE BEEN THINKING, ARCH... WHY DON'T YOU TREAT BETTY TO THAT SODA?
WHO HELPS YOU CRAM FOR YOUR MATH TESTS? BETTY! WHO DOES MOST OF YOUR HOMEWORK FOR YOU? BETTY! WHO...
I GUESS YOU'RE RIGHT, JUG...
BETTY'S BEEN A PEACH! ALWAYS IN THERE, PITCHING FOR ME! I'LL FIND HER AND BUY HER THE SODA!
ATT'A BOY, ARCH! BOY! WILL SHE BE HAPPY!
THERE SHE IS, ARCH!
HEY, BETTY! REMEMBER THAT SODA WE WERE TALKING ABOUT? HOW'S ABOUT YOU SHARING IT WITH ME?
I THOUGHT YOU WERE GOING TO ASK VERONICA? WHAT HAPPENED? DID SHE TURN YOU DOWN? SO NOW YOU THINK I'M GOOD ENOUGH, EH?
I DON'T LIKE SECOND-HAND INVITATIONS! DRINK YOUR SODAS BY YOURSELF!
YI-I-I-I!
ARCH,..SINCE THE BEGINNING OF TIME, MAN HAS FIGURED OUT EVERYTHING FROM THE SIMPLE WHEEL TO SPLITTING THE ATOM! I WONDER HOW LONG IT WILL TAKE TO FIGURE OUT A WOMAN'S MIND?
I THOUGHT YOU SAID SHE'D BE HAPPY?
The End

Archie's Girls
Betty and Veronica
"BEHAVIOR PATTERN!"
BETTY, I'M WORRIED! SOMETHING'S GOT TO BE DONE ABOUT ARCHIE AND REGGIE!!
I'VE BEEN TRYING TO DO SOMETHING ABOUT ARCHIE FOR YEARS!
by JOE EDWARDS
NO! I MEAN THEIR RIVALRY! THE WAY THEY TREAT EACH OTHER!!!
BOSH! TISH!...AND BALDERDASH....WHAT'S SO WRONG ABOUT A LITTLE INNOCENT RIVALRY!!
LOOK AT REGGIE! DOES HE LOOK LIKE A CRIMINAL OR SOMETHING?
HI REGGIE!
I'VE GOTTA GET OVER TO ARCHIE'S IN A HURRY! I'VE GOT SOMETHING FOR HIM!
WHAT IS IT?
RAT POISON!!
THERE! YOU SEE? HE'S BRINGING ARCHIE A GIFT OF---OF---.
RAT POISON

RONNIE! YOU WERE RIGHT! RAT POISON!! GOOD GRIEF!!!

W-WHY THAT FIEND! BUT SURELY ARCHIE ISN'T LIKE THAT!
GOLLY NO! ARCHIE IS NOT AS MEAN AND---

ARCHIE! ARCHIE!!! WAIT! WE WANT TO WARN YOU!!!

ABOUT WHAT?
REGGIE! HE'S GONE OVER TO YOUR HOUSE AND---

...TO MY HOUSE? GREAT!

NOW THAT HE'S OUT OF THE WAY, I CAN SNEAK OVER TO HIS HOUSE!!

I WANT TO SET THIS TRAP FOR HIM!! IT'S A SURPRISE!

S-SET A T-TRAP FOR HIM!

OMIGOSH! THIS IS SERIOUS THEY COULD KILL EACH OTHER!

YES!--AND IT'S ALL YOUR FAULT!
MY FAULT?

CERTAINLY! YOU KNOW YOU'RE THE REASON FOR THEIR RIVALRY!
BETTY, YOU'RE RIGHT!

...AND I'M GOING TO DO SOMETHING ABOUT IT! ---GO GET REGGIE!

-AND IF NECESSARY, DRAG HIM OVER TO MY HOUSE!
WHAT ARE YOU GOING TO DO?

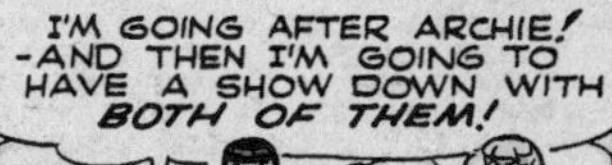
I'M GOING AFTER ARCHIE! -AND THEN I'M GOING TO HAVE A SHOW DOWN WITH BOTH OF THEM!

HEY! TAKE IT EASY! I SAID I'D COME, DIDN'T I??
SHUT UP, YOU...YOU MURDERER!

OUCH! LEGGO!
QUIET....YOU JUVENILE DELINQUENT!

NOW WHY CAN'T YOU TWO ACT LIKE BETTY AND I?
GOLLY! WE WERE TALKING ABOUT THAT THIS MORNING!!

YEAH-WE PROMISED EACH OTHER WE'D NEVER GET LIKE THAT!!!!

PETTY JEALOUSIES!
MEAN!
RESENTFUL!
SQUABBLES!

SO WE DECIDED WE'D TURN OVER A NEW LEAF!---- LIVE BY THE GOLDEN RULE!
YEAH! I EVEN DID REGGIE A FAVOR!

WELL, I TOOK CARE OF THOSE RATS THAT HAVE BEEN NESTING IN YOUR GARAGE!?
YOU DID!--AND I SET ONE OF MY MUSKRAT TRAPS BEHIND YOUR HOUSE LIKE YOU ALWAYS WANTED!

BOY, WHAT A PAL!
YEAH! WHY DON'T YOU GIRLS BE NICE TO EACH OTHER LIKE REGGIE AND I!
END

REGGIE.....

YOU PICKED A FIGHT WITH "RUNT" RILEY, AND HE BEAT YOU UP?
YEAH!

...I DARED HIM TO KNOCK A STICK OFF MY SHOULDER!!

—AN' HE GRABBED THE STICK AND ALMOST BEAT MY BRAINS OUT WITH IT!
R
END

Archie's Girls
Betty and Veronica in
"LIP SERVICE"
bill VIGODA
REGGIE, THAT GLEAM IN YOUR EYE SPELLS TROUBLE FOR SOMEONE! WHAT'S UP?
(:GIGGLE!:) THIS IS TOO GOOD TO KEEP TO MYSELF!

HEE, HEE! H-HERE'S HOW IT WORKS!
PRETEND THAT THIS POST IS SOME UNSUSPECTING GUY!

I SNEAK UP LIKE THIS, AND---GIVE HIM THE OLD, "GUESS WHO" TREATMENT!

YUK-YUK! AND WHEN I REMOVE MY HANDS, -----TEE, HEE! LOOK!
WHA---? B-B-BUT HOW---

HA, HA! SEE? RUBBER STENCILS GLUED ON MY HANDS AND SMEARED WITH LIPSTICK!

REGGIE!! YOU'VE JUST GOT TO PLAY IT ON ARCHIE!!
ARCHIE? BUT YOU KNOW HOW IT'S DONE!

HEE, HEE! BUT HE DOESN'T KNOW I KNOW!
?

HEY THAT'S RIGHT! I'LL GO LOOK HIM UP!

AHA! THERE'S THE POOR SUCKER NOW!

GUESS WHO?
YIPE!

OH IT'S YOU, YOU DARNED FOOL! FOR PETE'S SAKE, HOW CHILDISH CAN YOU GET?

WELL! YOU OLD GROUCH!! I GUESS I KNOW WHEN I'M NOT WANTED!!

HI, RONNIE! BOY DID YOU EVER SEE A GUY LIKE----
W-WHY ARCHIE ANDREWS!!

HOW DARE YOU FLAUNT YOUR PHILANDERING BEFORE ME? YOU-YOU CAD!! LOOK AT YOUR FACE!
?

GOLLY, IF I'D KNOWN YOU WANTED TO FLAUNT YOURS FIRST, I'D--I'D---
(:GIGGLE!:)

YIKE!
H-HOW DID T-THAT HAPPEN?
AS THOUGH YOU DIDN'T KNOW!!

IT HAD TO BE REGGIE! I DON'T KNOW HOW HE DID IT, BUT IT HAD TO BE HIM!

HMPH! TWO-TIMER!
?!?!?!?
HMPH! CONCLUSION-JUMPER!

WHAT WAS THAT ABOUT?
(:GIGGLE!:) REGGIE AND I ARE PLAYING A JOKE ON POOR ARCHIE!

TEE, HEE! AND HE CAN'T FIGURE OUT HOW HE GOT THE LIPSTICK ON HIS FACE!

HMMM! THAT'S TWO AGAINST ONE!

ARCHIE! WAIT! I'VE GOT NEWS FOR YOU!

PST-PSSST! BZZ-BZZZ!! VERONICA TOLD ME ALL ABOUT IT!!
AHA! SO THAT'S HOW HE DID IT, EH?

SURE! AND THEN RONNIE COMES ALONG AND HAS YOU IN A SPOT YOU CAN'T EXPLAIN YOUR WAY OUT OF!!

BETTY, YOU'RE A PAL! NOW, AT LEAST I'M PREPARED! I'LL FIX THAT RONNIE, BUT GOOD!

UH, UH! HERE WE GO AGAIN! THIS TIME HE'LL REALLY SQUIRM!

AHA! SO YOU CAD! ---BEEN AT IT AGAIN, EH ??
HUH?

TSK, TSK! OH DARN! IT'S SO TIRESOME, BEING IRRESISTABLE TO WOMEN!
WHA--?

IT'S ALL OVER REGGIE! HE'S WISE TO THE GAG!
HUH? HOW'D HE FIND OUT?

YOU MUST HAVE SLIPPED UP THE SECOND TIME YOU DID IT, AND HE CAUGHT ON!
I DON'T THINK SO! HE SEEMED---

---- WHAT SECOND TIME?---I ONLY DID IT ONCE!
WHAT?

YOU MEAN SOMEBODY'S STEALING MY STUFF!
I THINK SOMEBODY'S STEALING MY STUFF!
THE END.

JUGHEAD
HMM! PRETTY DOGWOOD!
GOSH, YOU KNOW LOTS ABOUT NATURE AND STUFF!

HOW DO YOU KNOW THAT'S DOGWOOD?

SIMPLE! I CAN TELL BY ITS BARK!

PENCILS: *HARRY LUCEY* INKS & LETTERS: *TERRY SZENICS*

ANYONE CAN SEE HE'S DEVOTED TO YOU! HE'D JUST RUN HOME TO HIS MASTER!
NOT IF YOU TAKE MY ADVICE, BETTY!

JUST RUB SOME SALT ON HIS NOSE EACH DAY! IN A WEEK HE'LL BE COMPLETELY YOURS!
SALT DOES THAT!?

THANKS, REGGIE! I'LL TRY IT!

CROOK! EMBEZZLER! SWINDLER! THAT WAS ONLY A STRAY MUTT FOLLOWING YOU!
WHY, JUGGIE, HOW YOU TALK! TSK! TSK!

I FORGOT "LIAR"! I SUPPOSE RUBBING SALT ON HIS NOSE WILL MAKE HIM LOVE HER?..
WELL...

THAT PLUS THE FACT THAT SHE'LL BE A SOFT TOUCH IN THE FOOD DEPARTMENT!

I THINK THAT WILL DO VERY NICELY, MR. SCHULTZ!
JA, BETTY! THIS STEAK IS SO TENDER YOU WOULDN'T EVEN HAVE TO COOK IT!

THAT'S THE IDEA!

VERONICA in "HATS ENOUGH!"

Betty
IN "WISER ADVISER"
OKAY! OKAY! SO, YOU'RE RIGHT, YOU YOU QUIZ KID!
GOLLY! I CAN'T HELP IT IF I HAPPEN TO HAVE A GOOD MEMORY!
OH!-OH!-LOOKS LIKE YOU RUBBED THAT CAT THE WRONG WAY!
WHO KNOWS? HE ALWAYS ARGUES WHEN WE'RE TOGETHER, THEN BLOWS UP WHEN I PROVE HE'S WRONG!
WHAT A JERK! THAT'S NO WAY TO GET A MAN!
I KNOW I WAS RIGHT!
SO WHAT? WOULD YOU RATHER BE RIGHT THAN ROMANCED?
IF YOU WANT ARCHIE, YOU'VE GOT TO BE A REAL DUMB BLONDE!
HOW'S THIS?
THAT'S IT BETTY!
PENCILS: BILL VIGODA INKS & LETTERS: JOE EDWARDS

OKLE, DOKLE, JUGGY! D-UH! I'LL MAKE BIG MOOSE LOOK LIKE EINSTEIN!

MAYBE JUGGIE'S RIGHT! I'LL TRY ANYTHING TO--

BETTY! OH, BETTY!

-COME HERE A MINUTE, WILL YOU?

BETTY, THIS IS MR. GREENBACK!
HOW DO YOU DO, BETTY!

D-UH! HOW DO I DO WHUT, MR. FATBACK?

ER-A-GREENBACK!
D-UH!-OH!-DON'T MIND IF I DO!

BETTY! WHAT'S COME OVER YOU?
WHO? ME? D-UH! NUTHIN'S COME OVER ME!

-DON'T SEE NUTHIN! DO YOU MR FATBACK? ANYTHIN' COMIN OVER ME?

OH FOR HEAVEN'S SAKE ! I'VE HAD ENOUGH OF THIS !
D-UH ! - HEY, ARCH ! WHAT'S EATIN' HIM ?
OH NOTHING !
- YOU KNOW THAT DAUGHTER OF HIS ? THE DUMB ONE !
D-UH ! SURE !
- WELL HE WAS LOOKING FOR A SMART YOUNG GIRL TO ACCOMPANY HER TO PARIS FOR THE SUMMER !
SACRE BLEU !
LATER
WELL, BETTY ! HOW DID IT WORK OUT ?
OH ! IT WORKED OUT FINE !
- I LEARNED THE SECRET OF HOW TO ACT REAL STUPID !!
YEAH ? WHAT IS IT ?
- FOLLOW YOUR ADVICE !!
END
Jughead
WONDER WHAT IT'S LIKE TO BE MARRIED TO THE SAME MAN FOR FIFTY YEARS ?
NOBODY KNOWS !
WHY NOT ?
- NO MAN IS EVER THE SAME AFTER HE'S MARRIED !

PENCILS: HARRY LUCEY INKS: RED HOMEDALE

JUGGY BID FIVE DOLLARS ON ONE OF THOSE "LOCKED TRUNK" DEALS AT AN AUCTION AND..
HAW! HAW! DON'T TELL ME HE GOT A TRUNK FULL OF LEFT-FOOTED SHOES?

OH, NO!
HIS WERE FOR THE RIGHT FOOT!
HUH?

HOLY COW! THEY MUST BE THE ONES THAT THE SHOE STORE LOST!

IF WE COULD GET BOTH SETS OF SHOES WE COULD SELL THEM BACK TO SAM AND MAKE A NICE PROFIT!
BUT WOULDN'T WE BE CHEATING JUGHEAD?

PERISH FORBID! WE'LL BUY THEM FOR WHAT HE PAID FOR THEM! HE'LL BE HAPPY TO GET HIS MONEY BACK!
I GUESS YOU'RE RIGHT!

..AND I COULD USE SOME EXTRA MONEY!
BUT JUST SO HE DOESN'T GET SUSPICIOUS, YOU BUY 'EM WHILE I GO TO WORK ON SAM!

HEH, HEH! TOO BAD I HAD TO RING BETTY IN ON THIS DEAL BUT I CAN'T AFFORD TO BE GREEDY!
SAM'S
SHOE OUTLET
KEEP YOUR CITY CLEAN

HI, SAM! I SAW YOUR AD IN THE MORNING PAPER!
DON'T REMIND ME!

LOOK, REGGIE, I'M IN NO MOOD FOR YOUR JOKES SO IF YOU DON'T MIND... HIT THE ROAD!
BUT I WANT TO BUY THOSE SHOES!

REGGIE! YOU DEAR, SWEET, LOVEABLE BOY! HERE... HAVE A CHAIR WHILE I GET THEM OUT OF THE STOCK ROOM!

MEANWHILE
BETTY, YOU ALWAYS SEEMED LIKE A SANE, SENSIBLE GIRL! ARE YOU SURE YOU WANT TO GO THROUGH WITH THIS?
YUP!

BUT THE SHOES ARE ALL FOR THE SAME FOOT! DON'T YOU WANT TO LOOK AT THEM?
I'LL TAKE YOUR WORD FOR IT! HERE'S YOUR MONEY!

OKAY! IF THAT'S THE WAY YOU WANT IT! CAN I HELP YOU WITH THE TRUNK?
NO, THANKS! I'M WAITING FOR MY BUSINESS PARTNER! HERE HE COMES!

DID YOU COMPLETE YOUR LITTLE TRANSACTION?
YOU BET!
BETTY! YOU MEAN YOU JOINED FORCES WITH THIS CHISLER?

'S'MATTER? AREN'T YOU SATISFIED WITH GETTING YOUR "FIN" BACK?
OH, SURE!...ONLY I HAVE A MILD DESIRE TO KNOW THE CAUSE OF YOUR INSANITY!

GENIUS IS THE WORD! IN THIS BOX ARE THE MATES TO THE SHOES IN YOUR TRUNK!
NO FOOLIN'? WHERE'D YOU GET 'EM?

WE PURCHASED THEM FROM SAM'S SHOE OUTLET FOR THE TRIFLING SUM OF TEN BUCKS!

NOW ALL WE HAVE TO DO IS MATCH THEM WITH THOSE IN THE TRUNK AND SELL 'EM BACK TO SAM!
THAT'S PRETTY SHARP, ALL RIGHT!

EEP!
ULP!
ANYTHING WRONG?

WOMEN'S SHOES!
CHEER UP! WHEN THE CIRCUS COMES TO TOWN YOU CAN SELL 'EM TO THE FREAKS!
The End

Veronica
in "MEMORIES!"
PLAYING THESE OLD RECORDS BRING SO MANY WONDERFUL MEMORIES BACK TO ME ARCHIE! THIS ONE REMINDS ME OF THE NIGHT WE PARKED DOWN AT THE BEACH!
CLICK!
...AND THE CAR RADIO KEPT ON PLAYING IT OVER AND OVER.... REMEMBER?
AND HOW! MY BATTERY RAN DOWN, AND IT COST ME $15 TO BE TOWED HOME AND POP TOOK IT OUT OF MY ALLOWANCE!

THE BAND PLAYED THIS THE NIGHT WE WENT TO OUR FIRST BARN DANCE!
NOPE! THE NIGHT BETTY THREW A SKATING PARTY, AND I FELL THROUGH THE ICE!
AH! THIS ONE I'LL NEVER FORGET! IT WAS THE DANCE WHERE I WORE MY VERY FIRST REAL EVENING GOWN!
TO ME.... IT'S HAVING TO STAY IN NIGHTS FOR ONE MONTH 'CAUSE YOU WOULDN'T GO HOME 'TILL THREE A.M.!

THIS ONE REMINDS ME OF THE FIRST PROM WE WENT TO!
IT REMINDS ME OF HOW MR. FLUTESNOOT FLUNKED ME IN BIOLOGY BECAUSE I WHISTLED IT IN THE LAB!

I STILL SAY THERE'S NOTHING THAT CAN BRING BACK MEMORIES LIKE THE OLD RECORDS ARCH! ISN'T IT WONDERFUL?
YEAH, THANK GOODNESS FOR THAT!
THE END.

SUPERINTENDENT HASSLE?!
WHAT ARE YOU DOING HERE?
HELLO, MS. PHLIPS! I'VE DECIDED TO FILL IN FOR MR. WEATHERBEE MYSELF!
PRINCIPAL
MS. PHLIPS
WRITER: BILL GOLLIHER
PENCILS: STAN GOLDBERG
INKS: BOB SMITH
Mr. Weatherbee
OPERATION FRUSTRATION
WHEN YOU CALLED LAST NIGHT TO TELL ME HE WAS UNDERGOING AN EMERGENCY TONSILLECTOMY, I BEGAN TO LOOK FOR A SUBSTITUTE!
THEN I HAD A WONDERFUL IDEA! WHY DON'T I JUST DO IT MYSELF?!
WHAT'S THE WONDERFUL PART?

THIS WAY I CAN BE IN TOUCH WITH THE STUDENTS AND FACULTY, AND SEE WHAT THIS PLACE REALLY NEEDS!

WEATHERBEE WILL HAVE SUCH A TIGHT SHIP WHEN HE GETS BACK, HE WON'T KNOW WHAT TO DO!
WEATHERBEE

SOON...
HE WHAT ?!
TEACHERS' LOUNGE

IT'S TRUE! HASSLE IS FILLING IN FOR THE BEE!
Oh, DEAR! IT MUST BE A SIGN OF THE APOCALYPSE!
COFFEE
KOFFEE KING

AH-HAH! THERE ARE MY TEACHERS! NOW GET OUT THERE AND DO YOUR THING!!
BUT IT'S OUR BREAK!

NO MORE BREAKS -- OR COFFEE! WE'VE GOT MINDS TO MOLD!
SWIPE
KOFFEE KING

FROM NOW ON, NO MORE TEACHERS' LOUNGE! IT'S BECOMING ANOTHER SUPPLY CLOSET!
GASP!
EVERYONE BACK TO CLASS!!
BUT WE'RE STILL ON LUNCH BREAK!

FROM NOW ON, LUNCH BREAK IS JUST FOR EATING, AND THEN BACK TO WORK!! THIS IS A SCHOOL, NOT A PLAYGROUND!!

LATER...
AFTER SOME THOUGHT, I'M CUTTING THE TIME BETWEEN CLASSES FROM TEN MINUTES DOWN TO THREE!
WHAT?!

BETWEEN THAT AND SHORTER LUNCHES, WE'LL PICK UP AN EXTRA 37 MINUTES OF CLASS TIME PER DAY!
ARE YOU HEARING THIS?!

THAT DOES IT! WE HAVE TO LET WEATHERBEE KNOW WHAT'S GOING ON HERE!

LATER, AT THE HOSPITAL...
HASSLE'S GONE POWER MAD!
I NEVER THOUGHT I'D SAY THIS... BUT YOU HAVE TO COME BACK TO SCHOOL-- QUICKLY!
ARCHIE

WHAT IS GOING ON HERE?!
MY FACULTY AND STUDENTS SAY I NEED TO GET BACK TO WORK!

I'M THE DOCTOR, AND I'LL DECIDE WHEN HE RETURNS TO WORK!
BUT IT'S AN EMERGENCY!

EVERYONE LEAVE MY PATIENT ALONE!
BUT--BUT--
BUT NOTHING! GO!!

WALDO! IT'S IMPORTANT THAT YOU GET YOUR REST! I'M KEEPING YOU ANOTHER DAY!
REALLY? WHAT SAY WE MAKE IT TWO?!

NEXT MORNING...
THAT'S ODD! IT'S AFTER EIGHT AND HASSLE'S NOT BARKING ORDERS!
YOU'RE RIGHT!

MS. GRUNDY! I JUST GOT A CALL FROM MRS. HASSLE!
MRS. HASSLE?! IS EVERYTHING OKAY?
NO! HASSLE HAD A SUDDEN CASE OF APPENDICITIS!
YOU DON'T SAY!

HE WON'T BE BACK! HE HAD TO HAVE HIS APPENDIX OUT!
THANK GOODNESS FOR THAT ANNOYING, USELESS ORGAN!!

I JUST HOPE HE ENJOYS HIS TIME AWAY FROM US AS MUCH AS WE WILL ENJOY OUR TIME AWAY FROM HIM!

MEANWHILE...
yawn! WHAT A PEACEFUL NIGHT'S SLEEP!
I'LL SEE WHAT'S ON TV!
RIVER HOSP
KLIK

TURN THAT OFF!!
WHAT?! I GOT A ROOMMATE OVER-NIGHT?!
IN THE NEWS...

SUPERINTENDENT HASSLE?!
WEATHERBEE?!

I JUST HAD MY APPENDIX OUT!
REALLY?!

IMAGINE WAKING UP IN THE SAME ROOM AS YOU!
YEAH! WHAT'RE THE CHANCES?

THIS IS A GOOD OPPORTUNITY FOR ME TO TELL YOU ALL THE THINGS I FOUND WRONG WITH YOUR SCHOOL...
AZETTE

LATER...
AND FURTHERMORE... BLAH BLAH BLAH BLAH BLAH...
Shhh!! IT'S A MIRACLE, DOC! I'VE HAD ALL THE REST I CAN TAKE! I'M HEADING BACK TO SCHOOL, PRONTO!
?!
END

Mr. Lodge in SNOW JOKE

Script & Pencils: Al Hartley / Inks: Jon D'Agostino / Letters: Bill Yoshida / Colors: Barry Grossman

GET THAT CAR OUT OF MY DRIVEWAY! I DON'T CARE HOW!

TAKE IT APART PIECE BY PIECE AND CARRY IT OUT IF YOU HAVE TO! BUT GET IT OUT OF HERE!
SLAM

WELL ???
I'M THINKING! I'M THINKING!

FOLLOW ME TO THE GARAGE, JUG!

HELP ME GET THESE SAILS OUT OF THE LOFT!

WE'LL TIE THE SAILS TOGETHER!

LET'S GET THEM OVER TO THE CAR NOW!

NEXT WE ATTACH THEM TO THE EXHAUST PIPE!

AND NOW I'LL START THE ENGINE AND INFLATE THEM!

LOOK AT IT RISE WITH THE WARM AIR, JUG!

WE'LL LET IT LIFT THE CAR UP A BIT AND THEN WE'LL PUSH IT OUT OF HERE!

OKAY, JUG...
PUSH!

OKAY, JUG!
THAT'S ENOUGH!

I SAID "THAT'S ENOUGH", JUG!

AHHH... THERE'S SOMETHING NOSTALGIC ABOUT A BLIZZARD!

TAKES ME BACK TO MY CHILDHOOD!

I'LL SLEEP WELL TONIGHT!

THUMP
THUMP
KNOCK
KNOCK
WHAT'S THAT?

KNOCK
KNOCK
ARCHIE!
WHAT DO YOU WANT?

UH... I GOT MY CAR OUT OF YOUR DRIVEWAY!

WELL, GOOD!
NOW GET OFF MY ROOF AND GO HOME!

UH... I CAN'T MR. LODGE!
WHAT DO YOU MEAN, "YOU CAN'T"?

MY CAR'S ON YOUR ROOF, TOO!
The END

MR. WEATHERBEE, MR. HASSLE IS HERE TO SEE YOU!
OH, GREAT! JUST GREAT!
JUST WHAT I NEED TO MAKE MY DAY COMPLETE!
WONDER WHAT KIND OF NUTTY IDEA HE'S COME UP WITH NOW!
Svenson
BEEP beep BEEP
Script: George Gladir / Art & Letters: Samm Schwartz / Colors Barry Grossman
WEATHERBEE, WE OF THE SCHOOL BOARD FEEL THE TIME HAS COME FOR RIVERDALE HIGH TO MOVE INTO THE TWENTY FIRST CENTURY!
SO SOON? WHY, THE TWENTIETH WAS HERE ONLY THIS MORNING! I'LL HAVE TO SET MY CLOCK AHEAD!
1

VERY AMUSING, WEATHERBEE, BUT WE'RE INITIATING A HIGH-TECH COMMUNICATIONS SYSTEM AND YOU'RE A PART OF THE NETWORK!
HIGH-TECH?

YES! TWO-WAY BEEPERS! ONE WILL KEEP US IN TOUCH AND THE OTHER IS FOR YOUR CUSTODIAN!
SVENSON NEEDS A BEEPER?

ALL YOU DO IS PRESS THE BUTTON AND IT SENDS OUT A SIGNAL TO THE OTHER'S BEEPER TO GO TO A PHONE AND CALL!

A BEEPER? VOT FOR DO I NEED A BEEPER?
IT WILL HELP YOU DO YOUR WORK MORE EFFICIENTLY!.. I HOPE!

BEEP BEEP
UH, OH! DERE GOES BEEPER! I BETTER CALL DER BEE!
BEEP

SVENSON, COME UP TO MY OFFICE! MY DESK DRAWER IS STUCK!
YA!

LATER
BEEP BEEP
BOINK
NOW VOT?
SVENSON! MY CHAIR IS SQUEAKING!
AGAIN?
MY WINDOW IS STUCK!
MY FILING CABINET IS LEANING!
SO IS TOWER OF PISA, BUT DEY DON'T BEEP ME!
BEEP BEEP
BEEP BEEP
BEEP
SHEE-EESH! EVEN VEN AY EAT!
SVENSON, THE GYM DOOR NEEDS PAINTING! SEE TO IT!
HOKAY!
TWO CAN PLAY GAME AS GOOD AS VUN! VE SEE HOW HE LIKE TO BE BEEPED ALL DER TIME!
THAT'S SVENSON'S BEEPER! IT MUST BE IMPORTANT!
BEEP
BEEP

YES, SVENSON?
VOT COLOR YOU VANT I PAINT DOOR?
GREEN! GREEN SOUNDS NICE!
BEEP
NOW WHAT?
VE OUT OF GREEN!
YOU CAN PAINT IT POLKA DOT FOR ALL I CARE!
BEEEEEEEP
HE'S JUST DOING THIS TO SPITE ME!
I'LL SHOW HIM! TWO CAN PLAY THIS GAME AS WELL AS ONE!
HE SHOULD BE ON HIS LADDER BY NOW!
RING!
HELLO, SVENSON?
NO-OOO! IT'S NOT SVENSON!
THIS'D BETTER BE IMPORTANT, WEATHERBEE! I'M IN THE MIDDLE OF AN IMPORTANT CONFERENCE!

..AND THE NEXT TIME YOU BEEP ME IT HAD BETTER BE SOME-THING IMPORTANT!

I'M NOT TAKING ANY CHANCES! THAT BEEPER STAYS HERE ON MY DESK WHILE I HAVE A SNACK!

YOO-HOO! FLUFFY! COME TO MOMMY!
VOT YOU LOOK FOR, MISS PHLIPS?

I BROUGHT MY CAT, FLUFFY, TODAY, SO I COULD TAKE HER TO THE VET AFTER SCHOOL, BUT SHE'S DISAPPEARED!

I'D BETTER FIND HER BEFORE SHE STARTS WANDERING THROUGH THE SCHOOL!
HERE, KITTY, KITTY! NICE KITTY!

OH, NO! NOT AGAIN! WHAT CAN HE WANT THIS TIME?
BEEP BEEP

WHAT DO YOU MEAN HE'S NOT THERE? HE'S BEEN BEEPING ME LIKE CRAZY THESE LAST TEN MINUTES!
AY DON'T KNOW! AY YUST FIX THINGS IN OFFICE!
LATER
MR. VEDERBEE, MR. HASSLE VANTS TO SEE US IN OFFICE, NOW!
HAND OVER YOUR BEEPERS! THEY'RE NOT TOYS TO BE TOYED WITH! HAND THEM OVER, NOW!

FROM NOW ON THIS SCHOOL IS STRICTLY LOW-TECH!

IT'S ABOUT TIME YOU FIXED MY COFFEE-MAKER!
YA! I GOT LOTS OF TIME NOW VE BACK IN DER TVENTIETH CENTURY!
END

Miss Grundy in "Perfectly Archie"

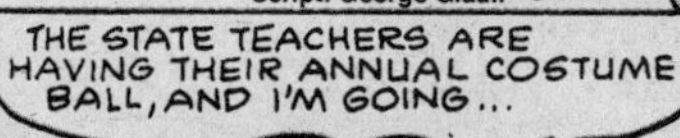

Script: George Gladir Pencils & Letters: Samm Schwartz / Inks: Rudy Lapick

MAN! THAT IS COOL! THAT'S REALLY COOL! I'M FLATTERED, MISS GRUNDY!
WHY DID YOU CHOOSE ARCHIE, MISS GRUNDY?

I WANT TO GO AS RIVERDALE HIGH'S MOST PICTURESQUE STUDENT!
HOW TRUE! THAT'S SO TRUE!

IT'S KIND OF HARD TO IMAGINE YOU LOOKING LIKE ARCHIE, MISS G.!
WAIT!

HOW DOES THAT GRAB YOU?
(GIGGLE) THIS IS SOMETHING ELSE!

I'LL PUT SOME FRECKLES ACROSS MY NOSE AND I'VE GOT A SWEATER AND SLACKS LIKE HIS!
CLOTHES ALONE DO NOT AN ARCHIE MAKE!
2

THAT'S RIGHT! TO BE AN ARCHIE, YOU'VE GOT TO ACT LIKE AN ARCHIE!
PERHAPS YOU CAN SHOW ME SOME..ER.. ARCHIEISMS!
FOLLOW ME!

WALK REAL SLOWLY, LIKE ME.. RIGHT PAST THE BEE.. MR. WEATHERBEE'S DOOR!

IF YOU CALL HIM "THE BEE" THEN I CALL HIM "THE BEE". I WANT TO DO THIS RIGHT!

..JUST UNTIL YOU GET PAST AND HE CAN'T CATCH YOU, SEE?
AND THEN?

RUN!

MMPH! THIS IS FUN!
YOU'RE CATCHING ON FAST, MISS G.!
ZONK!
ER...I THINK I'VE HAD ENOUGH PRACTICE FOR NOW!
YOU'RE A GREAT TEACHER, ARCHIE!

THAT EVENING:
(GIGGLE) TIME TO GET INTO MY COSTUME!

JUST WAIT UNTIL MR. WEATHE... I MEAN "THE BEE" SEES ME!

I FEEL LIKE GIVING MYSELF DETENTION!

THINK ARCHIE!
LOOK ARCHIE!
ACT ARCHIE!

I'M GLAD NONE OF THE NEIGHBORS SAW ME! NOW TO WHEEL OVER TO THE COMMUNITY CENTER!

GROOVY, BABY! LET IT ALL HANG OUT! LET'S ALL DO OUR OWN THING! COOL, MAN! COO...Ooo....

ULP! TH-THIS DOESN'T LOOK LIKE THE STATE TEACHERS' COSTUME BALL!

THE STATE TEACHERS' BALL IS NEXT WEEK! THIS IS A MEETING OF THE NATIONAL ASSOCIATION OF MUSEUM ATTENDANTS!

NEXT DAY..
HOW DID IT GO, MISS G.?
GIRLS, YOU WOULDN'T BELIEVE IT!

I MADE A PERFECT **ARCHIE** OF MYSELF!
END

Betty and Veronica IN "YOU CAN'T ALWAYS GET WHAT YOU WANT!"

Script: Frank Doyle / Pencils: Dan DeCarlo / Inks: Rudy Lapick / Letters: Bill Yoshida / Colors: Barry Grossman

BITTERLY COLD WEATHER! ICY WINDS NIPPING YOUR NOSE, AND BITING YOUR FINGERS AND TOES!
NICE! YOU OUGHTA SET THAT TO MUSIC!

COLDS, FLU, STUFFED-UP HEAD, OVER-WRAPPED BODY! SHORT DAYS AND LONG, DARK NIGHTS!
OKAY, OKAY!

I'D LIKE TO FEEL WARM WHEN THE SUN SHINES!
A BALMY BREEZE OF AT LEAST 55°!
YOU'RE RHYMING AGAIN!

TO RUN AROUND HALF, ER, THREE-FOURTHS, ER, SOMEWHAT BARE!
BAREFOOT, MAYBE!
CRUISE WEAR

I'VE HAD ENOUGH OF WINTER!
SPRING WILL BE HERE SOON!

NOT SOON ENOUGH FOR ME!
YOU KNOW WHAT, BETTY? YOU'RE RIGHT!

I AM? I MEAN YEAH, I AM!
I'VE HAD ENOUGH OF WINTER, TOO! LET'S DO SOMETHING ABOUT IT!
TUNA

WHAT? OFFER SACRIFICES TO THE SUN?
NO, SILLY! DON'T WE HAVE A MONDAY HOLIDAY THIS MONTH?

YEAH, SO WHAT?
SO, YOU AND I ARE GOING THAT WEEKEND TO WHERE THE SUN IS WARM AND THE BREEZES ARE BALMY!

WE'RE GOING TO HAWAII!!
HAWAII-?? OH, RON! OH, WOW!!
USA

C'MON! WE'VE GOT OODLES OF THINGS TO DO!
PARENTAL CONSENT, RESERVATIONS, SHOPPING, PACKING!
HAWAII! OH, WOW!
USA

AND SO THE PREPARATIONS BEGIN...
RON! THIS IS THE FOURTH MALL WE'VE BEEN TO TODAY!
I HAVEN'T FOUND JUST THE RIGHT SWIMSUIT YET, BETTY!
RIVERDALE MALL
3

AND CONTINUED...
YOU'LL NEED SOMEONE TO REPLACE YOUR BABY-SITTING JOBS THAT WEEKEND!
I WON'T FORGET, MOM!

RIGHT NOW I'M GETTING SOMEONE TO REPLACE ME AT THE COMMUNITY CENTER BAZAAR!
VERONICA'S HERE!

READY TO PICK UP OUR TICKETS?
YOU BET!

WITH THESE WE REALLY ARE ON OUR WAY! NO MORE COLD WEATHER!
NOT QUITE YET!
NYC
SEE
MEXICO

THERE'S STILL THE MATTER OF PACKING!
BUT I'M ALREADY PACKED!

WE NEED TO FINISH MY PACKING, SILLY!
HOLY TOLEDO!!
4

WE'RE ONLY GOING TO BE GONE THREE DAYS, RON!
I LIKE TO BE PREPARED FOR ANYTHING!

FINALLY! PUFF! PANT! I'M EXHAUSTED! I'M GONNA NEED THIS TRIP!
ME, TOO! IT'S BEEN ONE HECTIC WEEK!

PINCH ME, VERONICA! ARE WE REALLY HERE?
FEEL THAT SUNSHINE? THOSE BALMY BREEZES?
ROYAL HAWAIIAN HOTEL
TAXI

WHAT DO YOU THINK?
WOW! I CAN HARDLY BELIEVE IT!

AHH! THIS IS THE SUMMER I DREAMED OF!
IF ONLY RIVERDALE COULD BE LIKE THIS!

LET'S SIT AND THINK ABOUT EVERYONE BACK HOME, RON!
RUNNING AROUND IN MITTENS, COATS, HATS AND SCARVES!

DON'T WE JUST FEEL FOR THEM?!

HA-HA-HA
TEE HEE!
GIGGLE! SNORT!
GOOFY TEEN-AGERS!

THREE DAYS WHIZ BY, AND SOON...
HI, ARCHIE! WE'RE BACK TO THE ICE-BOX AGAIN!
ICEBOX? ARE YOU KIDDING?

IT WAS LIKE AN OVEN AROUND HERE WHILE YOU WERE GONE!
IT GOT SO HOT WE HADDA RUN AROUND IN SHORTS!
RIVERDALE BUGLE
80° WEEKEND
NEW RECORDS SET
UNUSUAL WEATHER

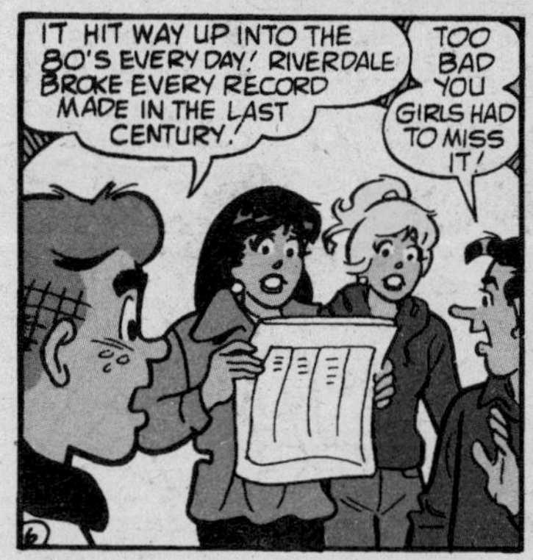
IT HIT WAY UP INTO THE 80'S EVERY DAY! RIVERDALE BROKE EVERY RECORD MADE IN THE LAST CENTURY!
TOO BAD YOU GIRLS HAD TO MISS IT!
6

WAAH!
TSK! THERE'S JUST NO PLEASING SOME FOLKS, IS THERE, POPS?!
END

Miss BEAZLY!
CROSS OUT ALL THE LETTERS IN BOXES CONTAINING AN ODD NUMBER TO DISCOVER WHAT CULINARY DELIGHTS ARE ON TODAY'S LUNCH MENU !!
The ANSWERS:
1. PORK PATTIES 2. BROCCOLI
3. OLIVE LOAF

Reggie
-in-
"RIVALS TO THE END"
DIG ARCHIE AND REGGIE RACING HEAD-TO-HEAD!

DIG ARCHIE AND REGGIE FINISHING NOSE-TO-NOSE!

CRACK

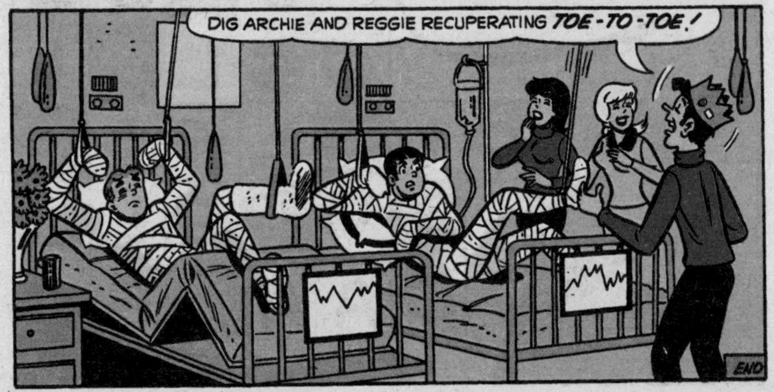
DIG ARCHIE AND REGGIE RECUPERATING TOE-TO-TOE!
END

SCRIPT & PENCILS: BILL GOLLIHER INKS: RUDY LAPICK
LETTERS: BILL YOSHIDA COLORS: BARRY GROSSMAN

ALL I NEED IS JUST A WARM BODY TO PUT IN THAT CLASS-ROOM!
HELLO DERE, MR. VEDDERBEE!

ARE YOU THINKING WHAT I'M THINKING?
YES! WE'VE FOUND OUR SUBSTITUTE!
VAT?!

MS. GRUNDY CALLED IN SICK AND WE COULDN'T GET ANYONE TO FILL IN FOR HER UNTIL NOW!
OH, NO!

I FACE DANGEROUS SITUATIONS HERE EVERY DAY! RICKETY LADDERS AND VORKING VITH ELECTRICITY...

...BUT I DRAW THE LINE AT FACING A CLASS FULL OF TEENAGERS!
DON'T WORRY! THERE'S NOTHING TO IT!

OKAY, BUT VAT SUBJECT VILL I BE TEACHING?
ENGLISH!
2

AH, FINE! AT LËAST DAT IS SOMETHING I KNOW GOOD!
UH... YEAH, SURE!

CLASS, MR. SVENSON WILL BE FILLING IN FOR MS. GRUNDY TODAY WHILE SHE'S OUT SICK!
YAY, SVENSON!
READ

YOU ALL HAD BETTER BE ON YOUR BEST BEHAVIOR!
IF NOT, WHAT'S HE GOING TO DO? CLEAN OUR CLOCKS? HAR! HAR!

AND SO...
SO, VAT ARE YOU STUDYING IN ENGLISH CLASS?
THAT WOULD BE DANGLING PARTICIPLES AND GERUNDS!

OOF! EVEN THOUGH I SPEAK THE ENGLISH LIKE A PRO, I DON'T KNOW MUCH ABOUT THOSE!
WHAT ARE YOU GOING TO TEACH US THEN?
READ

I DON'T KNOW! ANY IDEAS?
THERE MUST BE SOMETHING YOU'RE PASSIONATE ABOUT!

ISN'T THERE SOMETHING THAT YOU KNOW THAT YOU'D LIKE TO SHARE WITH OTHERS?
DA! MAYBE I DO HAVE SOME-THING!

AT DAY'S END...
MR. SVENSON, THANKS AGAIN FOR FILLING IN!
SURE! IT WAS MUCH MORE FUN DAN I IMAGINED!

NEXT MORNING...
WOULD YOU LOOK AT THIS! TRASH ON THE GROUNDS! SOME PEOPLE...
?
UH... THANKS, CHUCK!
RIVE
HIG

AHEM! MAY I HELP YOU GIRLS?

OH, WE WERE JUST CLEANING UP YOUR WINDOW! THERE WAS A DIRTY SPOT!
THANKS!
SOMETHING STRANGE IS GOING ON HERE!
MR. WEATHERBEE...
PRINCIPAL

MR. ANDREWS, WHAT BRINGS YOU PARENTS HERE?
I JUST WANTED TO THANK YOU! MR. SVENSON TAUGHT ARCHIE HOW TO POLISH WOOD! OUR STAIRCASE LOOKS LIKE NEW!
JUGHEAD WAXED THE KITCHEN FLOOR LAST NIGHT! WHAT A SHINE!
VERONICA CLEANED ALL THE CHANDELIERS IN THE MANSION!
SOON...
MR. SVENSON, WHAT HAPPENED IN YOUR CLASSES YESTERDAY?
I DECIDED TO TEACH THEM SOMETHING I'M PASSIONATE ABOUT...
...CLEANING!
THE MESSAGE MUST HAVE CERTAINLY GOT THROUGH!

I GUESS I VAS ABLE TO MAKE IT INTERESTING!
DAT... ER... THAT IS THE MARK OF A GOOD TEACHER!
5

MR. SVENSON, I'VE DECIDED TO GIVE YOU FIFTEEN MINUTES A WEEK TO WORK WITH KIDS!
BECAUSE A CLEAN SCHOOL IS A HAPPY SCHOOL!
YUMPIN' YIMINY! I'M A TEACHER!

A FEW WEEKS LATER...
SVENSON'S LITTLE CLASS IS PAYING OFF! IT'S HELPED HIS SELF CONFIDENCE AND THE KIDS ARE ENJOYING IT!

AND YOU'VE GOT TO ADMIT THE CAMPUS IS STAYING A LOT CLEANER!

I JUST WISH IT HADN'T HAD SUCH AN EFFECT ON THEIR WARDROBES, THOUGH!
END

Script: Frank Doyle / Pencils: Dan DeCarlo / Ink: Rudy Lapick / Letters: Vince DeCarlo / Colors: Barry Grossman

SEE? NOW YOU'RE IN FOR IT!
RIDICULOUS!

MR. WEATHERBEE!!
YES?

MY DADDY IS PRESIDENT OF LODGE ENTERPRISES!
YES?

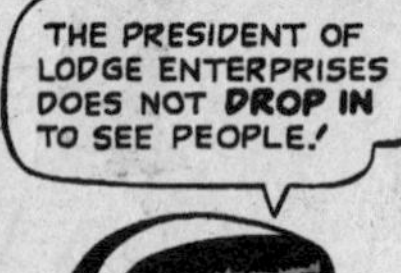
THE PRESIDENT OF LODGE ENTERPRISES DOES NOT DROP IN TO SEE PEOPLE!

ER- YOU MEAN I SHOULD DROP IN ON HIM?
BAKE SALE

HA, HA! THAT'S PRICELESS!
I'LL TELL DADDY, AND HE CAN PASS THE WORD TO HIS SECRETARY!
?

--- SHE WILL MAKE AN APPOINTMENT FOR YOU AT THE FIRST AVAILABLE OPPORTUNITY!

HMMM! ALL RIGHT, YOUNG LADY! JUST AS LONG AS YOU TELL YOUR FATHER!
OH, I'LL DO THAT!

VERONICA LODGE! HOW AWFUL! HOW RUDE! AREN'T YOU ASHAMED OF YOURSELF?
NOT IN THE LEAST!

DADDY HAS MORE IMPORTANT THINGS TO DO THAN HANGING AROUND A GRUBBY OLD SCHOOL!

YOU ARE AN INSUFFERABLE SNOB!
NONSENSE!

I AM MERELY AWARE OF MY SOCIAL POSITION!

LATER--
DADDY, MY PRINCIPAL, MR. WEATHERBEE, WOULD LIKE TO SEE YOU!
EGAD! WHAT DID YOU DO?

WHY, NATURALLY, I TOLD HIM YOU WOULD HAVE YOUR SECRETARY MAKE AN APPOINTMENT FOR HIM!

Y-YOU TOLD MR. WEATHERBEE **THAT?**
BUT OF **COURSE!**

NATURALLY, I TOLD HIM HE WOULD HAVE TO WAIT HIS TURN!
NATURALLY!

HMM! ALL RIGHT, DEAR! I'LL TAKE CARE OF IT!

MR. WEATHERBEE? THIS IS LODGE!
WOULD TOMORROW MORNING BE ALRIGHT?

GRACIOUS! I DIDN'T EXPECT AN APPOINTMENT BEFORE NEXT CHRISTMAS!

ULP! **PLEASE,** MR. WEATHERBEE! I'LL BE AT YOUR OFFICE AT NINE!

ER, BUT I'D LIKE THIS HANDLED **MY** WAY, IF YOU PLEASE!
I'LL EXPLAIN WHAT I HAVE IN MIND---

NEXT DAY–
IMAGINE HIM EXPECTING MY DADDY TO COME **HERE?**

A BIG TYCOON LIKE THAT! WHY, IT'S LAUGHABLE!

DADDY IS MUCH TOO IMPORTANT TO BE--- BE---

---**DADDY!!** WHAT ARE YOU DOING HERE?
WAITING UNTIL MR. WEATHERBEE IS READY FOR ME!

B-BUT, DADDY! HOW DEGRADING! YOU'RE A **RICH, BUSY** AND **IMPORTANT** MAN!

I DIDN'T GET **RICH, BUSY OR IMPORTANT** BY LOOKING DOWN MY NOSE AT OTHER PEOPLE, VERONICA!

AND BESIDES, MR. WEATHERBEE HAS A JOB THAT'S MUCH MORE IMPORTANT THAN MINE!
ULP! H-HE **DOES?**

I BUILD FACTORIES AND FORTUNES!
HE BUILDS MEN AND WOMEN!
NCIPAL

I'LL SEE YOU NOW, MR. LODGE!
SOMETIMES HE'S NOT TOO SUCCESSFUL!

WELL, RONNIE?
(SNIFF) G-GO AWAY, PLEASE!

DID I KEEP YOU WAITING LONG ENOUGH? DID IT WORK?
SHALL WE SEE?

VERONICA?

I'M WAITING TO SEE MR. WEATHERBEE, DADDY!
I'VE GOT SOME APOLOGIZING TO DO!

MAY I COME IN NOW, SIR?
(CHUCKLE) SHE'LL BE ALL RIGHT, NOW!
PRINCIPAL
THE END

Script: George Gladir / Pencils: Bob Bolling / Inks: Rudy Lapick / Letters: Bill Yoshida / Colors Barry Grossman

STUDENT-WHY-ARE-YOU-LATE?
I MISSED THE SCHOOL BUS.!

THAT-IS-NOT-AN-ACCEPTABLE-EXCUSE.!--- ONE-SHOULD-GET-UP-EARLY-ENOUGH-TO-ARRIVE-PROMPTLY.!

HERE-IS-YOUR-DETENTION-SLIP.!
KER-CHUNG!

SEE.! YOU DON'T EVEN HAVE TO TALK TO THE OFFENDING STUDENTS.!
FANTASTIC.!

AND THE COMPLETE SET-UP IS A MERE $50,000.!
YOU'VE JUST ABOUT SOLD ME.!

HEH.! HEH.! WATCH THE MACHINE GO TO WORK ON THIS TARDY STUDENT.!
2

STUDENT-WHY-ARE-YOU-LATE?
?
TSHUNG!

WHO'S TALKING?
THAT-IS-NOT-PERTINENT! WHY-ARE-YOU-LATE?

I WOULD HAVE BEEN ON TIME BUT, ER--- BUT JUST AS I WAS LEAVING HOME A HERD OF SHEEP BROKE THROUGH OUR FENCE AND I HAD TO DRIVE 'EM OUT!

??? THE MACHINE LET HIM THROUGH!

COMPUTER XR7, WHY DID YOU LET THAT STUDENT PASS?
WHIZ! RATTLE! FIZZ! - THE-STUDENT'S-EXCUSE-DID-NOT-COMPUTE!

UH, MR. WEATHERBEE, THAT'S THE FIRST TIME OUR COMPUTER HAS EVER FAILED TO ANALYZE AN ALIBI!
BUT IN ALL FAIRNESS-- WHO EVER HEARD OF SHEEP IN A RESIDENTIAL NEIGHBORHOOD?

YES, BUT THAT'S MY PROBLEM!--- I HAVE TO PUT UP WITH THAT SORT OF NONSENSE ALL THE TIME!

AHEM! LET'S SWITCH TO THE CLASSROOM MONITOR PART OF OUR SYSTEM!

OBSERVE HOW IT HAS CAUGHT A STUDENT FLYING A PAPER PLANE!

STUDENT-YOU-CANNOT-DENY-YOU-FLEW-THIS-PAPER-PLANE! THE-INCIDENT-IS-RECORDED-ON-FILM!
4

OF COURSE IT'S MY PLANE! I WON'T DENY IT!

I'M WORKING OUT A PROBLEM IN AERODYNAMICS!

GULP! THAT'S THE FIRST TIME MY MONITOR HAS EVER FAILED ME!
WHIZ
RATTLE
FIZZ
ZOW

AH! OUR ACCIDENT PREVENTER IS BEEPING! LET'S WATCH!

DANGER! A-SKATE-BOARD-IS-IN-THE-CORRIDOR!
THE WARNING GIVES US TIME TO STAND AGAINST THE WALL AND AVOID AN ACCIDENT!
PRINCIPAL

PRINCIPAL
PRINCIPAL
GEE! MR. WEATHERBEE ISN'T IN HIS OFFICE TO ACCEPT THIS SKATEBOARD I FOUND!
MAYBE HE'S OUT IN THE CORRIDOR!

SLAM!

I'M SORRY! THERE IS NO WAY I CAN HELP YOU WITH YOUR IMPOSSIBLE SCHOOL!

ARCHIE!
ER, I CAN EXPLAIN, MR. WEATHERBEE!

CONGRATULATIONS! YOU JUST SAVED OUR SCHOOL $ 50,000!
I DID?

YES! AND YOU ALSO HELPED MY MORALE! IT'S NICE TO KNOW I'M NOT THE ONLY ONE WHO CAN'T COPE WITH YOU!
END

Archie in

Script: Frank Doyle / Pencils: Stan Goldberg / Inks: Jon D'Agostino / Letters: Bill Yoshida / Colors: Barry Grossman

I JUST CAN'T WAIT UNTIL I'M OLD ENOUGH TO ASK HER FATHER FOR HER HAND IN MARRIAGE!
I DON'T KNOW IF YOU SHOULD JUST ASK FOR HER HAND, ARCH! IT WILL ALWAYS BE OPEN, ASKING YOU TO COME ACROSS WITH SOME BREAD!

OH, COME ON, JUG! RONNIE'S NOT LIKE THAT! SHE'S A VERY UNDERSTANDING GIRL!
OH, SURE! IF YOU'RE VERY RICH!

SHE'S GOING TO MAKE A GREAT LITTLE WIFE!
NOT THE WAY I PICTURE IT, OLD BUDDY!

I CAN SEE IT AS PLAIN AS DAY! YOU'RE MARRIED FOR JUST A COUPLE OF MONTHS, AND YOU'RE COMING HOME FROM WORK...
?
HI, HONEY! I'M HOME!

DON'T YOU HONEY ME, YOU DEADBEAT!
MOVIE STAR

AND LOOK AT YOU! YOU LOOK LIKE A BUM!
WELL, THIS IS THE ONLY SUIT OF CLOTHES I OWN ON THE SMALL ALLOWANCE YOU GIVE ME!

DO YOU REALIZE THE SACRIFICES I HAD TO MAKE THIS MORNING FOR MARRYING A CREEP LIKE YOU?
WHAT HAPPENED, MY PET? DID YOU HAVE A BAD DAY?
MOVIE STAR

I'LL SAY!--- I ONLY HAD ENOUGH MONEY ON ME TODAY TO BUY THREE NEW OUTFITS AT THE BOUTIQUE SHOP!

I HAD TO SWALLOW MY PRIDE AND LEAVE A TEN DOLLAR DEPOSIT ON THE FOURTH DRESS I LIKED, JUST LIKE A COMMON PEASANT!

WHY DON'T YOU GET ANOTHER JOB SO YOU CAN GIVE ME MORE MONEY?
BUT THERE'S ONLY 24 HOURS IN A DAY, SWEETIE, AND I'M ALREADY WORKING 20 HOURS WITH TWO JOBS!

IF YOU HAD ANY BACKBONE, YOU COULD GET A PART-TIME JOB SOMEWHERE TO WORK THOSE OTHER 4 HOURS!
GULP!
CLICK!

YES, MY LOVE! I'LL SEE WHAT I CAN DO ABOUT IT!
MY FATHER WAS RIGHT ABOUT YOU! YOU'RE A REAL GOOF-OFF!
T.V. GUIDE
CLICK!
CLICK!
CLICK!

GEE, RONNIE HONEY! HOW SWEET OF YOU! YOU PREPARED ME A NICE BIG T-BONE STEAK AND A DELICIOUS LOOKING SALAD!
OH, BOY! YOU'RE SUCH A GOOD WIFE! YOU KNEW I'D BE STARVING BECAUSE YOU NEVER MAKE ME ANY LUNCH OR BREAKFAST!

GET YOUR GRUBBY, DIRTY STINKY PAWS OFF MY STEAK!
?

BUT WHERE'S MINE, MY PET?
THERE'S A CAN OF BEANS IN THE CABINET AND YOU KNOW WHERE THE CAN OPENER IS!
SLURP!
SLURP!

HOW COME I DON'T GET ANY STEAK, LOVEY?
BECAUSE WE CAN'T AFFORD TWO STEAKS ON YOUR MEASLY LITTLE SALARY. THAT'S WHY! ANYWAY, YOU'RE USED TO THAT GARBAGE BETTY USED TO COOK FOR YOU!
SOAP
BEANS

NOW GET OUT OF HERE OR YOU'LL BE LATE FOR YOUR OTHER JOB!
I HAVE THINGS TO DO!

I HAVE TO FIND OUT WHERE I CAN HIRE A MAID TO DO ALL THIS HOUSE-WORK! IT'S JUST NOT MY THING!

DO YOU GET THE PICTURE, OLD BUDDY ?
?

OH, COME ON, JUG, YOU'RE EXAGGERATING!
RONNIE COULD NEVER BE LIKE THAT! I MEAN, COULD SHE ?

I JUST TELL IT LIKE I SEE IT, OLD PAL!
OH, ARCHIE! HAVE, I GOT NEWS FOR YOU!

YOU AND I ARE GOING TO A WEDDING THIS SATURDAY!
?

COUNT ME OUT, RONNIE! I'M JUST NOT READY FOR ANY WEDDINGS! I'M TOO YOUNG!
WHAT'S WITH HIM ? ALL I WANTED TO DO WAS INVITE HIM TO MY COUSIN'S WEDDING!
BEATS ME, RONNIE! MAYBE HE'S AT THE AGE WHERE WEDDINGS MAKE HIM CRY!
END

Veronica in "The SHOPPER"

Script: George Gladir / Pencils: Tim Kennedy

Inks: Rudy Lapick / Letters: Bill Yoshida

YOU'RE JUST FORTUNATE YOU HAD YOUR PHONE WITH YOU!
I NEVER GO SHOPPING WITHOUT IT!

FACE IT, VERONICA...
...YOU'RE A SHOPAHOLIC, AND IT'S GOT TO STOP!

MISS BRISSY, I'M TOLD YOU HAVE A HIGH SUCCESS RATE WITH COMPULSIVE SHOPPERS!
INDEED I DO, MR. LODGE!

MY DAUGHTER VERONICA NEEDS HELP!
BUT SHOPPING IS MY LIFE'S BLOOD! I CAN'T GIVE IT UP!

NOBODY IS ASKING YOU TO GIVE UP SHOPPING, MY DEAR!
"MODERATION" IS THE KEY WORD!

THE FIRST STEP IS TO GET RID OF YOUR CATALOGS AS SOON AS THEY ARRIVE BY MAIL...
Lacy's

...AND ALWAYS BRING ALONG A CALCULATOR WHEN YOU GO SHOPPING!
IT HELPS TELL YOU IF YOU ARE OVERSPENDING!

ARE THERE ANY SPECIAL STORES THAT TRIGGER YOUR SHOPPING SPREES?
MULLOCK'S, FOR ONE!
MULLOCKS

THEIR BEST CUSTOMERS GET A SPECIAL CREDIT CARD THAT ENTITLES THEM TO A 5% DISCOUNT!
THAT'S A FALSE ECONOMY, MY DEAR!
MULL

LOOK, EVERYONE! IT'S MISS LODGE!

THEY REALLY LIKE YOU HERE!
ACTUALLY, THIS IS NOT WHERE I DO MY SERIOUS SHOPPING!
WE HAVEN'T SEEN YOU IN SOME TIME, MISS LODGE!

WE'RE NOW GOING TO A SPECIAL OUT-OF-TOWN DISCOUNT MALL WHERE WE GET 50% OFF!
DID YOU SAY 50% OFF?
SPEKVILLE 15

BUT ALL OF THESE BRAND NAMES ARE SO PRICEY!
NOT WHEN YOU GET 50% OFF!
ARBANI'S

DON'T YOU JUST LOVE THE SMELL OF NEW CLOTHES, MISS BRISSY?
UH, YES, IT IS A PLEASANT ODOR!

AND THE WAY THE GARMENTS FEEL CREATES SUCH A FEEL-GOOD SENSATION!
QUITE SO!

I HAD NO IDEA THESE DISCOUNT OUTLETS EXISTED!
THE BEST IS YET TO COME, MISS BRISSY!

I KNOW OF A SPECIAL CONSIGNMENT SHOP NOT FAR FROM HERE!
"CONSIGNMENT SHOP"? BUT ISN'T THAT SECOND-HAND MERCHANDISE?

BUT THESE GARMENTS DON'T *LOOK* SECOND-HAND!
THAT'S BECAUSE THEIR RICH AND FAMOUS OWNERS WORE THEM ONLY A FEW TIMES!
Sale
R.L.

AND ONE CAN BUY THESE DESIGNER ORIGINALS FOR A *FRACTION* OF THEIR COST!
REALLY?

COME ON! THERE'S A SPECIAL BACK ROOM WHERE THEY KEEP THEIR *VERY BEST* BARGAINS!
YOU CERTAINLY KNOW YOUR WAY AROUND!

I CAN'T BELIEVE THESE PRICES!! *WOW! WOW! WOW!*

UH, VERONICA, DO ME A FAVOR!
WHAT, MISS BRISSY?

HIDE MY POCKET CALCULATOR WHILE I MAKE A FEW MORE PURCHASES!

WELL, I THINK I'VE SHOWN YOU MOST OF THE SHOPPING TRAPS I'VE FALLEN INTO!
YES, AND YOU'RE CONGRATULATED, VERONICA!
YOU'RE AWARE OF YOUR PROBLEMS...
...AND THAT'S THE FIRST STEP TO BEING CURED!
EXCUSE ME WHILE I PHONE YOUR FATHER!
TELEPHONE
MR. LODGE, I'M HAPPY TO SAY VERONICA IS DEFINITELY MAKING PROGRESS!
WONDERFUL!
BUT I'M AFRAID I CAN NO LONGER HANDLE HER AS A CLIENT!
WHY NOT, MISS BRISSY?
I JUST CAN'T AFFORD IT!
TELEPHONE
END

Mr. Svenson in Sock It to Me!
Mr. Svenson has just done his laundry, but he's having trouble matching up his socks! Can you find the odd sock?
A
B
C
D
E
F
G
H
I
J
K
The Answer: H

MR. WEATHERBEE GAG BAG

QUIT CHEMISTRY? YOU CAN'T JUST UP AND QUIT A SUBJECT IN THE MIDDLE OF A SEMESTER!
CHEMICAL REACTION
CHEMISTRY III
SORRY, PROFESSOR FLUTESNOOT! IT'S JUST TOO DANGEROUS FOR ME!
Jughead
Script: Frank Doyle / Art & Letters: Samm Schwartz
DANGEROUS? WHAT'S SO DANGEROUS ABOUT IT?
I JUST DON'T FEEL **SAFE** ANYMORE!
THE CONTINUED USE OF CHEMICALS MAY BE HAZARDOUS TO MY HEALTH!
THIS HAS GOT TO BE A GAG!
1

UH,OH! HE PUT HIS PLAN IN OPERATION!
WHAT PLAN?

JUGHEAD DOESN'T CARE MUCH FOR CHEMISTRY! AS A RESULT HE HASN'T BEEN GETTING VERY GOOD MARKS!
SO?

SO HIS WHOLE AVERAGE HAS DROPPED BECAUSE OF IT!
THEN WHY DOESN'T HE STUDY HARDER?

HE LIKES HIS PLAN BETTER!
HE SIMPLY WANTS OUT!
HE JUST CAN'T DROP IT LIKE THAT!

I DON'T KNOW! JUG IS PRETTY TRICKY!

QUIT? JUST LIKE THAT HE WANTS TO QUIT? NONSENSE!
2

HE'S WORRIED ABOUT HIS BODY!
HE SAYS THE CONTINUED USE OF CHEMICALS MAY BE HAZARDOUS TO HIS HEALTH!
REASON WITH HIM!

BE SENSIBLE, BOY! YOU'RE WORRYING NEEDLESSLY!

I'VE BEEN IN CHEMICALS ALL MY LIFE, AND LOOK AT ME!

ER..YES, SIR! THAT'S WHAT PUT THE IDEA INTO MY HEAD!

I WANT TO STOP, BEFORE IT'S TOO LATE!
MMPH!

STOP SMIRKING! IT'S NOT A BIT FUNNY!

F-FROM THIS SIDE, IT IS!

WAY I FEEL, A PERSON'S GOT A RIGHT... A DUTY TO PROTECT HIS OWN BODY FROM POSSIBLE HARM!

THAT'S ONE OF MAN'S MOST BASIC RIGHTS! AND IF IT'S NOT, IT SHOULD BE!

TO WHOM ELSE IS A MAN RESPONSIBLE IF NOT HIMSELF?
TO WHOM ELSE, INDEED!

WHEN THAT ROLL IS CALLED UP YONDER, WILL I BE FOUND WANTING BECAUSE OF A BODY CONTAMINATED BY CHEMICALS?
OR A MIND CONTAMINATED BY NONSENSE!

FLUTESNOOT, THIS NUT COULD START A WHOLE NEW WAVE OF STUDENT PROTESTS!
HE DOES HAVE THAT FANATICAL FERVOR!

WE COULD BE BACK TO MARCHES... PLACARDS... SIT-INS... THE WHOLE WORKS!
IT'S BEEN SO QUIET LATELY!

SO WE STRETCH A POINT AND LET THE KOOK HAVE HIS WAY!
ANYTHING IS BETTER THAN MAKING THE NATIVES RESTLESS!

ALL RIGHT, JUGHEAD! OUT OF RESPECT FOR YOUR-UGH-BODY... WE'RE GOING TO LET YOU DROP CHEMISTRY!
THANK YOU, SIR!

WELL? WELL?

I DID IT! I DID IT!

I ACTUALLY MADE THEM BEND THEIR SILLY RULES!
YOU'RE A GENIUS!

TO THE CAFETERIA! I'VE GOT TO HAVE A VICTORY LUNCH!
OUR HERO!
HE BEAT THE SYSTEM!

SIT DOWN, HERO! TELL US WHAT YOU'D LIKE! WE'LL GET IT FOR YOU!
SOMEBODY MAKE A LIST!

IS THAT THE BODY HE WAS SO CONCERNED ABOUT?
EGAD!

I WOULDN'T CRAM A MESS LIKE THAT IN MY GARBAGE DISPOSAL!
WE MUST REMEMBER... JUST TEACH THEM, DON'T TRY TO UNDERSTAND THEM!
CHOMP! SLURP!
END

Script: Frank Doyle
Art & Letters: Samm Schwartz
Colors: Carlos Antunes

HOMECOMING

HE'S UP TO SOME TRICK-ERY! JUG DOESN'T STICK HIS HEAD IN NOOSES LIKE THAT! I'M GONNA SEE WHAT HE'S UP TO!

A GUY DOESN'T HATE WOMEN ONE DAY AND GO LOOKING FOR THEM THE NEXT!

THERE'S NOTHING EITHER BRAVE **OR** FOOLHARDY ABOUT JUG!
HE'S GOT A GOOD REASON FOR WANT-ING US TO THINK HE WANTS ETHEL!

FIRST I'LL CHECK HER HOUSE AND MAKE SURE SHE'S NOT HOME!

OH? SHE'S REALLY OUT OF TOWN?
SHE LEFT YESTERDAY!

SHE AND MISS SPRINT THE COACH OF THE GIRLS' TRACK TEAM! THEY'LL BE GONE THREE DAYS!
I **KNEW** IT!

OH, IF SHE CALLS HOME, WILL YOU TELL HER I'VE **GOT** TO GET IN TOUCH WITH HER?

THAT PHONY! PRETENDING TO BE LOVE SICK FOR ETHEL!

HE **KNEW** SHE WAS OUT OF TOWN! HE WAS DARN SURE HE WOULDN'T RUN INTO HER!

WELL, **I'M** GONNA GET HER **BACK**! I'LL FIX **HIS** WAGON!
COACH SPRINT

YES, REGGIE! ETHEL AND THE COACH WENT TO CARTERVILLE!
DO YOU HAVE A PHONE NUMBER WHERE I CAN GET IN TOUCH WITH HER?

NO! ETHEL WAS GOING TO POP OVER TO WESTOWN TO VISIT A COUSIN TODAY!
A **COUSIN**! **WESTOWN**!

HEY, DOES ANYBODY KNOW ETHEL'S COUSIN IN WESTOWN?
I WANT TO GET HOLD OF ETHEL!

I'VE GOT TO GET HER BACK IN TOWN AS SOON AS POSSIBLE!
I DON'T KNOW HER!
NEITHER DO I!

DOESN'T ANYBODY KNOW ETHEL'S COUSIN? TIME IS OF THE ESSENCE! I'VE GOT TO GET HOLD OF ETHEL!
SURE! THAT'S HER COUSIN MATTIE!

YOU KNOW HER?
I HAVE HER NUMBER IN MY ADDRESS BOOK!

BEAUTIFUL, PAT! I'LL NEVER FORGET YOU FOR THIS!
YOU NEVER KNOW, DO YOU?

ETHEL? REGGIE, HERE! YOU'VE GOT TO COME HOME RIGHT AWAY! I'LL MEET YOU AT THE BUS STOP!
WHO'D HAVE BELIEVED IT?

TWO HOURS LATER
HO, HO! WAIT 'TIL THAT FOURFLUSHER JUGHEAD SEES WHAT I'VE GOT FOR HIM!
RIVER

DARLING
?

MOM CALLED! SIX OF MY FRIENDS CALLED! EVERYONE TOLD ME HOW FRANTIC YOU WERE THAT I WAS OUT OF TOWN!

LOVER, YOU NEVER HINTED THAT YOU FELT THAT WAY ABOUT ME! YOU SHY, SHY BOY!

OH, YOU SNEAKY CHARACTER! YOU HAD THIS WHOLE THING PLANNED FROM THE START!
YOU MEAN HE REALLY DOESN'T LOVE HER?
END

Script: Rod Ollerenshaw / Pencils: Rex Lindsey / Inks: Jon D'Agostino / Letters: Bill Yoshida / Colors: Barry Grossman

ONE DAY JUGHEAD WAS WALKING DOWN THE STREET!
WHAT A BEAUTIFUL DAY!
BOOM!
HEY! MY HAT!
WHOOSH!
OH, NO! GONE FOREVER! CHOKE
SLURP!
AND THEN... HEH, HEH
WELL, I STILL HAVE YOU, PAL!
GRRRRR
YOW! WHAT'S GOTTEN INTO YOU, HOT DOG?
RUFF!

MAN! WHAT'S HIS PROBLEM?
GGRRRRR
WHEW! SANCTUARY!
POP'S CHOC'LIT SHOPPE
AH, JUGHEAD! WHAT'LL IT BE? A HAMBURGER? STEAK? CHOPS...
YEAH, BUT I'M A LITTLE BROKE RIGHT NOW!
NO, PROBLEM! YOUR CREDIT IS GOOD HERE!
PUFF
SOMETHING'S FINALLY GOING GOOD TODAY!
HERE, THE HOUSE SPECIAL... BROCCOLI FLORETS!
DIG-IN!
OH! YUK...
PPTUIII!
IS SOME-THING WRONG?
THIS TASTES AWFUL!
OH, REALLY...?
3

WHADDYA WANT FOR NOTHING?...
BOOT!
GET OUTTA HERE, YA BUM! AND DON'T COME BACK... EVER!
EVER...?
POP'S SECRET ANTI-JUG POTION
HOT PEPPERS

AND HOW ABOUT...
WHAT A SIGHT FOR SORE EYES! MY BEST PAL...
ARCHIE!

GUESS AGAIN, NEEDLENOSE! I'M REGGIE'S BEST PAL!
EEP!

HE LOOKS A LITTLE DOWN ON HIS LUCK, DOESN'T HE, BUDDY?
THAT HE DOES, CHUM!
GASP!

MAIL FOR JUGHEAD JONES!
THANKS!
: F-FMEH :
THEY'RE "GOODBYE JUGHEAD" LETTERS FROM DEBBIE, JOANI AND ETHEL!
AND THEY'RE FORM LETTERS, TOO! I'VE BEEN DUMPED IN TRIPLICATE!
WELL, AT LEAST IT STOPPED RAINING!
KA-BOOM!
GOOD GRIEF!

THAT'LL SHOW THAT RAT!
IS AN IDIOT
HUH? WHAT'S GOING ON HERE?
NO. 2
ERASE! ERASE! ERAS
YOU'RE NOT THE ONLY ONE WHO CAN INFLUENCE THE CREATIVE TALENT AROUND HERE! I'M SENDING THE ARTIST ON A LITTLE VACATION!
...AND HERE'S MY VERSION OF THE STORY'S ENDING!
10¢ A THROW
GO APE! HIT THE BOOB AND WIN A BOOBY PRIZE!
CIRCUS
ADIOS!
ROTTEN TOMATO
ROTTEN TOMATO
THE END

Jughead *in* The CUT-UPS

Script: George Gladir / Pencils: Stan Goldberg / Inks: Rudy Lapick / Letters: Bill Yoshida / Colors: Barry Grossman

AND HE'S THE BEST AT MATHEMATICS! THERE'S NOBODY MORE QUALIFIED THAN HIM!
MAY WE SPEAK TO YOU A MINUTE, MR. WEATHERBEE?
?

SURE, FELLOWS! COME ON IN!
THANK YOU, SIR!

NOW WHAT SEEMS TO BE THE PROBLEM?

WELL, WE WOULD LIKE YOU TO HELP US OUT WITH A MATHEMATICAL PROBLEM!

HOW DO YOU DIVIDE A *CIRCLE* INTO *FIVE EQUAL PARTS*, MR. WEATHERBEE ?

THAT'S VERY SIMPLE, ARCHIE! FIRST YOU MEASURE THE DIAMETER!
CHECK!

THEN YOU MULTIPLY BY PI WHICH IS 3.14!
THAT GIVES YOU THE CIRCUMFERENCE -- WHICH YOU *DIVIDE* BY *FIVE*!

SEE? IT'S VERY SIMPLE!
THANK YOU, SIR!

DID YOU JOT THAT ALL DOWN, ARCHIE ?
I GOT IT, JUG!
3

I'M GLAD TO SEE YOU BOYS TAKING SUCH A GREAT INTEREST IN MATH.!
WELL, WE THINK THAT GETTING THIS PROBLEM CORRECT IS VERY IMPORTANT, MR. WEATHERBEE.!

I HAD THOSE BOYS FIGURED OUT ALL WRONG.!
I USED TO THINK THAT THEY REALLY WEREN'T CONCERNED ABOUT LEARNING ALL THEY COULD ABOUT A SUBJECT LIKE MATH.!

BUT THEY ARE GENUINELY TAKING AN INTEREST IN THEIR SCHOOL WORK.!

AH.! THE REWARDS OF TEACHING.!
IT MAKES ALL THE HARD WORK YOU PUT INTO IT WORTHWHILE WHEN YOU SEE SOMETHING LIKE THIS.!
4

IMAGINE BEING SO LUCKY AS TO BE TEACHING YOUNG FELLOWS LIKE ARCHIE AND JUGHEAD!

BEING ABLE TO SHAPE YOUNG, INQUISITIVE, SEARCHING MINDS!

WHO KNOWS WHAT GREAT MATHEMATICAL DISCOVERIES MAY COME FROM THIS SIMPLE BEGINNING?

AT LEAST I CAN ALWAYS SAY I HELPED IN MY OWN LITTLE WAY!
PIZZA

ONE SAUSAGE AND MUSHROOM PIZZA, AND CUT IT ACCORDING TO THESE DIRECTIONS!
END

Jughead in "Food Mood"

Script: G. Gladir / Pencils: S. Goldberg / Inks: M. Esposito / Letters: B. Yoshida Colors: B. Grossman

I KNOW HOW YOU FEEL, HOT DOG !!!

I'M ALWAYS HUNGRY, TOO!

KIBBLE

WELL...
GO AHEAD AND EAT !!!

HMMM... IT'S NOT FAIR, IS IT ???

WELL, HERE... TRY SOME OF MINE !!!
2

SORRY, PAL...
THAT'S ALL YOU CAN HAVE!!!

"PEOPLE FOOD" ISN'T GOOD FOR YOU!!!

I CAN'T STAND THE WAY HE'S LOOKING AT ME!!!
I'LL PUT HIM ON THE PORCH!!!

COME ON BACK IN!!!

A LITTLE BIT MORE WON'T HURT HIM!

LET ME PUT A LITTLE KETCHUP ON THAT!

WHAT FELLOWSHIP !!!
A MAN !!!
A DOG !!!
AND THEIR FOOD!!!
CHOMP!
SLURP!
GLOOP!

I'LL BET HE'LL LOVE CHILI !!!

HE CAN WASH IT DOWN WITH THIS COLA!!!
CHOMP!
COLA
CHOMP!

IT'S FUN TO SHARE ONE OF LIFE'S GREAT ADVENTURES!
SLURP!

BUT WE CAN'T OVERDO IT, PAL !!!

TOO MUCH OF THIS ISN'T GOOD FOR YOU!!!
SMACK!

BURP!

AND IT'S NOT TOO GOOD FOR ME EITHER !!!
END

Archie
-in-
"BOWL TOLL"
I JUST GAVE UP TRYING TO TEACH GIRLS THE ART OF BOWLING!

I WAS ALWAYS AT THEIR SIDE SHOWING THEM HOW!

BUT THEY KEPT MAKING THE SAME MISTAKE OVER AND OVER!

THEY KEPT DROPPING THE BALL!
YES!

HOW DID YOU KNOW?
END.

HOT DOG TV POLL PUZZLE
WHAT TYPE OF PROGRAMS ARE HOT DOG'S FAVORITE? FIND OUT BY BLACKENING ALL THE LETTERS THAT HAVE A DOT IN THEM! THE LETTERS LEFT ARE THE SHOWS HOT DOG REALLY GOES FOR -
BUT I'M WATCHING A FOOD SHOW, HOT DOG!
WHAT KIND OF SHOW DO YOU WANT?
T S F E U N
V J R N S Y
A C N I W M
U A L C K A
Y R X
N T
O F O
N S
HOT DOG
ANSWER - FUNNY ANIMAL CARTOONS

Professor Jughead's Educational Corner

IF IT RAINS DURING A DATE, THE GAL MUST CARRY THE UMBRELLA.

THE BOY MAY HOLD THE UMBRELLA ONLY WHEN THE GIRL CARRIES HIM ACROSS A PUDDLE.

WHEN A GIRL PICKS UP HER DATE IN HER DADDY'S CAR SHE SHOULD ARRIVE WITH A FULL TANK OF GAS...

SINCE THIS WILL SAVE THE BOY THE EMBARRASSMENT OF ASKING HER TO PAY FOR THE GAS.

WHEN TREATING A BOY TO DINNER, DON'T BE SO CRUDE AS TO SLIP HIM THE MONEY AT THE TABLE...

GIVE HIM YOUR FULL ALLOWANCE **BEFORE** ENTERING THE RESTAURANT.

HE SHOULD DO ALL THE DIAL SWITCHING WHILE SHE DOES THE HOMEWORK.

BUT PROFESSOR, HOW COME SOME GIRLS DO NONE OF THOSE THINGS AND ARE STILL POPULAR?
YOUNG LADY, MY METHODS WORK ONLY ON NORMAL TEENAGE BOYS LIKE *MYSELF*!

MY METHODS DO NOT APPLY TO THE 95% OF THE MALE POPULATION WHO ARE **GIRL-CRAZY NUTS**!

FRAUD!
CHARLATAN!
FAKE!

MY NEXT LECTURE WILL BE ON "THE DANGER OF GIVING LECTURES"!
RIVERDALE 10 MI
END

Archie
HENRY SCARPELLI
CRAIG BOLDMAN

YOU'RE ANGRY AND FRUSTRATED!
HOW CAN YOU TELL?
THAT'S THE SAME LOOK YOU HAVE WHEN ARCHIE IS AROUND!

I TOLD YOU I DON'T NEED ARCHIE!
DADDY, US KIDS GREW UP ON ELECTRONICS!

I CAN'T GET THIS THEATER SYSTEM TOGETHER!
LEAVE IT TO ME!

LET'S SEE... THE COMPONENT VIDEO THING GOES HERE...
COAXIAL CABLE HERE... AUDIO OUTPUT... HMM... HDMI...

WELL, YOU LOOK HAPPY! GLAD WE CALLED ARCHIE?
YES...

...HE CAN'T DO IT, EITHER!

Script: George Gladir / Pencils: Stan Goldberg / Inks: Mike Esposito / Letters: Bill Yoshida / Colors: Barry Grossman

THE RIVERDALE LITERARY REVIEW BOUGHT A POEM FROM ME!

AND THEY BOUGHT IT FROM BETTY COOPER, NOT "PAGE TURNER"!

THEY WANT ME TO SEND MORE POEMS!

HERE ARE SOME GOOD ONES!

NEXT MONTH...
DAD, THEY BOUGHT ANOTHER POEM!

THE FOLLOWING MONTH...
THE MAGAZINE WITH MY POEM JUST CAME OUT!

RIVERDALE LITERARY

I'M GOING TO SHOW IT TO ALL MY FRIENDS!

THAT'S MY POEM!
YEAH, RIGHT! GIVE ME A BREAK!

JUST BECAUSE YOU HAVE THE SAME NAME AS A FAMOUS WRITER...
WHAT?

YOU MEAN THERE'S ANOTHER BETTY COOPER?
YOU'RE NOT KIDDING, ARE YOU?

SHE'S BEEN CONTRIBUTING TO THAT MAGAZINE FOR YEARS!
DO YOU THINK THEY THOUGHT I WAS HER?

PROBABLY! AND THEY'LL SUE YOU FOR TAKING MONEY UNDER FALSE PRETENSES!

LATER...
DON'T LISTEN TO VERONICA! YOU DIDN'T DO ANYTHING WRONG!
I'M GOING TO GO TO THE MAGAZINE AND CLEAR THIS UP!

HERE IT IS!
RIVERDALE LITERARY REVIEW

BETTY COOPER?
YES?

YOU'RE BETTY COOPER?
YOU! YOU TOO?

YOU'RE BOTH BETTY COOPER?
I'M THE ONE WHO SENT IN THE POEMS!

I DIDN'T MEAN TO DECEIVE ANYONE! I DIDN'T KNOW THERE WAS ANOTHER BETTY COOPER!

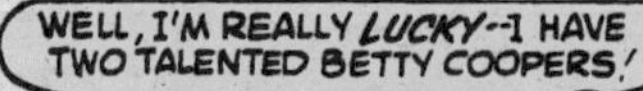
WELL, I'M REALLY *LUCKY*--I HAVE TWO TALENTED BETTY COOPERS!

YOU MEAN YOU *STILL* WANT ME TO CONTRIBUTE?
YES! YOU HAVE REAL *TALENT!*

I GUESS I SHOULD USE A *PSEUDONYM* TO AVOID CONFUSION! I HAVE ONE I THOUGHT OF...

I'LL LET YOU IN ON A LITTLE *SECRET!* BETTY COOPER *IS* MY PSEUDONYM!

MY *REAL* NAME WOULD HAVE BEEN *RIDICULOUS* FOR A *WRITER!*
WHY? WHAT *IS* IT?

PAGE TURNER!
END

Betty in "LIFE IS BUT A DREAM" OR SHE WAS SPOKESPERSON AT A BICYCLE CONVENTION

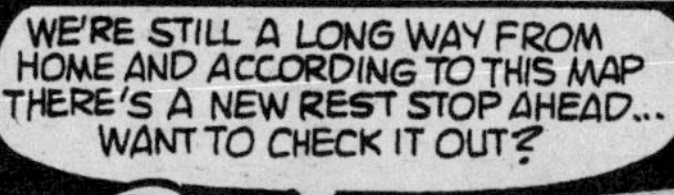

SOON..
THIS IS ONE PACKED REST STOP!
THEY'RE DIRECTING US TO ITS THIRD LEVEL!
SINCE THIS REST STOP IS OVERCROWDED, YOU'RE ONLY ALLOWED 45 EARTH MINUTES HERE!
THE INTERGALACTIC POLICE ARE VERY STRICT ON TIME LIMITS!
BETTY! BETTY, HONEY... WAKE UP... WE'VE COME TO A REST STOP!
HUH?! GUESS THIS MEANS I'VE GOT TO STOP RESTING!
I LEFT THE AIR ON TO KEEP CARAMEL COMFORTABLE!
HERE'S THE DRIFT TUBE TO THE MAIN PAVILION!
OH! I FORGOT MY CAMERA! I'M GOING BACK FOR IT!
SINCE WE ONLY HAVE 45 MINUTES, GO ON AHEAD AND I'LL CATCH UP WITH YOU AT THE MAIN PAVILION!
MEET US AT THE GAMMA RAY GRILL!
NOW WHERE DID I PACK MY CAM-?
2

CARAMEL! COME BACK!

OH, GREAT! INSTEAD OF HEADING FOR THE MAIN PAVILION, SHE'S CUTTING OUT FOR HER ANCESTRAL HOME!

DUMB EARTHLING!!!
GET OUT OF THE WAY!!
THOSE SASSY SATURNIANS! THEY'RE ALL OVER THE GALAXY!
POOR TIPPERS, TOO!

(PUFF! PUFF!) I'VE BEEN CHASING CARAMEL FOR FORTY MINUTES AND I'VE FINALLY CORNERED HER IN THIS TOWERING TRUMPET TREE!

I HATE TO LEAVE ON SUCH A SOUR NOTE!

OOF!!

IT'S A TOUR BUS OF MOUSE PEOPLE FROM PLANET RODENTIA!

THEY'RE TERRIFIED OF CARAMEL...
...AND THEY'RE SURE TRYIN' TO SHAKE US OFF!
SQUEAK!
SQUEAK!
SQUEAK!

(GULP!) NOW WE'RE HEADED FOR THAT MOUSE-HOLE SIZED OPENING!
THEY'RE GONNA GIVE US A HIGH VELOCITY BRUSH OFF!

WE'RE OVER AN ACTIVE BUBBLE GUM SPRING... AND THAT MAKES ME REAL...

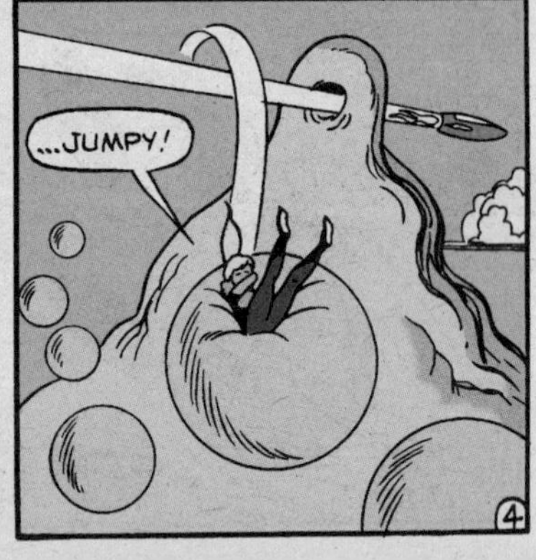
...JUMPY!

SHARPEN YOUR CLAWS, CARAMEL...
WE'VE REACHED THE THIRD LEVEL!
BLAM!
?
MOM! DAD! *THEY'RE GONE!!*
THE EARTH SHIP LEFT THREE MINUTES AGO! THEY WILL BE ALLOWED TO RETURN IN *FIVE* DAYS!

WE CAN'T ORBIT THIS ASTEROID FOR FIVE DAYS... WE HAVE JUST ENOUGH FUEL STICKS TO REACH EARTH!
AND ALL THE MONEY BETTY HAS ARE THE TWO MERCURY DIMES I GAVE HER!

(GROAN!) SHE'S YOUR DAUGHTER, ALWAYS LATE!
AND THOSE TWO MERCURY DIMES WON'T GET HER VERY FAR!
FAR ENOUGH! *LOOK!*

RENT A ROCKET
INSERT DIMES FROM MERCURY ONLY

I'VE PUT THE ROCKET ON REMOTE RETURN!
BETTY! BETTY, HONEY! WE'RE COMING TO A REST STOP!
FOR REAL?
LOOK! AN EXHIBIT ON THE FUTURE! WANT TO TAKE IT IN?
FUTURAMA
CARS
TRUCKS

THANKS, DAD, BUT FROM NOW ON I'M TAKING MY FUTURE ONE DAY AT A TIME!
?

SHE'S YOUR DAUGHTER!
THE END

Betty and Veronica in "A Fan's Fan"

Script & Art: Holly G! / Letters: Bill Yoshida / Colors: Barry Grossman

WHAT PART ARE YOU GOING TO TRY OUT FOR?
CLAUDIA, OF COURSE!
Josie

BUT CLAUDIA IS SUPPOSED TO BE 26 YEARS OLD!
SO WHAT?
SMILE
TIGERS

A LOT OF 26 YEAR OLD ACTRESSES PLAY TEENS, SO WHY NOT VICE-VERSA?
I'LL NEED TO LOOK OLDER AND MORE SOPHISTICATED WITH A SOUTHERN FLAIR!
HEY, BETTY, MAY I BORROW YOUR LACE FAN?...

IT'D BE JUST PERFECT TO COMPLETE MY OUTFIT!
OKAY!

HOW DO I LOOK?
OKAY!
2

JUST OKAY?! I HAVE TO LOOK PERFECT!
YOU LOOK PERFECTLY OKAY!

AND SO...
I'M VERONICA LODGE, HERE TO SEE THE PRODUCER!
PLEASE, TAKE A SEAT!

PSST! RONNIE, YOU'RE NOT HOLDING THE FAN RIGHT!
I AM TOO!

ARE NOT!
AM TOO!
ARE NOT!
AM TOO!

LET ME SHOW YOU HOW TO HOLD IT!
HEY!
LADY PRETTY
MOONMA
ZIP!

GIVE THAT BACK!
IT'S MY FAN!

GIVE ME THAT!
NO WAY! AND I'D LIKE TO SEE YOU TRY!

GOTCHA!

GIVE IT - GIVE IT - GIVE IT!

GOT IT!

NO YOU DON'T!

GIVE IT BACK!
NAH!

GIVE IT UP, COOPER!

HI, I'M THE PRODUCER! I ASSUME YOU'RE VERONICA LODGE?
UH-OH!
SPACE BUG

GR-UH-GGG- THAT IS ... I'VE ... SORRY!
DON'T BE...

THE MOMENT I SAW YOU I KNEW YOU WERE JUST PERFECT!
REALLY!?

THE NEXT DAY...
HI, VERONICA, DID YOU GET A PART IN THAT TV MOVIE?
YES!

SHE GOT THE ROLE OF CLAUDIA'S IMMATURE, IRRESPONSIBLE YOUNGER SISTER, BUFFY!
End

Dear Diary,
Little did I expect such a simple thing could lead to such a special outcome...
WHAT'S IN THAT BOX, MOM?
SOME ITEMS GRANDMA HAS DECIDED TO GIVE US!
Betty in Really Special
SCRIPT: KATHLEEN WEBB
PENCILS: STAN GOLDBERG
INKS: JOHN LOWE

SHE AND GRANDPA ARE TRYING TO PARE DOWN THEIR BELONGINGS!

SHE THOUGHT WE MIGHT LIKE THESE THINGS!
OOO! LOOK AT THE OLD JEWELRY!

WOW! LOOK AT THESE GLOVES!
Ah! GRANDMA'S EVENING GLOVES!

HOW ELEGANT THEY LOOK!
SHE WORE THEM TO MANY LOVELY FUNCTIONS!

DO YOU WANT THEM, MOM?
HEAVENS! I'VE NO USE FOR THEM!

POLLY?
I'VE GOT MY OWN PAIR!

LOOKS LIKE THEY'RE YOURS, KIDDO! UNLESS DAD WANTS THEM!
I'D LOOK SO REFINED WORKING IN THE YARD IN THEM! NO THANKS!

GUESS THEY'RE MINE! COOL! THEY MAKE ME FEEL SO GRAND!

BEFORE I PUT THEM AWAY, I'LL TRY THEM WITH ONE OF MY FORMAL DRESSES!

GOSH! THEY MAKE THIS OLD DRESS OF MINE LOOK SPLENDID AGAIN!

POLLY! TAKE A LOOK AT THIS!
?

IS THAT A TEAR, HAL?
JUST SOMETHING IN MY EYE...

...AFTER SEEING HOW GROWN UP OUR BETTY HAS BECOME!
SHE'S DEVELOPED INTO SUCH A BEAUTIFUL YOUNG WOMAN!

YOU'RE RIGHT! THOSE GLOVES REALLY GIVE THAT DRESS A GLAMOROUS TOUCH!
I ONLY WISH THERE WAS AN EVENT I COULD WEAR THEM TO!

AS IT IS, I'LL HAVE TO WAIT WEEKS FOR THE FIRST FORMAL DANCE OF THE SCHOOL YEAR!
!

SAY, WHAT DO YOU THINK OF...
BZZ... BZZ... BZZ...
?

HAL, I THINK THAT'S A LOVELY IDEA!
Shh! I WANT IT TO BE A SURPRISE!

BETTY, WHY DON'T YOU FIX UP YOUR HAIR AND MAKE-UP SO WE GET THE FULL EFFECT!?
OKAY, MOM!

HOW DO I LOOK?
FABULOUS! LET'S GO!

DADDY? YOU'RE ALL DRESSED UP! WHAT--?
WELL, I HAD TO GET SPIFFY MY-SELF, TOO!

ESPECIALLY SINCE I'M TAKING SUCH A BEAUTIFUL GIRL OUT WITH ME!
MOM?

IT WAS YOUR FATHER'S IDEA, HONEY! ENJOY!
HAVE FUN!

"And we did, dear Diary! First was dinner out with a great father-daughter chat...

"Then for a memento of the evening, Daddy took me to an expensive portrait studio...

He confessed the reason for the evening was not only to give the gloves a night out..."
WELL, AFTER REALIZING MY LITTLE BABY HAD GROWN UP, I WANTED TO GET TO KNOW THE LOVELY YOUNG WOMAN SHE'S BECOME!
AWWW, DADDY!

LOOKS LIKE GRANDMA'S GLOVES ARE OFF TO A BEAUTIFUL START OF MAKING MANY MORE HAPPY MEMORIES!
END

Betty and Veronica in "A CRITICAL CONDITION"

Script: Hal Smith / Pencils: Dan DeCarlo / Inks: Jimmy DeCarlo / Letters: Bill Yoshida / Colors: Barry Grossman

THIS ONE GETS A BIG THUMBS UP FROM ME! I LOVED THE PLOT, THE CINEMATOGRAPHY AND, MOST OF ALL, THE STAR!

I'M AFRAID I DISAGREE! I THOUGHT IT WAS UNREALISTIC AND PRETENTIOUS AND THE STAR TURNED ME OFF!

WHAT?
YOU WOULDN'T KNOW A GOOD FILM IF IT BIT YOU ON THE NOSE!

MAYBE WE'D BETTER GO ON TO OUR NEXT FILM!
GGGG
ROLL IT!!

THIS ONE FEATURES JUGHEAD JONES, AND IT'S CALLED THE VAMPIRE STRIKES BACK!
2

GIVE ME A BREAK! IT SHOULD BE CALLED "TOP GOON!"
TEE HEE!

I KINDA LIKED THAT! I THOUGHT IT WAS A CUTE SPOOF ON HORROR FILMS!
OH, GET REAL...

THE ONLY HORROR IN THAT FILM IS BEING FORCED TO SIT THROUGH IT!
WELL, I GUESS WE SPLIT ON THAT ONE!

ROLL THE NEXT ONE!

THIS ONE STARS BETTY COOPER LOOKING FOR HER PET DUCK AND IT'S CALLED "ABSENCE OF MALLARD!"

YOU MEAN ABSENCE OF TALENT! THE STAR HAS ALL THE CHARISMA OF A SEA SPONGE!

OH, YEAH ? WELL I THOUGHT THE STAR WAS MUCH MORE REAL THAN THE PHONY IN THE FIRST FILM!

YEAH? WELL I GIVE THIS BOMB TWO THUMBS DOWN!
AND I GIVE IT TWO THUMBS UP!

ROLL THE LAST FILM!!

THIS FILM FEATURES ARCHIE ANDREWS AND IT'S CALLED "DIAMONDS ARE AN EFFORT!"

NOW THIS STAR I LIKE!
AT LAST! SOMETHING WE CAN AGREE ON!

HEY!
4

THAT ONE WOULD HAVE BEEN TWICE AS GOOD WITHOUT THAT GOOFY BLONDE CHEERLEADER!
OH, YEAH? WELL I THOUGHT THAT WAS THE BEST SCENE IN THE FILM!

WELL, BOYS, HOW DID YOU LIKE THE VIDEO WE MADE?
I THOUGHT IT WAS AN ORIGINAL IDEA...

AND THE CO-HOSTS WERE CHARMING, BUT ALL THAT ARGUING GOT OLD FAST! I GIVE IT A MARGINAL THUMBS UP!
I DIDN'T LIKE IT AS WELL AS YOU DID, ARCH! EXCEPT FOR THE VAMPIRE BIT, IT WAS A SNORE! A THUMBS DOWN FROM ME!
WHAT?! AFTER ALL THAT WORK WE PUT INTO IT!
YEAH!

HOW WOULD YOU LIKE ME TO STICK MY THUMB IN YOUR EAR AND USE YOUR HEAD FOR A BOWLING BALL?
HEY!
THIS'LL MAKE A GREAT VIDEO! I'LL CALL IT "GOOFBUSTERS!"
DOM'S DELI
END

Betty
INFLATION JUBILATION
Script: Gladir / Pencils: Amendola / Inks: D'Agostino
Letters: Yoshida / Colors: Grossman
I STILL DON'T KNOW WHY YOU CAN'T COME ALONG, ARCHIE!
IT'S THIS INFLATION, RONNIE! THEY'VE PRICED THE TICKETS TOO HIGH FOR ME THIS YEAR!
TER TRANSIT
CHARTERED
BUS STOP
RIVERDALE HIGH SKI OUTING MEETS HERE
JAPAN
GRT. BRITAIN
ITALY
HAWAII
"INFLATION"! I'M SICK AND TIRED OF THAT WORD!
THAT'S ALL I EVER HEAR FROM YOU, LATELY!
ONE WAY
DON'T WALK
COME ON, RONNIE!
WELL, I HAVE TO GO NOW! TA! TA!
1

HI, ARCHIE! I THOUGHT EVERYBODY BUT ME WENT ON THE SKI OUTING!
NO, THE TICKETS WERE JUST TOO EXPENSIVE THIS YEAR!
CHEER UP! WE CAN STILL HAVE OUR SKI OUTING! RIGHT HERE IN RIVERDALE!
DON'T BE RIDICULOUS! THEY DON'T EVEN RENT SKIS IN RIVERDALE!
HOW ARE WE GOING TO SKI HERE?
WITH A LITTLE INGENUITY!
?
FIRST, WE REMOVE THE WHEELS FROM OUR SKATEBOARDS-
NEXT, WE TIE ON OUR MINI-SKIS!

AND AWAY WE GO.!
WHEE.! THIS IS FUN.!

YOU KNOW, I SORT OF MISS THE OLD SKI LIFT.!
HMM.! THAT CAN BE ARRANGED, TOO.!

MOOSE OWES ME A FAVOR FOR HELPING HIM PASS HIS MATH.!
?

MOOSE, PLEASE TAKE THIS ROPE UP THE HILL AND THEN THROW ONE END OF IT DOWN TO US.!
D-UH, SURE, BETTY.!

THAT'S IT, MOOSE.! KEEP PULLING.!
HEY.! THIS IS JUST LIKE THE SKI LIFT.!
3

BETTY, YOUR "SKI RESORT" HAS EVERYTHING BUT A SKI JUMP!
AND WHAT MAKES YOU THINK WE DON'T HAVE ONE?
RIVERDALE PLAY GROUND
YOU'RE KIDDING!
YOU'LL SEE!

ARCHIE, YOUR SKI JUMP AWAITS YOU!
WELL, I'LL BE---

FIRST, LET ME PUT SOME SOFT SNOW WHERE YOU'LL BE LANDING!

WHEE!

FANTASTIC!

RIGHT NOW, THE GANG IS PROBABLY GATHERING AROUND THE FIRE PLACE FOR HOT COCOA.!
AND WHAT MAKES YOU THINK WE CAN'T DO THE SAME?

VOILA.! A THERMOS OF HOT COCOA.!
BETTY, YOU'RE TOO MUCH.!

SIGH! WE'RE GOING TO HAVE TO GO ON MORE OF THESE "INFLATION DATES".!
TV

EXCUSE ME.! WE'RE TAKING A SURVEY OF PEOPLES' OPINIONS.!

HOW HAS INFLATION AFFECTED YOU?

IT'S THE GREATEST THING THAT'S EVER HAPPENED TO ME.!
END.

Script: **Bill Golliher** Pencils: **Tim Kennedy** Inks: **Ken Selig**
Letters: **Bill Yoshida** Colors: **Barry Grossman**
Editor-In-Chief: **Victor Gorelick** President: **Mike Pellerito** Publisher: **Jon Goldwater**

I GET TO TRAIN AND PERFORM WITH THE CLOWNS FOR THE OPENING PERFORMANCE OF THE DINGLING BROTHERS CIRCUS HERE IN RIVERDALE!
THAT SOUNDS LIKE A BLAST!
DINGLING BROS.
CIRCUS

YOU CAN BET WE'LL ALL BE THERE TO LAUGH AT YOU!
BELIEVE ME, THIS IS ONE TIME I WON'T MIND!

I START MY TRAINING TOMORROW!
ARCHIE, I THINK YOU'LL DO GREAT!
POP'S

REALLY, REGGIE?! THANKS!
OF COURSE! YOU'VE GOT EXPERIENCE! YOU'VE BEEN MAKING A FOOL OF YOURSELF FOR AGES!

THE NEXT DAY...
CAN I HELP YOU, YOUNG MAN?
YES, I'M ARCHIE ANDREWS! I WON THE RADIO CONTEST TO BE A CLOWN FOR A DAY!

OH, GREAT! WE'VE BEEN EXPECTING YOU!
COME ON! I'LL INTRODUCE YOU TO THE REST OF THE GANG!
COOL!
2

HEY, BOYS! THIS IS ARCHIE! HE'S GOING TO BE JOINING YOUR RANKS FOR THE OPENING PERFORMANCE!
IS THAT SO?

CONGRATULATIONS!
LET'S CELEBRATE!

... WITH SOME PIE!

SAY, WHAT'S THE BIG IDEA!?
I'M SORRY ABOUT THAT... HE'S RUDE!

LET ME WASH IT OFF FOR YOU!
SPLASH!

WHAT'S WRONG WITH YOU GUYS? ARE YOU NUTS?!
WE CERTAINLY ARE! TEE-HEE!

YOU SEEM GOOD NATURED ENOUGH! I THINK YOU'LL WORK OUT FINE!
WHAT? THAT WAS SOME KIND OF A TEST?
CONVENTION

OF COURSE! NOT EVERYONE'S CUT TO BE A CLOWN!
BUT YOU'VE GOT WHAT IT TAKES TO FILL OUR SHOES!

YEAH! WE'LL BE GLAD TO SHOW YOU THE ROPES!
HEY! PUT ME DOWN!

AND SO...
TAKE THAT!
WOW! A TRIPLE PIE TOSS! ARCHIE, YOU'RE A NATURAL!

YOU'RE GREAT ON THE UNICYCLE! YOU'VE GOT WONDERFUL BALANCE!
OF COURSE! I'VE BEEN BALANCING TWO GIRL-FRIENDS FOR YEARS!

THE BIG NIGHT...
ARCHIE, ARE YOU READY FOR YOUR DEBUT??
I SURE AM!

FINE! LET'S SEE HOW YOU'RE GOING TO LOOK!
KOFF! KOFF!
SOON...
WOW! I'M A CLOWN! I'M REALLY A CLOWN!
AND SO...
AND NOW, IN THE CENTER RING, THE DINGLING BROTHERS CLOWNS!
HAR! HAR! THERE'S ARCHIE!
HEY, HE'S HILARIOUS!
GET HIM, ARCHIE!

FINALLY...
THANKS FOR THE HELP, GUYS!
BUT OF COURSE, ARCHIE! WE COULDN'T HAVE DONE IT WITH-OUT YOU!
YEAH! YOU WERE GREAT!
CLAP! CLAP!
SAY, WHO ARE YOU TWO? I DON'T REMEMBER YOU FROM REHEARSALS!

BETTY AND VERONICA ?! WHAT ARE YOU DOING ?
WE'RE SO PROUD, WE DECIDED TO SNEAK ON FOR THE GRAND FINALE TO JOIN YOU!

NOW COME ON! LET'S YOU AND I GO CELEBRATE!
NO WAY! HE'S COMING WITH ME!
HEY! THE CROWD LOVES THIS!
HAR! HAR! HAR!

NEXT DAY...
LET ME GET THIS STRAIGHT! THE CIRCUS ASKED YOU GUYS TO STAY ON FOR THE REST OF THE RIVERDALE PERFORMANCES?
BUT OF COURSE!
THEY SURE DID! THEY LOVE US!

THAT'S RIDICULOUS! WHEN IT COMES TO THE CLOWN BUSINESS YOU GUYS ARE JUST AMATEURS!
HMMPH! IS THAT SO?

SOON...
WE'VE BEEN THINKING REGGIE! YOU'RE RIGHT! WE ARE AMATEURS! IN FACT, THERE'S SOMETHING WE'D REALLY LIKE TO BRUSH UP ON!
OH, YEAH? WHAT'S THAT?

PIE THROWING, OF COURSE!
END

Script: Mike Pellowski / Pencils: Stan Goldberg / Inks: Henry Scarpelli / Letters: Bill Yoshida / Colors: Barry Grossman

LAND-HO, LADS! OUR FEARFUL TRIP IS AT AN END! WE HAVE FOUND OUR ROUTE TO THE INDIES!
COLUMBUS?
A MINUTE AGO HE WAS ADMIRAL PERRY, FINDING THE NORTH POLE!
OFFICE

SOMETIMES I THINK HE STUDIES TOO HARD!
HE BECOMES ONE WITH EVERYTHING HE'S LEARNED!

THE TIME CREPT BY WITH INCREDIBLE SLOWNESS! HIS HEART HUNGERED FOR ROMAN COMPANIONSHIP!
WHO IS HE NOW?
BEATS ME!

BUT, SUDDENLY... "WHAT'S THIS? IT CAN'T BE!...BUT IT IS!!
HOLD ON! I THINK HE'S GOING TO TELL US!

-A FOOTPRINT!! A REAL HUMAN FOOTPRINT!!"
ROBINSON CRUSOE!!
OF COURSE!!
2

"BUT, SOFT! WHAT LIGHT THROUGH YONDER WINDOW BREAKS?"
MAN! HE JUMPS ABOUT! NOW HE'S *ROMEO!*

ISN'T THAT ROMANTIC? HE THINKS OF *ME* AS *JULIET!*
SAYS WHO?

WHAT'S GOIN' ON? AND HOW CAN IT GO ON WITHOUT *ME*?
IT'S ARCHIE!

HIS IMAGINATION IS RUNNING WILD AGAIN!
HMPH! THAT'S NOT THE WAY I'D PUT IT!

-TWO BRICKS SHORT OF A LOAD! HIS ELEVATOR DOESN'T GO TO THE TOP! -HIS PORCH LIGHT IS DIM!
HYUK!
DON'T BE CRUEL!

SOMETIMES ARCHIE IS MORE INTENSE THAN MOST OF US!
CAMPERS ARE "IN *TENTS!*" ARCHIE IS "*INSANE!*"
SLURP!
3

AH! HOW SWEET IT IS!

YOU'RE A BETTER MAN THAN *I* AM, GUNGA DIN!
ARCH! I'M NOT GUNGA DIN! I'M YOUR PAL, JUG!
GUNGA DIN WAS A *WATER BOY*!
I KNEW THAT!

ARE WE HOLDING A SEMINAR IN THE HALLWAY, STUDENTS?
SORRY, MR. WEATHERBEE!

ARCHIE'S IMAGINATION IS RUNNING WILD AGAIN!
HE KEEPS *LIVING* ALL THE THINGS HE'S STUDIED!

THAT'S *YOUR* FAULT, GERALDINE! YOU PROGRAMMED THE BOY!
THEY *ALL* HAD THE SAME LESSONS!

BUT HIS MIND IS MORE MALLEABLE! MORE EASILY IMPRESSED!
"MALLEABLE" MEANS SOFT AS A GRAPE!

LASSIE! LASSIE! HOME! GET HELP! THE QUICKSAND'S GOT ME.!!
OH, DEAR!
SCHOOL DANCE

WE'VE GOT TO SHOCK HIM BACK TO REALITY SOMEHOW!-- SHAKE HIM LOOSE!
ALLOW ME! I CAN SHAKE HIM LOOSE, IF ANY-BODY CAN!

DARLING! KISS ME, MY SWEET! WHERE MAY WE GO, WHERE WE CAN BE ALONE?

FRANKLY, MY DEAR, I DON'T GIVE A DARN!
EEP! HE'S RHETT BUTLER!!

(SIGH!) VERONICA NEVER DID TAKE REJECTION LIGHTLY!!!
D-UH! I COULDA BEEN A CONTENDER!!
END

Archie in Spellbound

Script: George Gladir / Pencils: Tim Kennedy / Inks: Ken Selig / Letters: Bill Yoshida / Colors: Barry Grossman

ONE CONSOLATION... THE LIFT LINE ISN'T VERY LONG!

...AND I GET TO SHARE A LIFT WITH THIS LOVELY LASSIE!

ARE YOU HERE FOR THE WOMEN'S SNOWBOARD-ING CONTEST?
I DIDN'T EVEN KNOW THERE WAS A CONTEST SCHEDULED!

UH-OH! SOMETHING'S WRONG!
...OUR LIFT IS COMING TO A HALT!
WHIRRRR

WE REGRET THERE MAY BE A DELAY OF SEVERAL HOURS BEFORE THE LIFT IS REPAIRED!
AND LUCKY ME TRAPPED WITH YOU!
OH, DEAR! I'M ONE OF THE CONTEST JUDGES!

FORTUNATELY, WE'RE NEAR THE TOP OF THE HILL!
LOOK! SOME-ONE IS COMING TO HELP US DOWN!
SHUCKS!

LOOKS LIKE ALL THE CONTESTANTS ARE WAITING FOR YOU!
SNOWBOARD CONTEST

WE MAY HAVE TO CANCEL THE EVENT!
I'M TOLD OUR OTHER JUDGE IS STRANDED BELOW!
DARN!

WAIT! YOU'RE A SNOWBOARDER!
HOW'D YOU LIKE TO JUDGE OUR GIRL CONTESTANTS?

HEY! DOES A CAMEL LIKE DRINKING WATER?
OF COURSE I'LL HELP JUDGE THE EVENT!

LOOK AT HER DO A 720!

THE CONTESTANTS ARE SIMPLY BREATHTAKING!
IN MORE WAYS THAN ONE!

LATER...
HMM! NOW WE NEED SOMEONE TO HAND OUT THE TROPHIES!
GUESS WHO'S VOLUNTEERING!

FIRST PRIZE GOES TO MEGAN SAGE!

THANK YOU!
SMACK!

SECOND PRIZE GOES TO GRACE MORIZAWA!
I'M THRILLED!

THIRD PRIZE GOES TO ZOE HOLMES!
WHAT AN HONOR!

ARE YOU HAPPY WITH THE RECEPTION YOU'RE GETTING?
SIGH! I'D BE EVEN HAPPIER IF THERE WERE MORE PRIZES TO HAND OUT!
4

MY CELL PHONE!
BRINNNG!

ARCHIE, WE WON'T BE ABLE TO COME UP UNTIL THE LIFT IS REPAIRED!
I'LL BE WAITING, RON!

HOPE YOU HAVE YOUR DANCING SHOES ON! WE'RE HAVING A VICTORY DANCE AT THE INN UP HERE!

AND STILL LATER...
WE FINALLY MADE IT TO THE TOP!
POOR ARCHIE!! WE'VE KEPT HIM WAITING SO LONG!

SOUNDS LIKE EVERYBODY IS IN THERE!
WE'LL HAVE TO ASSURE ARCHIE THIS WILL NEVER HAPPEN AGAIN!

... I'LL SAY IT WON'T HAPPEN AGAIN!
END

Script & Pencils: Bob Bolling / Inks: Jim Amash / Letters: Bill Yoshida / Colors: Barry Grossman

RISE AND SHINE, SON.! TIME TO GET UP AND SHOVEL THE OLD SNOW AWAY FROM THE HOUSE!

SNOW? SNOW IS SO PEACEFUL--- SO RELAXING--- LIKE A BIG WHITE BLANKET--- MAKES ME WANT TO SLEEEEP.!

PLOP!

ARCHIE!

YOU WANTED SOMETHING, POP?
THE SNOW OUTSIDE ON THE SIDEWALK? I WANT IT REMOVED.!

AND I DO MEAN NOW.!
SHEESH.! WHY DIDN'T YOU SAY SO IN THE FIRST PLACE?

SEE, MARY? TO GET THAT BOY WORKING, ALL YOU NEED IS A FIRM HAND!
NOT TO MENTION A BIG MOUTH!

HE'S NOT REALLY A LAZY BOY! IT'S JUST THAT HE OCCASIONALLY LIKES TO GOOF OFF!

LIKE RIGHT NOW FOR INSTANCE!

ZZZ

ARCHIE! WAKE UP!
POP

SURE, POP! I'M MOVING NOW!
JUST RESTING THE RETINAS!

WHUMP!

GIGGLE!

LAUGH ALL YOU WANT! AT LEAST HE'S GETTING THE JOB DONE!
SCRAPE
SCRAPE

MARY, IT'S TIME TO FACE FACTS! OUR BOY HAS THE BLAHS TODAY!
PLOP!

HE'S COMPLETELY WITHOUT ENERGY! THERE'S NO WAY HE'LL WAKE UP TODAY!
RING!
IT'S VERONICA!
BOING!

YES, LOVE?
ZOOM!

OF COURSE, SWEETUMS-- DON'T WORRY--- A LITTLE SNOW CAN'T SEPARATE US--- BE WITH YOU SOON!
BE HOME LATER, DAD! VERONICA'S EXPECTING ME!
ARCHIE!
5

SOMETHING WRONG ?
OUR SIDEWALKS STILL NEED SHOVELING!

NO SWEAT! BE DONE IN A JIFF!
WISK!

GASP!
FLOOSH!
WHISK!
ZIP
ZOOM!

CAN'T STAY AND CHAT! VERONICA'S WAITING!

GASP! A GIRL LIKE VERONICA SHOULD RUN FOR GOVERNMENT, THEN THE COUNTRY'D NEVER HAVE ANOTHER ENERGY CRISIS!
END

Archie in "WAITING ROOM"

Script: Mike Pellowski / Pencils: Tim Kennedy / Inks: Henry Scarpelli / Letters: Bill Yoshida / Colors: Barry Grossman

FOR EVERY DR. YOUNG IN THE WORLD, I WONDER IF THERE'S A DR. OLD!
NAH! THAT'S SILLY!

MAN, WHAT A CROWD! THAT'S A SIGN OF A GOOD DOCTOR!

COULD I SEE DR. YOUNG FOR A SECOND?
SIGN THE BOOK, PLEASE!

B-BUT I ONLY WANT TO TELL HIM---
YES! YOU'LL BE CALLED IN TURN! HAVE A SEAT, PLEASE!

I GUESS YOU CAN'T BUCK THE SYSTEM! I COULD BE HERE ALL DAY!

RIGHT HERE! ON AND OFF! IT'S EXCRUTIATING!
I KNOW! I KNOW!
2

IT MAKES YOU WALK KIND OF BENT OVER ?
EXACTLY! THIS IS AS FAR AS I CAN STRAIGHTEN UP!

I GET THIS MUSCLE SPASM! I GO TO TURN MY HEAD, AND-SNAP!

I GO AROUND LIKE THIS UNTIL I CAN GET TO THE DOCTOR!
EEP!

HAH! YOU WANT TO BE SCARED?-WELL I GOT THESE SPOTS BEFORE MY EYES!
SPOTS ?

FLOAT AROUND ALL THE TIME! MAKES YOU THINK YOU'RE OUT IN SPACE!

I'VE HAD THOSE! COMES AN' GOES! KNOW WHAT I MEAN ?
YEAH! WHAT ARE THEY ?
3

I CALL 'EM "SPOTS BEFORE MY EYE"!
BUT YOU KNOW WHAT'S WORSE?
WHAT?

WHAT I GOT NOW!
ALLERGIES!

ITCH AND SCRATCH! ITCH AND SCRATCH! ALL DAY- ALL NIGHT! NO LET UP!
SCRATCH!
SCRATCH!

I'M TELLING YOU, KID, IT'S ENOUGH TO DRIVE YOU BATTY!
IT SOUNDS AWFUL!
SCRATCH!
SCRATCH!

HAH! I GOT A BRUISE ON MY HEEL, PLAYIN' RACQUET BALL LAST NIGHT!

SHUCKS! I'LL BE LIMPIN' AROUND ON MY TOE FOR A MONTH!
4

(GULP!) I'VE HAD ENOUGH OF THIS! I'VE GOT TO GET OUT OF HERE!

YOU CAN TAKE MY NAME OFF THE LIST, MISS! I'VE GOT TO GO!

ACK! WHAT A PLACE! THAT POOR LADY, ALL BENT OVER--- THE MUSCLE SPASM -- ITCHY ALLERGIES---

-- SPOTS -- RACQUET BALL FOOT- HOO BOY!
DID YOU SEE HIM, ARCHIE?

YOU'D BETTER TRY THE PHONE AGAIN, POP!
I'M TOO SICK TO HANG AROUND A DOCTOR'S OFFICE!
SCRATCH!
SCRATCH!
HOBBLE! HOBBLE! HOBBLE!
END

SCRIPT: MIKE PELLOWSKI PENCILS: BOB BOLLING INKS: AL MILGROM
LETTERS: BILL YOSHIDA COLORS: BARRY GROSSMAN

DRAMA 101 A.
HEH! HEH! IT'S SORT OF LIKE DÉJÀ VU ALL OVER AGAIN!

MINUTES LATER...
I'D BETTER CHECK THE BACK HALL AGAIN!
RING!

DRAMA 101 A.
WHOOPS!
HUH?

ARCHIE, ARE YOU OKAY?
HUH? AH... YES! I'M A-OKAY, SIR!

OH! GOOD! HA! HA! IT'S LIKE DÉJÀ VU ALL OVER AGAIN!

WHOA! WAIT JUST A MINUTE HERE! THIS IS DÉJÀ VU ALL OVER AGAIN!

CALM DOWN, WALDO! WHAT YOU NEED IS A NICE CUP OF COFFEE IN THE TEACHERS' LOUNGE!
TEACHERS LOUNGE

LATER...
NOW I FEEL MUCH BETTER!
HELLO, MR. WEATHERBEE!

HELLO, MR. MORGAN! HOW ARE YOUR DRAMA CLASSES THIS TERM?
FINE! IN FACT WE'LL BE PUTTING ON A SMALL SHOW OF SKITS IN ABOUT A WEEK OR SO!

THAT'S GOOD! I LOOK FORWARD TO SEEING IT!
TEACHERS LOUNGE

SPEAKING OF SEEING THINGS, HERE COMES ARCHIE AGAIN!
3

WHOOPS!
GASP! THIS CAN'T BE HAPPENING! ...CAN IT?

A-ARCHIE? ARE YOU...
UH-OH! I'M A-OKAY, SIR!

DÉ-JÀ VU IS ONE THING, BUT THIS IS JUST TOO WEIRD!

ARCHIE, PLEASE GET TO WHEREVER YOU'RE GOING BEFORE THE NEXT BELL RINGS!
YES, MR. WEATHERBEE!
THERE HAS TO BE A LOGICAL EXPLANATION FOR THIS!
RIVERDALE HIGH

MINUTES LATER...
RING!
THERE'S THE BELL NOW! I'LL JUST...

DRAMA 101 A
OH, NO!
WHOOPS!

NO PROBLEM, SIR... I'M OKAY!
HEH! HEH! OF COURSE YOU ARE!

I'M THE ONE WHO NEEDS TO TALK TO THE SCHOOL NURSE... AND THAT'S WHERE I'M GOING... RIGHT NOW!

SORRY I'M A BIT LATE FOR CLASS, ARCHIE! WHAT ARE YOU DOING DOWN THERE?
I'M PRACTICING MY PRAT-FALL FOR THE DRAMA SKIT I'M IN!

YOU REMEMBER, IT'S A SLAP-STICK COMEDY BIT... I SLIP ON A BANANA PEEL!
OH! THAT'S RIGHT! HOW IS IT COMING?
TERRIFIC! I'VE BEEN REHEARSING IT ALL MORNING AND I THINK I'VE GOT IT!
END

Archie in "BETTER THAN THE REAL THING"

Script: Mike Pellowski / Pencils: Tim Kennedy / Inks: Rudy Lapick / Letters: Bill Yoshida / Colors: Barry Grossman

I'M SURPRISED YOU WANT TO BE COOPED UP LIKE THIS...
ESPECIALLY SINCE YOU'RE SO GOOD AT SNOW-BOARDING!

C'MON! GRAB YOUR BOARD AND WE'LL HEAD FOR THE SLOPES!
UH... OKAY...

LATER...
NOW ISN'T IT MUCH MORE FUN TO CARVE REAL POWDER?

BETTY! HOW'D YOU EVER LURE HIM AWAY FROM HIS DUMB SNOW-BOARD GAME?
IT WASN'T EASY...

ARCHIEKINS, I'VE BEEN DYING TO HAVE YOU IMPROVE MY TECHNIQUE!
GIRL! THERE'S NOTHING WRONG WITH YOUR TECHNIQUE!

NOW HOLD ME REAL TIGHT OR I'LL FALL!

OOPS! I ALMOST FELL!
...YOU'LL HAVE TO HOLD ME MUCH TIGHTER, ARCHIE!

THAT'S BETTER... MUCH BETTER!

I THINK I'M MAKING PROGRESS!
I'LL SAY!

LATER...
RIGHT NOW I COULD GO FOR A NICE HOT CHOCOLATE!
SO COULD I!
UNFORTUNATELY, THERE'S A VERY LONG LINE AT THE SNACK STAND!
SNACKS
3

I KNOW...
LET'S ALL GO TO THE FAMILY CHALET FOR A QUICK SNACK BREAK...
... I'LL PHONE SMITHERS TO HAVE EVERYTHING READY!

UH... I DON'T THINK THERE'S ROOM FOR THREE!
YOU'RE RIGHT!! THERE ISN'T!

YOU DRIVE, BETTY... AND I'LL SIT ON ARCHIE'S LAP!

OH, GOOD! IT LOOKS LIKE SMITHERS HAS EVERYTHING READY!

WOULD YOU ALSO LIKE SOME WHIPPED CREAM ON YOUR HOT CHOCOLATE?
YES... I WOULD!

HOW'S THAT?
JUST SUPER!!
4

UM... I'D ALSO LIKE SOME, VERONICA...
BUT OF COURSE!

OH, DEAR! IT'S ALL GONE...
... SO SORRY!
SPRITZ!

AND NOW LET'S GO BACK TO THE SLOPES FOR MORE SNOWBOARDING!

...IT'S MY HAIRDRESSER!

I FORGOT ALL ABOUT MY SPECIAL APPOINTMENT...HE'S COMING HERE!

AND SINCE IT'S ONLY A SHORT DISTANCE TO THE SLOPES, WHY DON'T YOU TWO WALK OVER... ...I'LL JOIN YOU IN ABOUT AN HOUR!

BETTY, THAT'S NOT THE WAY TO THE SLOPES!
I KNOW!
SO WHERE ARE WE GOING...?
TO WHERE I PARKED MY CAR!
...AND NOW WE'RE GOING BACK TO YOUR PLACE!
RIVERDALE 2 MILES
BACK TO MY PLACE? HOW COME?
ANDREWS
BECAUSE YOU'RE SO RIGHT, ARCHIE...
...VIDEO SNOWBOARDING IS MUCH BETTER THAN THE REAL THING!
END

Script: Mike Pellowski / Pencils: Stan Goldberg / Inks: Rudy Lapick / Letters: Bill Yoshida / Colors: Barry Grossman

HE'S SUING US FOR A MILLION DOLLARS FOR LOSS OF INCOME BECAUSE OF HIS INJURIES!
TV

SURELY, HE CAN'T BE SERIOUS!
I'M GOING TO SEE A LAWYER!

I'M AFRAID HE DOES HAVE A CASE, MR. ANDREWS!
WHAT?

I DON'T EVEN HAVE A MILLION DOLLARS!
OH, DON'T WORRY ABOUT THAT!
THE JUDGE WILL PROBABLY REDUCE THE AWARD TO YOUR LIFE'S SAVINGS!
ISN'T THERE ANYTHING WE CAN DO?
YES...
2

I COULD HIRE A PRIVATE DETECTIVE TO PROVE HE'S *FAKING* HIS INJURIES AND THEN, THERE ARE *APPEALS*...

FORGET IT! THAT WOULD TAKE MY LIFE'S SAVINGS!

JUG, DAD AND THE BURGLAR WILL BE AT A *HEARING* TODAY!
SO?

SO, WE'LL *FOLLOW* THE BURGLAR AND *CATCH* HIM FAKING HIS INJURIES ON *VIDEO!*

ARCH, THIS IS A PRETTY ROUGH PART OF TOWN!
SPIKE'S TRAVEL AGENCY
TOURS TO PLACES WITH NO EXTRADITION
ED'S BURGLAR TOOLS
SPIKE'S PAWN SHOP
WE FENCE ANYTHING!
3

WE COULD GET OUR CAR AND CAMERA RIPPED OFF!
YOU'RE RIGHT!

I RECOMMEND WE DO A QUICK 180!
RIGHT!

SKREEEEE!!

DAD, WE HAVE GOOD NEWS AND BAD NEWS!

GIVE ME THE BAD NEWS!

WE FOLLOWED THE BURGLAR AND LOST HIM AND GOT A TICKET FOR MAKING AN ILLEGAL U-TURN!

AND THE GOOD NEWS?
WE DIDN'T GET OUR CAR OR CAMERA STOLEN!

DILTON'S A GENIUS! MAYBE HE CAN HELP!
I DOUBT IT!

I'LL ACCESS THE DATA-BASE OF THE LAW LIBRARY AND CROSS-REFERENCE PERTINENT FACTS!
DILTON'S LAB

HOURS LATER...
THAT'S IT! I'VE GOT IT!

YOUR HONOR, ACCORDING TO AN 1863 STATE LAW THAT WAS NEVER REPEALED...

ANY PERSON ENTERING ONTO THE PROPERTY OF ANOTHER MUST TIE HIS HORSE TO A HITCHING POST AND CARRY A LIGHTED KEROSENE LANTERN!

FAILURE TO COMPLY RELIEVES THE PROPERTY OWNER OF ALL LIABILITY FOR INJURY!

I DON'T HAVE A *HORSE!* THERE WAS NO *HITCHING* POST! I DON'T HAVE A KEROSENE LANTERN!

IN *LIGHT* OF THIS *EVIDENCE*, I DECLARE THE PLAINTIFF'S CLAIM *NULL* AND *VOID*!

CASE *DISMISSED!*
WHAT?
YAAAY!!

TO *CELEBRATE*, I'M TAKING US ALL OUT TO DINNER, INCLUDING *YOU*, DILTON!

ME? *REALLY*?
SURE! *YOU* CAME UP WITH THE HITCHING POST *DEFENSE*!

SO YOU CAN *HELP* US PUT ON THE *FEEDBAG*!
END

ARCHIE in DELI DALLY

SHE MIGHT FIND YOU SPECTACULARLY UNIMPRESSIVE IF SHE MET YOU!

WELL, I DON'T THINK SHE'D FALL FOR A ZERO LIKE YOU!!

I'LL TAKE MY CHANCES OVER YOURS ANY DAY!
GOOD LUCK WITH THAT PROJECT, CHIEF!

YEAH, RIGHT! GOOD LUCK TO ME! LATER DAYS, MOONBATS!
WHATEVER!
SHOVE

THAT REGGIE THINKS HE CAN GET ANY GIRL HE WANTS!
YUP!

GULP! ONLY, I DON'T KNOW ANYTHING ABOUT KELLIE!
I DO!
2

H-huh? WHAT? Y-YOU DO?!
YEAH! I KNOW PLENTY!

I KNOW THAT HER DAD OWNS THAT NEW DELI ON THE CORNER OF LAMBERT AND FERDINAND PLACE!
Oh?

SHE WORKS THERE EVERY DAY AFTER SCHOOL 'TIL 6:00, AND MOST EVERY SATURDAY!
YES...YES... WHAT ELSE?

WHAT ELSE? Oh, YEAH-- THE TURKEY IS A LITTLE DRY, BUT THE BRISKET IS TO DIE FOR! MMM... THE CHICKEN, THE HAM... yum!
JUG!

SNAP OUT OF IT, JUG! THIS ISN'T ABOUT YOUR STOMACH!!

IT'S ABOUT MY HEART!
Oh, YEAH-- THAT!

LISTEN, JUG.. I'VE GOT A WAY FOR ME TO GET A LEG UP ON THAT REGGIE AS FAR AS KELLIE IS CONCERNED!
GROAN! DON'T TELL ME--IT'S A PLAN THAT INVOLVES ME!

PRECISELY! BUT YOUR MEALS ARE ON ME! HERE'S THE PLAN!
COUNT ME IN!

THE NEXT DAY...
OKAY, JUG! YOU KNOW THE DRILL! GO TO THE DELI EVERY DAY THIS WEEK AND ORDER A SANDWICH...!
ANDREWS

YEAH... AND THEN FIND OUT AS MUCH AS I CAN ABOUT KELLIE!

OPERATION DELI-WATCH IS UNDER WAY!
SLURP!

DAY ONE...
ULP!

DAY TWO...

DAY THREE...

THAT NIGHT....
SO, JUG -- AFTER THREE DAYS, WHAT INFORMATION DID YOU GET?

hmm... INFORMATION? WELL, um... THE HAM AND CHICKEN ARE GOOD; THE TURKEY IS A LITTLE DRY, BUT THE --
CHIPS

YEAH, YEAH! THE BRISKET IS TO DIE FOR! ... WHAT DID YOU LEARN ABOUT KELLIE?!
RIVERDALE

Oh, um... NOT MUCH! SAY BUDDY, THIS MIGHT NEED A LITTLE MORE RESEARCH!

RESEARCH? THREE DAYS AND I'VE GOT NOTHING?! I CAN'T AFFORD YOUR RESEARCH! YOU'RE FIRED!!

WHO DOES HE THINK I AM? MR. GOTTBUCKS?!
I'M JUST A PART-TIME LIBRARY SHELVER!
I'LL GO AND TALK TO KELLIE MYSELF!

NEXT DAY...
I DON'T NEED SOMEONE ELSE TO DO MY FOOT WORK!

BESIDES--ONLY A LOSER WOULD DO THAT!

WHA-?

JUG?!
SHE'S A GREAT KID!
SHE'S INTO VIDEO GAMES AND COMIC BOOKS!
PLUS, HER DAD OWNS A DELI!
SORRY, ARCH... BUT MY STOMACH TRUMPS YOUR HEART!
END

Archie in "RACE CHASE"

Script: George Gladir / Pencils: Stan Goldberg / Inks: Rudy Lapick / Letters: Bill Yoshida / Colors: Barry Grossman

CAN I SEE THE DEMONSTRATION?
NO! YOU'RE A JINX!

DON'T BE A MEANIE, DADDY! YOU KNOW ARCHIE IS VERY INTERESTED IN SNOWMOBILES!

LOOK AT THE ONE HE BUILT ALL BY HIMSELF!
SO HE'S THE ONE WHO'S RESPONSIBLE FOR THAT JUNKYARD MONSTROCITY!
IT FIGURES!

MR. LODGE, WOULD YOU CARE TO USE MY SECRET FUEL IN YOUR SNOWMOBILE?
NO, DILTON! I CAN'T RISK USING ANY EXPERIMENTAL FUEL!
SUPER SONIC FUEL

HOWEVER, I'LL BE GLAD TO TAKE YOU TO THE DEMONSTRATION!
GEE! THANKS, MR. LODGE!

I WISH I COULD SEE THE DEMONSTRATION!
WE CAN! WE'LL FOLLOW ALONG IN YOUR SNOWMOBILE JALOPY!
LODGE SUPER

BUT I DON'T HAVE ENOUGH FUEL TO TAKE US TO THE TEST AREA!
HMM! THERE MUST BE FUEL AROUND HERE SOMEWHERE!

LOOK! DILTON LEFT HIS SPECIAL FUEL BEHIND!
GOOD! WE'LL TAKE IT ALONG!
SUPER SONIC FUEL

I THINK THAT'S THE TEST AREA DOWN IN THE VALLEY!
PUT! PUT! PUT!

WHY ARE WE SLOWING DOWN?
'CAUSE WE RAN OUT OF GAS!

IT'S A GOOD THING YOU BROUGHT ALONG DILTON'S CAN!
HURRY! MY DAD'S SNOWMOBILE IS ABOUT TO START!
GLUG! GLUG! GLUG!

GEE! ALL OF A SUDDEN MY SNOWMOBILE JALOPY IS ACTING MIGHTY PECULIAR!
SUPER SONIC FUEL

ZOOM!

ALL RIGHT, MIKE, LET HER GO!!
LODGE SUPER X-11

WOW! LOOK AT MY BABY ACCELERATE!
ZOOM!
LODGE SUPER X-11

HEY! THERE'S ANOTHER SNOWMOBILE IN THIS TEST RUN!
AND IT'S GOING EVEN FASTER THAN LODGE'S!
V-VROOM!

?
ARCHIE! THIS IS DANGEROUS! WHAT'S GOING ON ?
GULP! I THINK IT HAS SOMETHING TO DO WITH DILTON'S FUEL!

CONGRATULATIONS, YOUNG MAN! YOU JUST BEAT OUT LODGE'S SUPER X-12!
HUH ?

WOULD YOU BE INTERESTED IN SELLING YOUR SNOWMOBILE AS A PROTOTYPE ?
WE'LL GIVE YOU THREE MILLION FOR IT!
THREE MILLION ?!!
CONTRACT

DON'T ANY OF YOU WANT TO KNOW THE TIME OF MY SNOWMOBILE ?
SORRY, LODGE! YOUR SNOW-MOBILE IS ALREADY OBSOLETE!
LODGE
SUPER X-12

I KNEW IT! HE'S A JINX! A JINX!

BAD NEWS, DADDY! THEY CAN'T USE ARCHIE'S SNOWMOBILE AFTER ALL!
REALLY?

THEY SAY IT'D BE TOO EXPENSIVE TO MASS PRODUCE!
---IT SEEMS THAT ALL THE SCRAP PARTS HE USED BELONG TO COMPANIES THAT NO LONGER EXIST!

LOOKS LIKE WE'LL HAVE TO BUY YOUR SNOWMOBILE, MR. LODGE!
CONTRACT

I WONDER HOW ARCHIE'S SNOWMOBILE BEAT MINE? I'D BETTER TAKE A GOOD LOOK AT IT!

PLEASE, MR. LODGE! DON'T GO NEAR IT! YOU MIGHT SCRATCH IT!
END

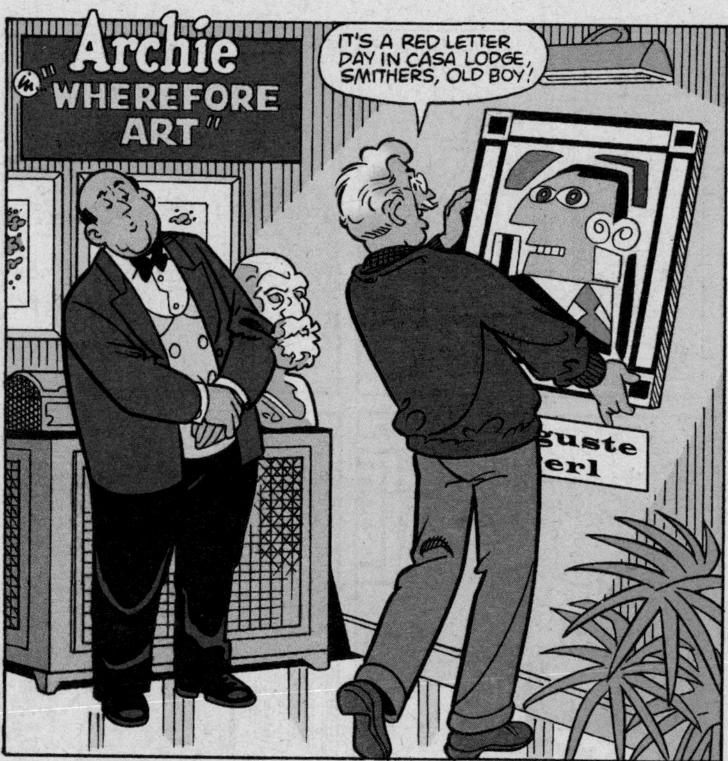

Script: Kathleen Webb / Pencils: Stan Goldberg / Inks: John Lowe / Letters: Bill Yoshida / Colors: Barry Grossman

HAVE I GOT A SURPRISE FOR YOU!
WHAT IS IT?

NO NO, DON'T LOOK YET! LET ME SET IT UP!

WON'T SHE BE THRILLED TO FIND OUT I'M GOING TO BE AN ARTIST!

IT HAS TO BE ON THE WALL FOR THE FULL EFFECT!
Auguste

AH! I'LL PUT IT UP HERE! THE PERFECT SPOT!

I'LL JUST PUT THIS OLD THING ASIDE FOR THE TIME BEING!
August
Perl
2

LOOKS JUST LIKE IT BELONGS, IF I DO SAY SO MYSELF!
Auguste Perl

OKAY, VERONICA, YOU CAN COME IN NOW!

WELL? WHAT DO YOU THINK?
ER... WOW!

IT'S YOU!
I WAS AFRAID YOU WERE GOING TO SAY THAT!

NOT QUITE THERE, HUH?
THE FRAME IS VERY NICE!
Auguste Perl

I GUESS I WON'T BE A FAMOUS PAINTER!
BUT YOU TRIED, AND THAT'S WORTH A SLICE OF GASTON'S CARROT CAKE! COME ON!

WELL! YOU CERTAINLY WASTED NO TIME, DOWLING!
I HAVE TO SEE IT!

I DON'T BELIEVE IT! YOU LOCATED AN AUGUSTE PERL?
DON'T TAKE MY WORD, DOWLING! IT'S HANGING IN THE GALLERY!

TRY NOT TO BREATHE ON IT! I PAID A PRETTY PENNY FOR THAT MASTER-PIECE!
HEH! HEH!

GOOD GRIEF! LODGE IS LOSING HIS MARBLES FOR REAL!

WELL?
YOU MUST BE JOKING! YOU PAID MONEY FOR THAT?

WELL... PERLS DON'T COME CHEAP!
LODGE! TELL ME SOMEONE DIDN'T TRICK YOU INTO THINKING THAT IS AN AUGUSTE PERL!!!
4

THAT AMATEUR EFFORT WOULDN'T FOOL A CHILD! IT WOULDN'T FOOL MY DOG!
LODGE OLD MAN, I THOUGHT YOU HAD A BETTER EYE THAN THAT! I'M STUNNED!

WELL, DON'T FRET, OLD BOY! AT LEAST THE FRAME IS NICE!

I'D BETTER PUT YOUR DAD'S PICTURE BACK UP BEFORE I FORGET!

I'LL DO YOU A FAVOR AND NOT MENTION THIS DEBACLE TO OUR FRIENDS IN THE ART LEAGUE!

HOW COULD I HAVE BEEN SO WRONG? I COULD HAVE SWORN IT WAS A GENUINE AUGUSTE PERL!

ER... DOWLING? LODGE! SO GLAD YOU ENJOYED MY LITTLE...ER...JEST!
YES, OF COURSE I WAS JOKING!

I'LL GIVE THAT ART DEALER A PIECE OF MY MIND! SELL ME PHONY MERCHANDISE, WILL HE?!

WHERE ARE YOU GOING, DADDY?
TO RETURN THIS HORRID PIECE OF JUNK!

GEE, I THOUGHT IT WAS NICE!
ME, TOO! BUT, HEY!

WHY NOT?
AS LONG AS HE'S GOT NOTHING BETTER TO HANG!
END

Archie in "I FORGOT"

FIND THE WORDS SHOWING WHAT ARCHIE HAS FORGOTTEN TO BRING TO SCHOOL!

Archie
IN
"HAPPY CHAPPY"

OOPS!

OOF!

SKI VALLEY LODGE

I HAVE BAD NEWS, EVERYBODY!
---AN APPROACHING BLIZZARD WILL MAKE SKIING IMPOSSIBLE FOR A FEW DAYS!

YAHOO!!
END.

Betty and Veronica in "Best Test"

Script: George Gladir / Pencils: Jeff Shultz / Inks: Al Milgrom / Letters: Bill Yoshida / Colors: Barry Grossman

FORGET IT!
HMPH! HE'S JUST AFRAID TO PICK THE BEST IDEA... MINE!
WHAT? YOU REALLY DO THINK YOU'RE BETTER THAN ME, DON'T YOU?

"THE TRUTH IS THE TRUTH! FOR EXAMPLE, I'M THE BEST IN TENNIS!"
THAT'S THE MATCH POINT! DON'T LOOK SO BURNED UP, BETTY!
GRRR!

BIG DEAL! YOU'VE TAKEN TENNIS LESSONS SINCE YOU WERE TWO AND YOU HAVE YOUR OWN COURT!
SO SUE ME!

"HA! I'M BETTER THAN YOU IN MOST OTHER SPORTS!"
WOW! A THREE POINTER!
SWISH!

RAH! RAH! WELL, I'M A BETTER CHEERLEADER!
GIMMIE A..."N"... GIMMIE AN..."O"... NO! YOU'RE NOT!

"OKAY! FORGET SPORTS, LET'S TAKE A TRIP TO THE MALL!"
SALE
DOTTIE'S DRESS SHOP

"I'M THE BEST SHOPPER!"
I'LL TAKE THAT AND THAT AND THAT!

"NOT! I GET MORE FOR MY MONEY AND I'M A BETTER BARGAIN HUNTER!"
I GOT ALL THIS FOR THE SAME RRICE AS THAT!

SO YOU SEE, I'M THE BEST SHOPPER!
I DON'T BUY THAT STORY!

OKAY, WELL WHO'S THE BEST COOK?
GULP!

"YOUR CAKES DON'T FALL... THEY PLUMMET!"
COOKING CLASS

"BIG DEAL! I'M AT MY BEST WHEN IT COMES TO PLANNING A DINNER PARTY!"
SEAT BETTY COOPER FAR AWAY FROM ARCHIE ANDREWS!

"I'M A BETTER STUDENT!
BETTY, YOU DO SO WELL IN SCIENCE, YOU SHOULD STUDY MICRO-BIOLOGY!
TEST TODAY
B-
A+

"I KNOW MORE ABOUT THE LATEST FASHIONS!"
WOW! CHECK OUT RON'S NEW MICRO-MINI!

I WAS ELECTED CLASS PRESIDENT!
I WAS VOTED PROM QUEEN!
VOTE FOR BETTY!
RON RULES!

YOU KNOW... THIS IS SILLY!
I AGREE! WE BOTH HAVE DIFFERENT STRENGTHS AND WEAKNESSES!

I GUESS THAT'S WHAT MAKES US BEST FRIENDS!
RIGHT!
SMACK!
4

GIRLS, I CHANGED MY MIND! I DECIDED IT IS SAFE TO GIVE YOU MY HONEST OPINION!

SORRY, BETTY, BUT I LIKE RON'S IDEA BEST!
THAT'S UNDERSTANDABLE!

WHAT ARE YOU TALKING ABOUT?! BETTY'S IDEA IS JUST AS GOOD AS MINE!
HUH?

HEY! WHY DON'T WE COMBINE OUR IDEAS INTO A COMMON THEME?
WOW! THAT'S THE BEST IDEA I'VE HEARD ALL DAY!

HUMPH! SOME HELP YOU WERE, REGGIE!
W-WHAT DID I DO?
END

Betty in
CONSOLATION
YOU SEEM PRETTY EXCITED ABOUT SOMETHING!
IT'S THIS E-MAIL I JUST GOT FROM VERONICA, SIS!
SHE AND HER FAMILY ARE SPENDING THEIR VACATION IN HAWAII!
SCRIPT: GEORGE GLADIR
PENCILS: STAN GOLDBERG
INKS: RICH KOSLOWSKI
SHE ALSO E-MAILED ME THESE GREAT PHOTOS THEY TOOK IN HONOLULU!!
HAWAII AIRPORT

AND WHAT DO WE HAVE BACK HERE IN RIVERDALE?... NOTHING BUT SNOW, SNOW, AND MORE SNOW!!

AND COULDN'T THE SNOW HAVE WAITED UNTIL WE GOT BACK TO SCHOOL?
SO THAT WE COULD HAVE GOTTEN A FEW MORE DAYS OFF?

SO THAT'S THE WAY THINGS STAND IN RIVERDALE, RONNIE. WE ALL ENVY THE FAB TIME YOU'RE HAVING IN HAWAII!
KLIK KLIK KLAK
R
R

I THINK THAT'S ARCHIE CALLING ON MY CELL. I WONDER WHAT HE WANTS. I'LL GET BACK TO YOU LATER...

HI, BETTY! I WAS GOING TO SUGGEST WE SPEND THE DAY AT THE MALL... BUT THE HEAVY SNOW HAS IT CLOSED!
RIVERDALE MALL
CLOSED

SO COME ON OVER HERE!
MY SIS BOUGHT SOME SNOWSHOES WE CAN USE ON A HIKE! I'LL MAKE A LI'L LUNCH BASKET WE CAN TAKE WITH US!

BOY! I CAN'T REMEMBER WHEN WE HAD SO MUCH SNOW!
WE SHOULD HAVE NO TROUBLE TREKKING THROUGH THE DRIFTS IN THESE!
THESE ARE THE VERY LATEST, AND THEY'RE VERY COMFY!
YEAH!
LET'S GO UP NOB HILL! LOOKS LIKE CHUCK AND NANCY ARE UP THERE TUBING WITH JUG!
I BET IT'S FUN!
HI, GUYS!!
YOU TWO ARE WELCOME TO TRY THE TUBE!
wheee!
BUMP
3

I HAVE TO TAKE A PHOTO OF YOU TWO!
HA!HA!!

AND ANOTHER OF YOU TWO STRUGGLING TO GET UP!

WHAT DO WE DO NOW?
BRRR! I'M ALL FOR GOING INSIDE SOMEWHERE!

HOW ABOUT THE NEW BOWLING ALLEY IN TOWN... I HEAR IT'S STILL OPEN DESPITE THE SNOW!
I'M ALL FOR IT!

RATS! ANOTHER GUTTER BALL! I THINK MY FINGERS ARE STILL FROZEN!
1
2
3

JUG, TAKE ONE OF ME CONSOLING ARCH FOR THROWING ALL THOSE GUTTER BALLS!
AND A SHOT OF ME CONSOL-ING BETTY FOR HAVING THE CONTENTS OF HER LUNCH BASKET FREEZE!

RIVERDALE LANES
AND HOW ABOUT ONE MORE TO REMIND US OF THIS TERRIBLE WINTER!
YES!

SO WHAT'S GOING ON BACK IN RIVERDALE?
BETTY SAYS THAT THE WEATHER HAS BEEN AWFUL!

I'VE PRINTED OUT SOME OF THE PHOTOS SHE SENT WITH HER E-MAIL!

RIVERDA
LA
1
2

IT'S BEEN TWO DAYS SINCE I E-MAILED VERONICA ABOUT THE HORRIBLE WEATHER WE'VE BEEN EXPERIENCING! ... I WONDER WHY I HAVEN'T HEARD BACK FROM HER!

BECAUSE HERE SHE COMES UP OUR DRIVEWAY!
?!

? VERONICA, I THOUGHT YOU WERE GOING TO BE IN HAWAII FOR A FEW MORE DAYS!
SO DID I!

... BUT I DECIDED TO COME BACK EARLY FOR SOME CONSOLATION!
CONSOLATION FOR WHAT, IN HEAVEN'S NAME ?!

SOB! FOR ALL THE FUN I'VE BEEN MISSING OUT ON BACK HERE IN RIVERDALE!!
?!
END

Betty and Veronica in "CLOTHES" MINDED!

Script: Barbara Slate / Pencils: Jeff Shultz / Inks: Al Milgrom / Letters: Bill Yoshida / Colors: Barry Grossman

WHY DIDN'T YOU MENTION WE WERE SHOPPING FOR DRESSES, TOO?
ARE YOU KIDDING? AT THESE PRICES WE'D HAVE TO GO HALVES ON A PAIR OF EARRINGS!

YEAH! WHO ARE WE KIDDING? HOW CAN WE AFFORD DECENT NEW GOWNS TO WEAR TO THIS DANCE?
MAYBE WE'LL FIND SOMETHING ON THE BARGAIN RACK!
BARGAIN RACK

THIS IS IT?!
OF COURSE ALL OUR STRING BIKINIS ARE HALF OFF!
SARA

I GUESS IT WON'T BE TOO BRIGHT TO WEAR A BIKINI IN JANUARY!
BUT IT WOULD BE ATTENTION GETTING!

HI, ARCHIE! WHAT ARE YOU UP TO?
GETTING FITTED FOR MY TUX FOR THE DANCE!
TUXED

I JUST HOPE THEY DON'T MEASURE WHAT'S IN MY WALLET!
TUX

YOU KNOW, NANCY, THIS WHOLE THING SEEMS RIDICULOUS!
WHAT DO YOU MEAN? THE PROCEEDS ARE GOING TO CHARITY!
COMICS

THAT'S JUST IT! THIS DANCE AND OUR FLEA MARKET WAS TO RAISE MONEY FOR CHARITY AND HERE WE ALL ARE SPENDING MONEY ON OURSELVES!

OH, COOL IT, BETTY! JUST BECAUSE YOU CAN'T AFFORD A NICE OUTFIT, DON'T TAKE AWAY OTHER PEOPLE'S FUN!

ALL I'M SAYING IS THE LESS MONEY WE SPEND ON OUR-SELVES, THE MORE WE COULD GIVE TO CHARITY!
THAT'S A GOOD POINT!

ARE YOU SAYING WE SHOULD MAKE IT A CASUAL DANCE?
I DUNNO, THAT SOUNDS SORT OF BORING!

DIDN'T WE MAKE ENOUGH CHARITY MONEY FROM THAT FLEA MARKET? ALL WE WERE LEFT WITH WAS A BUNCH OF OLD CLOTHES!
YEAH, NOBODY WANTED TO BUY OUT-OF-STYLE CLOTHES!
3

OF COURSE! THAT'S IT!
WHAT?! DID I MISS SOMETHING?

WE'LL HAVE AN *OUT-OF-STYLE DANCE!*
?

I THINK THE POOR GIRL'S GONE KOOKY! BUT LET'S HUMOR HER!
WHAT'S AN *OUT-OF-STYLE DANCE?*

EVERYONE WHO'S GOING GETS TO BUY AN OUTFIT TO WEAR FROM OUR FLEA MARKET LEFTOVERS!
UGH!

WE COULD PLAY OLD RECORDS AND DO OUT DATED DANCES!
THAT SOUNDS GREAT! WHAT DO YOU THINK, VERONICA? *VERONICA?!*

OH, WELL! MAYBE IT WILL GROW ON HER!
4

THE NIGHT OF THE DANCE...
BETTY, WHAT A WONDERFUL IDEA! EVERYONE'S HAVING A GREAT TIME! AND WE GOT RID OF THOSE OLD CLOTHES!
THANKS, MS. GRUNDY!
STAYIN' ALIVE! STAYIN' ALIVE!

OH, GERALDINE! WOULD YOU CARE TO DO THE "MONKEY" AGAIN?
LEAD ON, DISCO KING!

WHERE'S VERONICA? HAVE YOU SEEN HER?
OH, LOOK! THERE SHE IS, OVER THERE I *THINK*!

VERONICA, WHAT'S WITH THAT GET-UP?
SINCE I'M GOING ALONG WITH THIS OUT-OF-STYLE IDEA, I DECIDED I SHOULD AT LEAST BE THE **MOST** OUT-OF-STYLE!
JUST GO TO THE YMCA
END

Script: Kathleen Webb / Pencils: Stan Goldberg / Inks: Al Milgrom / Letters: Bill Yoshida / Colors: Barry Grossman

(SIGH) I WAS ALL OF SEVEN THE FIRST TIME I WAS KISSED!
A NEIGHBOR'S BOY BY THE NAME OF HERBIE PICKLESEYMER DID THE DEED!

ARCHIE AND I WERE SIX! HE GAVE ME A FLOWER! I PRESSED IT INTO MY DIARY!
THAT'S BETTER THAN I GOT!

HERBIE PICKLESEYMER GAVE ME THE MEASLES, THEN HE MOVED AWAY!
I'M GLAD YOUR FIRST KISS WAS BETTER!
SO AM I!

I'D BETTER MAKE SURE EVERYTHING'S READY!

LET'S SEE NOW... THE CHERRY FLAVOR LIP CAKE IS ALL FROSTED...

I HAVE PLENTY OF CHOCOLATE CANDIES...

AND JUST TO KEEP THE KISSES COMING, I HAVE SOME DRIED MISTLETOE FROM CHRISTMAS!

BING
BONG
HE'S HERE! HE'S HERE!

WHO'S HERE?
ARCHIE! MUMSY... COULD YOU-?
OF COURSE, DEAR!
BING

COME ON! LET'S LEAVE THEM SOME PRIVACY!
WHO'S GOING TO LEAVE *ME* SOME PRIVACY?

ARCHIE! DARLING! HAPPY ANNIVERSARY!
FLOWERS? FOR *ME*?

MMMMMMMM

WAIT A MINUTE! YOU'RE NOT MY ARCHIEKINS!
TOO BAD!!

THE NAME'S JOSH! I'M HERE TO DELIVER FLOWERS FOR MRS. COOPER!
OH!

ER... I'M NOT ARCHIE, BUT I MIGHT MAKE A GOOD SUBSTITUTE!
SOME OTHER TIME!

JUST A GUY DELIVERING FLOWERS FOR YOU, MOM!
FOR ME?!?

SHE'S NOT THE ONLY ONE WITH AN ANNIVERSARY! REMEMBER THE OLD COFFEE BEAN CAFE?
OUR FIRST DATE! YOU REMEMBERED!!

THAT WAS SWEET OF DADDY!
(SIGH) BUT IT LOOKS LIKE ARCHIE FORGOT!
BING BONG
4

SWEETIE! YOU REMEMBERED!!

(GASP) IT'S *YOU* AGAIN!
YEAH! HERE! HAPPY ANNIVERSARY!

BY THE WAY, I'M STILL AVAILABLE IF YOUR BOY-FRIEND ISN'T!
THANKS, BUT NO THANKS!
BRRRING

I GOT YOUR FLOWERS, ARCHIE! THANK YOU FOR REMEMBERING, BUT... WHERE ARE YOU?
AT HOME, SICK! I CAUGHT THE MEASLES FROM THAT NEW KID, RALPH PICKLESEYMER!

PICKLESEYMER?! H-HOW...
HE GAVE THEM TO VERONICA, AND SHE GAVE THEM TO ME!

Y'KNOW, MOM, SOME THINGS ***NEVER*** CHANGE!
ESPECIALLY WHEN IT COMES TO PICKLESEYMERS, DEAR!
TV
END

Betty and Veronica in "THAT'S INCREDIBLE"

Script: Mike Pellowski / Pencils: Dan DeCarlo / Inks: Henry Scarpelli / Letters: Bill Yoshida / Colors: Barry Grossman

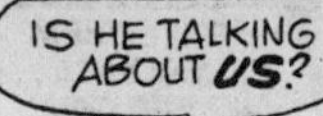

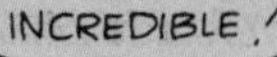

WHAT DID YOU MEAN WHEN YOU SAID WE WERE CHAMPS IN OUR OWN WAY ?
WELL, YOU BOTH HAVE LOTS OF MEDALS AND TROPHIES !

RONNIE WAS MISS RIVERDALE - QUEEN OF THE WINTER CARNIVAL -- MISS GREAT LEGS OF 2013 AND LOTS MORE !
TRUE ! ALL TRUE !

BETTY WON THE AMERICAN HISTORY MEDAL, STUDENT OF THE YEAR, THE GENERAL EXCELLENCE MEDAL, THE SCIENCE AWARD !
SO ?

YOU NOTICE RONNIE'S AWARDS ARE ALL PHYSICAL ! YOU KNOW - BEAUTY STUFF !

BETTY'S AWARDS ARE ALL FOR HER MENTAL ABILITIES !
SEE ? NO COMPETING !

SO THERE'S NO REASON FOR ENVY OR JEALOUSY OR ANY OF THAT DUMB STUFF !

HEY, LISTEN, I'VE GOT TO SPLIT! I'LL SEE YOU GIRLS LATER!

INCREDIBLE! HE REALLY BELIEVES IT!
HE MAKES YOU SOUND STUPID AND ME UGLY!

NO ENVY? NO JEALOUSY? HOW NAIVE CAN YOU GET?

I'VE ALWAYS ENVIED YOUR TROPHIES!
REALLY?

WELL I'M TIRED OF BEING A HEAD! I'D LIKE TO BE A BOD FOR A CHANGE!

YOU SILLY TWIT! YOURS IS MORE IMPORTANT AND MEANINGFUL!

YOU'VE GOT IT ALL UPSTAIRS!
BULLY FOR ME!
ALK

I'D LIKE A LITTLE IN THE ATTIC, AND MAYBE SOMETHING IN THE BASEMENT!

SAY! WHY NOT?
WHY NOT WHAT?

WHY DON'T WE SWAP A FEW OF THE ONES THAT DON'T HAVE OUR NAMES ENGRAVED ON?
THAT'S AN INCREDIBLE IDEA!

HOW WOULD YOU LIKE TO MIX THESE WITH YOUR BRAINY TROPHIES?

MISS GREAT LEGS OF 2013, MISS APPLE BLOSSOM FESTIVAL, JUNIOR HIGH PROM QUEEN, PRIZE PROFILE CONTEST WINNER-- FIRST PRIZE!
WOW!
4

NOW WE'LL GO TO YOUR PLACE AND SEE WHICH ONES YOU'RE WILLING TO PART WITH!
GREAT!

THIS WAY WE'LL BOTH LOOK MORE WELL-BALANCED - MENTALLY AND PHYSICALLY!
RIGHT! ALL-AROUND CHAMPIONS!

HEY! WHAT'S WITH ALL THE TROPHIES?
MUM'S THE WORD, BETTY

ER - JUST A FEW OF BETTY'S AWARDS! THEY GOT DINGY AND SHE HAD THEM PROFESSIONALLY POLISHED!
LET'S SEE WHAT THEY'RE FOR, BETTY!

HMM! THE JUDGES KNEW THEIR STUFF! I WOULD HAVE VOTED THE SAME WAY!

HE BELIEVED I WON THESE! THAT'S INCREDIBLE!
SEE? I TOLD YOU WE COULD GET AWAY WITH IT!

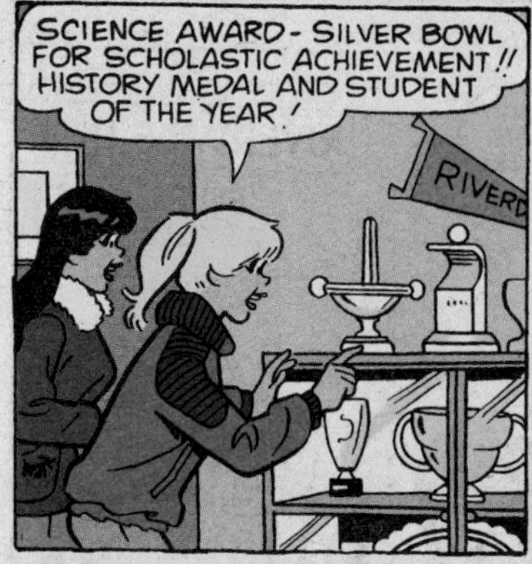
SCIENCE AWARD - SILVER BOWL FOR SCHOLASTIC ACHIEVEMENT !! HISTORY MEDAL AND STUDENT OF THE YEAR !
RIVERD

I LOVE IT ! NOW OUR TALENTS WON'T SEEM ALL SO ONE-SIDED !

MORE TROPHIES ?
ER - THESE ARE RONNIE'S !! WE'RE TAKING THEM TO GET POLISHED !

SCIENCE AWARD ? STUDENT OF THE YEAR !?!
NOW THAT'S INCREDIBLE !

I THINK YOU PUT A DENT IN YOUR SILVER BOWL FOR SCHOLASTIC ACHIEVEMENT !
THAT POINT ON HIS HEAD RUINED IT !
I'LL GET BY WITH THESE THREE !!!
The END

TOMOKO, THIS IS A WONDERFUL HUMAN INTEREST STORY YOU'VE WRITTEN ABOUT MOOSE!...
...AND HIS CONSTANT STRUGGLE TO KEEP HIS GRADES UP SO HE'D BE ELIGIBLE TO PLAY FOOTBALL!
RIVERDALE HIGH
BLUE and GOLD
BLUE and GOLD
MILK
SCRIPT: GEORGE GLADIR
PENCILS: STAN GOLDBERG
INKS: JOHN LOWE
Betty in MAKING the GRADE

I GUESS THE DUDE DIDN'T STRUGGLE HARD ENOUGH!
THE LATEST GRADES HAVE JUST BEEN POSTED AND MOOSE IS NO LONGER ELIGIBLE TO PLAY!
oh, NO!
oh, YES! COME AND SEE FOR YOURSELVES!

OH, MOOSE! THIS IS TERRIBLE!
≡GULP!≡ D-UH, I GUESS THIS JUST PROVES I'M A GREAT BIG DUNDERHEAD!
LIST of ACADEMICALLY INELIGIBLE

BETTY, THIS SEEMS SO UNFAIR! MOOSE WORKS SO HARD TO KEEP HIS GRADES UP!
MAYBE WE CAN GET THE PRINCIPAL TO DO SOMETHING ABOUT IT!
DO YOU REALLY THINK SO?
NEVER UNDERESTIMATE THE POWER OF THE PRESS!
SIR, IS THERE SOMETHING THAT CAN BE DONE TO HELP MOOSE?
MAYBE HE CAN HAVE ANOTHER CRACK AT THE EXAMS HE FAILED?
THIS IS HIGHLY IRREGULAR!

BUT I DID READ TOMOKO'S ARTICLE... AND WAS QUITE MOVED BY IT!
LET'S HAVE ANOTHER LOOK AT ALL HIS EXAM RESULTS!

HMM... THIS IS ODD! NONE OF HIS GRADES WERE GREAT... BUT IT WAS HIS FAILURE TO TAKE HIS P.E. EXAM THAT DID HIM IN!
?BUT PHYSICAL EDUCATION IS HIS STRONGEST SUBJECT!!

MOOSE! HOW COULD YOU POSSIBLY FAIL PHYS-ED!
D-UH, IT'S A LONG STORY, BETTY!!

"I WAS ON MY WAY TO SCHOOL ON EXAM MORNING WHEN I SAW A HOUSE ON FIRE!

KOFF-KOFF! MY INFANT CHILD IS STILL INSIDE!
HER BEDROOM IS THERE!
"WITH ALL THE SMOKE, I HAD TROUBLE MAKING MY WAY...
KOFF! KOFF!

"FINALLY, I DID MANAGE TO LOCATE THE CHILD...

"AND BRING HER SAFELY TO HER MOM!"
OH, THANK HEAVENS! MY BABY IS ALIVE!!

"BY THE TIME I GOT TO SCHOOL THE P.E. EXAM WAS OVER! I HAD MISSED IT!"
MNASIUM
BUT, WHY DIDN'T YOU TELL ANYONE ABOUT THE FIRE?
D-uh, IT NEVER OCCURRED TO ME!
BESIDES, I JUST FIGURED MY OTHER GRADES WOULD DO ME IN!
LATER...
THE MOTHER CONFIRMS WHAT HAPPENED... SHE SAYS THE CHILD'S RESCUER RUSHED OFF BEFORE SHE COULD GET HIS NAME!
TO THIS DATE NO ONE KNOWS WHO IT WAS!!
RIVERDALE HIGH PRES
BLUE and GOLD
BETTY COOP
EDITOR-IN-CHIEF
SO THAT'S WHY MOOSE MISSED HIS EXAM!
I'LL HAVE IT RESCHEDULED IMMEDIATELY!
D-uh, IS IT OKAY IF I DO MY PUSH-UPS WITH ONE HAND? THE OTHER IS STILL A LITTLE BRUISED!
HE'S UNBELIEVABLE! EVEN WITH ONE HAND HE'S PASSING!
AMAZING!
PHYS. ED DEPT.

FRIDAY NIGHT...
MOOSE WAS A ONE-MAN WRECKING CREW TONIGHT!
RIVERDALE WINS 20 TO 7 THANKS TO HIS 13 TACKLES... AND THE FOUR FUMBLES HE CAUSED LAKEVIEW TO HAVE!

THE GAME BALL IS YOURS MOOSE!
D-uh, I DON'T DESERVE IT!!
MASO
R

IT BELONGS TO THOSE TWO GIRLS WHO GAVE ME MY SECOND CHANCE TO PLAY!!
COACH

LIKE I SAID, TOMOKO, NEVER UNDER-ESTIMATE THE POWER OF THE PRESS!
THE END

Archie in "CHARM CHATTER"

Script: George Gladir / Pencils: Stan Goldberg / Inks: Henry Scarpelli / Letters: Bill Yoshida / Colors: Barry Grossman

WE'RE VERY CROWDED RIGHT NOW! THEY'RE FILMING A MOVIE HERE!
BUT WE HAVE RESERVATIONS!

I'M AFRAID THIS IS ALL WE CAN OFFER YOU, MR. DOILEY!
IT'S NOTHING MORE THAN A BROOM CLOSET!

BUT I'M AFRAID WE HAVE NOTHING FOR YOU, MR. ANDREWS!
GULP!

HA! HA! DID YOU FORGET TO RUB YOUR LUCKY RABBIT'S FOOT?
HMPF!

WAIT! ONE OF OUR GUESTS IS ABOUT TO CHECK OUT!

YOU CAN HAVE HIS SUITE AT OUR REGULAR ROOM RATE!
THAT'S SUPER!

WOW! WHAT A BIG ROOM!
I'D INVITE YOU TO SHARE IT WITH ME, DILTON---

---BUT SINCE YOU DON'T BELIEVE IN MY CHARM, YOU WOULDN'T BE COMFORTABLE HERE!
HMPF!

THE SIZE OF A ROOM ISN'T IMPORTANT SINCE WE'LL BE OUTDOORS MOST OF THE TIME!

HEY! WATCH WHERE YOU'RE GOING!

YOU JUST BROKE MY SKIS!
I'M TERRIBLY SORRY!

YOUR CHARM IS CERTAINLY GETTING YOU OFF TO A GOOD START!
HOW ARE YOU GOING TO SKI WITHOUT SKIS?

COME WITH ME!
?
SKI SHOPPE

MY MOTHER RUNS THIS SKI SHOP!
PLEASE LET ME REPLACE YOUR SKIS!

BUT THESE SKIS ARE MUCH BETTER THAN THE ONES I HAD!
YOU'LL ALSO NEED MATCHING SKI BOOTS, SKI SUIT., GLOVES---

AFTER ALL THE UPSET I CAUSED YOU, IT'S THE LEAST I CAN DO!

CHALK UP ANOTHER ONE FOR MY RABBIT'S FOOT!
SKI SHOPPE
I DON'T BELIEVE THIS! I DON'T BELIEVE THIS!

LOOK AT ALL THE NEWSMEN AROUND!
THE DESK CLERK SAID THEY WERE SHOOTING A MOVIE HERE!

ANY OF YOU BOYS SEE BROOKE TATUM, THE TEENAGE STAR?
IS **SHE** HERE?

COME ON! LET'S GO UP DEVIL'S HILL!
I DON'T THINK WE SHOULD RISK IT, ARCHIE!
SKI LIFT

AH! BUT I'VE NOTHING TO FEAR, AS LONG AS I HAVE MY CHARM!

I KEEP TELLING YOU THERE IS NO STATISTICAL EVIDENCE TO SUPPORT YOUR SILLY BELIEF!

UH, OH!
IS SOMETHING WRONG?
DO NOT DISTURB SKI LIFT OPERATOR

THE SKI LIFT IS **JAMMED!**
THEY'RE GOING TO BE STUCK UP THERE FOR HOURS!

SOME GOOD-LUCK CHARM!
...YOUR SKI LIFT IS JAMMED!

I DON'T MIND IN THE LEAST BEING STUCK UP HERE!
?

LOOK WHO'S HERE WITH ME--- **BROOKE TATUM** THE MOVIE STAR!
HI!

ARCHIE! HOW ABOUT THROWING DOWN YOUR LUCKY CHARM TO ME?
YOU WON'T NEED IT UP THERE!
---PLEASE, ARCHIE! PLEASE!
END

M. Pellowski • T. Kennedy • A. Milgrom

YOU HAVE SUCH A NICE, FRIENDLY PERSONALITY! I'VE DECIDED TO MAKE YOU OUR STORE GREETER!
WOW! COOL!

EXACTLY WHAT DO I SAY?
THERE IS NO STANDARD WELCOME! JUST SAY SOMETHING LIKE... "HELLO! WELCOME TO VALUEMART! I HOPE YOU ENJOY SHOPPING HERE..." AND SMILE!
I CAN DO THAT, SIR! IN FACT I'LL MAKE PEOPLE FEEL VERY WELCOME!
HAHA! GOOD! I'M SURE YOU WILL!
IN AWHILE...
HELLO! WELCOME TO VALUEMART! I HOPE YOU ENJOY SHOPPING HERE!
THANK YOU, YOUNG MAN!
LATER...
HELLO, SIR! WELCOME TO VALUEMART! I HOPE YOU...
HUMMPH! OUTTA MY WAY, SONNY!
YEOW! HEY, MISTER... YOU RAN OVER MY TOE!!
SORRY, BUT I DID TELL YOU TO CLEAR A PATH!
TIME PASSES...
HELLO! WELCOME TO VALUEMART! I HOPE YOU ENJOY SHOPPING HERE!
...AND PASSES...
H-HELLO! WELCOME TO VALUEMART! I-I HOPE YOU ENJOY SHOPPING HERE...
2

ARCHIE ?!
UGH ?!

HELLO! WELCOME TO VALUEMART! I HOPE YOU ENJOY SHOPPING HERE!
EASY, ARCHIE! YOUR SHIFT IS OVER! YOU CAN GO HOME NOW!

THE NEXT DAY...
I'M TELLING YOU, JUG! IF I UTTER THAT BORING GREETING ONE MORE TIME MY BRAIN WILL EXPLODE!
WELL CHANGE IT! JAZZ IT UP. MR. BROWN SAID THERE IS NO STANDARD GREETING!
VALUEMART

HEY! YOU'RE RIGHT! MAYBE I'LL TRY SOMETHING NEW... LIKE A RHYME OR TWO! SEE YA!
GO FOR IT, ARCH! SO LONG!

WHEN ARCHIE GOES TO WORK...
WELCOME TO VALUEMART... A FUN PLACE TO SHOP... YOU'LL LIKE IT SO MUCH, YOU WON'T WANT TO STOP!
TEE HEE! HOW CUTE!

LATER...
WELCOME TO VALUEMART A PLACE THAT IS NICE... YOU'LL FIND IT TO BE A SHOPPER'S PARADISE!
HUMPH! I HATE POETRY, SONNY!

AT THE END OF THE DAY...
WHEW! IT'S A GOOD THING MY SHIFT IS OVER! I'VE RUN OUT OF RHYMES!

THE NEXT WEEKEND...
THE RHYMING THING WENT OKAY, BUT I'M TRYING SOMETHING NEW TODAY!
COOL! MAYBE I'LL STOP BY LATER AND CHECK IT OUT!
EMART

INSIDE THE STORE...
HELLO! OUR BARGAIN PRICES WILL MAKE YOU FEEL LIKE DANCING!

LATER...
WELCOME TO VALUE-MART! STOP AND ENJOY THE SHOW!
HUH?

TA-DAH!
BRAVO, YOUNG FELLA! YOU FINALLY GOT MY ATTENTION!
CLAP! CLAP!

AH-HUM!
OH! HI, MR. BROWN! HOW DID YOU LIKE MY NEW WELCOME BIT?

IT WAS INTERESTING, ARCHIE, BUT TO TELL THE TRUTH... IT'S A BIT MUCH! THIS IS A STORE, NOT THEATER!
OH! RIGHT, SIR!

I WONDER HOW ARCH'S NEW ROUTINE HAS WORKED OUT?
VALUEMART

THERE HE IS NOW WITH A CUSTOMER!
HELLO!

WELCOME TO VALUEMART! I HOPE YOU ENJOY SHOPPING HERE!
WHAT THE...?

HEY, ARCH! WHAT HAPPENED TO YOUR NEW BIT?
WELL, JUG, LET'S JUST SAY...

I HAD THE WELCOME MAT PULLED OUT FROM UNDER ME!
?
The END

Betty and Veronica in "SPRING AHEAD"

Script: Kathleen Webb / Pencils: Dan DeCarlo / Inks: Jimmy DeCarlo / Letters: Bill Yoshida / Colors: Barry Grossman

WE JUST GOT IT IN YESTERDAY, MISS LODGE!
HER ENTIRE SPRING COLLECTION!
NEW FOR SPRING
OOOOO!

THERE ARE EVEN SOME PIECES I CAN AFFORD!
I CAN'T WAIT 'TIL SPRING TO WEAR THEM!

WHY SHOULD WE?
YOU SAID THAT BEFORE...

...BUT THIS TIME, THERE IS A PERFECTLY GOOD REASON FOR WAITING!
WHAT'S THAT?

MAYBE YOU HAVEN'T NOTICED, BUT IT IS SNOWING OUTSIDE! WE'LL FREEZE TO DEATH!
PISH TOSH!

WE CAN WEAR HEAVY COATS TO SCHOOL!
ONCE WE'RE THERE, WE'LL TAKE 'EM OFF! WE'LL HAVE SCHOOL HEAT TO KEEP US WARM!

AND WE'LL HAVE THE SMOLDERING OF THE BOYS TO KEEP US WARM!
OKAY! YOU TALKED ME INTO IT!

NEXT DAY:
I'M GLAD YOU DECIDED TO DRIVE US TO SCHOOL IN YOUR HEATED CAR!
WE'D HAVE FROZEN TO DEATH WALKING THERE!
VL 1

NOW FOR THE UNVEILING!
BE SURE TO WATCH ALL THE MALE EYES ON US!

B-R-R-R!!!

M-M-MR. SVE-SVE... SVENSON...WHA-WHA-WHAT HAPPENED TO THE HEAT?
DER SCHOOL BOILER IS ON BLINK! IT BAIN STUCK AT 45 DEGREES!

IT FEELS MORE LIKE 45° BELOW!
S-SO MUCH FOR SHOWING OFF OUR S-SPRING CLOTHING!

ARCHIE, AREN'T YOU COLD?
NOPE! NOT WITH A HEAVY SWEATER AND MY JACKET ON!

HEY! GREAT LOOKIN' BLUE LIPSTICK, RON!
SHE'S NOT WEARING LIPSTICK!

YOU'RE NOT WEARING PURPLE FISHNET STOCKINGS EITHER, I TAKE IT?
N-NOT THE LAST TIME I LOOKED!

DERE! DAT OUGHT TO FIX DE BOILER!
IT SHOULD VARM UP NOW!
CLANK!
CLANK!

?- THAT'S FUNNY! IT'S STARTING TO FEEL WARM AROUND HERE!
SVENSON MUST HAVE GOTTEN THE BOILER FIXED!
4

BETTY! NOW'S OUR CHANCE! TAKE YOUR COAT OFF!
WOW! LOOK AT THAT!

WHEW! THEY'VE GOT THE RIGHT IDEA! IT'S TOO HOT FOR SWEATERS AND SLACKS!
I'M GOING TO CHANGE INTO MY GYM CLOTHES!

PHEW! IT MUST BE OVER 90 DEGREES!
I MAY CHANGE INTO MY SWIMSUIT IF IT KEEPS UP!

WE DON'T HAVE PROBLEMS WITH OUR STUDENTS FOLLOWING RIVERDALE HIGH'S DRESS CODE, SUPERINTENDENT HASSLE!
YOU WON'T SEE REBELS OR TROUBLE -MAKERS HERE!

!

BOY! I DIDN'T REALIZE HOW HOT IT REALLY IS!
YEAH! MISTER WEATHERBEE'S SWEATING SO MUCH, IT LOOKS LIKE HE'S CRYING!
END

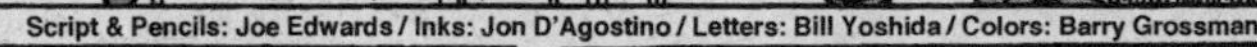
Script & Pencils: Joe Edwards / Inks: Jon D'Agostino / Letters: Bill Yoshida / Colors: Barry Grossman

STOP THINKING WITH YOUR FISTS! DON'T YOU HAVE A GENTLER SIDE?

YOU'RE NOT HAPPY WITH ME, MIDGE?
NOW YOU'VE GOT IT, MR. BRAWNY!

11
CRUNCH

MOOSE, YOU LET THE OTHER TEAM WALK OVER YOU!
I-I KNOW, COACH!
4

WHAT'S GOTTEN INTO YOU-? THERE'S NO FIGHT IN YOU!
SORRY, COACH! I WAS THINKING OVER WHAT MY GIRL SAID TO ME!
COACH

BETTY, YOU WOULDN'T BELIEVE WHO I SAW WITH MOOSE!
I KNOW,-- VERONICA!

THE TWO HAVE BEEN QUITE THICK NOW THAT MIDGE HASN'T BEEN AROUND!
REALLY?

LATER:
MISS VERONICA WILL SEE YOU NOW AT THE HOUSE!

MY! MY! SO VERONICA'S BUTLER IS DELIVERING MESSAGES, EH?

HI, REGGIE! DID YOU SEE MOOSE?
YES! AND I KNOW WHERE HE'S AT... VERONICA'S HOUSE!

YOU'VE GOT TO BE KIDDING... SHE'S NOT HIS TYPE!
OKAY, MIDGE! COME ON, I'LL SHOW YOU!

SSSH! I DON'T WANT HIM TO THINK I'M :KOFF: CHECKING UP ON HIM!
PSSST! HE'S INSIDE!
3

MOOSE, YOU'RE DOING VERY WELL!
THANKS TO *YOU* AND *SMITHERS*...

...I'M GETTING *LESSONS* IN *HOW* TO *BE* A *GENTLEMAN*! - D-UH!

I NEVER KNEW THERE'S SO MUCH TO LEARN - LIKE HOW TO SIT, WALK AND TALK!

SO THAT'S *WHERE* HE'S BEEN DISAPPEARING!
HA HA!

ALL RIGHT, MOOSE! WALK THE WAY I SHOWED YOU... HEAD UP...

HA HA! THIS IS RICH! MOOSE TRYING TO BE A *GENTLEMAN*! MY SIDES ARE HURTING!
4

VERY GOOD! YOU'RE LEARNING TO DRINK A CUP OF TEA LIKE A TRUE GENTLEMAN!

I'D LIKE TO GO OVER YOUR SPEECH LESSON! REMEMBER YOUR DICTION-- ENUNCIATE...

'OW NOW BROWN COW
THE RAIN IN SPAIN FALLS MAINLY IN THE PLAIN

OOOOH! THIS IS TOO MUCH! I'M BUSTING!

I JUST CAN'T WAIT TO SPREAD THIS NEWS... HA! HA! HE'LL BE A LAUGHING STOCK!
5

YOU CHANGED YOUR MIND ABOUT ME? WHAT DID IT?

YOUR TRYING TO CHANGE CHANGED ME! I'M PROUD OF YOU!

I'M TOUCHED THAT YOU WOULD GO TO SUCH TROUBLE FOR ME!

WOW! LOOK! REGGIE'S GOT A BLACK EYE!

HONEST, MIDGE! I DIDN'T DO IT!

I KNOW! I DID!
?
END

Reggie  IT'S ALWAYS THE SAME OLD STORY ON A WEEKEND SKI TRIP

Script & Pencils: Bob Bolling / Inks: Jon D'Agostino / Letters: Bill Yoshida / Colors: Barry Grossman

THE WAIT IS SO MONOTONOUS YOU WISH FOR SOMETHING TO DO---
YAWN

AND YOU GET YOUR WISH-- THERE IS SOMETHING TO DO---
NO CARS BEYOND THIS POINT WITH-OUT SNOW CHAINS
SPLASH!
2395

AND THEN WHEN YOU FINALLY MAKE IT TO THE SKI LODGE YOU'RE TOLD---
NO VACANCY

BUT THE MANAGER REMEMBERS THERE IS STILL ONE ROOM AVAILABLE--- AND YOU CONGRATULATE YOURSELF ON YOUR GOOD FORTUNE!

---UNTIL YOU SEE YOUR ROOM---
JANITOR'S SUPPLY ROOM

THE NEXT MORNING YOU GET UP BRIGHT AND EARLY BECAUSE YOU WANT TO AVOID THE CROWD FOR BREAKFAST---
R-R-RING!

ONLY TO DISCOVER EVERYONE ELSE HAD THE SAME BRILLIANT IDEA---
CAFETERIA LINE
ME!
HERE!

AFTER BREAKFAST YOUR COLD NUMB HANDS FUMBLE WITH YOUR FROZEN BOOT-LACES---
BRRR

YOU FINALLY SUCCEED IN GETTING ON YOUR SKIS---

PLOP!
---ONLY TO TRIP IN THE SLUSH AROUND THE LODGE---

AFTER MUCH STRUGGLING YOU SUCCEED IN RIGHTING YOURSELF---

ONLY TO BE SQUIRTED IN THE FACE BY SOME PASSING HOTDOGGER---

AFTER MUCH WAITING IT'S FINALLY YOUR TURN---

AND OF COURSE YOUR ANSWER IS ---
YOU BET IT WAS!
THE
END

Reggie
THE RULES
SPLAT
PLOP
Script: G. Gladir
Art & Letters: S. Schwartz
THERE'S ONLY ONE GUY SNEAKY ENOUGH TO DO THAT!
AND THERE HE IS!
CREEP! THROWING AT US WHEN WE WEREN'T LOOKING!
OF COURSE! WHEN ELSE?
JUST TO PROVE I CAN BE FAIR, I'LL TAKE ON THE TWO OF YOU IN A SNOWBALL FIGHT! NO THROWIN' WHEN NOT LOOKIN'!
YOU'RE ON!
1

DILLY, WHERE ARE YOU GOING? COME BACK!
I'M NOT RUNNING AWAY! YOU HOLD HIM OFF 'TIL I GET BACK!

THIS SHOULD TAKE CARE OF MISTER MANTLE! THE DOILEY R.F.S.T. M-1! MY RAPID FIRE SNOWBALL THROWER!

THE SECOND HE SHOWS HIMSELF.. POW!
THIS SHOULD DO IT!

HAW! THIS IS GONNA BE GOOD!

RAT-A-TAT-TAT-TAT-TAT

NO FAIR! OFFICIAL RULES OF SNOWBALL FIGHTS STATE THAT ONLY ONE SNOWBALL AT A TIME MAY BE THROWN!
TIME OUT!

COME WITH ME, JUG! THIS CALLS FOR AN ENTIRELY DIFFERENT TYPE OF ATTACK!
GOT ANOTHER GADGET, DILLY?

LATER
HEY! HOW LONG ARE YOU GONNA STALL? WHEN'RE YOU GOING TO START THROWIN'?
RIGHT NOW!

JUST ONE WAS ENOUGH!
END

REGGIE'S WINTER SPORT WORD PUZZLE

LOOK FOR WORDS THAT DESCRIBE THE WINTER SCENE! WORDS MAY BE READ FORWARDS, BACKWARDS, UP, DOWN AND DIAGONALLY! THE WORDS ARE IN A STRAIGHT LINE AND THEY NEVER SKIP A LETTER! SOME WORDS OVERLAP AND SOME LETTERS ARE USED MORE THAN ONCE!

WORD LIST

1. BOBSLED
2. GOALIE
3. HOCKEY
4. HOTDOGGING
5. ICE
6. JUMP
7. LODGE
8. PUCK
9. SKATING
10. SKI
11. SLALOM
12. SLOPE
13. SNOWBALL
14. SNOWMAN
15. SNOW-MOBILE

S	F	G	E	L	M	P	Q	S	T	X	E
A	K	E	C	E	D	H	K	B	N	L	O
G	B	I	C	E	G	I	J	O	I	L	U
N	S	L	O	P	E	D	H	B	Y	A	R
I	Z	A	T	Q	S	O	O	S	Q	B	Y
G	P	O	Q	R	C	M	K	L	Q	W	W
G	O	G	N	K	W	A	M	E	L	O	K
O	V	I	E	O	T	V	J	D	Y	N	X
D	X	Y	N	I	M	O	L	A	L	S	K
T	Z	S	N	O	W	M	A	N	H	C	Z
O	V	G	C	Y	D	V	F	E	U	G	Q
H	O	C	K	E	Y	A	B	P	M	U	J

NOTE: SAMPLE WORD "ICE"! SCORE A POINT FOR EACH WORD YOU FIND PLUS TEN ADDITIONAL BONUS POINTS FOR UNCOVERING THE ONE WORD THAT APPEARS TWICE!

TURN UPSIDE DOWN FOR ANSWERS

DILTON
IN
MEET
TREAT

GEE, MOOSE! I'D SURE LIKE TO MEET THAT NEW GIRL!

---BUT I'M TOO SHY!

JUST LEAVE IT TO ME, DILTON!
?

END

Jughead® in GIVE ME A Sign
I THOUGHT RIVERDALE WAS GETTING ITS FIRST STARSTRUCK'S COFFEE!
NOT ANY-MORE!
COMING SOON
STAR STRUCK
HERE!
YOU SCARED STARSTRUCK'S COFFEE AWAY FROM RIVER-DALE, DADDY?
YOU BET I DID! MR. STARSTRUCK AND I ARE OLD BUSINESS RIVALS!
WHEN I MADE IT KNOWN THAT I'M OPENING MY OWN CHAIN... HE TURNED AND RAN!
LODGE COFFEE CO.
LODGE ICE COFFEE
LODGE COFFEE
Script: Craig Boldman Pencils: Rex Lindsey Inks: Rich Koslowski Letters: Jack Morelli Colors: Barry Grossman
Editor-In-Chief: Victor Gorelick President: Mike Pellerito Publisher: Jon Goldwater

FRANKLY, THE POOR BOY'S NOT UP TO ANOTHER BATTLE ROYALE WITH OL' H.P. LODGE!
AS I RECALL, THAT "BATTLE ROYALE" ALMOST FRAZZLED DADDY AS WELL!
IT WAS A HAPPY DAY WHEN THEY ABANDONED THEIR FEUD!
HEY--IF YOU'RE GOING TO THROW THAT SIGN AWAY, I'LL TAKE IT OFF YOUR HANDS!
BE MY GUEST... BUT WHY DO YOU WANT IT?
MAYBE I'LL MAKE IT INTO A PLANTER!

whew!
THIS THING'S MORE UNWIELDY THAN IT LOOKS!
I'LL JUST LEAVE IT OUT HERE WHILE I POP IN FOR A SODA!
FOR LEASE
COMING SOON
HERE

I FEEL LIKE SCOUTING POSSIBLE LOCATIONS FOR LODGE COFFEE SHOPS!

WHAT THE--?!
FOR LE
COMING SOON
STAR STRUCK
ERE!

SO STARSTRUCK HASN'T ABANDONED HIS PLANS! HE'S OPENING A SHOP IN RIVER-DALE AFTER ALL!

WELL, THAT WAS REFRESHING!
HEY! WHEELS!

YOU KIDS WANT TO HAUL THIS FOR ME FOR A FEW BLOCKS?
SURE, MR. JUGHEAD!

JUST LEAVE IT AT THE CORNER OF 3RD! I'LL CATCH UP!
TSK! OLD PEOPLE!
COMING SOON
STAR STRUCK
HERE!

WHA?! ANOTHER! STARSTRUCK'S BEEN BUSY!
COMING SOON STAR STRUCK HERE!
HE'S BUYING UP LOCATIONS RIGHT UNDER MY NOSE! I MUST BE SLIPPING!
NOW BACK TO THE CHORE!
A BIT LATER...
THIS BREEZE DOESN'T MAKE IT EASY TO TOTE THINGS!
OH, GREAT! THERE GOES MY HAT!
YOU WAIT HERE!
WHAT?
SPUTTER!
COMING SOON STAR STRUCK HERE!
BANK
RIVERDA

DON'T TELL ME THE BANK IS TURNING INTO A LATTE JOINT! IT'S MADNESS!

THAT BREEZE IS GETTING WORSE, NOT BETTER!

EEPS! THERE GOES THE WHOLE DARNED THING!!
WHOOSH

ZIPP
COMING SOON
STAR STRUCK
HERE!
CLONK

DEFACING PICKENS PARK WITH PREMIUM-PRICED COFFEE? THAT'S TOO MUCH!
COMING SOON
STAR STRUCK
HERE!

I'VE BEEN ASLEEP AT THE SWITCH! STARSTRUCK HAS TAKEN OVER THE TOWN!

GLAD TO SEE YOU, ARCH! HOW ABOUT A LIFT?
SURE! IF YOU DON'T MIND STOPPING AT VERONICA'S ON THE WAY!
LEAVE THAT THING OUTSIDE! WE'LL FIND SOMETHING TO SECURE IT TO THE CAR BETTER!
RIGHTO!
COMING SOON
STAR STRUCK
HERE!
NO! NO!
NOT IN MY OWN HOME!
COMING SOON
STAR STRUCK
HERE!
STARSTRUCK? IT'S LODGE! I SURRENDER! I CALL A TRUCE! I'LL STOP MY PLANS IF YOU STOP YOURS!
?
?
?
?
STAR STRUCK
PRESIDENT
... AND THAT'S WHY RIVERDALE IS THE ONLY TOWN WITHOUT PREMIUM-PRICED DESIGNER COFFEE!
REFILL, MISTER? IT'S FREE!
Coffee 75¢
JAVA JO
THE END

JUGHEAD! YOU SHOULDN'T BE EATING SO LATE AT NIGHT!
WHY NOT, MOM? I WAS HUNGRY!
Jughead IN
Food Fright!
WHEAT BREAD
MILK
YOU'RE ALWAYS HUNGRY! DON'T YOU KNOW EATING BEFORE YOU GO TO SLEEP CAN GIVE YOU NIGHTMARES?
BURP! DON'T WORRY, MOM! I NEVER HAVE NIGHT-MARES!
NOW THAT I'VE HAD A MIDNIGHT SNACK, I CAN GO TO BED AND PEACEFULLY DREAM ABOUT BREAKFAST!
GOOD! LET'S GET TO SLEEP! WE'LL CLEAN THIS UP IN THE MORNING!
Script: Craig Boldman / Pencils: Rex Lindsey / Inks: Rich Koslowski
Letters: Bill Yoshida
Colors: Barry Grossman

I ALWAYS REST BETTER ON A FULL STOMACH!
HUH? I THOUGHT YOU ALWAYS SLEPT ON YOUR BACK!
GOOD NIGHT, JUGHEAD!
'NIGHT, MOM!
YAWN! SLUMBER CITY HERE I COME!
Z Z Z Z
SNORE! SNORE! Z Z Z TOSS
GAH! AWK! TURN! Z Z
WELCOME TO FOODLAND
SNORT! HUH? WHAT TH...? WHERE AM I?
FOODLAND! WHAT KIND OF NUTTY PLACE IS THIS?
BUTTERFLY
FRENCH FLY
CRINKLE CUT FRENCH FLY
HEY! CHECK IT OUT! A GROVE OF REFRIGERATOR TREES!
I COULD USE A SNACK!
RINGG!
HUH?
EEK! CLOSE THE DOOR! THE SALAD IS DRESSING!

TWEET! TWEET! FREEZE, FOOD FUGITIVE!
YOU'RE UNDER ARREST FOR RAIDING A REFRIGERATOR WITHOUT A PERMIT!
GULP! TALKING HOT DOGS!
W-WHO ARE YOU?
I'M DETECTIVE FRANK FURTER AND HE'S MY DEPUTY DOG, SARGE FRYDAY!
DON'T MOVE OR I'LL BEAN YOU WITH MY CLUB SANDWICH!
WHERE ARE YOU TAKING ME?
TO COURT, YOU SNACK THIEF! YOU'RE IN A REAL JAM!
BURGER COUNTY COURT
ARE WE THE NEXT SODA CASE IN COURT?
YES! SO DON'T GET SHOOK UP AND POP OFF AT THE MOUTH!

YOU'VE GOT A LOT OF CRUST TELLING ME YOU DON'T HAVE ANY DOUGH, YOU CRUMB! ARE YOU WACKY?
OF COURSE! I'M WRY BREAD!
SO, YOU'RE THE BIG CHEESE! FRANKLY SIR, YOUR ALIBI IS FULL OF HOLES!
WELL, SURE, JUDGE MINT! I'M SWISS!
GE MINT

WHAT ARE YOU HERE FOR?
I WAS CAUGHT HANGING AROUND WITH A BAD BUNCH!
SAY, WHAT KIND OF FOOD ARE YOU?
I'M NOT FOOD! I'M HUMAN AND I'D LIKE TO GET OUT OF HERE!
I LIKE YOU, BANANA NOSE! I'LL HELP YOU GIVE THOSE GUYS THE SLIP!
HEY, YOU! YOU'RE NEXT!
NOW! BANANA NOSE! SPLIT! RUN FOR IT!
YEOW! THANKS!
STOP!
WHOA!
AH-HA! THE OLD BANANA PEEL IN THE PATH TRICK ALWAYS WORKS!
PUFF! PUFF! THEY'RE STILL AFTER ME!
COME BACK! YOU'LL SPEND THE REST OF YOUR SHELF LIFE IN THE COOLER FOR THIS!
GROUND BEEF
GULP! N-NOW WHICH WAY!?
DON'T ASK ME! I WOULDN'T TELL YOU THE TRUTH! I'M FULL OF BOLOGNA!
SCREECH!
4

LOOK! THAT POTATO HEAD RAN OFF THE CLIFF!
NOW HE'LL BE A MASHED POTATO!
YIKES I'M FALLING! AAHHHH!
YEOW!
THUMP!
JUGHEAD! ARE YOU OKAY?
Y-YES, MOM! I JUST HAD A BAD DREAM AND FELL OUT OF BED!
A BAD DREAM? WHAT WAS IT ABOUT?
FOOD!
WHERE ARE YOU GOING NOW?
I'M GOING DOWN TO THE KITCHEN!
THAT NIGHTMARE MADE ME HUNGRY! I NEED A SNACK!
SIGH-
THE SLURP END

Jughead in SKI-CART CATASTROPHE

Script: George Gladir / Pencils: Sal Amendola / Inks: Jon D'Agostino / Letters: Bill Yoshida / Colors: Barry Grossman

VERY IMPRESSIVE!
BETTY, IT'S THE LATEST FAD IN WINTER SPORTS!
ARCHIE, TELL ME--- DOES IT WORK?
DON'T KNOW! JUGHEAD IS GOING TO TEST IT NOW!

JUGGIE, WHY DID YOU VOLUNTEER TO TEST THIS MONSTROSITY?
ARCHIE OFFERED ME TEN BURGERS!

BUT WHAT IF THE SKI-CART HAS AN ACCIDENT?
NO PROBLEM, BETTY!

I ALREADY ATE THE BURGERS!

JUG, YOU'RE CRAZY TO RIDE THIS CART FOR TEN BURGERS!
I SHOULD HAVE HELD OUT FOR TWELVE?
2

OHHHHH--- WHAT'S THE USE?
READY?
READY!

BE VERY CAREFUL, JUGHEAD!
I DON'T WANT YOU TO DAMAGE THE SKI-CART!

IT'S WORKING! IT'S WORKING!
GASP! I DON'T BELIEVE IT!
HMMMM--- NOT BAD! THIS SKI-CART IS A LOT OF FUN!

WHIIZZZZ!
HA! HA! BETTY THOUGHT THE SKI-CART WAS DANGEROUS! YUK! YUK!

TWANG!!
WHOMP!

I KNEW HE'D HAVE AN ACCIDENT!
IT DOESN'T LOOK SERIOUS!
I HOPE NOTHING'S BROKEN!

WE'RE IN LUCK!
WE ARE ???

YEAH! THE SKI-CART'S ALL RIGHT! NOTHING'S BROKEN!
PAT! PAT!

ER---ARCH, I DON'T THINK THE SKI-CART'S SAFE!
LISTEN TO THE MAN, ARCHIE!

NONSENSE! JUG'S MERELY A CLUMSY DRIVER!
WATCH HOW IT HANDLES UNDER MY EXPERIENCED HANDS!

SAY-Y--- THIS IS FUN! IT'S A GREAT RIDE!

ULP!
?

YIPES!!! THE LAKE!!!

SPLATTERY!!!

EVERYTHING COMES FROZEN TODAY!
YOU'RE NOT KIDDING!
FROZEN FO
PIZZA
MIXED FRUITS
END.

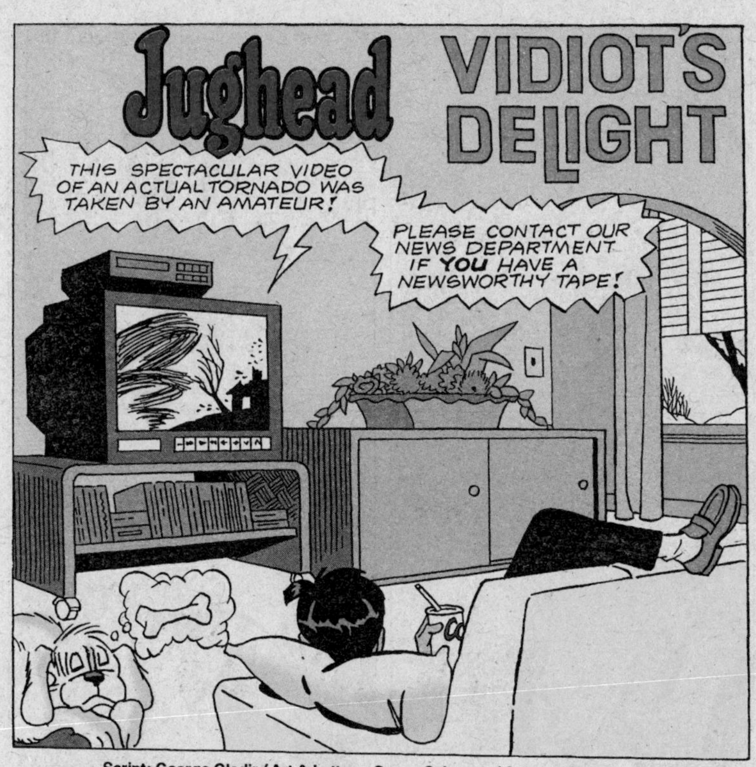

Script: George Gladir / Art & Letters: Samm Schwartz / Colors: Barry Grossman

ALL THIS JOGGING AND DIETING MAKES A MAN HUNGRY!
I THINK I'LL TREAT MYSELF TO A SNACK!
HOT FRANKS
SODA

RATS! NOTHING SEEMS TO BE HAPPENING IN TOWN TODAY!

OH, WELL, I GUESS I'LL HAVE TO SHOOT MY FRIENDS AND ACQUAINTANCES!
CHOMP

HI, MR. W! MIND IF I TAKE SOME MOVIES OF YOU EATING?
GOODNESS! I'LL BE THE LAUGHING STOCK OF MY **WEIGHT LOSERS CLUB** IF I'M SEEN PIGGING OUT!

ER.. I SEEM TO HAVE LOST MY APPETITE! I CAN'T EAT ANY MORE!
AW, THAT'S TOO BAD! I REALLY WANTED TO GET YOU ON FILM!

LET ME MAKE IT UP TO YOU! HERE! GET YOURSELF A DOZEN OR SO HOT DOGS AND A FEW SODAS!
THAT'S VERY KIND OF YOU, SIR! I ACCEPT!

REGGIE, IF MOOSE EVER SAW US TOGETHER HE'D GO WILD!
HE DOESN'T SCARE ME! BESIDES, HE'S OUT OF TOWN!
WHAT DO YOU KNOW? REGGIE AND MIDGE! MOOSE MUST HAVE GONE AWAY!
THIS COULD MAKE A GOOD VIDEO!
UH-OH! JUG! WITH A CAMCORDER! THIS COULD BE TROUBLE!
OH, NO! IF MOOSE EVER SEES IT....
STOP! DON'T MOVE!
HUH?
BEFORE YOU DO ANYTHING, TELL ME.. ARE YOU FEELING OKAY?
I AM!
YOU DON'T LOOK WELL!
I DON'T?
I THINK YOU LOOK UNDER-NOURISHED!
I DO?
HERE! GO SNACK IT UP SOMEWHERE FAR AWAY BEFORE YOU COLLAPSE!
GEE, REG! THIS IS REALLY NICE OF YOU!

I WAS HOPING YOU'D DO THAT! CHECKMATE! I WIN!
QUIET!
LIBR

THAT MAKES TEN GAMES IN A ROW I'VE WON! YOU'RE LOSING YOUR TOUCH, CUZ!
LITTLE CREEP! IF HE WASN'T MY COUSIN I'D---

I BEATCHA I BEATCHA I BEATCHA! I'M THE NEW CHAMP
HEE
HAW
QUIET
HUSH
SHADDUP

IF WORD OF THIS EVER GETS OUT I'LL BE THE LAUGHING STOCK OF TOWN!
HI, DILLY!
A-B

WHAT'S WITH THE CAM-CORDER?
HOW'D YOU LIKE ME TO TAKE SOME MOVIES OF THE TWO OF YOU PLAYING CHESS?

I WOULDN'T! I'D HATE IT! IN FACT, I FORBID IT! IT'S A NO-NO! YOU CAN'T DO IT! IF YOU DO I'LL SUE!
SHEE-E.. PEOPLE ARE SURE UP-TIGHT ABOUT MY CAMCORDER!

THEY'VE EVEN PAID ME NOT TO SHOOT THEM!
SHREWDIE! HE'S ASKING FOR A BRIBE!

HERE, JUG! GO AWAY AND HAVE A GOOD TIME ON ME... AND FORGET ABOUT THE CHESS GAME!
CHESS GAME? WHAT CHESS GAME?

WHAT'RE YOU WATCHING, DAD?
LOOK! THEY'RE SHOWING MORE VIDEO CLIPS MADE BY AMATEURS!

THERE'S LOTS OF MONEY TO BE MADE TAKING PICTURES WITH A CAMCORDER!
TRUE!

AND EVEN MORE BY NOT TAKING PICTURES WITH A CAMCORDER!
END

BUMP!
Jughead
THERMOS BE A BETTER WAY
KLUNK!
Boldman / Lindsey / Koslowski / Yoshida / Grossman
OWOW OW!
DON'T WORRY! IT'S UNBREAKABLE STAINLESS STEEL!
MORTAR SHELL?
NO, GOOFUS! IT'S A THERMOS BOTTLE!

YOU KNOW HOW TOUGH IT IS TO GET THROUGH THAT LONG MORNING STRETCH UNTIL LUNCH!
FOR YOU, MAYBE!

RIGHT! I GROW LISTLESS FROM LACK OF NOURISHMENT! LIFELESS! DIZZY! SURLY!
YOU'RE A HUMAN WRECK, ALL RIGHT!

BUT NO MORE! WITH THIS AT MY SIDE, A REJUVENATING SNACK IS ALWAYS WITHIN MY REACH!

THIS BABY CAN KEEP A QUART OF SOUP BUBBLING HOT ALL DAY! DOUBLE INSULATED!
YEAH, BUT...

GRUNDY TOLD YOU NO MORE EATING IN CLASS!
THAT'S THE BEAUTY OF IT!

A THERMOS HOLDS LIQUIDS! YOU DON'T EAT LIQUIDS!
SLOSH!
2

THAT'S A TECHNICALITY!
NOT AT ALL! I'M BETTING MISS GRUNDY WILL SEE MY POINT OF VIEW!
SSLUURRRRR
PPPPPPPPP
ENGLISH
MS. GRUNDY
3

RIV
CRASH!
SO WHAT DID MR. WEATHERBEE SAY?
NOT A WORD!
GREAT INVENTION! EVEN HOURS AFTER FILLING THE THERMOS, I CAN STILL HAVE STEAMING HOT SOUP! IT'S INSULATED!
YOUR BRAIN IS INSULATED! KEEP THAT LETHAL WEAPON FAR FROM ME! SIT OVER THERE! YOU'RE AN OUTCAST!

HMM! THE STOPPER IS JAMMED!
NO WONDER! YOU'VE BEEN TREATING IT LIKE A SOCCER BALL!
AH! HERE IT COMES!
POP!
AAAA!
THERE GOES MY SNACK!
JUG, THAT THERMOS HELD BUBBLING HOT SOUP!
NO, I SAID IT CAN HOLD BUBBLING HOT SOUP!
IT SO HAPPENS, TODAY I WAS IN THE MOOD FOR ICE COLD LEMONADE!
THE END

Jughead in "TREASURE HUNT"

Script: George Gladir / Pencils: Dan DeCarlo Jr. / Inks: Jimmy DeCarlo / Letters: Bill Yoshida / Colors: Barry Grossman

YOU NEVER KNOW WHAT YOU'LL FIND IN THE SAND THIS TIME OF YEAR!
SHORE POINT EXIT 3

HURRY UP, JUG! I WANT TO COMB AS MUCH BEACH AS POSSIBLE!

WOW! WHAT LUCK! I FOUND SOMETHING ALREADY!
BEEP! BEEP!
GREAT! START DIGGING!

WHAT IS IT?
MONEY?
JEWELRY?
NOPE! IT'S A BOTTLE CAP!

MUCH LATER-
IT'S HOPELESS, ARCH! ALL WE'VE FOUND ARE 10 BOTTLE CAPS, 6 PENNIES AND A BENT SPOON!
I'M NOT GIVING UP!

LET'S START BACK, IT'S GETTING LATE!
HEY! WAIT A MINUTE! WHAT'S THIS?
BEEP BEEP

IS IT ANOTHER BOTTLE CAP?
NO, IT'S SOME-THING REALLY NICE... A LOCKET!

HEY! THAT IS VALUABLE!
LOOK! THERE'S AN INSCRIPTION ON IT! "TO MY BEST GIRL, MANDY, LOVE FOREVER!"

THAT WILL BE EASY TO SELL! THEN YOU'LL HAVE ENOUGH MONEY TO GO TO THE DANCE FOR SURE!
I KNOW! BUT I FEEL KINDA FUNNY ABOUT SELLING IT!

I BET IT HAS A SPECIAL MEANING TO SOMEONE!
TRUE! BUT SENTIMENTALITY WON'T BUY DANCE TICKETS! WHAT WILL YOU DO WITH IT?

I'LL PUT AN AD IN THE PAPER! THEN IF NO ONE CLAIMS IT, I'LL SELL THE LOCKET!
ATTAWAY, ARCH! I'M PROUD OF YOU!

I'M KINDA PROUD OF MYSELF!
BESIDES... WHO KNOWS? MAYBE THE OWNER WILL GIVE YOU A GENEROUS REWARD!

DAYS LATER:
HI, MOM!
ARCHIE, SOMEONE CALLED AND IDENTIFIED THE LOCKET! HERE'S HER ADDRESS!

SHE SOUNDED EXTREMELY GRATEFUL!
GRATEFUL ENOUGH TO OFFER A REWARD?

SHE DIDN'T SAY!
THANKS, MOM! I'LL DRIVE THE LOCKET OVER TO HER RIGHT NOW!

THE HOUSE SHOULD BE UP AHEAD! GEE, MAYBE MANDY WILL BE A LIVING DOLL!
BEACH DR.

THIS IS THE ADDRESS!
KNOCK
KNOCK

ER, HELLO! I'M ARCHIE ANDREWS! ARE YOU MANDY?
YES! I'M MRS. MANDY MORGAN!

IS THIS YOURS?
MY LOCKET! YOU'RE THE ONE WHO FOUND IT! OH, THANK YOU, THANK YOU!

PLEASE COME IN!
THIS WAS A GIFT FROM MY LATE HUSBAND! I THOUGHT IT WAS GONE FOR GOOD!

I WISH I COULD GIVE YOU A REWARD, BUT I LIVE ON A FIXED INCOME AND...
THAT'S OKAY! I'VE BEEN REWARDED IN A WAY, REALLY!

HOW ABOUT SOME COOKIES AND MILK? MY NIECE IS VISITING! SHE JUST BAKED A FRESH BATCH!
THAT SOUNDS GREAT, MRS. MORGAN! THANKS!

MISS TEEN QUEEN!!
JUDY, THIS IS THE NICE BOY WHO FOUND MY LOCKET AND RETURNED IT!

HIS NAME IS ARCHIE ANDREWS!
HIS NAME SHOULD BE SIR GALAHAD! DO YOU ALWAYS HELP DAMSELS IN DISTRESS?
5

I... I TRY TO!
GOOD, THEN MAYBE YOU CAN HELP JUDY! SHE'S THE GUEST OF HONOR AT THE COUNTRY CLUB DANCE!
AND SHE DOESN'T HAVE AN ESCORT!

WOULD YOU BE MY DATE, ARCHIE, PLEASE!?
GULP! I'D BE DELIGHTED TO, JUDY!

THE DAY OF THE BIG DANCE!
HUMPH! ARCHIE DIDN'T EVEN HAVE ENOUGH MONEY FOR TICKETS... AND HE ENDS UP ESCORTING MISS TEEN QUEEN! HOW?
YOU MIGHT SAY HE FOUND A BURIED TREASURE!
R
END

Veronica in "JET LAG JITTERS"

Script: George Gladir / Pencils: Stan Goldberg / Inks: Rudy Lapick / Letters: Bill Yoshida / Colors: Barry Grossman

VOOM!
SOMEONE LEFT THE VOLUME UP!

WHAT DID YOU SAY?
I SAID SOMEONE LEFT THE VOLUME UP!

BOOM!

TURN IT DOWN!
I CAN'T HEAR YOU! I'LL TURN THE TELEVISION DOWN!

LET ME GIVE YOU A HAND!
THAT'S OKAY, MR. LODGE, I CAN HANDLE IT!

THERE, MR. LODGE, ISN'T THAT BETTER?
LET ME AT HIM!
PLEASE, DADDY, YOU DON'T MEAN IT! YOU'RE JUST TIRED!

YOU'RE RIGHT, RONNIE! I AM TIRED!
I DON'T KNOW WHY! IT'S ALMOST NOON TIME!

DADDY WAS OVERSEAS YESTERDAY! IT'S 4 A.M. WHERE HE WAS AND HE HASN'T ADJUSTED YET! HAVEN'T YOU EVER HEARD OF JET LAG?
YEAH!

ME, TOO! WHERE'S MY BED?
UPSTAIRS, DADDY!

NOW, ARCHIEKINS, LET'S GET OUT OF HERE AND LET DADDY SLEEP!
3

LATER-
WELL, WE'VE BEEN OUT FOR A WHILE! THINK IT'S SAFE TO GO BACK TO YOUR HOUSE?
I SUPPOSE SO, IF WE'RE QUIET!
RIVERDALE SHOPPING MALL
PIZZA CITY
214

NOW JUST TAKE IT SLOW!
RIGHT!

RING!

WHY DID YOU RING THE BELL?
I ALWAYS RING THE BELL WHEN I COME OVER... I FORGOT, THAT'S ALL!

ARCHIE, GET OUT OF HERE! JUST GO HOME!

RONNIE, WHO RANG THAT BELL?!

NEVER MIND, DADDY! JUST LIE DOWN HERE ON THE COUCH AND REST!

GEE, I FEEL BAD! I KNOW RONNIE IS MAD AT ME! I KNOW WHAT I'LL DO...

I'LL GIVE HER A CALL!

WHAT'S THAT?
RING!
5

ARCHIE!
I'VE GOT TO FIND A PLACE WHERE I CAN GET SOME REST!

OKAY, RONNIE, IF THAT'S THE WAY YOU FEEL, I MIGHT AS WELL GO HOME AND GO TO BED!

HI, MOM! HI, DAD! I'M GOING TO BED!
NO, ARCHIE! NO!

WHAT DO YOU MEAN, NO?
THERE'S SOMEONE SLEEPING IN YOUR BED!

MR. LODGE THOUGHT SINCE YOU WERE ALWAYS OVER AT HIS PLACE, HE COULD GET A GOOD REST HERE! BESIDES, THE POOR MAN LOOKED SO TIRED!
End

Betty and Veronica in LATE STARTERS

Script & Pencils: Dick Malmgren / Inks: Jon D'Agostino / Letters: Bill Yoshida / Colors: Barry Grossman

'BYE, MOM!
DON'T FORGET YOUR BOOKS!

'BYE 'BYE, DEAR!

WATCH OUT FOR THE MAILMAN!

THUMP!!

MY GOODNESS! ARE YOU ALL RIGHT?

IS YOUR HOUSE ON FIRE?
NO!--- SHE'S LATE FOR SCHOOL!
2

VERONICA! HURRY OR YOU'LL BE LATE!

FORGET MY BREAKFAST! I WANT TO DIET ANYWAY!

WHERE'S MY JACKET?
HURRY!

HERE YOU GO!

MY BOOKS, WHERE ARE MY BOOKS?
RIGHT HERE!

'BYE, DADDY!
'BYE 'BYE, DEAR!
3

HEY! LOOK OUT!
OH, NO!

FUMP!

ARE YOU OKAY?

I'M GOING TO HAVE TO FIND A DIFFERENT PROFESSION!

I'D FEEL A LOT SAFER BEING A QUARTERBACK ON THE RIVERDALE RAMS FOOTBALL TEAM!

HI, RONNIE!
HI, BETTY!

HOLD THAT DOOR!

HURRY! THE BELL'S ABOUT TO RING!

R-RINGGGGGGG!

IF THEY WORKED AS HARD AT THEIR SCHOOL WORK AS THEY DO GETTING TO SCHOOL ON TIME, THEY BOTH WOULD BE HONOR STUDENTS!
END

I CAN'T BELIEVE IT! THE WEEKEND IS ALMOST HERE AND I HAVE NO PLANS!
DIDN'T CHUCK ASK YOU OUT?
RIVERDALE SCHOOL NEW
Betty and Veronica IN GIRLS' NIGHT OUT

NO! HE'S GOING TO A LECTURE BY SOME FAMOUS COMIC BOOK ARTIST!
DON'T FEEL BAD, NANCY!
ICK!
I GOT DUMPED, TOO. MOOSE IS GOING TO SOME SPORTS CARD SHOW!
SCRIPT: PELLOWSKI
PENCILS: GOLDBERG
INKS: AMASH

I'M IN THE SAME FIX. I WAS HOPING ARCHIE WOULD ASK ME TO THE "SMASHIN' KUMQUATS" CONCERT.
Hmph! ASK YOU?!
THE PLAN WAS FOR ARCHIE TO ASK ME TO THE CONCERT!
WELL... DID HE?

GULP! NO! MY WEEKEND SOCIAL CALENDAR IS ENTIRELY BLANK.
DON'T FEEL BAD, GIRLS. I HEAR THOSE TICKETS ARE IMPOSSIBLE TO GET!
RIVERDALE SCHOOL

SIGH! I GUESS WE CAN ALL LOOK FORWARD TO ONE BIG, BORING, GUY FREE WEEKEND!
HEY! WAIT A MINUTE, WHO NEEDS GUYS ANYWAY??
WHAT DO YOU MEAN, RON?
WHY DON'T WE HAVE A GIRLS' NIGHT OUT!?

I BET MY FATHER CAN SCORE TICKETS TO THE "SMASHIN' KUMQUATS" CONCERT. DADDYKINS HAS FRIENDS IN THE MUSIC BUSINESS!
WOW! THAT WOULD BE TOTALLY AWESOME!

AFTERWARDS, WE COULD GO OUT TO EAT!
RON'S RIGHT! WHO NEEDS GUYS TO HAVE FUN? A GIRLS' NIGHT OUT SOUNDS GREAT--COUNT ME IN!
RIVERDALE

ME, TOO!
FORGET THE GUYS! GIRLS RULE THIS WEEKEND!
ABSOLUTELY!

A DAY LATER...
HI, BETTY! I HAVE WONDERFUL NEWS! DADDYKINS GOT FOUR TICKETS TO THE CONCERT THIS WEEKEND!
YIPPIE!! THIS WILL BE A GIRLS' NIGHT OUT TO REMEMBER!

HEY, NANCY-- GUESS WHAT? RON GOT US TICKETS TO THE "SMASHING KUMQUATS" CONCERT!
HUH? OH! REALLY? THAT'S... uh, SUPER.

YOU DON'T SOUND VERY EXCITED ABOUT OUR GIRLS' NIGHT OUT. WHAT'S WRONG?
TO TELL THE TRUTH, CHUCK ASKED ME TO GO TO THAT LECTURE WITH HIM AFTER ALL!

I TOLD HIM I'D THINK ABOUT IT. NOW THAT OUR PLANS ARE SOLID I'LL TELL HIM "NO THANKS". HEH! HEH! WHO NEEDS GUYS?
HOLD ON! YOU AND CHUCK HAVE BEEN DATING A LONG TIME... YOU'D RATHER BE WITH HIM, WOULDN'T YOU?

BE HONEST NOW!
WELL, CHUCK DID SAY THIS WILL BE A REALLY INTERESTING LECTURE! THE ARTIST IS VERY FAMOUS!

SAY NO MORE! WE UNDERSTAND!
whew!
YOU UNDERSTAND WHAT?
4

NANCY IS GOING OUT WITH CHUCK ON SATURDAY, SO IT'LL BE JUST THE THREE OF US.
CHEER UP, MIDGE! RON GOT TICKETS FOR THE "SMASHIN' KUMQUATS" CONCERT! ISN'T THAT GREAT NEWS?
OOPS!

OH, NO! NOT YOU TOO?!
HEH! HEH! WOULD YOU BELIEVE MOOSE ASKED ME TO GO TO THE SPORTS CARD SHOW?

DON'T BOTHER TO EXPLAIN. JUST GO AND ENJOY YOURSELF!
THANKS! MAYBE WE CAN GET TO-GETHER SOME OTHER TIME!

WELL, BETTY, IT LOOKS LIKE WE'LL BE GOING TO THE "SMASHIN' KUMQUATS" CONCERT ALONE!
I GUESS SO!
WHAT?! YOU HAVE TICKETS TO THE SMASHIN' KUMQUATS?
THAT'S THE CONCERT OF THE YEAR!
5

I TRIED EVERYWHERE TO GET TICKETS!
I WAS TOO BROKE TO EVEN TRY! THAT'S WHY I DIDN'T ASK ANYONE OUT THIS WEEKEND!

I GUESS WE'LL JUST SIT AROUND POP TATE'S ON SATURDAY WHILE YOU TWO ARE HAVING FUN AT THE CONCERT!
hmmm...

ON SATURDAY...
YAHOO! THIS IS TERRIFIC!!
IT SURE IS! THIS TURNED OUT TO BE A FANTASTIC EVENING AFTER ALL, RON!
SMASHING KUMQU
KUMQUATS
KUMQUATS
SMASHING KUMQUATS

YOU'RE RIGHT, BETTY! ESPECIALLY SINCE WE GOT TO BRING THE GUYS ALONG ON OUR GIRLS' NIGHT OUT!!
CLAP
END

Betty IN "THE GIFT"

Script & Pencils: Bob Bolling / Inks: Al Milgrom / Letters: Bill Yoshida / Colors: Barry Grossman

SOON...
GROAN! HOW MUCH LONGER IS THIS GOING TO TAKE?
WE'RE JUST ABOUT DONE, MS. LODGE... JUST A COUPLE MORE PINS!

THE GOWN WILL BE READY TOMORROW AFTERNOON, MS. LODGE!
IT BETTER BE!... MY PARTY'S ONLY TWO DAYS AWAY!

WHAT ARE YOU GOING TO WEAR TO THE PARTY?
I DON'T KNOW!... I WANTED TO BUY A NEW OUTFIT, BUT MY MONEY'S KIND OF TIGHT!
JOE'S

... AND MISS GRUNDY SAID WE NEED TO BUY A BOOK FOR LITERATURE CLASS! HAVE YOU GOTTEN YOURS YET, RONNIE?
I TOLD SMITHERS TO GET IT FOR ME ON AUDIO CASSETTE!
WHO HAS TIME TO READ?

DON'T WORRY ABOUT AN OUT-FIT! YOU CAN BORROW ONE OF MINE!
OH, NO!... I COULDN'T...!

OOPS! I ALMOST FORGOT! I'VE GOT A BABYSITTING JOB TONIGHT! I'D BETTER GET ON OVER THERE!
BUT WHAT ABOUT YOUR DRESS?
2

WELLLL, I'LL PICK IT UP TOMORROW! THANKS, YOU'RE A PAL!
DON'T MENTION IT...
...TOO OFTEN!

THE NEXT DAY...
CATCH YA LATER, ARCH!
OKAY, MAN!
HI, BETS! WHAT'S UP ?

HEY, ARCH, DON'T YOU THINK THOSE EARRINGS WOULD BE GREAT FOR VERONICA?!
YEAH! THEY'RE NICE, BUT I'VE ALREADY BOUGHT HER A PRESENT!

NO! I WANT TO GET THEM FOR HER! BUT I CAN'T BUY EARRINGS AND THE COMPLETE WORKS OF O. HENRY!
YOU DON'T HAVE TO BUY THAT BOOK!

MY DAD'S GOT IT AT HOME COLLECTING DUST ON A SHELF... HE WON'T MISS IT!
BUT DON'T YOU NEED IT, TOO?

NOPE! I'VE GOT MISS HAGGLY, AND WE'RE DOING POETRY FIRST!
OH, ARCHIE! YOU'RE THE GREATEST!
3

THEY'LL LOOK GREAT ON VERONICA, WON'T THEY?
YEAH, SHE'LL LOVE THEM!

THANKS AGAIN, ARCHIE! I COULD KISS YOU!
HEY! WHAT'S STOPPIN' YA?

I JUST HOPE THEY HAVE MY DRESS READY...
WHAT!?!

WHY THE LITTLE POOR-MOUTHING SNEAK HAD ARCHIE BUY HER THE EARRINGS I WANTED!

... AND AFTER I PROMISED TO LEND HER A DRESS!
FRUITS

OH, WELL! I'LL KEEP MY WORD, BUT I KNOW JUST THE DRESS I'LL LET HER BORROW! HEH! HEH!
EARRING EN
EARRING ENCLAVE

THE NEXT NIGHT AT VERONICA'S PARTY...
YEAH! YOU'RE QUITE A KNOCK-OUT TONIGHT!
YOU MIGHT EVEN BE ECLIPSING THE PARTY GIRL HERSELF!
OH, THANKS, GUYS!
BETTY! THAT'S A LOVELY OUTFIT!

VERONICA, I JUST CAN'T THANK YOU ENOUGH FOR LETTING ME BORROW...
OOPS!
SORRY!
THE BAND'S STOPPED! THAT'S MY CUE TO OPEN GIFTS!
I THINK YOU KNOW WHAT THIS ONE IS... BUT DO THE HONORS, DAUGHTER!
WHATEVER YOU SAY, DADDY!
OH, IT'S MY ANNUAL PORTRAIT!
HUH?
?
HEY! BETTY'S WEARING THE SAME DRESS!

OH, BETTY DEAR! I'M SORRY... I COMPLETELY FORGOT ABOUT THAT!
THAT'S OKAY... HERE'S YOUR PRESENT!

I NEED SOME AIR!
NOW WE KNOW HOW SHE COULD AFFORD THAT RITZY OUTFIT!

SHUT-UP, BIG MOUTH!
W-W-WHAT? ... WHO?...

VERONICA, YOU'D BETTER GET THAT MYSTERY FRIEND OF YOURS TO APOLOGIZE TO ME!
OH, SHUT-UP, REGGIE! IT LOOKS LIKE I HAVE SOME APOLOGIZING TO DO, TOO!

HEY, BUCKAROO! THERE'S NO PARTY GOING ON OUT HERE, IS THERE?
I JUST FEEL LIKE BEING ALONE!

IF IT'S THE SIMILARITY A THEM OUTFITS THAT'S BOTHERING YA!... I KNOW JUST THE THING!
BRRRRR!

THERE! YA JUST HANG ON TO THIS! IT'S THE PERFECT ACCESSORY!... BESIDES... YOU'RE SHIVERIN' LIKE A PRAIRIE DOG IN A RATTLER'S DEN!
OH, NO... I-I CAN'T... WELL... THANKS!

I INSIST! NOW COME ON IN! WE'VE GOT A PARTY TO LIVEN UP!
YOU'RE ON!
END

Script: Mike Pellowski / Pencils: Jeff Shultz / Inks: Al Milgrom / Letters: Bill Yoshida / Colors: Barry Grossman

HEY! WATCH IT!
YO! WHASSUP, SNOW BUNNIES?!

IF YOU BABES ARE UNATTACHED, *THIS* COOL DUDE IS AVAILABLE! GET MY DRIFT?!

GET LOST, YOU SNOW FLAKE!
YEAH! WE'RE NOT INTERESTED IN CRUDE GOONS!
HMPH!

SUIT YOURSELVES, DUDETTES! SEE YOU AROUND!
I HOPE NOT!
SWOOSH!

LATER...
WE'VE BEEN ON THE SLOPES FOR HOURS, AND HAVEN'T MET A SINGLE NICE GUY!
MAYBE WE'LL HAVE BETTER BOY LUCK DOWN BY THE SKATING POND!

THAT AFTERNOON AT THE POND...
THAT'S A GREAT FIGURE EIGHT, BETTY!
THANKS, RON! WHEN IT COMES TO SKATING, EIGHT IS MY LUCKY NUMBER!

HA! SOME LUCK! THERE'S NOT A GUY IN SIGHT!!

HEY, GIRLS! YOU'LL HAVE TO CLEAR THE ICE!
YOU SPOKE TOO SOON! HERE COMES A PACK OF PRE-TEENS!

OH, REALLY? WELL, WE'RE PAYING GUESTS AT THE LODGE, AND WE'RE STAYING! THERE'S PLENTY OF ROOM TO SKATE!
OKAY! IF THAT'S THE WAY YOU WANT IT!

BUT WHEN WE START OUR HOCKEY GAME, YOU'RE ON YOUR OWN!!
DON'T BLAME US, IF YOU GET KNOCKED DOWN OR HIT WITH THE PUCK!
GULP!

YOU BOYS ARE REALLY RUDE!
HA! SO GO BACK TO THE LODGE AND COMPLAIN! SEE IF WE CARE!

THAT'S JUST WHAT WE'LL DO! YOU WISE GUYS DON'T KNOW WHO YOU'RE DEALING WITH!
WHIRRR!
HUH? WHAT'S THAT SOUND?

YIPES! A SNOWMOBILE!
HEY, OUTTA THE WAY! KEEP THE TRAIL CLEAR!

GRR ... NANCY WAS SURE WRONG ABOUT THIS PLACE! EVERY BOY WE'VE MET HAS BEEN CRUDE OR RUDE!
URP! I THINK THE BOY ON THE SNOW-MOBILE HAD A TATTOO ON HIS FOREHEAD!
ZOOM!

THAT DOES IT! LET'S HEAD FOR THE OFFICE! THE MANAGEMENT IS GOING TO GET A PIECE OF MY MIND!
YOU GO, GIRL!

WE HAVE A COMPLAINT!
GEE WHIZ! CAN I HELP YOU, MISS? I'M JON!

HUH? JON? I HAVEN'T SEEN YOU BEFORE!
I COVER THE OFFICE WHILE MOST GUESTS ARE OUT ON THE SLOPES! I'LL GET THE ASSISTANT MANAGER FOR YOU!

HMM...JON IS KINDA CUTE!
AND HE'S VERY POLITE, TOO!

HI, LADIES! I'M BART, THE ASSISTANT MANAGER! HOW CAN I BE OF ASSISTANCE?
AREN'T YOU KIND OF YOUNG TO BE IN CHARGE?

ACTUALLY, I'M A COLLEGE STUDENT! MY DAD OWNS THE PLACE! I ONLY WORK THE AFTERNOON SHIFT!
OH, THAT'S WHY WE HAVEN'T SEEN HIM BEFORE! WE'VE BEEN SPENDING OUR AFTERNOONS OUTSIDE!

RON EXPLAINS THE PROBLEM...
I'M SORRY ABOUT THE HOCKEY TEAM AND THE REST! I'LL TAKE CARE OF IT!
THAT'S NICE OF YOU! THANKS!
5

CALL ON ME ANYTIME! MEANWHILE, LET ME TRY TO MAKE AMENDS!

JON, PLEASE ESCORT BETTY AND VERONICA TO THE LODGE AND GET THEM A HOT DRINK! I'LL JOIN YOU IN A WHILE!
SURE, BART! IT'LL BE MY PLEASURE!

FOLLOW ME, LADIES! THIS HALL IS A SHORTCUT!
WE'RE RIGHT BEHIND YOU, JON!

GENTLEMEN, WOULD YOU KEEP THESE LOVELY LADIES COMPANY WHILE I FETCH THEIR DRINKS?
WE SURE WILL!

AND TO THINK WE EVER DOUBTED NANCY'S STORY!
ALL ALONG WE WERE JUST IN THE WRONG PLACES AT THE WRONG TIMES!
END

FUN FASHIONS
BETTY, VERONICA, MIDGE, NANCY ETHEL
BETTY
BETTY
I ♥ JUG

HENRY SCARPELLI
CRAIG BOLDMAN
Archie

HAVE YOU NOTICED THAT ARCHIE IS ALWAYS UNDERFOOT ?

ALSO OVERFOOT... BEHIND FOOT... ON FOOT... IN FRONT OF...

OOPS!
TRIP!

OOPS!
TRIP!

YOWP!
TRIP!

WHOOPS!
TRIP!

THAT ARCHIE CERTAINLY IS CLUMSY...

... I'VE TRIPPED OVER HIM FOUR OR FIVE TIMES!

Veronica Punch This!

VERONICA'S TAKING OUT HER FRUSTRATIONS THE RIGHT WAY FOR ONCE. OUT OF THE 4 SHOTS BELOW, 2 ARE EXACTLY THE SAME. TRY AND SEE WHICH 2 ARE THE SAME.

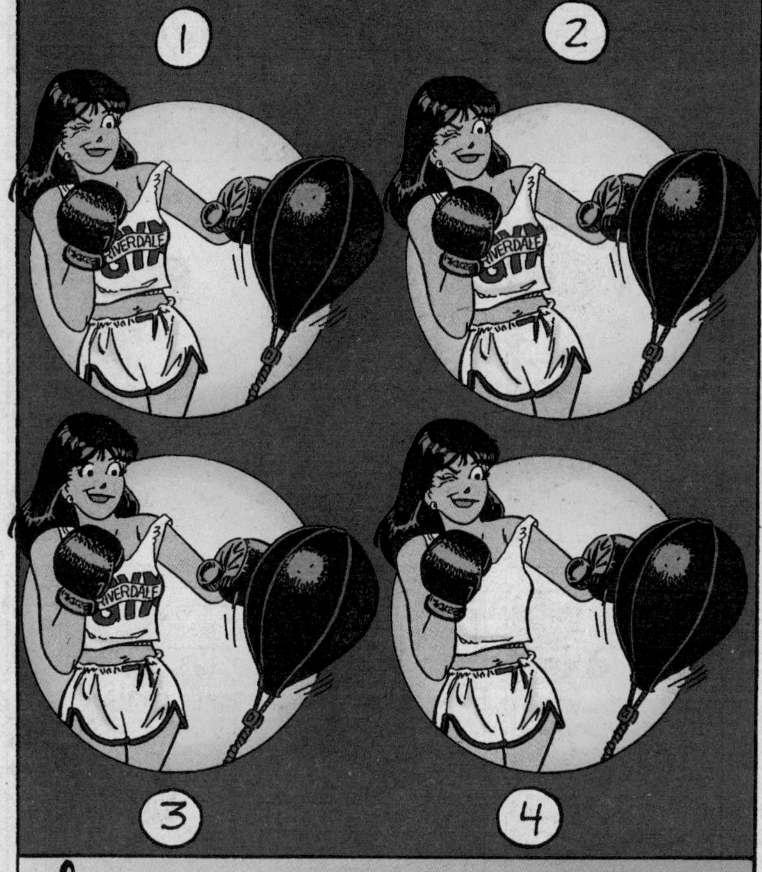

Answer : 1 AND 2 ARE THE SAME.

Script: Frank Doyle / Pencils: Dan DeCarlo / Inks: Rudy Lapick / Letters: Bill Yoshida / Colors: Barry Grossman

HEY, LOOK AT THAT CUTE LAMP!
IT LOOKS LIKE THE ONE IN THE MOVIE!
Antiques

I'M GOING TO BUY IT! IT'LL REMIND ME OF THAT HUNKY GENIE FROM THE MOVIE!

BOY, THAT THING IS DIRTY! WE'LL HAVE TO CLEAN IT!
IT WAS EXPENSIVE, TOO! $100!
Antiques

YOUR FATHER'S GONNA KILL YOU! HE WAS JUST ON YOUR CASE FOR OVER-SPENDING!
NOT TO WORRY, BETTY DEAR!

MOM AND DAD ARE OUT OF TOWN! WE'LL FIX UP THE LAMP AND THEY'LL THINK THEY ALWAYS HAD IT AROUND!

A LITTLE BIT OF THIS METAL POLISH AND...

POOF
EEK! WHAT'S THAT?

OMIGOSH! IT'S A GENIE! LIKE IN THAT MOVIE!
I'M NOT THAT GENIE! I'M HIS SECOND COUSIN, HORACE!

HORACE? WHAT KIND OF ARABIAN NAME IS THAT?
ARE YOU GOING TO INSULT ME OR MAKE A WISH?

I'M SORRY!
DO WE REALLY GET TO MAKE A WISH?
SHE DOES!

SHE BOUGHT AND RUBBED THE LAMP, SO I MUST SERVE HER!
NOW THIS IS A FAITHFUL EMPLOYEE!

GO AHEAD! MAKE A WISH, RONNIE!
LET'S SEE! I HAVE EVERYTHING! THIS IS DIFFICULT!

I KNOW! MAKE THIS HOUSE LIKE SOMETHING OUT OF "ALADDIN, THAT ARABIAN DUDE!"
BOING
OOH!
AHH!

NOW COULD YOU MAKE THE HELP LOOK LIKE THE 40 THIEVES?
EGADS!
YOWZA!
SACRÉ BLEU!

CAN YOU DO A BIT OF A MAKEOVER FOR ME?
OF COURSE, MISS VERONICA!

LOVELY, SIMPLY LOVELY!
GEE, WHAT ABOUT ME?

I MUST WARN YOU, YOU'VE USED UP THREE WISHES! YOU GET ONLY ONE MORE!
HOW COME YOU GIVE FOUR WISHES?

WELL, WITH THE RECESSION AND ALL, IT HELPS BUSINESS!
4

LET'S SEE! THERE'S GOT TO BE ONE MORE THING THAT I WANT!
OH NO! SHE'D BETTER NOT...

SOMETHING THAT I'VE ALWAYS HAD THE DESIRE FOR...
PLEASE DON'T EVEN THINK ABOUT IT!

ARCHIE!!!
SHE THOUGHT ABOUT IT!

THAT'S IT! ARCHIE AS MY SERVANT TO DO EVERYTHING I SAY! THIS IS WHAT I'VE LIVED FOR!
BOING
HUH?

THAT'S NOT FAIR, VERONICA! I DON'T HAVE A GENIE TO DO MY WORK FOR ME!

NOBODY'S STOPPING YOU FROM FINDING YOUR OWN GENIE!
MAYBE YOU'RE RIGHT!
5

GOOD! THEY'RE STILL OPEN!
OPEN
Antiqu

HELLO! DO YOU HAVE A GENIE FOR SOME-ONE ON A BUDGET?
ER-I-UM MEAN A GENIE LAMP?
?
UCLA 89

I HAVE THESE LAMPS THAT GO FROM $ 20 TO $ 50...
THEN THERE'S THIS OLD RUSTY THING FOR $ 5...

I'LL TAKE IT!
OKAY! IT'S YOURS!
CHEAPSKATE!

AT BETTY'S...
DARN! I'VE BEEN CLEANING THIS THING ALL NIGHT!
I GUESS NO GENIE WOULD LIVE IN SUCH A CRUDDY LAMP!

HEY, TOOTS! I RESENT THAT!
?!
CONTINUED

GENIE HI-JINX
CHAPTER 2
OH, GOODY! MY VERY OWN GENIE! NOW MY WISHES CAN COME TRUE!
HEY, KID! WATCH THE SILK! I ONLY GET TO THE DRY CLEANERS EVERY ONE HUNDRED YEARS!

IT SEEMS LIKE YOU ALREADY KNOW THE RULES SO WHAT CAN I DO FOR YOU?
FIRST I WANT ONE OF THOSE COOL HAREM-TYPE OUTFITS!

AND SECONDLY I WANT ARCHIE ANDREWS!
ZAP
MY, THIS MUST BE SOME GUY FOR YOU TO USE A WISH ON!
7

MEANWHILE...
YOUR BEVERAGE, MADAM!
THANK YOU, ARCHIE, MY BOY! HOW ABOUT SOME MORE GRAPES?!

ZAP!
ARGHH! I'M DRENCHED!

WHOO-BOY! I MUST'VE MESSED UP SOMEWHERE!
NO! THAT'S HIM! THAT'S MY ARCHIE!

OKAY, YOU TWO-BIT SHYSTER! WHAT HAPPENED TO MY FOURTH WISH?
I DUNNO! IF I DIDN'T KNOW BETTER, I'D SAY IT WAS ANOTHER GENIE!

WELL, IT'S SATISFACTION GUARANTEED! SO HERE'S YOUR ARCHIE BACK!
THAT'S MORE LIKE IT!
RE-ZAP

MEANWHILE...
WAH!
SHEESH! TURN OFF THE WATERWORKS, KID! I'LL BRING HIM BACK!
8

SQUEAL!
MAN, IT DOESN'T TAKE MUCH!

AND...
RE-ZAP!
THERE! HE'S BAAACK!
GOOD! NOW KEEP HIM HERE!

IT MUST BE VERONICA'S GENIE! HE KEEPS ZAPPING ARCHIE BACK!
C'MON, GIRLY! LET'S GO CONFRONT THIS PUSHY PUFF OF SMOKE!

SOON...
HE SHOULD KNOW IT'S AGAINST THE GENIE CODE TO RE-ZAP SOMEONE ELSE'S ZAP!
RING!

YES...
WE'RE HERE TO SEE MS. LODGE AND HER GENIE!
YOU!
YOU!

I SHOULD'VE KNOWN ONLY YOU WOULD RE-ZAP MY ZAPS!
IF I KNEW IT WAS YOU, I WOULD HAVE DOUBLE RE-ZAPPED!

I TAKE IT YOU TWO HAVE MET!
YES! WE WERE MARRIED FOR A WHILE!
THE LONGEST ONE THOUSAND YEARS OF MY LIFE!

IT WAS NO PICNIC IN THE SAHARA FOR ME EITHER, TOOTS!
OH, THAT DOES IT! TAKE THIS!
ZAP

SO, YOU WANT TO PLAY ROUGH, HUH?
OUCH! THAT WAS A LITTLE TOO CLOSE FOR COMFORT!
ZAP

I BELIEVE IT WAS SAFER TO TRY TO GET ARCHIE THE OLD-FASHIONED WAY!
I'M WITH YOU, BUT HOW DO WE GET RID OF THESE GROUCHY GENIES?
10

AH-HA! I THINK I'VE GOT IT! WHERE'S YOUR BROOM CLOSET ?!
IN THE KITCHEN! BUT THIS IS NO TIME TO CLEAN UP!

SOON..
MY MOTHER WARNED ME ABOUT YOU!
YEAH! WELL, THEY SHOULD WARN PEOPLE ABOUT YOUR MOTHER'S LOOKS!
YOO-HOO!

BEAT IT, KID! YOU'RE INTERRUPTING US!
YEAH!
NOT FOR LONG!

WHOA! HELP!
WE'LL BE TRAPPED! TOGETHER!!
WHOOSH

WHAT'LL WE DO WITH THEM NOW?
I KNOW! LET'S GO TO DADDY'S NEWEST SITE!

SOON..
A TIME CAPSULE, HUH?
YEAH! WHO KNOWS, AFTER A HUNDRED YEARS MAYBE THEY'LL BE GETTING ALONG!
FUTURE SITE OF THE LODGE TOWER
2014 A.D. TO BE OPENED 2114 A.D.
THE END

Betty and Veronica in ICE RAGE!
RIVERDALE COMMU
POND
ADMISSION
$1.00 PER PERSON
SKATE RENTALS
..... $3.00
I'M SORRY I CAN'T HANG OUT TODAY.
I JUST STARTED MY NEW JOB HERE AT THE POND, RENTING OUT ICE SKATES.
Ruiz / Milgrom / Williams / Grossman
FINE, BETTY! BE THAT WAY!
I'LL JUST FIND SOMETHING ELSE TO DO...
...LIKE KEEP ARCHIE ALL TO MYSELF WHILE BETTY IS FROZEN AT THE POND!

... AND I KNOW EXACTLY HOW TO ORGANIZE THE PERFECT DISTRACTION!
HEE HEE HEE!
?

LATER AT LODGE MANOR...
AHH... THE HOUSE IS FINALLY COMPLETELY CLEAN!
AT LAST, A MOMENT TO RELAX!
SMITHERS!
SMITHERS! I'M HAVING A FEW GUESTS THIS AFTERNOON.

COME! WE HAVE MUCH TO PREPARE!
SIGH YES, MISS...
Welcome to
VACATIONLAND
POP SMITHERS

WHILE BETTY'S BUSY WORKING, I'M GOING TO KEEP ARCHIE OCCUPIED AS MUCH AS POSSIBLE!
IN WINTER, THERE AREN'T TOO MANY PLACES ARCHIE CAN GO SWIMMING! FORTUNATELY, I HAVE MY INDOOR POOL!

I'M ALSO GOING TO INVITE THE WHOLE GANG OVER. ARCHIE LOVES HAVING HIS FRIENDS AROUND!

Hmm... WITH EVERYONE COMING, WE'RE GOING TO NEED MORE ROOM IN HERE. COULD YOU MOVE THE LOUNGE CHAIRS OVER THERE, SMITHERS?
YES, MISS.

WHILE YOU DO THAT, I'M GOING TO START CALLING EVERYONE.

HELLO, ARCHIEKINS! I'M HAVING SOME OF THE GANG OVER FOR A LITTLE POOL PARTY...
WHEW! HOW DID THIS CHAIR GET SO HEAVY?

...AND I WAS WONDERING IF YOU'RE INTERESTED IN ATTENDING...
YOU ARE?
THAT'S TERRIFIC!
Huff Puff WHEEZE!
3

SOON AFTER...
GASTON! I'M HAVING SOME FRIENDS OVER AND WE'LL NEED REFRESHMENTS!
OUI, MISS! I SHALL PREPARE A FRESH HAM!
THANK YOU, GASTON. JUGHEAD JUST LOVES YOUR HAM.
JUGHEAD?!?

IN ZAT CASE...
LATER STILL...
NOW, YVETTE, MAKE SURE YOU KEEP FILLING THE SNACK TRAYS!
SIGH! YES, MISS!
AND LATER STILL...
WHILE BETTY IS WEARING MORE LAYERS THAN A POLAR BEAR, ARCHIE WILL FLIP OVER MY NEWEST SWIMSUITS.
DING DONG!
AH! THAT MUST BE THE GANG!

HELLO, EVERYONE...
HEY, RON!
A POOL PARTY IN THE WINTER! ONLY YOU, RON...

OH, JUST A SPONTANEOUS LITTLE IDEA I HAD!
WOW! WHAT A SPREAD!

SAY, WHERE'S BETTY? DIDN'T YOU INVITE HER?
OH, POOR BETTY IS STUCK WORKING AT THE ICE POND RENTING SKATES.

AT THE ICE POND?
SAY, I HAVEN'T BEEN SKATING IN A LONG TIME!

ME EITHER.
I WONDER IF BETTY CAN GET US IN?
HEY! WE CAN EAT AT THE SNACK SHACK BY THE POND!
YEAH!
B... BUT... BUT... BUT...

LET'S GO SKATING!
YEAH!
I'M IN!
YEAH! WE CAN ALWAYS GO SWIMMING IN THE SUMMER!

LATER, AT THE POND...
ARCHIE, THIS IS SO SWEET OF YOU GUYS TO COME AND SEE ME!
AWW, NO PROBLEM, BETTY. THIS IS A BLAST!

WELL, YOU'D BETTER ENJOY IT AS LONG AS THE COLD HOLDS OUT!
WHAT ARE YOU TALKING ABOUT, JUG?

I THINK THERE'S A WHOLE LOT OF HEAT COMING YOUR WAY!
?
THE END

Script: George Gladir / Pencils: Dan DeCarlo / Inks: Jimmy DeCarlo / Letters: Bill Yoshida / Colors: Barry Grossman

AS YOU GET READY FOR SCHOOL, YOU DISCOVER YOUR CAT HAS SHREDDED YOUR HOMEWORK! YOU LOSE ANOTHER TURN!
---YOU ALSO LOSE YOUR TEMPER!
AND YOU EAT SO FAST.... YOU ALMOST GET INDIGESTION!
12
9
3
6
YOU ADVANCE TO SCHOOL BUS STOP IN TIME, SO YOU DO NOT LOSE TURN... JUST YOUR BREATH!
SCHOOL BUS STOP
BUT YOU WISH YOUR BUS SEAT NEIGHBOR HAD LOST HIS BREATH! HIS BREAKFAST MUST HAVE BEEN PIZZA WITH GARLIC AND ONION TOPPINGS! HIS BREATH FORCES YOU BACK TWO SPACES!
R
YOU ADVANCE TO YOUR SCHOOL LOCKER!

YOU PICK A FATE CARD! THE CARD SAYS:
FATE CARD
YOUR LOCKER IS JAMMED... LOSE TURN!
YOUR FRIEND VOLUNTEERS TO OPEN YOUR LOCKER FOR YOU... YOU'RE ALL SET TO ADVANCE FIVE SPACES IN ECSTASY!
R
UNFORTUNATELY YOUR DEAR FRIEND CAN'T OPEN THE LOCKER EITHER!
...BUT HE MANAGES TO GET SOMEONE ELSE WHO CAN OPEN YOUR LOCKER!
17
THE DEAR FRIEND THEN ASKS YOU TO MEET HIM AT POP TATE'S RIGHT AFTER SCHOOL! WOW! YOU ARE READY TO ADVANCE TEN SPACES TO YOUR FIRST CLASS!
R
...ACTUALLY, YOU FLY THE TEN SPACES TO YOUR FIRST CLASS!

YOU FIND OUT YOU DON'T HAVE TO HAND IN YOUR SHREDDED COMPOSITION BECAUSE YOUR REGULAR TEACHER IS ABSENT! ADVANCE TWO SPACES!
I'M YOUR SUBSTITUTE TEACHE MY NAME IS MRS. ROGERS
YOUR LOVE RIVAL GETS CAUGHT PASSING A NOTE! SHE HAS TO GO BACK TEN SPACES TO DETENTION!
DETENTION
THE GAME IS BEGINNING TO GO YOUR WAY! THE CHEM TEACHER HANDS YOU YOUR EXAM PAPER! YOU GET AN A+! ADVANCE FOUR SPACES!
A+
YOU DISCOVER YOUR MOTHER PACKED YOUR FAVORITE SANDWICH AND DESSERT FOR LUNCH! ADVANCE THREE MORE SPACES!
LUNCH ROOM
TIME FLIES AND THE DISMISSAL BELL RINGS BEFORE YOU KNOW IT! ADVANCE FIVE ADDITIONAL SPACES!
R-R-RING
AS YOU WAIT FOR YOUR DEAR FRIEND, YOU FEEL LIKE THE BIG WINNER IN TODAY'S GAME!

YOU MEET YOUR DEAR FRIEND AND YOU SAY, " ISN'T LIFE LIKE A GAME ?"
HE AGREES THAT LIFE IS LIKE A GAME... A GAME CALLED "MONOPOLY."
THE PRINCIPAL HAS GIVEN HIM A FATE CARD...
FATE CARD
DETENTION
GO DIRECTLY TO DETENTION
DO NOT GO HOME -
DO NOT GO ON DATE
UNFORTUNATELY NEITHER YOU OR HE HAS A "GET OUT OF DETENTION FREE CARD."
DETENTION
AS YOU LEAVE SCHOOL YOU DISCOVER YOUR RIVAL HAS WON TODAY'S GAME AND YOU'VE LOST IT!
DETENTION ROOM
YOU GO BACK TO START AND HOPE THINGS WILL BE BETTER IN TOMORROW'S GAME!
The End

Veronica in "MESSTERPIECE"

Script: Mike Pellowski / Pencils: Jeff Shultz / Inks: Rich Koslowski / Letters: Bill Yoshida / Colors: Barry Grossman

YES, AND WE HAVE TO STAY ABSOLUTELY MOTIONLESS!
IT SOUNDS HARD!

IT'LL BE WORTH IT! ALL THE BEST PEOPLE WILL BE THERE, AND I'LL PROBABLY GET MY PICTURE IN THE PAPER!

HOW WILL WE KNOW IT'S YOU AND NOT THE REAL MONA LISA?

OUT! OUT! OUT! OUT!
I'M GOING! I'M GOING!!

AND IF YOU ATTEND THE SHOW, DON'T DO ANYTHING TO EMBARRASS ME!

LATER...
YOU'RE GOING TO THE COLISEUM SATURDAY? SO AM I!
YOU ARE?
2

YES! I'M GOING TO THE CAT SHOW!
THE WHAT?

CAT SHOW! CAT SHOW!
GESUNDHEIT!

NO, SILLY! THE CAT... SHOW! I'M TAKING MY CARMEL THERE!
YOU'RE SELLING CANDY?

CARMEL IS MY CAT! I'M ENTERING HER IN THE SHOW!

THE DAY OF THE SHOW...
RIVERDALE COLISEUM
BOAT SHOW-- CAT SHOW
AUTO SHOW--
LIVING PAINTINGS
THERE'S A PARKING SPOT!

THANKS FOR GIVING CARMEL AND ME A LIFT, ARCHIE!
MEOW!
CARMEL

KEEP AN EYE ON CARMEL, WHILE I FIND OUT WHERE TO GO!
OKAY!
MEOW!

I'M GETTING THIRSTY! THERE'S A WATER FOUNTAIN!
CARAMEL

OOPS!

CARAMEL, COME BACK HERE!!

OH, NO!

CARAMEL, DON'T GO IN THERE!!
LIVING PAINTING

VERONICA IS ALLERGIC TO CATS!

NEXT IS THE MONA LISA!

AH·AH·AH·AH...

CHOOOO!
MONA LISA

THE NEXT DAY...
VERONICA DID WANT TO GET HER PICTURE IN THE PAPER!
DO YOU THINK SHE'S SEEN IT YET?

WHY DON'T YOU ASK HER?
MONA SNEEZA
END.

Webb / Goldberg / Scarpelli / Yoshida / Grossman

BUT DAA-DEE, I'M FREEZING!! CAN'T I TURN IT UP A BIT?
AND WATCH OUR HEATING BILL GO UP, TOO?
SORRY, BETTY, BUT WE'VE HAD SOME PRETTY HIGH HEATING BILLS ALREADY THIS WINTER!
I'M TRYING TO KEEP THEM FROM GOING ANY HIGHER!
GAS ELECTRIC BILL
YOU'LL HAVE TO FIND SOME OTHER WAY TO KEEP WARM!
WHY DON'T YOU TAKE A NICE WARM BATH, HONEY?
AFTER YOU GET OUT, DRESS IN WARM LAYERS TO KEEP IN THE HEAT!
OKAY, MOM - I'LL GIVE IT A SHOT!

AHH! MOM WAS RIGHT! I'M AS WARM AS TOAST, NOW!
TOO BAD I CAN'T STAY IN HERE ALL DAY!

NOW... MY THERMAL UNDERWEAR, PLUS SOME NICE WARM SWEATERS...
...PLUS MY PLAID WOOL SLACKS... AND MY BIG FUZZY SLIPPERS...

AND, VOILA! MOM WAS RIGHT! I'M WARM AGAIN!

...AT LEAST FOR A FEW MINUTES!
NOW I'M C-COLD AGAIN!

WHAT'S MAKING IT SO COLD TODAY, MOM? THE TEMPERATURE ISN'T EVEN BELOW ZERO!
IT DOESN'T EVEN FEEL THIS COLD WHEN IT SNOWS!

IT'S THE HUMIDITY, DEAR! MAKES IT SEEM EVEN COLDER THAN IT IS!
HERE, HAVE A CUP OF COCOA!

DAD'S GOT A FIRE GOING-- YOU COULD CURL UP BEFORE THAT!
I'LL GET A AFGHAN OFF MY BED AND A GOOD BOOK TO READ...

...ONE THAT TAKES PLACE IN THE SAHARA OR SOMETHING!
AHH... HERE WE ARE! "DESIRE IN THE DESERT!"
DESIRE IN THE DESERT

WHOA! "HE PRESSED HIS LIPS FIERCELY AGAINST HERS, AS HOT AS THE DESERT WINDS THAT BLEW OVER HER BARE SHOULDERS!"
OH, WHO AM I KIDDING? EVEN THAT DOESN'T WARM ME UP!
I'M FATED TO BE FROZEN!
I COULD HAVE BEEN WARM AND HAPPY ON THE SKI SLOPES TODAY! BUT OH, NO!
IT HAD TO GO AND RAIN INSTEAD!
MAYBE I'LL JUST GO BACK TO BED!
BING BONG
WOULD YOU GET THAT, BETTY DEAR?
ARCHIE!
H-H-H-HE-HELLO, B-B-B-BUH-BETTY! C-C-C-CAN I C-C-CUH-COME IN?
YOU POOR BABY! YOU FEEL LIKE AN ICICLE!
COME INTO THE LIVING ROOM BY THE FIRE!

HERE! HAVE SOME HOT COCOA!
AND LET'S PUT THESE EXTRA SLIPPERS OF MY DAD'S ON YOUR FEET!

TH-THANKS! SOME FEELING IS STARTING TO RETURN!
SNUGGLE UP UNDER MY AFGHAN!

THERE...NOW, ISN'T THAT COZY?
MMM! I'LL SAY!

IS IT WARM IN HERE, OR IS IT JUST ME?
(SIGH) JUST RIGHT!

HEY, I FOUND OUR SPACE HEATER, IF BETTY'S STILL TOO COLD!
THAT'S NICE, BUT I DON'T THINK SHE NEEDS IT RIGHT NOW...

... SHE'S FINALLY FOUND HER OWN PERSONAL SOURCE OF HEAT!
END

Script: **Mike Pellowski** Pencils: **Fernando Ruiz** Inks: **Jim Amash**
Letters: **Bill Yoshida** Colors: **Barry Grossman**
Editor-In-Chief: **Victor Gorelick** President: **Mike Pellerito**
Publisher: **Jon Goldwater**

I HAVE TO GO TO THE STORE! I WON'T BE LONG!
OKAY, MOM! THE WATERBOY WILL BE HERE!
BOY, MOM SURE HAS A LOT OF PLANTS! THERE MUST BE ANOTHER WAY TO DO THIS THAT'S MORE FUN!
YES! THE SUPER SOAK WATER GUSHER GUNS I BOUGHT LAST SUMMER!
THEY'RE UPSTAIRS PACKED AWAY IN MY CLOSET!
MINUTES LATER...
HOOKAY, PLANTS! ARNOLD IS BACK... AND READY FOR ACTION!

DO NOT BE AFRAID, MY LITTLE LEAFY FRIENDS! I'M HERE TO TERMINATE YOUR DRYNESS!
HASTA LA VISTA THIRST!
SQUIRT! SQUIRT! SQUIRT!
TAKE DAT, YOU HANGING BASKET CASES!
I MUST APPROACH THE NEXT ROOM WITH EXTREME CAUTION!
AH-HA! DID YOU THINK YOU COULD HIDE FROM THE WATER BOY?

HERE'S H2O IN YOUR BULLSEYE!
UH-OH! I'M RUNNING LOW ON WATER PRESSURE!
IT'S TIME FOR THIS MUSCLE MAN TO GET PUMPED UP!
THUNK! THUNK!
NOW DAT TAKES CARE OF YOU!
AND YOU!
AND YOU! NOW THERE'S NOT A DRY PLANT LEFT IN THE HOUSE!
SQUISH!
SLOSH!
4

A WHILE LATER...
I WONDER IF ARCHIE FINISHED HIS CHORES!
HI, MOM! I'M JUST ON MY WAY OUT!
HELLO ARCHIE, ARE ALL THE PLANTS WATERED?
ABSOLUTELY, BABY! I GAVE DEM ALL A GOOD SOAKING!
WELL...I SEE YOU DIDN'T DIE OF BOREDOM!
NOPE! ACTUALLY... IT WAS KIND OF FUN FOR ONCE!
FUN? UH-OH! I BET THERE'S SOMETHING ABOUT THIS I'M BETTER OFF NOT KNOWING!
END

Archie in... "CHILL OUT"

Script: Mike Pellowski / Pencils: Stan Goldberg / Inks: Mike Esposito / Letters: Bill Yoshida / Colors: Barry Grossman

EGAD! I CAN'T STAND THAT SIGHING! IT'S DRIVING ME NUTS!
ME, TOO!
SIGH!

HEY! I HAVE AN IDEA THAT MIGHT THAW OUT ARCHIE!
WHATEVER IT IS, I HOPE IT WORKS!
HO-HUM!

ARCHIE, WHY DON'T YOU INVITE YOUR FRIENDS OVER FOR A PARTY TONIGHT?
REALLY, MOM? IS IT OKAY, POP?

SURE! ANYTHING TO CURE YOU OF THOSE ANNOYING BLAHS!
COOL! I'LL GET ON THE PHONE RIGHT NOW!

A BIT LATER
EVERYONE IS COMING! THIS SHOULD BE A GREAT NIGHT!
GOOD! I JUST HOPE THE WEATHER COOPERATES! IT LOOKS LIKE SNOW!

THAT EVENING...
HEY! HI, GIRLS! COME ON IN!
HI, ARCHIE!
COLA

I KNEW I WAS COMING, SO I BAKED A CAKE!
OUR CHEF MADE SOME OF HIS SPECIAL DIP! WE KNOW HOW FAST FOOD GOES AT A PARTY!

SPEAKING OF DIP... HI, REGGIE!
YO! WHAT'S UP, CARROT-TOP? NOW THE PARTY CAN BEGIN! MANTLE IS HERE!

OTHER GUESTS POUR IN...
DUH...THANKS FOR INVITING US! THIS IS A SUPER IDEA!
I'M HERE, ARCH, AND SO IS MY APPETITE! WHERE'S THE FOOD?

THE PARTY IS A BIG HIT, FRED! WHY DO YOU LOOK WORRIED?
THE WEATHER IS TURNING REALLY NASTY!

LATER THAT EVENING...
ATTENTION, EVERYONE! I JUST HEARD THERE'S A WINTER DRIVING ADVISORY IN EFFECT FOR THE REST OF THE NIGHT!
UH-OH!

THAT MEANS IT'S TOO DANGEROUS FOR ANYONE TO DRIVE HOME! YOU'LL ALL SPEND THE NIGHT HERE!
WE'LL PHONE YOUR FOLKS!

HEY! WHO CARES ABOUT THE STORM?
SPENDING THE NIGHT HERE WILL BE FUN!
CLICK
CHERRY COLA

IT LOOKS LIKE ARCHIE'S WINTER BLAHS ARE FINALLY CURED!
THANK GOODNESS!

YO! ARCH! WE'RE OUT OF SODA! IS THERE ANYTHING ELSE TO DRINK?
GULP! GEE... I DON'T THINK SO!
COLA
COLA

WE'RE OUT OF CHIPS AND PRETZELS, TOO!
I THOUGHT WE HAD PLENTY!
HEY, ARCH! THE TV JUST WENT OFF! THE CABLE IS ON THE FRITZ BECAUSE OF THE STORM!
OH, NO!
CLICK CLICK
NO SODA! NO SNACKS! NO TV! GULP!
AND THE BLIZZARD HAS US TRAPPED! WHAT A PARTY!
SIGH! THIS IS DEPRESSING!
I KNOW! I FEEL AN ATTACK OF THE WINTER BLAHS COMING ON!
RUMBLE
SIGH!
HO-HUM!
SIGH!
NO, MARY! NO! NO! WE'LL BE LISTENING TO THAT ALL NIGHT!
END

Archie in FLICKS TRICKS

Script: George Gladir / Pencils: Howard Bender / Inks: Jon D'Agostino / Letters: Bill Yoshida / Colors: Barry Grossman

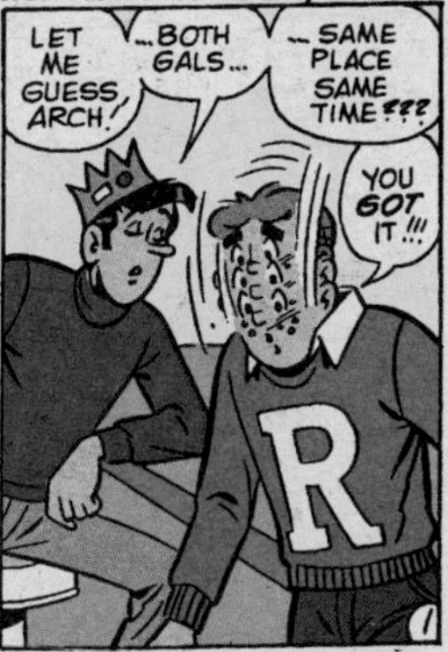

ARCH ... HOW DO YOU GET INTO THESE MESSES ???
I DON'T KNOW... THEY JUST HAPPEN!

I MADE A FRIENDLY LITTLE DATE WITH BETTY!
... TO SEE THE NEW FLICK...

AND THEN VERONICA CALLED...
...SHE WANTED TO GO TO THE SAME FLICK...
...AND I CAN'T SAY NO TO VERONICA !!!
SIGH!

NOW LISTEN...
I'LL BRING VERONICA TO THE MOVIE AT SEVEN !!!
WE'LL SIT ON THE RIGHT SIDE!

YOU SIT A FEW ROWS BEHIND US!
WHEN I LEAVE TO GET BETTY...
...DON'T LET VERONICA OUT OF HER SEAT !!!

BETTY AND I WILL SIT ON THE LEFT SIDE !!!
ARCH! THIS IS CRAZY !!!

SEVEN THAT NIGHT-
ARCHIE, YOU SEEM ALL UPTIGHT !!!
WHO ME ???
CARE FOR SOME POPCORN ?

SIT DOWN, ARCH !!! WE JUST GOT HERE!
POPCORN !!!
GOT TO GET POPCORN !!!

SORRY I'M LATE, BETTY!
CARE FOR SOME POPCORN ???
YOU BOUGHT POPCORN ALREADY ???

I LOVE POPCORN !!!
HERE... LET'S SIT ON THE LEFT SIDE!
YOU SEEM NERVOUS, ARCH!

OH, I'M FINE !!!
...BUT THIRSTY !!!
GOT TO GET A SODA!
?

HERE'S YOUR POPCORN, VERONICA !!!

WHAT'S WITH YOU, ARCHIE ?
THE BOX IS EMPTY !!!
EMPTY ?

WELL, I'LL... UH... SEE THE MANAGER ABOUT THIS !
...BE RIGHT BACK !!!

HERE, BETTY...
I GOT TWO STRAWS WITH THE SODA !
THANKS, ARCH !

DO YOU LIKE CANDY ???
SURE, ARCH... BUT...

I'LL GET SOME !

HERE'S A FULL BOX OF POPCORN, VERONICA !
OH GOODIE !!!

WAIT!
I FORGOT TO PUT BUTTER ON IT!

ARCHIE... I DON'T CARE IF YOU PUT WHIPPED CREAM ON IT!!!

DID YOU GET THE CANDY???
CANDY???
I THOUGHT I WENT FOR WHIPPED CREAM???

ARCHIE, WHAT'S WRONG WITH YOU???
OH NOTHING! I...UH...
LADIES AND GENTLEMEN!!!

AS A PRECAUTION, WE'VE PUT THE LIGHTS ON...
...AND ASK YOU TO LEAVE THE THEATRE...
...NO NEED TO PANIC...
...JUST A VERY MINOR FIRE IN THE PROJECTION ROOM...

ARCHIE, WHY ARE YOU CRAWLING ???
CAN'T LET VERONICA SEE ME WITH BETTY!
UH, JUST CHECKING FOR SMOKE!

ARCHIE SENT ME FOR YOU, VERONICA!
HE VOLUNTEERED TO FIGHT THE FIRE!!!

HE'S PROBABLY THROWING POPCORN AT IT...

ALL RIGHT, FOLKS...
THE FIRE IS OUT...
YOU MAY RETURN TO YOUR SEATS!!!

BETTY!!!
ISN'T THIS A SURPRISE???
WHO'S THAT WITH YOU?
WHAT DO I DO NOW, ARCH?
WAIT IN THE CAR!
I MAY HAVE TO LEAVE FAST!
THE End

Script: Mike Pellowski / Pencils: Stan Goldberg / Inks: Mike Esposito / Letters: Bill Yoshida / Colors: Barry Grossman

HEALTHIEST PASTIME IN THE WORLD, KIDS! SHOWS THE OL' BODY WHO'S IN CHARGE!

YOU KNOW, THEY'RE RIGHT! LOOK AT THOSE OLD TIMERS MOVE!
AND THEY'RE NOT EVEN SHIVERING!

HEY! WHAT DO YOU SAY? ARE YOU FEELING MACHO?
I'VE ALWAYS BEEN IN FAVOR OF GOOD HEALTH!

TOMORROW MORNING?
IF A BUNCH OF GRANDPAS CAN DO IT, SO CAN WE!
SLAP

NEXT A.M.
GOOD GRIEF, ARCHIE! WHAT IN THE WORLD IS THAT OUTFIT FOR?
CLOMP
CLOMP

JUG AND I ARE GRABBING A QUICK DIP IN THE RIVER, MOM!
ARE YOU CRAZY?
GOES WITH THE AGE, MARY!
2

WE SAW THE OLD GUYS IN THE POLAR BEAR CLUB YESTERDAY--- OOPS! THERE'S JUG!
DING! DONG!

READY WHEN *YOU* ARE, A.A.!
WE'RE OFF, MOM!

AT LEAST THEY *RECOGNIZE* THE FACT!
PARDON THE PUN, BUT THOSE TWO TURKEYS WILL CHICKEN OUT!

WELL, IF IT ISN'T THE CLOWN PRINCES OF RIVERDALE! WHAT ARE YOU TWO SUPPOSED TO BE?

A COUPLE OF SOON-TO-BE HEALTHY POLAR BEARS!
DO YOU MAKE ANY SENSE OUT OF THAT STATEMENT?
NO MORE THAN I *EVER* GET OUT OF THOSE TWO!

DOES THIS TELL YOU ANYTHING?
SCREECH!!

T-THEY'RE WEARING SWIM TRUNKS!
WE'RE GOING FOR A DIP IN THE ICY RIVER!

THAT'S WHAT THEY ARE, ALL RIGHT! A COUPLE OF DIPS!
IT'S A PASTIME FOR THE TRULY MACHO!

THIS I'VE GOT TO SEE!
WOULDN'T MISS IT FOR THE WORLD!

YIKES! NOW THAT I'M HERE...
I KNOW! BUT THE GIRLS ARE WATCHING!

SQUELCH THAT SCREAM! PRETEND TO ENJOY IT!
GRRK!
4

B-B-B-BOY! T-T-THAT'S GREAT!
FEELS L-LIKE A M-MILLION B-B-BUCKS!

HMPH! WE COULD DO THAT!!
EEP! RON!!

OKAY! LET'S MAKE A GROUP EARLY MORNING PLUNGE TOMORROW!
PICK US UP AT MY PLACE!

ARE YOU CRAZY? YOU WANTA GO THROUGH THAT TORTURE AGAIN?
HEY! WE CAN'T BACK DOWN NOW!

ARE YOU OUT OF YOUR MIND, RON? I'M ALLERGIC TO SELF-INFLICTED PAIN!
WE'VE GOT TO GO THROUGH WITH IT!

CAN'T LET THEM THINK THEY'RE BRAVER THAN WE ARE! BE AT MY HOUSE AT EIGHT!
5

NEXT MORN-
I'M DOING THIS UNDER PROTEST, YOU KNOW!
NO SWEAT, SWEETIE!

SWEAT IS THE LAST THING I EXPECT TO DO!
FOLLOW! BEING RICH HAS ITS ADVANTAGES!

(GASP!) YOUR INDOOR, HEATED POOL!! B-BUT---
NOBODY SPECIFIED WHERE THIS WINTRY PLUNGE SHOULD TAKE PLACE!

SHEESH! LOOK AT THAT! WHAT DO YOU SAY ABOUT THAT KIND OF CHEATING?
HOW ABOUT, "IF YOU CAN'T BEAT 'EM - JOIN 'EM"?
END

Archie in ANY PORT IN A STORM

YOU'RE WELCOME TO RELAX AT MY PLACE LATER WITH HOT CHOCOLATE AND COOKIES!
Hmmm...

SOUNDS LIKE A GOOD IDEA! IF I DON'T GET ANY MORE HOMEWORK, I'LL THINK ABOUT IT!
I'LL BE WAITING!

I HEAR HAGGLY REALLY LEANED ON YOU TO HIT THE BOOKS!
UH-HUH.

I MIGHT GO TO BETTY'S LATER FOR A LITTLE PAMPERING!
YOU WON'T GET MUCH THERE!

COME OVER TO MY PLACE INSTEAD, ARCHIEKINS... I'LL HAVE SMITHERS BUILD US A ROARING FIRE...

... AND HAVE GASTON PROVIDE GOURMET COCOA, RICH CHOCOLATE BROWNIES, AND DELICIOUS PASTRIES!
YUM!
2

SOUNDS GREAT, LOVE-BUG! AFTER I FINISH MY HOME-WORK, I'LL BE OVER!
I'LL LOOK FORWARD TO IT!

SOUNDS GOOD TO ME, TOO! SLURP! I THINK I'LL MOSEY OVER AS WELL!

I'M SURE THERE'LL BE MORE FOOD THAN EITHER RON OR ARCH CAN EAT! I'LL BE GLAD TO CLEAN UP THE LEFTOVERS!

LATER...
THERE! I HAD TO FIT MY TWO HOURS OF STUDY AROUND BASKETBALL PRACTICE AND DINNER!
WHUMP
8:30

...BUT I KEPT MY PROMISE! NOW I CAN HEAD TO RON'S!
I'LL LET HER KNOW I'M ON MY WAY!
MONSTER TRUCK
BEEP
BOOP

WHERE ARE YOU OFF TO IN THIS WEATHER?
RON'S! TO JOIN ARCHIE FOR SOME HIGH CLASS COCOA AND COOKIES!

SLOBBER! I CAN ALMOST TASTE THOSE GOODIES NOW!
SLURP!

WHOOPS! BETTER WATCH THE SLOBBERING IN THIS COLD WEATHER! MY TONGUE MIGHT FREEZE!

WE FIND ARCHIE, ALSO BATTLING THE ELEMENTS!
THIS MAY NOT HAVE BEEN THE BEST WEATHER TO GO VISITING IN--!
WHOOSH

I CAN'T MOVE MY FROZEN FEET MUCH FURTHER!

I'LL NEVER MAKE IT TO VERONICA'S IN THIS STORM!

I'D BETTER FIND SANCTUARY WHERE I CAN!
COOPER

POOR ARCHIEKINS! YOU BRAVED THIS CRUEL WEATHER JUST TO SEE ME!
ACTUALLY, I DIDN'T--

DIDN'T WHAT?!
ER... I MEAN, IT DIDN'T LOOK LIKE IT WAS THAT BAD WHEN I STARTED!

NO MATTER! HERE! SIT BEFORE THE FIRE AND WARM UP!

I BAKED THESE COOKIES JUST FOR YOU!
THEY'RE DELICIOUS!

POOR RON! I JUST COULDN'T MAKE IT TO HER PLACE! I HOPE SHE'S NOT TOO LONELY!

TECHNICALLY, NO...!
WHERE DID I GO WRONG?!
NOT ENOUGH VARIETY IN THE COOKIES... AND MORE WHIPPED CREAM ON THE COCOA!
END

Script: Mike Pellowski / Pencils: Tim Kennedy / Inks: Rudy Lapick / Letters: Bill Yoshida / Colors: Barry Grossman

"FOR THE LAST THREE WEEKS, WE'VE SPENT OUR FRIDAY AFTERNOONS SITTING IN A ROOM WITH THE BEE..."

"WE'VE GROWN SICK OF SEEING THAT FACE..."

ONE TIME, WE WERE HAVING A PAPER AIRPLANE CONTEST WHEN THE BEE WALKED INTO THE ROOM...

ANOTHER TIME WE GOT CAUGHT SKATING IN THE BACK HALL ...
WHOOPS! BUSTED!
STOP RIGHT THERE, YOU THREE!

WE ALSO GOT NABBED EATING IN THE SIDE HALL!
ARE YOU THE GUYS WHO ORDERED THE PIZZA DELIVERED?
YES! WHAT DO WE OWE?
THE PRICE YOU'LL PAY IS DETENTION!

THERE WERE ALSO OTHER REASONS, LIKE PRANKS THAT BACKFIRED!
RIGHT! AND SILLY LITTLE ACCIDENTS AND MISHAPS!

"THE END RESULT WAS THAT WE SPENT THE LAST THREE FRIDAYS WITH THE BEE!"

BUT NOT TODAY! WE'RE FINALLY FREE... FREE OF THE BEE!!
GOOD FOR YOU! SO WHAT PLANS DO YOU HAVE NOW?

WE'RE GOING TO HANGAROUND A BIT AND THEN DRIVE DOWN TO POP TATE'S TO CELEBRATE!
HAVE FUN! I'VE GOT TO RUN!

LEAVING EARLIER THAN USUAL ON A FRIDAY, MR. VEDDERBEE?
YES, SVENSON! BELIEVE IT OR NOT, NO ONE HAS DETENTION TODAY!

LATER, IN THE SCHOOL PARKING LOT...
WHAT'S WRONG, ARCH?
I DON'T KNOW! THE ENGINE WON'T START!
CLICK!
WHIRRRR!

GREAT! EVERYONE HAS ALREADY GONE HOME AND WE'RE STRANDED HERE ON A FRIDAY!
HEY! HERE COMES A CAR!

ARE YOU BOYS HAVING CAR TROUBLE?
GULP! YES, MR. WEATHERBEE!

HOP IN! I'LL GIVE YOU A LIFT!
I-THANK YOU, SIR!

WELL, BOYS! WHAT DO YOU KNOW? HERE WE ARE TOGETHER AGAIN!
The End